The Crocodile Bride

Ashleigh Bell Pedersen

The

Crocodile Bride

HUB CITY PRESS
SPARTANBURG, SC

Cover Design: Emily Mahon
Lead Book Design: Meg Reid
Author Photo © Bailey Toksöz
Proofreaders: Megan DeMoss,
Kendall Owens, Stephanie Trott

Library of Congress
Cataloging-in-Publication Data

Pedersen, Ashleigh Bell, author.
The crocodile bride / Ashleigh Bell Pedersen.
Spartanburg, SC : Hub City Press, [2022]
Identifiers: LCCN 2021058463
    ISBN 9781938235917 (hardback)
    ISBN 9781938235924 (epub)
Subjects: LCGFT: Bildungsromans.
Classification:
    LCC PS3616.E2895 C76 2022
    DDC 813/.6—dc23/eng/20211220

LC record available at https://lccn.loc.gov/2021058463

This book is a work of fiction. References to real people, events, establishments, organizations,
or locales are intended only to provide a sense of authenticity, and are used fictitiously. All other characters,
and all incidents and dialogue, are drawn from the author's imagination and are not to be construed as real.

Hub City Press gratefully acknowledges support from the National Endowment for the Arts,
the Amazon Literary Partnership, South Arts, and the South Carolina Arts Commission.

Manufactured in the United States of America
First Edition

HUB CITY PRESS
200 Ezell Street
Spartanburg, SC 29306
864.577.9349 | www.hubcity.org

This novel is dedicated to...

Mimz, for telling me stories
Oils, for reading me stories
and Chuck Kinder, for believing in mine

Canst thou draw out leviathan with an hook? or his
tongue with a cord which thou lettest down?
Canst thou put an hook into his nose? or bore his jaw
through with a thorn?
Will he make many supplications unto thee? will he
speak soft words unto thee?
Will he make a covenant with thee? wilt thou take
him for a servant for ever?

Job 41:1-4 *King James Bible*

Lay your hands, gently lay your hands.

Carey Landry, "Lay Your Hands Gently Upon Us"

PART ONE:
Stones and Spiders

1.
Staying Modest

June 1982

S unshine was standing waist-deep in the lake when she discovered the stones trapped inside her chest, one behind each bare nipple. They felt raw and tender in the cold water so she stood and cupped her palms against each to soothe them, and that's when she felt them there: two strange, tucked-away treasures.

Aunt Lou hated the word *nipple* and instead said *buttons* when she had to call them anything at all. She also hated the words *fart* and *anus* and, for some reason, *nostril* and *toenail clippings*. (JL said these words whenever she got the chance, just to get on her mother's nerves—always at great risk, Sunshine thought, since Aunt Lou did not like it when JL got smart.) If Sunshine's own nipples worked like real buttons, she could unfasten each one, pluck out the misplaced stones, and pocket them for safekeeping.

But even through her goggles she could see, too, that the nipples themselves were bigger—no longer buttons at all, but two pink, puffy mounds. Underneath were the stones and she could push them back and forth a bit, just like with her kneecaps, only her kneecaps had been there all along and these stones were what JL would call *une surprise*, oon soo-prees-eh.

3

Speaking French was another way for JL to annoy her maman. Aunt Lou insisted that JL and Sunshine never mistake themselves for Cajuns; the Turners, she said, were swamp people only in proximity and not at heart. JL only ever replied with a mournful, "*Oui, oui...*" and pretended to take a drag of a cigarette.

The morning was swollen with humidity, like overripe fruit about to burst. On their walk to the lake, steam had curled off the grass that grew in the ditches along Only Road. They'd crossed into the woods and strolled single-file down the path, carrying towels and cans of ginger ale and peanut butter sandwiches and the half-deflated yellow inner tube. Bluestem tickled their bare legs and the pines smelled sweet.

As they walked, JL had said, "I'm glad it's just us. I like when it's just us," and Aunt Lou pretended to react with shock.

"My daughter, saying something nice? Sunshine, call a doctor."

By the time they reached the lake, JL was ignoring them both, lips puckered like she'd sucked on a sour wedge of lemon. Instead of playing Beauty Pageant or swimming with Sunshine, she'd flopped back on her towel and declared she was going to get so tan that the pale skin underneath her freckles caught up to the color of the freckles themselves. "I'm going to be one smooth color by the end of today," she said, closing her eyes, "like caramel."

Aunt Lou told her that this (a) was impossible, and (b) would mean Joanna Louise should be careful what she wished for, as her freckles were a bit on the orangey side. "Might wind up an Oompa Loompa," Aunt Lou cautioned.

Now, as Sunshine stood in the water, confused and excited by her discovery, JL was still lying belly-up on the nearby shore, roasting in the sun. Sunshine squinted toward her and saw something else that she hadn't noticed before: JL had breasts.

Two apple halves beneath an olive green bikini top.

Little green hills on a flat, pale landscape.

Nearby, Aunt Lou swam past—legs kicking, long freckled arms wheeling slowly backwards. The sky was a watery blue.

If Aunt Lou wasn't around—swimming her slow backstroke in wide circles around Sunshine—she could go and plop on the sand next to her cousin and ask her to look at the nipples. To feel for the stones.

JL could tell her what they meant and what they were called and whether or not Sunshine should be worried.

LATER THAT SUMMER, SUNSHINE would decide that the stones were to blame for all that happened. They were, she would eventually see, the first of several curses. She would connect the signs she had missed that day like weaving string for a cat's cradle, finger to finger to finger: the two stones. The set of red dust boot prints across the floorboards. The unseen ghost in the tangerine living room and the too-much-bourbon.

But *before* the later, she stood waist-deep in the water and decided, for now, to keep the stones secret. She strapped on her goggles and, seeing Aunt Lou was still swimming backstroke, turned and swam right up to the yellow rope.

THE LAKE WAS NOT actually a lake but a wide, brackish bayou with a pale crescent of beach and a dilapidated picnic table in the shade of an old oak.

On this side of the lake, several springs bubbled up from deep underground and turned the water a cold, clear jade. Aunt Lou said that everyone thought the whole of Atchafalaya was all muck and mosquitoes but that places like this side of the lake were their best-kept secret. That winter, Sunshine's fifth-grade class had learned about the rise and fall of the Roman Empire, and Sunshine had pictured the ancient baths looking like this part of the lake, a jeweled green, the togas billowing under the water like sails. (For their history project, Tommy Hutton had made a poster of the Roman baths, but all the people bathing were women with huge breasts that bulged out from under their togas, and Miss Collins had sent Tommy to Principal Murphy to be paddled.)

Where the spring water met brackish water, the jade color turned abruptly opaque with silt. The shore opposite was crowded with tupelo and cypress, the water carpeted in a leafy layer of duckweed. Once, out in Moss Landry's bateau, Sunshine and Billy and Moss had watched, shocked, as a gator leapt from under the duckweed and snatched a mama duck sitting on her eggs in the hollow of a rotting tupelo. On the Fingertip side, Sunshine had only ever seen one gator anywhere close to their swimming hole—a young three-footer moving sluggishly in the cold water, already turning back for the warmer shore. Still, someone had long ago tied up a yellow safety rope to emphasize the boundary you could already plainly see in the water's change of color.

"Never, ever let me catch you swimming under that yellow rope," Aunt Lou reminded them every summer—and Sunshine obeyed, but she liked to put on her goggles and swim up to the edge.

Billy had given her the goggles for her birthday last summer. They had a red rubber strap and their lenses were made from the good kind of plastic that didn't easily fog up. She rose to the surface for a breath and checked that Aunt Lou wasn't paying attention, then ducked her head under again. In the clear water, a school of minnows scattered like arrows. Sand drifted and swirled. The water just past the yellow rope was a strange, shadowy green. How thrilling to know that there, so close, only a few breast strokes away, was a whole other world.

She imagined she was in the Black Bayou now. That she was lost in all that murky water.

She watched as from that clouded green emerged the head of the crocodile. At first he was just a dark shadow, and then the shadow began to materialize, solidify, and she realized that looming before her was the head of that huge old beast—so close that she could reach out and touch its crisscrossed teeth, run her hand along its hide. A shiver ran from her neck to her toes and she turned and swam fast and hard away from the rope and the imagined crocodile, before rising to the surface again, panting.

"Will you stop all the splashing?" Aunt Lou snapped, rubbing water from her eyes. Then, as though the two topics were related, Aunt Lou added, "And sugar, it's about time you start wearing a top when you swim. You hear?"

"Yes ma'am," Sunshine said, though she wasn't sure what Aunt Lou meant, exactly.

"Look at Joanna Louise," Aunt Lou continued, squinting at Sunshine. Aunt Lou was lean but had a belly curdled with stretch marks, and a wide behind Nash liked to grab when he'd had a beer or two. *These biscuits'll make a grown man weep*, he'd say, and Aunt Lou always rolled her eyes or slapped at his hand but she never seemed mad, not really. "You don't see her running around without a shirt on."

Of course—she understood now. Aunt Lou had noticed the stones. She glanced down at her bare chest and felt her cheeks flush.

She'd only ever worn bathing suit bottoms to swim, or underwear, or sometimes nothing at all—depending on what she could find in her dresser drawers, depending on whether she or Billy had remembered to pull the clothes from the rusting washer that hogged the small balcony off the kitchen and smelled of mildew. (More than once, Sunshine had opened the washer to find their moist, forgotten clothes covered in a layer of soft gray mold, like the feathers of the chicks they'd raised in her second-grade classroom.)

When she looked up again, Aunt Lou was staring at her with a look on her face like she'd stepped on something sharp. "Look," she sighed. "It's okay to be naked with just us girls—but around Nash, or your daddy, you stay modest." She began to move toward shore, taking long slow strides through the shallow water.

Sunshine called after her. "Aunt Lou—what's *modest*?"

Aunt Lou turned back to look at her expression that said, *If you're being sassy, watch out*—but then, seeing Sunshine was not being sassy at all, she grinned (a runt of a grin, but still) and said, "It just means you keep your top on."

EVEN BEFORE THE STONES, the early-summer season had felt different than in years past.

In September, Sunshine would start middle school, which meant sharing a bus with high schoolers. This *would* have meant that JL—who would be in ninth grade—would also be on the bus, which took both middle and high schoolers into St. Cadence, but Aunt Lou and JL would be moving in with Nash at the end of the summer. JL would take the bus to her new school in Lafayette from the house Nash was renovating for them, and Sunshine would walk to the bus stop by herself, down Only Road and over the tracks to where the paved road (sun-bleached, pocked with potholes) dead-ended at I-79. She'd get dropped off each morning in front of the low brick building with casement windows and a sports field with a weed-strewn track and no playground.

The idea of sixth grade, and of no longer living across from JL, worried her. There were no other children in Fingertip. In the spring, when Aunt Lou told her about the move, Sunshine had asked hopefully who would be moving into the pink house once they left.

Aunt Lou had scoffed. "I don't think anyone's moving into these old houses anymore, sugar. This place is dying on the vine."

Even worse than the move was that JL wouldn't even be around for most of the summer. Caroline Murphy, who was JL's *best* friend (not Sunshine, JL did not have to say), was taking her all the way to Arkansas, in the Ozark Mountains, where Caroline Murphy's cousin ran a camp that she and a friend could attend entirely for free. JL said there was horseback riding and canoeing and that she would probably kiss boys. By the time JL got back, the summer would be nearly over.

With this new mystery of the stones, and now of *staying modest*, the whole summer felt more uneasy—like a boat tilting too far to one side. Over the tree line on the opposite side of the lake, clouds were stacking themselves like fat white boulders.

Sunshine followed Aunt Lou back to the beach, then wrapped her towel around her like a cape and kept it there so it covered her chest. JL rolled onto her stomach and ate her peanut butter sandwich, and Sunshine drank her lukewarm ginger ale. From the woods, cicadas sang. Aunt Lou showed them a picture of Princess Diana in *LIFE* and asked if they thought she should cut her hair like that, short and feathered.

JL looked at Princess Diana for a long beat, then took another bite of her sandwich. "Please, no," she said through a full mouth. "You'd look like a Cheeto."

Even though JL was being smart, Aunt Lou laughed, and Sunshine couldn't help but laughing too, and for a moment, the tilting boat wobbled back into precarious balance.

LATER THAT AFTERNOON, HER hair tangled and crisp, the sun just dipping toward the tree line behind the yellow house, Sunshine changed from the bathing suit bottoms she'd been wearing all day into clean underwear and clean shorts—but no top, yet. Now that she was alone, she wanted to examine the pink mounds and the stones underneath.

The room was hushed. The green wallpaper made her feel that she was underwater again, not in the lake or the Black Bayou but the sea, and the white daisies strewn across it were floating sea anemones. She could breathe in that quiet water, keep nice and cool.

She looked down at her bare chest again and confirmed (with dismay and excitement, hand in hand) that they were still there.

They looked nothing like JL's. Not yet. She tried to think back to whether she had noticed these changes in JL before today. Had JL's breasts begun as stones? And if her own stones had arrived so suddenly, what if they kept growing all afternoon? And overnight? What if they swelled and swelled, pushing the puffy mounds into apple halves? What if within only a few days they looked like Ms. Mouton's—breasts so large and cushiony that Ms. Mouton's back had developed a hunch? Or what if the stones didn't grow at all, but sank down into Sunshine's stomach and she had to squeeze them out her belly button, and how bad would that hurt?

A familiar roar and clatter from down the road broke the underwater-quiet of her bedroom—Billy was already home from the coast, hours early.

She pulled on her largest T-shirt, then ran down the hall and through the little living room to the screened porch. The pickup was just pulling up the drive, and Sunshine peered down for signs of what kind of mood he'd brought back to the yellow house.

2.
June Moods

Sunshine waved down to Billy through the porch screen. He stuck one sun-browned arm out the window and waved back. "What's poppin', Fred?" he called, grinning. His Bob Dylan cassette was playing loudly. *Lord knows I've paid some dues*, Bob Dylan was singing.

The mood seemed good and bright. Sunshine slipped on her sandals and, the screen door slamming behind her, darted down the wooden steps and across the plywood plank they'd laid down over the muddiest patch of yard—Sunshine's very own bridge to Terabithia, Billy had started calling it, which was a reference to a book he hadn't read but that Sunshine had read in school and told Billy all about. When she got to the part about Leslie dying, Billy's eyes had filled with tears.

Billy was already out of the truck and when Sunshine ran up he picked her up under the armpits and swung her around like he'd never been happier to see a person. She let out a small scream and he pulled her close, her feet still off the ground, and said, "Sunshine, my only Sunshine." His words were muffled and hot against her shoulder. (*My brother's the kind of man who can make you feel like the darn whole sun is shining on you*, is what Aunt Lou liked to say, *for better or worse*—and Sunshine always felt proud that she and

Billy shared something in that way, that her name was the same as the way
Billy could make people feel.) She could smell his day all caught up on his
shirt: the gasoline from the machine he operated in the warehouse and,
underneath that, the salty ocean air that poured in through the open warehouse doors, out over the dock where the boats came each morning to load
their stock for the rigs. She could smell, too, his body odor mixing with his
Right Guard, and something about the salt and gasoline and his body and
his Right Guard made Sunshine feel so good that, once he finally put her
down, she wanted to ask Billy to swing her again.

But she didn't, because it was best not to show too much around Billy.
Best to keep things nice and even, Steady Freddy. If you got it wrong, if
you misinterpreted his mood, if you asked for too much, you were bound
for disappointment—and so she didn't say anything.

Instead, she hopped along behind him, then kicked off her sandals
before following him inside. Only Road got so muddy that the soles of
everyone's shoes in Fingertip were perpetually stained red if not fully
caked in mud, and someone had long ago spread the rumor that if you
walked in your house with red soles, haints would come from the woods
and track your blood-colored footprints like an invitation. Haints were
worse than ghosts, Billy said. Ghosts could be scary, sure, they at least
had a soul, they had memories. Haints were tricksters at best, he said,
and most were just plain evil. They'd follow you inside and commit who
knew what kind of mischief. (Aunt Lou said this was nonsense and that
she kept her shoes by the front door simply because she valued a clean
floor and *that* was the end of *that*.)

Today, though, Sunshine had the lingering smells of Billy's shirt and
the feeling of him lifting her up and she didn't even notice that he hadn't
removed *his* shoes—and she didn't notice, either, the red dust boot prints
over the hardwood floors.

And while she did notice the next day and soaked a rag in water and
lemon oil and carefully mopped them up, she knew it was too late. Some
kind of haint—a terrible one, capable of turning hands into spiders—
must have followed her and Billy over the bridge to Terabithia (moving
quietly, leaving no footprints of its own), climbed the steps to the yellow
house, and followed those red boot prints right inside.

THE YELLOW HOUSE WAS just shy of forty years old and already an old lady. She creaked and groaned and smelled funny. She tilted, exhausted, to one side. Sunshine once took a purple jawbreaker and dropped it on one side of the little living room; down it rolled with a mouse-sized roar until it clacked against the baseboard. The wallpaper—which Billy said Grandma Catherine had put up herself, when he was still inside her belly—bubbled in places and was speckled with mold in others; the floorboards wore pale, irregular patches like birthmarks where the varnish had worn off. In the kitchen, the cupboard doors were buckled with humidity. The butterfly-shaped stain on the black-and-white linoleum lay aged and lifeless.

Behind the house, bluestem grew nearly as tall as Sunshine and ironweed reached even higher—its reedy buds revealing, every August, flowers like bursting purple suns. When Billy or Sunshine hung wet laundry on the line out back, they sang loud songs to scare off rattlers coiled in the overgrowth. Just past the grassy yard stood a shallow grove of shrubby pines, and beyond those trees, to the south and southwest of Fingertip, were the taller pine woods. Deep in those woods is where you could eventually—if you went far enough—find the Black Bayou, which Billy said he had been to, once, but wouldn't say how or when or what happened. He'd told her Grandma Catherine's stories many times over, but of his own he only shook his head, green eyes twinkling. He told her, "Some stories you gotta keep right there in your pocket, Fred."

Their yellow house sat high up on stilts because it was, according to Billy, ever-sinking. He said one day it would plunge all the way down into the underworld. The soft wet earth kept the house cooler and slaked the thirst of the enormous oak—grown so large its fingers scraped at Sunshine's window on one side and stretched out across Only Road on the other—but the moisture also bred relentless mosquitos, and when it rained the ground was like a cake drowned in milk.

Sunshine imagined that their soft spot of earth gave way not to the underworld but to an enormous cave with its own lake and trees and sky and animals. She imagined what *une surprise* it would be for that world below when, one day, their underground blue sky began to pull apart like cotton candy as first the pilings punched their way through and then the whole yellow house dropped down.

In that underground world, just she and Billy would be in charge. Billy would be all June moods, no storms, and up above them, right in the middle of that blue sky, would be a large house-shaped hole that peered back up into Fingertip. The neighbors would gather around the hole and drop down bundles of fig pies and cartons of cold milk tied to the end of a string. Aunt Lou would come all the way from the new house to peer down at them and cry; JL would say, *It's whatever, babe. . . .* But she would secretly miss Sunshine and from time to time would launch, from the lip of the hole, paper airplanes with notes scrawled inside, explaining the things JL learned in the library books that neither of them were allowed to read but which JL always did anyway.

When Tommy Hutton called Sam Lancaster a *scrotum*, Sunshine, knowing by the way Miss Collins, belly fat with a baby by then, had gone a reddish-purple that *scrotum* was not a word to ask Aunt Lou about, had come home and asked JL about it instead. But JL had only lorded the knowledge over her. "I probably shouldn't tell," she said. "Someday, when you're *muh-toor* enough, I'm sure you'll learn for yourself."

Sunshine imagined how, after JL wrote down the things she knew in the paper airplanes notes, it would be a nice soo-prees-eh if JL took a clumsy and tragic fall down through the house-shaped hole in the sky.

AUNT LOU LIKED TO say that Sunshine got her wild imagination from Billy, and Billy told Sunshine to take that as a compliment. He said Grandma Catherine was the same way, and also sweet as a peach. "My sister, on the other hand, is a bit on the straight-and-narrow side," he said. "And anyway, she was too little to remember the best stories."

One of the best stories, Billy said, was when he was a little boy and Aunt Lou was still a baby. It was back before they got the stilts in place and the yellow house still sat low to the ground, and one night, during a bad storm, the house up and floated away. When the Turners woke up the next morning, the house was drifting in slow circles around the lake and an alligator had made itself a home on the living room sofa (ornately carved and rose-pink, brought along with Grandma Catherine from Tennessee). It was Grandma Catherine's idea to take two stiff straw brooms and use them as oars—she leaned out one window and Billy leaned out the other, and they rowed the house back home on a river of muddy floodwater to that soft plot of land where it belonged. Finally, ten-year-old Billy took his slingshot and fired a blue-and-yellow marble right between the alligator's eyes. His aim was true and the thing was dead straight away.

"What did you do with the gator?" Sunshine asked, each time he told the story.

"I'll tell you what I did, Fred: I made a fine alligator-skin purse for my mama, boots for my daddy, and a whole stockpile of alligator meat that lasted our family a whole forty days and forty nights. We ate like kings."

Someone thought up the idea to put the house up on stilts to stop it from floating away again and everyone in Fingertip came to help. The Moutons, Moss Landry, the Lanes, the Solomons. The DeBlancs and the Martins. Little Jake and Janey Buttersworth—who later died of heartbreak or worry or both when her son, Big Jake, went off to Vietnam. But in that moment they were all there, encircling the yellow house—the whole of Fingertip as it was after the Second World War, when the houses were all occupied, when there were still children growing up in several of the houses, when some of the men hunted on the pig paths, when Grandma Catherine and John Jay were alive and not in black-and-white. Already pit-stained when they arrived, the October sun beating down, the neighbors reminded each other to lift with their legs. They put their hands underneath and with a *one-two-three* they heaved the whole thing up. The yellow paint shone like light itself. Aunt Lou was so little she only pretended to help by holding her arms straight up, but her fingers just grazed the underside of the house. ("Useless," Billy teased her, when he told this story.)

Then John Jay himself—Sunshine's grandfather—dressed casually for the only time in his adult life in jeans and a sweat-and-dirt-streaked T-shirt, so that he looked just like any of the other men there, knelt down right in the mud and rolled the fat pilings under the house, setting them one by one in their rightful place.

Above John Jay, the beams under the house were like the ribs of a whale. He righted each piling as the neighbors held up the house over him.

"Only good thing he ever did for us," Billy said. Then just like that, the story was over.

So far in Sunshine's lifetime, the pilings had not begun to sink and the house had not floated away. All that had ever happened was that the yard flooded with a couple inches of water after bad storms, and they put down the bridge to Terabithia in front of the porch steps so they didn't have to sink ankle-deep.

It was the indoor storms that threatened to flood, but they were of a different sort than the kind of storms that brooms or even a circle of pit-stained neighbors could help you handle.

THE KITCHEN WAS BRIGHT with late afternoon light. Billy was squatting low, putting his beer in the fridge. "You know how come I'm home early, baby girl?"

"How come you're home early?" she said, and began unpacking the grocery bags—placing the peanut butter on its proper shelf, placing the Wonder Bread next to it and the cereal boxes lower down, lined up neatly side by side.

"Because—well, hold on. Let's just do this proper, now." Billy cracked open a beer and took a sip of the foam that rose to the top. "The *reason* is that ol' Billy here got himself a promotion, is why. Finished up my work early, tied up loose ends, and got the hell out of there to celebrate."

Sunshine gasped with pleasure. She gave Billy a high five and then shook her hand from the sting of it. "Does a promotion mean more money?"

"Oh yes, *indeed*," Billy said, in an Irish accent that always made Sunshine laugh.

"Three cheers for Billy!" she said. She'd been practicing her Irish accent, too, and though it came out all wrong now, she hopped up and down in a jig, and then Billy did a jig, too, and shouted, "We got the damn luck o' the Irish, Fred!" and the kitchen floor bounced under their weight. Sunshine was laughing so hard she had to lean back against the counter. They were both out of breath and some of Billy's beer had splashed on the black-and-white linoleum.

Around most other people, Sunshine knew how to close herself up. At school, she followed the line leader down the beige tile hallways and made sure to never goof off or lollygag like the teachers didn't like you to do. She was good at saying *yes ma'am* and *no ma'am* and at being quiet when she was supposed to be quiet, which was most of the time. But when Billy was in a good mood, a June mood, his accents and stories and jigs and laughter made her feel like she couldn't close herself up even if she wanted to, and it felt like what Aunt Lou said about Billy and sunlight. Like the roof had been torn right off of the yellow house all together and light filled it like gold.

Billy had already finished his beer, and he reached into the refrigerator to get another. Sunshine would go to the Lust Outpost tomorrow and get the things he'd forgotten, laundry detergent and dish soap and milk for cereal (but he'd remembered the cereal itself—a box of Honey Nut Cheerios for him and a box of Lucky Charms for her).

"Yep, some good news indeed, I'll tell you what, Fred. It's worth celebrating, huh?"

Now she could hear it: *Some good news, indeed.* She could hear how there was something else.

It reminded Sunshine of when they had all gone to see *Peter Pan* at the St. Cadence Theatre and Peter Pan's shadow raced around the Darlings' room playing tricks on him—that was like the something in Billy's voice. Something tricky and unsewn from the rest of him.

Billy was standing at the sink, drinking his beer and staring out over the trees, and even though he'd said nothing Sunshine worried the good mood was turning already. She smelled rain. In the yellow house, it could rain indoors even when out over Fingertip, the weather was clear.

Cautiously, feeling for some reason a need to reassure, to soothe, she went up to Billy and put two arms around his waist.

To her relief, he grinned. "Well heya, Fred." He put the arm holding his beer around her shoulders.

"I'm so proud of you," she said, staring up. She was short for her age and the top of her head reached just past Billy's ribs. "About the promotion."

He smiled again, then removed his arm so he could sip his beer, and Sunshine breathed in a whiff of that salt water smell, and the rain inside the yellow house held off.

THAT EVENING, AFTER BILLY called Aunt Lou to tell her the good news, things turned A-okay again. Sunshine giggled when she heard Aunt Lou screech with joy through the phone receiver. Aunt Lou cooked up Salisbury steak and made ambrosia salad, which was mostly marshmallows and the only kind of salad Sunshine liked. The meal was also Billy's favorite, and Aunt Lou only ever made it on special occasions.

At the dining table, Sunshine and JL sat next to one another. JL's arms were pink with too much sun and her freckles had only darkened. She looked nowhere close to caramel and Sunshine felt a pinch of satisfaction. The grown-ups talked loudly and laughed and clinked their glasses, and JL turned to Sunshine and said, "Sunny, do I have anything in my teeth?" then grinned wide, her teeth coated in a thick layer of chewed-up salad. Sunshine laughed so hard she started to choke and Billy had to reach over and pound on her back, and Aunt Lou gave JL a *look*.

JL joking with her was a good sign. Maybe after dinner she could pull JL into her bedroom, just the two of them, and Sunshine could lift her too-large T-shirt and show her the changes in her body.

"Well, cheers to this promotion," Aunt Lou said, and raised her gin rickey toward Billy. "I'm so proud of you, Billy."

AFTER DINNER, AUNT LOU said they should skip the dishes ("My girl got herself a buzz," Nash said, and Billy snickered) and play Monopoly. JL stood up quickly—the smell of baby powder lingering—and, without saying anything to Sunshine, took the telephone into her room and shut the door quietly behind her. The green telephone cord ran all the way from the kitchen through the dining room and then through the little hallway, like a narrow river (in which all of JL's knowledge and secrets passed, without Sunshine hearing). As they settled around the coffee table, picking their Monopoly pieces (Sunshine chose the thimble) and shuffling the cards, peals of laughter escaped from the space under JL's bedroom door and cut through the living room like a knife through soft fruit.

The walls in Aunt Lou's house were painted the color of vanilla ice cream and in the lamplight at night they took on a soft tangerine glow. (Sunshine wondered if Aunt Lou's new house would glow like this at night. She doubted it. She had seen it once, before Nash had started working on it, and it was big and old, its dingy white paint peeling off like dry skin and its windows covered in plywood.) She sat cross-legged on the hardwood floor and the folds behind her knees were slick with sweat. Outside, the twilight still held the day's gathered-up heat, and through the open windows Sunshine could hear the shrill call of the toads.

"I'm just so darn proud of you," Aunt Lou said to Billy, sipping her gin rickey. A bright wedge of lime clung to the edge of her glass. "It's like the tides are turning, huh? It's like God gave you a gift."

"Seems to me it's more like *Reagan* did the giving," Billy said. He was leaning forward in his chair, jiggling one leg.

Aunt Lou giggled and Nash grunted, "Huh," and Sunshine laughed along with Aunt Lou, although she didn't really get the joke.

In the middle of the game, Sunshine heard the door behind her crack open, and she turned to watch her cousin pad barefoot into the kitchen. JL came back with a glass of strawberry Yoo-hoo and leaned against the archway that divided the living and dining rooms. Sunshine watched as JL licked the pink mustache off her upper lip, then dragged the back of her wrist across her mouth to wipe off any trace of milk or spit. Her lipstick smeared. (JL wore lipstick now, even inside the house—and incredibly, Aunt Lou didn't even seem to care.)

"But I thought things were bad down there," JL said from the archway.

"Hmm?" asked Aunt Lou. She was leaning back against the couch, in between Nash's legs and fanning herself with a magazine. Nash—his eyes a little red and puffy-looking—was playing with her hair. "Oh, 'Go to Jail'? Darn it all. I was just there!" She moved her little silver hat over to the Monopoly jail then looked up at JL. "Bad down where?"

"On the coast," JL said.

"Oh," Aunt Lou sighed. "I guess I need to read the news now and then, huh?"

"Caroline's uncle's coming to live with them for the summer and work for her dad. Mr. Murphy said it's 'cause he can't get work in oil.'"

The room fell quiet. Sunshine shot her cousin a glare. She knew JL probably enjoyed having made a statement that had this effect on the grown-ups. It was like she was trying to peel off pieces of their happiness—more money, better moods, fewer storms—like you'd peel off the shell of a crawdaddy, bit by bit.

She felt suddenly protective of Billy. But who cared about Caroline Murphy's uncle? Billy was doing better than him. Sunshine should feel proud.

"Nash?" she said. "It's your move."

Nash leaned forward to examine the board, but Aunt Lou was still looking up JL. "Well, *your* uncle got work and then some," she said, and reached over to pat Billy's knee. Sunshine gave Billy an encouraging smile—to remind him things were A-okay. But Billy, too, was watching JL, too, a funny look on his face that Sunshine didn't quite recognize.

"*Okay then,*" JL said, her words drawn out for emphasis. She put both arms up as though she were being arrested. She was annoyed. "That's just what the Murphys said, is all." Then she took her glass and padded in her bare feet into her bedroom. Sunshine watched her go, and as JL clicked the door shut behind her, their eyes met for just a brief moment.

"She's turned into a bit of a pill these days," Aunt Lou said.

The mood in the room had shifted again. It was like an unhappy ghost had drifted into the center of that tangerine glow and made everything colder and duller. Then Billy stood and said, "It's about that time," which meant he was going to get another beer. Nash raised a hand like he was at a restaurant and said, "Grab me one, brother?"

"Nash, it's your *turn*," Sunshine snapped.

Aunt Lou's eyes darted to Sunshine in surprise, and she opened her mouth to say something—but Nash reached for the dice and said in his Southern belle accent, "Excuse *me*, Miss Turner, I do *declare* I must have gotten too much *sun* today," and both Aunt Lou and Billy burst into laughter, and their laughing made Sunshine laugh, too, and the tangerine living room turned bright again.

ON TOP OF AUNT Lou's old Magnavox were framed photographs of Sunshine and JL when they were still little, and another of Billy and Sunshine at the lake when Sunshine was just a baby. Her blonde hair sticking straight up. Face sticky-looking, cheeks pink. Billy was smiling so big for the camera that Sunshine, when she looked at this picture, felt jealous of the version of herself—a baby who had made Billy so happy without even realizing it.

There was also a photograph, in a tarnished silver frame, of Grandma Catherine and John Jay. Aunt Lou had told Sunshine about the photograph, once. How they had just gotten married, how they were standing on the courthouse steps in Nashville, Tennessee, holding up their wedding certificate.

The photograph was in black-and-white, which was how Sunshine would always imagine them, the grandparents she had never met and that Billy did not like to talk about much: Two black-and-white figures on courthouse steps. Grandma Catherine skinny and squinty-eyed from smiling, John Jay tall and lean and dark-haired.

Billy and Aunt Lou didn't ever call John Jay *Dad* or *Daddy*—he was just John Jay, and for some reason Sunshine had done the same with Billy for as long as she could remember.

"She looked so pretty that day, didn't she?" Aunt Lou had said to Sunshine, years ago. It had been on a night like this one, when they were playing games and the grown-ups were drinking. "And he was such a dapper man. Don't they look happy?"

As Aunt Lou smiled at the photograph, Billy had come back into the room from the kitchen, beer in hand, and he'd burst into laughter. "What a bunch of horseshit," he said, and there had been something hard in his voice despite the laughing.

From the couch, JL had met Sunshine's eyes and raised her eyebrows. "Excuse me?" Aunt Lou had said. "Why on earth...?"

Billy had only muttered, "Hey, tell whatever stories you gotta tell, sister," and then, instead of returning to the small green easy chair where he always sat at Aunt Lou's, he had walked right out the front door and they had not seen him again the rest of the night.

Still, Sunshine loved to look at dapper John Jay, who looked a little like Billy but taller and without a beard. She especially loved looking at Grandma Catherine, smiling brightly beside her new husband. Pretty and slender-armed. Freckle-nosed like Sunshine.

"And the best," Billy said, "goddamn storyteller you'd ever met."

SUNSHINE WONDERED IF THEY would play games like this in Aunt Lou's new house—or if Billy would want to drive all the way to Lafayette just for Monopoly and beers.

They had in fact never once finished a game of Monopoly that Sunshine could remember, which was annoying tonight because she owned both Boardwalk and Park Place. Since Nash had talked in his Southern belle voice the mood had changed for the better, but she could see the grown-ups were getting tired and a little bored. Billy bought Pacific Avenue without any bragging at all except a half-hearted "Yeehaw," and when Aunt Lou got released from jail, she yawned, and then it was Nash's turn again.

"Remind me, Sunny," said Nash, reaching for the dice and muffling the yawn he caught from Aunt Lou. "Does this game ever end?"

Billy said, "Holy shit, no kidding." Then he clapped his hand over his mouth and widened his eyes dramatically at Sunshine.

She giggled. "You owe me *two* dimes now. That was the second time."

Billy was supposed to give her a dime every time he cursed. It had been Aunt Lou's idea that spring, after Billy stubbed his toe on a chair leg and shouted the F word. Billy now owed Sunshine over twenty dollars, but Billy often talked about how there was *never any money* and so Sunshine hadn't ever asked him to pay up. Maybe, she thought, the promotion meant she could remind him of what he owed, and she could take that twenty dollars and stash it in the piggy bank in her room that, until now, contained only a few pennies and a single dollar bill she'd once found suspended like a tiny flag in the tall grass along Only Road.

She could tell that, despite how the game had slowed, Billy didn't want the night to end, either. "How 'bout we retire to the Turner porch for a nightcap and a smoke or two?" he said.

A slow breeze drifted in from the open windows. Aunt Lou craned her head toward Nash, and the uneven, copper-colored braid he had made in Aunt Lou's hair fell down over her shoulder. "What do you say, baby? Change of location? Dear *Lord*, I'm gonna regret this decision tomorrow."

MOSS LANDRY WAS THE one who taught Sunshine about June moods. He lived next door to Aunt Lou and had been one of the first to move to Fingertip, back when it was brand new, and he was the only true Cajun, Aunt Lou said. For better or worse.

Moss said June moods were when you found yourself loving everything and everyone around you and it all loved you back and sometimes for no reason at all, one way or the other. When the feeling in your body was like the sweet-bitter smell of wet dirt dug up, and when you had a kind of buzz in your head and maybe you didn't even know why. The best and truest June moods only happened in June, Moss said. After that, the summer sank in good and heavy.

This was the feeling as they traipsed across Only Road; Sunshine could feel its buzz in the air. Billy had finally had what Aunt Lou once called *a little luck*.

"All your daddy needs is a little luck," she'd said. "He's got so much potential."

They were swimming at the lake on an unseasonably warm day last winter, just her and Aunt Lou. JL was at a sleepover in St. Cadence. The water was cold and the cypress trees were bare and stark against the blue sky.

"What's *potential?*" she asked, shivering.

"C'mon, sugar," Aunt Lou said. "Let's get you out before you turn into an ice cube." They made their way to the beach. Sunshine didn't have any stones, then, just regular old buttons she never thought about one way or the other, and a pair of underwear. "*Potential* just means someone could have or be a lot more than they are right now."

Sunshine felt confused. "How would Billy be different?" she asked, wrapping her towel around her shoulders like a cape.

Aunt Lou put on her terrycloth cover-up. It was a bright pink-orange, like the inside of a grapefruit, and zipped up in the middle. Once, Nash had called it her Sexy Old Lady Robe and Aunt Lou had slapped at his arm, laughing. "I just like to keep covered up, okay?" she had said, and Nash had said, "Yeah. I noticed that."

"I'm not sure quite how to explain it, sugar," Aunt Lou told her, wringing out her hair. The water made dark little splatters on the terrycloth. "But all I mean is that your daddy is smart and hard-working. With a little luck I think he'll be a little happier. That's all. Does that make sense?"

FIREFLIES BLINKED IN THE darkness along Only Road. In the distance burned the steady star of the Lust Outpost, and Sunshine could hear oldies drifting faintly from its open door.

The Lust was Fingertip's only grocery and only bar. It was once called the Last Outpost, according to the grown-ups who had been around long enough to remember it, but someone had long ago whited out the "a" in the stenciled letters on its sign, and no amount of repainting could restore use of its original name in the minds and mouths of anyone in Fingertip.

Down on the opposite end of the road, just past the yellow house, hung the dark curtain of woods. The sight of the woods at night always made Sunshine shiver—but as she felt that familiar surge of fear, Billy grabbed her T-shirt sleeve and pulled her up against his waist. He said "Heya, Fred," and she said, "Heya, Billy," and giggled. Aunt Lou and Nash were ahead of them, making their way up the porch steps.

At the edge of their yard, one arm hooked around Billy's waist, Sunshine looked back over her shoulder toward JL's window. The June mood had made her almost forget about the stones, or at least ignore them, but now she felt again her desire to talk to JL, the feeling so strong it was like a gust of wind, and she wanted to break away for just a moment and race back and knock on JL's window and say, *Hey, I have something I have to ask you about, a secret.*

But JL's curtain was drawn shut, burning pink in the darkness, and Sunshine didn't want to risk ruining the mood of the evening.

Later, of course, she'd look back at that June mood—and on herself—with disgust.

Didn't she already know that anything could happen? Didn't she already know that a little luck could turn? Hadn't the storms in the yellow house showed her that anything could change at any moment? Stones could be born inside your chest. Bourbon could poison. Ghosts could drift into a room and turn the whole mood sour. Rain could pour from your ceiling and your daddy could tell stories one minute and turn so silent it was like something—a haint, maybe, who had followed red-dust footprints inside a yellow house—had stuffed his mouth with cotton.

She knew she was in part to blame. She hadn't been paying close attention. Otherwise, she might have unhooked her arm from Billy's waist as they crossed Only Road and gone back to ask JL about the stones.

The order of things may have unfolded differently.

The summer might have remained bathed in the same tangerine glow as Aunt Lou's living room.

But she kept her arm around Billy, fooled by the fireflies and the distant music, and they crossed the yard and over the plywood bridge to Terabithia.

3.
Spiders

T he trouble could start anywhere—but Billy said that it was mostly
because of bourbon. "Beer's A-okay, Fred, but bourbon—oh, boy.
Bourbon can be dangerous." That's what he once told Sunshine after an
especially bad week, when he'd missed work for two days in a row and
Jimmy Devereux had called the yellow house and Sunshine had told him
Billy wasn't feeling well.

That was the truth, wasn't it? But as Jimmy asked after Billy, rain
poured down from the ceiling as she talked and sloshed around her
ankles.

Aunt Lou called them *moods*. Not storms. But Aunt Lou didn't see
how bad they could get—or if she did, she didn't see how they felt to
Sunshine. It wasn't Aunt Lou's fault. She didn't see, couldn't see, how
it could be blue-skied over Fingertip, but pouring down rain inside the
yellow house.

How Sunshine had to watch out for Billy, then, because she knew how
to swim and Billy did not.

"Shit, I know you're just a kid," Jimmy said, on the other side of the
telephone line. "But goddamn, there are only so many times I can have an

employee do this. I've got work that needs to be done, you know? I love the man but he needs to goddamn show up." He paused to take a deep breath. Then, as though defeated, he said, "Shit, honey. I'm sorry. Can you just—can you wake his ass up?"

"Okay, sure. Yes, sir," Sunshine had reassured him. She wanted Jimmy to believe that Billy would show up—that he would wake up, at the very least. Jimmy had always been nice to her. He sent Billy home with Devereux & Co. hats and T-shirts or sometimes a few pieces of candy, and when Sunshine occasionally went into work with Billy, Jimmy had paid her a dollar an hour to do odd jobs like wash the windows of the office or organize the drawers of Jimmy's big metal desk.

She hung up the phone, embarrassed, and did not wake Billy. All day and into the evening, the door to his bedroom opened only long enough for him to shuffle to the bathroom. Sunshine could hear through the door the long, heavy stream of pee. Without flushing, he shuffled back out again.

Late that night, when she didn't think Aunt Lou would notice, she'd crossed Only Road to JL's window and climbed inside and fallen asleep.

That storm was back in the fall, at the start of Sunshine's fifth grade school year. Jimmy had taken Billy back, like he'd always done. Since then, things seemed to be going A-okay, Steady Freddy. Aunt Lou speculated that Jimmy must have had a come-to-Jesus with Billy because he sure did seem to have stepped it up in the Moods Department.

It had been a good year in the yellow house, for the most part.

A good year in the Storms Department.

Billy had still been worried about money most of the time, but he sometimes stayed on the coast on Fridays and fished off the pier for both extra cash and food for the yellow house. The waitresses at the 79 Dine gave him and Sunshine discounts on pancakes and free coffee, and Aunt Lou made dinners for everyone and Nash often bought the groceries.

The storms that had crossed through the yellow house those last months were ones that only Sunshine knew about—not Aunt Lou or Jimmy Devereux, she didn't think—and they weren't so bad. Since that September, the worst had lasted only a day or two. Other times, they'd passed so quickly that Sunshine thought she might have imagined them.

ON THE SCREENED PORCH of the yellow house, Aunt Lou sent Nash home when he started talking nonsense, his words slurring together. "Go to bed, you idiot," she said, but she looked happy when she said it, and then she herself didn't leave until long past midnight.

"I got a second wind!" she kept saying, as though her second wind were a prize she'd won on her Piggly Wiggly receipt. *I got a free bottle of dish soap! I got a free loaf of Wonder Bread! I got a second wind!* Then she'd open another beer, and when they ran out of beer she poured them both bourbon. Robert Johnson sang through the open living room windows, his voice riding low and then high again when you least expected it. Ms. Mouton twice shouted at them through her open bedroom window to shut up, you Turners, couldn't an old lady get a moment's peace in this neighborhood? Billy turned the volume down after the second time but he added in a whisper that Old Mouton needed to learn to cut loose now and again.

Aunt Lou said, "Sunshine Turner, I hope you remember that your Aunt Lou here knows how to cut loose now and again."

"Yeah," Billy said. He put a cigarette in his mouth and flicked a match. The glow illuminated his face for a brief moment, his dark beard newly threaded with silver. "She's only a stick-in-the-mud approximately nine-ty-nine-point-nine percent of the time."

Aunt Lou leaned across the orange crate (the crate Billy said Sunshine had arrived in as a baby, the NATURE'S ORIGINAL! logo painted beside a pile of oranges now mostly faded) and plucked the cigarette from Billy's mouth. She took a drag of it herself.

Sunshine loved when Billy and Aunt Lou were like this together, laughing like children over secrets they wouldn't share with her. Neither smoked except when they were drinking together, which was rare enough because Aunt Lou did not much like it when Billy got drunk. Billy said smoking was the one bad habit he refused to get stuck on, and Aunt Lou said it was disgusting except for on nights like this, when she seemed to forget anything bad she had ever said about smoking or drinking. She'd found a half-empty pack of Marlboros in one of the kitchen drawers and brought it out to Billy triumphantly. They sat in the iron rockers on either side of the Florida orange crate, feet bare, heads leaning back.

Now and then throughout the night, Billy let Sunshine have a sip of his beer, and after the third or fourth sip she started to feel pleasantly fuzzy and light. She imagined Billy and Aunt Lou inside the yellow house back when they were kids like her. From where she sat with her back against the porch wall, she could see the two of them through the screen door. One head dark, one head red. The boy raised a pale, skinny arm in a wave. He nudged his sister with an elbow but she didn't wave back. She only looked at Sunshine with wide eyes.

Then grown-up Lou said something to grown-up Billy, and when Sunshine glanced at the doorway again there was no one there. Through the screen she could see the record player along the opposite wall. Robert Johnson had stopped singing and there was only the empty *click-click-click* as the record spun its fruitless circles.

. . .

THE NEXT DAY, HEAD throbbing, day sweltering, Lou would turn on the AC unit in the green-tiled bathroom on full blast. She would sit on the closed seat of the toilet in a towel (even alone, she preferred a tightly drawn towel around her naked body), goose bumps forming on her arms and thighs, head in hands. When she was sufficiently chilly and her nausea had mostly passed, she would stand, slightly dizzy, and draw a hot bath.

She twice glanced at the door to make sure it was locked—an old habit—before hanging the towel on a hook and allowing herself to sink down among the bubbles with a sigh. She traced the pale pink stretch marks that mapped her belly, and, unbidden, a memory from the previous evening came back to her.

It was possibly nothing.

Probably, almost definitely nothing, she decided, and it was the deciding that allowed her to pull the memory back into view like drawing a curtain back from a window.

She felt herself leaning back in between Nash's legs, Billy to her right in the easy chair, Sunshine on the floor across from her, nose and cheeks sunburned from the lake. She'd let them stay out too long. Hardly even June and Sunshine's hair was already crisp-looking from just a little sun and water; she'd buy her some conditioner and remind her to use it. Under Sunshine's tank top was the hint of breasts that Lou had first noticed in the water that day.

Just little nubs. Soft, sweet buttons.

(The actual names of body parts always felt sticky in her mouth, like the words themselves should exist in private. Under clothes and under quilts. Behind sheets covered in blackberry vines.)

She could feel, remembering the board game after dinner, the feeling of the sofa against her back, and of Nash's jeans against her bare arms—scratching at her own sunburned arms—and the firmness of his calves beneath them. She and Billy were doing okay. He seemed alternately happy about his promotion and then dazed, as though his mind were not quite fully in the room anymore. She thought he was probably drunk—and why not? A person was allowed to celebrate.

The fact of Billy getting promoted—it was worthy of celebration.

It wasn't just the money, though that would certainly be helpful. It was that for any troubles in his past—the bouts of depression that could last a week or even more, the drinking—Jimmy Devereaux saw the good in him. Recognized his hard work. Her brother didn't say so but she imagined he felt validated. Appreciated. Not since he'd gotten the job eleven years prior had he truly good news to share.

That afternoon, when he had called to tell her, he'd sounded happy.

And she knew that it was more than that. To rise at all in this world was to refute the person their father had told Billy he was, either indirectly or, often enough, directly.

Lou sometimes wondered if Billy's dark moods, his sensitivity, were solely because of John Jay—because of the things he told Billy about himself, and because Billy believed them. She tread lightly with Billy because of this; because she knew he was sensitive, for one, but also because she had seen the way their father had treated him, and she didn't want to cause him more pain than he'd already been caused in this life.

In the early spring, when she'd told him about the move to Lafayette, she had tried to do so as gently as possible.

(It hadn't worked. She'd felt the tension between them even before she'd shared the news aloud.)

But now there would be more money, despite the recession. Now his hard work had paid off; now her brother had something, finally, to feel good about. Good things, hard-earned good things, were happening for both of them—and for a moment, lying in the bathtub, she smiled.

IT WAS IN THE middle of Monopoly that Joanna Louise emerged from her bedroom and walked barefoot through the living room to the kitchen. She returned with a glass of strawberry Yoo-hoo and stood in the archway, sipping it as she paused to watch the game.

Two things came back to Lou as she traced her stretch marks in the green bathtub.

The first was how her daughter, sipping her strawberry milk, looked suddenly like a stranger to her. Or not a stranger, exactly—but a strange version of herself. Just that afternoon, eyes closed against the sun, Joanna Louise had looked so young. Lou remembered how she would watch her daughter sleep when she was still a baby. Those moments were pockets of quiet in Robert Dalton's house. But now, standing in the arched entry of the living room, with her red hair loose and the curls softened and her lips darkened with lipstick—though Lord knew why, as Joanna Louise was apparently spending the bulk of the evening alone in her bedroom—her daughter had transformed herself, as though by magic, into an almost-adult.

She was so moody these days, her daughter. She used to love Monopoly and, like Sunshine, was the only one of the family who cared enough about the game to try and play until the bitter end.

Now her bare legs, in cut-off denim shorts, were long and lean. Now she leaned in the archway, her shorts accentuating the curve of her hip. It was as though until this moment Lou had been watching a film preview of her growing daughter, and then the film somehow dissolved and the actress stepped off the screen and into her living room.

Her shoulders. Her breasts. Her jutting hip and lean legs. Her glass of strawberry milk.

Lou had resisted rising hastily—knocking over drinks, sending Monopoly cards scattering—and going to her redheaded girl. She wanted to put her hands on her daughter's face and her lips on her mouth, to taste the too-sweet strawberry. She would pull back, hands still gripping her freckled, pretty face, and look directly into her daughter's eyes and remind herself that Joanna Louise was still a child.

No—rather, she would remind Joanna Louise that she was still a child, and that she, her mother, was letting her know that Joanna Louise would need to ask her permission to (1) wear her lipstick, and (2) look the way she looked tonight. With her glass of strawberry milk. Her long freckled legs.

IN THE BATHTUB, LOU took the pink folded washcloth from the tub's edge and dipped it in the hot water, then dragged it across her breasts and let it rest there like soft armor.

SHE HAD ONLY WATCHED Joanna Louise for a moment. A crescent of pink stained the rim of the glass. Then Joanna Louise made the comment about things being bad on the coast, something about her friend's uncle, and Lou had worried Billy would be offended. It had come across as if Joanna Louise were doubting him.

There was something else, too—the second thing about that evening, which Lou had not had time to think about and consider until now, in the quiet of the bathroom, the warmth of the water. There was her daughter, and there was the way her brother had watched her daughter.

Lou had turned away from Joanna Louise with her throat choked up and glanced, for some reason or another, toward Billy. He was slumped down, legs spread, resting his beer on one thigh. His eyes were turned up toward Joanna Louise.

His eyes had bothered her. Or they hadn't bothered her then, rather. She was warm-feeling from the gin, from Nash's hands running through her hair. But they bothered her now. It was a certain look on his face. She couldn't think why, exactly, only that the look reminded her of something. And of course it was probably nothing to worry about.

Probably not a something at all.

But still, in the bathtub, the AC roaring so that Lou was cocooned by sound and by that peach-skin washcloth covering her breasts and soft light filtered through the steamed-up window, it was the image of Joanna Louise and of the strawberry milk and of the look on her brother's face that rose to the surface of her mind, and hovered.

HER BROTHER HAD CHANGED over the years, though.

He was troubled, yes—but his heart was good. When they were children, he'd made a fort for them, tacking a sheet diagonally across the corner of the bedroom so the fort was three-walled: green wallpapered walls on one side and a bedsheet with blackberry vines running across it on the other. While John Jay raged beyond the closed door of their childhood bedroom, they huddled inside the fort. If she was crying, Billy would pretend to pluck a piece of fruit from the blackberry vine and hand it to her. If she was not yet playing along, he'd say, *Go on, eat up*, and pretend to gobble a handful himself. *Dewishush*, he'd say, his mouth fat with invisible blackberries. *We can make a pie, Lou Lou.* He whispered the same stories their mother told them on better nights and made Lou fill in the details he pretended to forget. *Do you remember, Lou Lou? D-d-do you remember what she did with that old c-c-crocodile's heart?* No matter how hot a summer evening, Lou's whole body shook on those nights. Her teeth chattered. Billy would wrap a blanket around her and keep talking, keep telling her stories and making her answer his questions. (*She buried it underground*, she'd say.) He'd keep plucking blackberries from the vine until the house grew quiet and still again.

THAT WAS ALL TRUE, but so was this:

She was sixteen, in late spring. The May evening so hot that sweat pearled along her upper lip; she wore only a tank top and underwear. Through the window over her bed, she could hear the high chirping of a tree frog.

This was years after they had dismantled the fort, though they still shared the bedroom. Instead, several sheets hanging across a rope and secured with clothespins acted as a dividing wall. There was a lemon-yellow sheet and the sheet with the blackberry vines they had used for their fort. The cotton nubby after so many years, the blackberries faded to dusty blue.

The kind of quiet that fell after one of John Jay's rages took awhile to settle into a true quiet.

Even with no movement, no shouting, no banging, no hitting, the quiet hummed for an hour or more with something alive and quietly popping, like bonfire embers not yet gone out. And on this night when she was sixteen, the true quiet had not yet arrived.

She'd been reading *Jane Eyre* for school. Over her nightstand lamp she'd draped a sheer, silky scarf that her mother said had belonged to *her* mother, Margaret Bell. The scarf over the lampshade cast her side of the room in a pink glow, her tank top and underwear the color of a ripened peach.

(That was a detail she would remember later, many times over: the strange choice of her clothing, or lack thereof, with a teenage brother—nearly a man—in the same room, with only the curtain of sheets between them.)

During John Jay's outburst, which was brief enough that Billy had not gone to intervene—to both her relief and disappointment—she had tried to focus on the book but had only managed to reread the same paragraph several times in a row. Only as the true quiet settled, like a child finally succumbing to a fevered sleep, had she begun to absorb the words again. Jane was wandering the moors, and she could hear Mr. Rochester calling to her from far away. *Jane, Jane.* Lou could almost hear his voice echoing in the bedroom. She imagined she was Jane, walking on and on across the moors. Her skirts rustling. The moors rolling like the sea in all directions. Green and daisy-covered. *Jane, Jane.*

Then Billy had knocked.

When they'd divided their bedroom years before, still just children, they had established an unspoken rule that they knocked on the wall outside of the drawn curtain.

Shave and a haircut.

If it was all right to come in, the other would respond with a double knock.

Two bits.

If they weren't dressed or for one reason or another did not want the other person around, they'd say, *Hang on* or *Go away* or *Can a person get a little privacy in this goddamn house?*

Lou had learned early on in her teenager years to be modest. If she wore too few clothes around her father, she risked his attention. Unlike the fathers of many of her friends, who wielded belts or the threat thereof, John Jay didn't hit Billy or Lou. He instead reserved the hitting for his wife, and he might instead comment on Lou's too-thin arms, or her freckles, or some other characteristic she could do little to change. He had recently told her that she better watch what she ate, that her thighs (in their bell bottoms, stylishly fitted at the hips) were starting to look thick as Virginia hams. Of course, she also risked his attention if she did not put in enough effort: On several occasions, he declared in his haughty Tennessee drawl that her hairstyle was old-fashioned and plain. When neighbors put together an Easter cookout at the lake, he told her that her pastel dress made her look tired and washed out; couldn't she try a little color? She had learned more than modesty; she had learned how to hide.

So, when Billy knocked, she pulled her sheet up around her, all the way up to her armpits with a reflexive haste.

Then she raised her knuckles to the bedside wall, and knocked back.

(Her first mistake, she recalled now. Or perhaps the first mistake had been her lack of clothing. The second, her invitation—*two bits.*)

Billy stepped around the curtain. Her eyes were still on the page of her book but she could sense him watching her. Saying nothing.

"What?" she said after a moment, startled by his silence, and then irritated. His hair was uncombed and fell in heavy bangs across his forehead. Pimples spattered both cheeks. "I'm reading." She scanned the page for where she'd left off.

But still he stood there. She slid her eyes toward him again. He was leaning against the green flowered wall behind him. He was skinny but strong, his muscles corded from the years of playing baseball—though he had been kicked off the team earlier that spring for showing up at practice drunk. He had been different in those last couple of years, her brother, and she excused the way he'd started drinking—not every day, she didn't think, but often enough—because she knew what it was like to want to escape. Who could blame him for finding an easy way of doing so?

Dark fuzz shadowed his upper lip. His eyes looked swollen. She wondered if he had been crying or drinking, or both.

Then all at once, before she thought to ask what he was doing, to say anything at all, he was moving toward her, was on top of her, pressing her shoulders down into the mattress. The strength of his hands surprised her. His fingers dug into her skin. His mouth pressed against hers with such force that without meaning to she cried out, but her voice sounded muffled and weak.

She had never kissed a boy before. She tried to seal her mouth shut but his tongue pushed its way through. He tasted like liquor. Another muffled noise rose in her throat but she caught herself, because as this happened she had the thought that no matter what, she could not let their mother hear or see.

She pushed against his shoulders as hard as she could, then slapped at him, at his shoulders, and then, feeling increasingly frantic, at his ears. Fear rose up in her so powerfully that she felt a wave of nausea. Then, somehow, her hands found Billy's chest and she pushed with a strength she hadn't known she possessed.

As though suddenly waking from sleepwalking, her brother scrambled backwards and stood up, panting. He looked away from her. He coughed. Her bedsheet had fallen away in the tussle and she scrambled to pull it over her body again. Several pages from her book had been torn out and had drifted to the floor like leaves.

Billy's cheeks were flushed. He stood near where he'd first come in, back to the dresser, and he held up his hands as though a searchlight had turned on him. His green eyes were wide. "I'm sorry," he said, and he sounded like he might cry. "I'm sorry. I'm sorry."

In the bathtub, Lou remembered how their mother used to say, ever since Billy was a child, that he should be an actor. The good looks—the dark hair with his light eyes. And, when he outgrew his stutter, a honey-tongued charm. The way he appeared to be someone one minute—sweet, funny—and then, when Lou least expected it, cold and distant, and in the very next moment, someone she felt sorry for, and wanted only to reassure.

"No, no," she'd whispered that night, the sound barely escaping her lips, "I'm sorry."

He'd retreated to the other side of his room, and the makeshift wall with its faded blackberries fell back in place, and Lou hadn't once spoken of it. Not to Billy or to anyone else. Certainly not to Nash. She kept it to herself, the taste of him. The way she couldn't lift her arms the next day without pain.

But, she thought, dunking the washcloth in the warm water and laying it over her bare breasts once more, things were different back then, in the yellow house. It was no wonder that Billy had reacted in the way he did, back then. The drinking, that kiss.

And besides, hadn't she in some ways, in some very critical ways, contributed to his advance? Was she on some level inviting his gaze—trying to play sexy like her girlfriends at school? Had he seen, in a narrow gap between the sheets, her teenage body stretched out on her bed, the peach-tinted underwear, before he knocked? Seen the dark of her nipples (how she hated that word!) through the thin, ribbed cotton of her tank top? Her bare legs? That was a critical lapse in her own judgment, and the look on his face in the warm lamplight of her living room the night before, when they played Monopoly, the look on his face as her daughter sipped her strawberry milk, had only been a shadow that most men possessed.

Men would be men, wouldn't they?

And so, the bath growing tepid, the window and the green tiles of the bathroom beaded with moisture, Lou let her concern fall with a *plunk* into the bathwater and sink under the mounds of bubbles.

• • •

IT WAS LATE WHEN Aunt Lou finally left the yellow house—long after she'd sent Nash back home—and Sunshine watched her step over the bridge to Terabithia and then trip on a tree root and curse. She called back over her shoulder, "Don't say a word, you two! I did that on purpose."

"She owes you a dime," Billy drawled. "You can remind her of that tomorrow." He was sitting in one of the iron rockers, slumped low in the dim light from the living room window, and he turned his head slowly toward Sunshine and grinned.

The night felt suddenly hushed, like a blanket had fallen over all of Fingertip. Although Billy's eyes were closed and she felt like she might fall asleep herself, it felt so nice sitting with him, just Billy, that she swallowed a yawn and said, quietly, "Heya, Billy?"

Eyes still closed, he said, "Heya, Sunny?"

"Feel like telling a story, maybe?"

"Good lord. No rest for the weary, huh?" He paused and sighed dramatically. "Hell, okay now. Here's a story, Fred." His words slurred together a little; he opened his eyes and looked at her. "It's a secret story, Fred, and you're the only one I can tell."

She giggled again, although both his eyes and his mouth were unsmiling.

Later, she would feel stupid about that laugh. It was the kind of thing Miss Collins would say was *inappropriate*. Miss Collins loved to tell her students what was appropriate or inappropriate. The girls who did not like Sunshine because she lived in a place that wasn't on the school map and because her hair was sometimes not combed and she sometimes forgot to take a bath for several days had once encircled her on the playground, all six of them. They held one another's hands and sang, "Cinderelly, Cinderelly, clean your hair and clean your belly," to the tune of the song the mice sang in *Cinderella*. Miss Collins had scolded the girls but then pulled Sunshine aside after school and said to her that showing up to school without being properly bathed was inappropriate. That night, Sunshine had scrubbed her body with a soapy washcloth until her skin turned bright pink.

But inappropriate laughs were different. You couldn't scrub clean an inappropriate laugh no matter how many times you tried.

"Come on over here," Billy said. He held his glass of bourbon with one hand and patted his lap with the other.

On the Florida orange crate stood several empty beer cans and Aunt Lou's still-full glass of bourbon and an ashtray with a small, stumpy forest of cigarette butts sprouting from it. She could hear the record churning and wanted to go inside and put on Lead Belly or Muddy Waters or Bob Dylan, but she hadn't sat on Billy's lap in a long time, and the night had felt so good. Even though her eyelids were heavy she still didn't want it to end.

She eased herself back onto Billy's thighs, but she could feel, as soon as she lay awkwardly back against him, that she was too big for lap-sitting.

Billy grunted and said, "Mercy, Fred!" He belched, and it smelled like Salisbury steak. "You been sneaking candy bars behind my back?"

"No," she said, and laughed again. Something taut had stretched itself inside her belly like a warning, but she slumped low and nestled her head back against Billy's shoulder. His neck was warm and damp. Her legs fell to either side of his and her toes reached the floorboards. She let out a sigh.

"Well, if you've been hiding candy bars," he said, and started to rock the chair back and forth, "hide them no more. I'm goddamn starving."

"What's the secret?" she said, through her laughter.

Against the porch screen, stitched together in places with dental floss, the wings of moths and june bugs clanged. The june bugs would fly away for a moment, as though realizing their mission was pointless, then forget and come plowing into the screen all over again.

"You're the only one I can tell, Fred," said Billy. "So if I say it, you can't tell no one else. Not your cousin, not Nash, not anyone. Definitely not my sister."

The chair groaned as it rocked. Sunshine's bare feet on the rough porch floorboards went from tiptoes to flat, tiptoes to flat.

"Okay," she said, and although the taut thing was still in her belly, she felt excited that there was something Billy would share with only her. "I won't tell," she promised.

"Okay then. I didn't get—well, shit. Here it is, all right? I didn't get any promotion, Fred."

She laughed loudly this time. A high-pitched, nervous laugh.

"Yeah, I know. Seems like a joke, huh? But this is the truth, Fred. Your daddy Billy here, well, the truth is that instead of a promotion, he got laid off. Goddamn laid off. See what I mean, Fred?"

She laughed again. "You teasing?" She couldn't see his face so she couldn't tell.

"It ain't the best story I ever told, I guess—huh, Fred?"

Then Billy did something he hadn't ever done before in front of her, not once. He started to cry. They rocked back and forth, and his voice when he spoke again was strange and choked. "I couldn't tell the truth about it earlier. Can you understand that, Fred? I didn't want to disappoint everyone. The way my sister's always on top of me about money. About you. Well, shit." His tears ran down his cheek and onto his neck where her own face was pressed, their skin hot and wet. Billy took a deep, shaking breath. "That's the truth of it, I guess."

Sunshine didn't know what to say. She knew what being laid off meant—it meant that *never any money* was lasting, not just a thing Billy said before payday. It meant Billy and Aunt Lou would fight, if Aunt Lou found out. Unlike Caroline Murphy, they did not have a rich cousin who owned a business where Billy could work, and all of this meant that the rain inside of the yellow house would fill the house faster than it could drain and that Billy could drown in it.

Billy put his arm around Sunshine's belly, hooking her against him. He said, "I didn't plan on telling you that," and his words tickled her ear. She flinched, as though one of the june bugs had made its way through an unrepaired hole in the screen and aimed for her ear. "You must think your old man is pretty pathetic, huh?"

Later, she would wonder why she hadn't protested, hadn't reassured.

Later, she wanted to go back in time and tell Billy: *No, no, I don't think that.* To tell him he was Billy, her Billy, King of Stories. King of Making Her Laugh 'Til She Peed.

Rescuer of Strawberries in Florida Orange Crates.

He was still crying, catching his breath. "I'm sorry, Sunshine. I'm sorry."

He said this again, and then again, his breath hot in her ear, "I'm sorry, I'm sorry," and as he repeated the words, as his crying finally calmed, a single hand began to slide up under her shirt.

She thought at first that he meant to tickle her, and she contracted her stomach, tightening it against the coming attack. She almost laughed again. But the hand lifted itself so just the fingers were touching and her T-shirt became a small tent. Inside the tent, the hand was a spider, large and five-legged, rough-skinned and warm, and the spider slid its legs over the ticklish skin of her belly and up to her chest and over one puffy, raw nipple. Not a button, not an eye, but a tender and bruised-feeling nipple with something hard underneath.

Gently, at first, like pinching a fig to test for ripeness, the spider legs squeezed. Then rougher. Rubbing. As though trying to root out and swallow her stones.

Billy's mouth stayed pressed against her ear. "I'm sorry, I'm sorry," he drawled and slurred, but the words sounded tinny and percussive. Then they dropped away all together, and there was only Billy's hot breath and the bugs flapping against the screen and the *shkk shkk shkk* of the whirring, musicless record. Both hands were spiders, now, and they moved around under her shirt, grabbing and searching and rubbing. She was already sore and the spiders agitated the raw skin and she bit her lip, hard, so she would not yell out. It seemed important to stay silent, as though it wasn't happening at all. Billy groaned and where her body rested against the crotch of his jeans she could feel something shift, turn firm.

As she let the spiders poke and prod, a movement caught her eye. She saw that to her left, in the rocker Aunt Lou had left vacant, sat a woman. Sunshine couldn't quite make out her face in the shadows, but she saw her slender arms, smooth and glowing in the lamplight from the window, and she could see the red in her hair. It was Grandma Catherine, Sunshine knew. She was holding a Mason jar of water on her lap, ice cubes lightly clinking as she rocked. "Oh, darlin'," she whispered. "He's got much better stories than *that*."

Sunshine closed her eyes. When she opened them again there was no one there except her and Billy, and the spiders were pulling themselves out from the tent of her shirt. She could see them clearly in the light that spilled softly from the living room.

Just hands. Not spiders at all.

Billy's voice, too, was back to normal. He said, "It's past your bedtime, huh, Fred? Pretty late by now."

"Yes," she whispered. She climbed off of his lap, stiffly. It felt as though her whole body was filled up with sand. Maybe she had fallen asleep, she thought, and dreamed the whole thing.

That would explain why Billy was acting like nothing had happened.

(Days later, she would wonder if Billy had been the one to fall asleep. He'd been drinking beers all night, since he first got home. Then bourbon too. Maybe he'd told her about being laid off because he was talking in his sleep, and he hadn't realized he was crying, or his hands had mistaken her for someone else entirely—a girlfriend Sunshine did not know about, or her own mother.)

She stepped inside the house. The little girl and boy she'd seen earlier were gone and there was no Grandma Catherine, either. It was just the empty yellow house, now, and the too-late hour. Billy spoke again, and she turned to peer around the door, afraid of what she was going to see. But there he was, still—just Billy. Eyes bloodshot and tired. Hands on his belly. She could see the hair on the tops of his fingers. He looked startled, his eyebrows raised and his eyes wide, like he'd just seen something that scared him. A haint, maybe. Tracking red dust footprints.

She suddenly felt sorry for him and wanted to tell him not to worry about anything, but he spoke first, squinting at her from the rocker. "Just stay quiet, okay? Just stay quiet, Fred. I promise I'll make it all right."

She said, "I promise," but her throat was so dry that hardly any sound came out at all.

4.
The Crocodile

Fingertip, 1950s

C atherine Turner began the story in the yellow house, her children close against her body, one on each side. Her girl, four years old, with red, curly hair after her own; her boy, just turned six, with dark hair like his daddy's.

Story time was in one of the twin beds in the room her children shared. All around, the green wallpaper with the daisies strewn across it. She had picked it herself, papered the walls herself, her son inside her belly. At story time, the green and the tendrilled flowers made Catherine feel they were inside a fairy tale. She began:

A very long time ago, deep in the forest at the end of the road, was a place called the Black Bayou.

In this bayou lived a very large, very old crocodile.

Nobody knows how a crocodile came to be in this part of the world. There are no other crocodiles here, of course. Alligators, yes, but crocodiles are even more frightening—and this crocodile was larger and more ferocious than even the biggest alligator, and he was very lonely.

(*Why was he lonely?* Billy asked. His soft fingers were curled around her pinky.

Because he didn't love anybody, Catherine said.

Oh, said Billy, *that's s-sad.*)

The Black Bayou was old as the sea and its water black as oil. All around it, the woods were green and wild, with cypress trees taller than any castle. In the summer, swarms of horseflies blotted out the sky, and snakes coiled in the shade of the sawgrass, and there were black bears and red wolves and wild boars with quick tempers. The ferns grew so thick on the forest floor that children were known to disappear inside of them, never to be seen again.

(*What happened to the children?*

Nobody knows. Do you want me to tell this story?

Yes ma'am.

Okay then. Hush, now.)

Of course, the crocodile was never in danger. He was the king, and he ruled the black water and the forest that cupped the bayou shore like the palm of a hand.

He had cracked, yellowed teeth like blades; his hide was a muddy green; the plates along his back were thick and impenetrable. He gobbled up wooden boards punched through with rusty nails as though they were fresh-baked biscuits. Countless fishing boats and cargo barges, their captains and crew, their wives and children, attempted shortcuts to the city only to find themselves lost forever to the crocodile's enormous belly. When from time to time some arrogant hunter or another shot at the crocodile, the musket balls only lodged themselves in his hide like cloves in a Christmas orange and caused—at worst—a mild rash.

Bones and treasures, the wares of merchants and pirates and thieves, piled up inside of him, and the crocodile began to develop a taste for these delicacies. For jewels and pearls and gold watches, and for diamond rings and gold-plated spoons. He liked the cold metals that clinked pleasantly against his teeth. He enjoyed the smoothness of pearls as they slid down his throat. He loved these delights as much as he loved the crunch of human bones.

Those travelers who escaped with their lives (though rarely all of their limbs) warned others of the Black Bayou. *Travel by land,* they cautioned, *for a great beast lurks and he'll eat you whole! You'll live out your days in the dark of his belly!*

So it was that eventually, people stopped passing through the Black Bayou at all. Villagers kept their distance. Native tribes hunted elsewhere. Merchants took the long route to the city. All at once, the crocodile's enormous appetite was left unsatisfied—and so he began to eat up the world around him.

He swallowed the palmettos that spiked the shoreline, the lily pads, the snapping turtles, a wagon wheel encrusted with rust and small snails. He swallowed whole families of alligators, then he chewed his way through their marshy den, teeth gnawing through the mud as though it were chocolate cake, licking his lips in what was, unfortunately, only a brief moment of satisfaction.

The more he ate, the hungrier the crocodile became. In one single day, he ate a fallen, water-logged tupelo, beginning at the algae-slick branches, munching his way through the softened trunk, and finally slurping up the wet, mossy roots like noodles. When fog rolled in each night, he ate the low-hanging clouds. He ate the muddy shoreline, biting off chunks of red earth, and he ate the oaks and the pines and even the huge old cypress. Always, he soon found himself hungry again.

The Black Bayou grew wider and deeper as the crocodile ate more and more—and he would have *kept* eating, would have eaten straight through the entire forest until he had no home left, until his world was all treeless water and great big sky, had the girl not arrived.

SHE STOOD ON THE shore one summer morning as though already home.

Her simple white dress was torn to the knees and her feet were bare. She wore her dark hair in two long braids, and her skin was the color of milky coffee.

Her bare arms were bruised. A fresh cut ran across one cheek.

The sun hadn't yet risen over the tree line and pink clouds reached across the sky. What an easy morning meal this girl would have made—but the crocodile felt something strange and unfamiliar stir in his lonely crocodile heart.

He blurted out: *Don't you know I could eat you whole?*

But you won't, said the girl, and apparently certain of her words, she walked straight into the water—right up to the crocodile. She stood before him, waist-deep. Her white dress ballooned around her. *Instead,* she said, *you'll allow me to fetch your heart from your belly, and it will build me my home, and no one will ever hurt me again.*

Build you your home? sputtered the crocodile, quite genuinely confused. *With my own* heart? *Look at me, girl. Look at my teeth.* He bared his teeth for her. *Look at my jaws.* He opened his jaws for her, then snapped them shut again. The force blew wisps of hair back from smooth brown forehead. *I could* eat *a house, but I cannot possibly build you one.*

You won't build it for me, she said. *I'll bury your heart in the ground, and a house will build itself on top of it.*

And what will you give me in return? asked the crocodile.

Many things, said the girl.

Pearls? asked the crocodile slyly, hopefully. *Rubies? Emeralds? A barge full of human bones?* His mouth watered at the thought.

I'll give you the gift of my hands, said the girl—and before the crocodile could argue, she placed both of her hands on top of his large, lumpy crocodile snout. She closed her eyes.

The girl's hands were small but warm, and they felt on the crocodile's hide like how jewels and bones and flesh tasted in his mouth. They felt sweet like rain, or like the smell of pine trees after the sun had warmed them. When this strange girl took her hands away, the crocodile could still feel their warmth and their taste and their smell—and all at once, the crocodile was no longer hungry.

As though under her spell, the crocodile opened his jaws wide so that she might crawl inside. When she came back out again, the girl carried in her arms the crocodile's heavy heart, red and warm and beating.

As she had promised, she took the crocodile's heart into the forest and buried it deep in the earth. The crocodile had never before noticed his own heartbeat, but now he could hear its rhythm from underneath the forest floor: *Da dum. Da dum. Da dum.* When the girl finally arrived back at the bayou shore, it was approaching noon. She was streaked with dirt, and her long black braids were loose and untidy. The bruises that had ringed her arm, however, had almost disappeared, and there was a pale scar where the cut on her cheek had been.

Do you see? said the girl, wiping sweat from her brow with the back of her hand.

See what? asked the crocodile.

My house, just there—and she pointed through the leafy trees, dripping with moss, to where the crocodile could make out, sitting upon a shallow ridge, a little red house.

A house as red as the heart buried beneath it.

I'll be safe here, said the girl, and she turned to the crocodile and smiled.

(*Does she still live on the Black Bayou?* Billy whispered, his cheek hot against his mother's bare arm. On Catherine's other side, Lou had fallen asleep. *Is the crocodile's heart still buried?*)

IF ON THAT DAY, any local had ignored what they had heard about the ravenous crocodile, about his bottomless appetite, and dared to visit the Black Bayou—if they had been watching the shore from the forest, pressed safely against the trunk of a cypress, they would have seen this: standing before the enormous crocodile, a small, black-haired young woman with milky-coffee skin, the hem of her white dress trailing behind her like a wedding gown.

PART TWO:
Sea Anemones

5.

Goldfish Keepers

Before she plastered the walls of what would become the children's bedroom with green wallpaper strewn with daisies, she was not Catherine Turner, but Catherine Elyse Booker of Portland, Tennessee.

She was born in 1919, just as the country tipped gratefully forward into a new decade and away from the First World War. Both her father, a veteran-turned-postman, and her mother, a schoolteacher, were already in their early forties and had reconciled themselves, having tried and miscarried several times already, to a childless life. That their infant daughter arrived splotchy-faced and wailing, head thick with her mother's red hair, was a pleasant and welcome surprise.

Perhaps she sensed from a young age the heartache her parents had already endured from their miscarriages—or perhaps she sensed the illness slowly rising in her father. Whatever the reason, Catherine seemed to understand from infancy—with the exception of her screeching entry into the world—that it was best to be quiet. Best not to disrupt. As a baby, she slept through the night and kept to a reliable feeding schedule. In school, she raised her hand and did not speak until spoken to—and even then, she did so quietly. She minded her mother, whose sternness and reserve made her a beloved grammar school teacher and a distant (though not unkind) parent. In the evenings, Catherine sat on the arm of her father's reading chair, head leaning against his, and listened as he taught her about the plants he studied in his spare time.

The Bookers lived in a white house with green gingerbread trim on a spacious corner lot, where the only disruption to the property's general sense of peace came when the Malverns' territorial rooster, Pontius Pilate, made his way up the sidewalk and attacked any animal or human who happened to be nearby.

Catherine preferred the back yard anyway. On summer days, she lay in the grass between her father's garden plots and played pretend with Rosie, a rag doll with black yarn for hair and mismatched buttons for eyes: one brass, one shaped like a rose. Together, she and Rosie sometimes explored a narrow, tangled thicket of woods that bordered their yard (and seemed, when Catherine was very young, to be vast). They discovered the hollow of a huge old oak big enough to sit inside and hid from imaginary dangers. There were witches and ghosts. There was a prowling wolf. (She could hear its heavy footfall nearby, slow and menacing.) Catherine brought treasures inside the hollow and lined them up around herself and Rosie in protective circles—a tarnished baby spoon, stones she'd once found in the creek at the edge of Portland and brought back home in the pocket of her skirt, acorns, a rusted old key. The hollow smelled sweet and mineral, of rotting wood and the earth that dirtied her clothing.

Many years later, when she moved to the place called Fingertip, the sweet scent of rotting wood she sometimes encountered along the piney paths and the smell of mud along the road or along the shore of the lake would take her back to the hollow of that oak tree, and the bliss she found in there in the company of Rosie, and of her own imagination.

ONLY AROUND HER FATHER did Catherine share the stories that occupied so many hours of her childhood. In school, she was so quiet that students teased that she was mute. But her father had a way of coaxing from her the words she otherwise kept tucked away. In the evenings, they settled into his study after dinner, a stack of books on the floor beside his reading chair. "Who did you and Rosie meet today?" he'd ask—and before they looked at sketches from *Wildflowers of the Southern U.S.* or *Trees of Appalachia*, Catherine would describe the witches that disguised themselves as blackbirds in the woods, or the troll who came searching for Rosie, eager to kidnap her for himself, only to be turned to dust when he came too close to the magic stone she had set just at the entry of their hollow tree.

Finally, when she finished telling her story to completion and answering her father's questions about the size of the troll (so that he should know just how frightened to be himself), or the sound of the witches' cries (so that he could tell the difference between regular blackbirds and otherwise), he opened that evening's book.

TALMADGE BOOKER WAS KNOWN and well-liked in Portland. He was tall and lean, with a loping gait and friendly blue eyes. By the time Catherine attended grammar school, his hair—which stuck up in a feathery cowlick at the crown of his head—was the color of tarnished silver. Tiny flakes of dandruff powdered his stooped shoulders. Talmadge was the only creature, human or otherwise, whom Pontius Pilate seemed to tolerate. For as long as Catherine could remember, her father kept a pail of feed in the mudroom specifically for the rooster, and on his walk to the post office each morning, he tossed Pontius Pilate a handful.

In most ways, Talmadge was his wife's opposite. While Margaret Bell took comfort in daily rituals—grading papers and planning lessons, sipping tea and reading the morning paper—Talmadge was full of small, spontaneous surprises. He kept Werther's Originals in his pocket and left them hidden for his daughter at random—under her pillow, in the pocket of her winter coat. When he learned that Catherine, at age fourteen, didn't know how to foxtrot, he made her stand on his shoes and danced with her around the living room as she threw her head back and laughed.

Sitting in his study one evening when she was still very small, he told her that simply reading about plants was too dull for a springtime evening. He took Catherine's hand in his, and together they walked the moonlit sidewalks of Portland, looking for the flowers and herbs and trees they'd seen in his books. They found morning glory vines along a neighbor's picket fence; they found a black cherry tree by the Methodist church. They found pine trees and Talmadge quizzed Catherine on whether they were Virginias or loblollies. They returned to the house with the ginger-bread trim, luminous under the full moon, at nearly midnight; Catherine was so tired that Talmadge carried her the last blocks on his shoulders, and she'd stacked her hands in his feather-soft hair and rested her chin on top of them. "See, Cathy?" Talmadge whispered, as they reached the front porch, "Sometimes you just have to see a thing for yourself to really know it by name."

AFTER HIGH SCHOOL, CATHERINE remained with her parents and took on part-time secretarial work at a small law firm next door to the post office. The work was well-suited to someone who preferred minimal conversation, and mostly involved typing up various letters or taking dictation. In the second-floor office, tall windows overlooking South Street diffused the room with soft blue light, and through the window next to her desk she could see across the alley to the brick wall of the Post Office next door, on which a faded advertisement for Mitchell's Hardware (which had gone out of business a few years back, during the worst of the Depression) was painted.

She found the view comforting, and her pleasant daily routines were interrupted only by the occasional approach of Mr. Geraldson (the gentler of the two lawyers) who now and then might clear his throat softly, and say, "Catherine, dear? A message came from next door. I wonder if you might just go and see about your father?"

And so, well accustomed to the role her mother had inexplicably given up long ago, Catherine excused herself to go and see.

PORTLAND, TENNESSEE, WAS A small and slow-moving town; the post office could easily accommodate an absent employee, and because Talmadge's supervisor, Roy Washburn, had also fought in the war and, rumor had it, medicated his own troubles with a steady supply of liquor even during working hours, Talmadge managed to keep his job. Furthermore, the problems in a small town could all but disappear behind polite smiles and the unspoken tenet that a man's business was his business. Talmadge's illness was overlooked whenever possible. When it wasn't being overlooked, it was alluded to rather than spoken of; even Margaret Bell remained mostly silent on the subject, and when discussion could not possibly be helped she referred to them only as *spells*.

When as an adult she reflected on her childhood, Catherine could recall that the spells had been happening all along—but they were so mild, and her mother so swift to tend to them, and the matter of their existence so generally ignored, that she hadn't known it, not really. Talmadge had occasionally arrived home from the post office, his bushy gray eyebrows knit in concern, complaining about misplacing something that they hadn't owned in years. His mother's porcelain tea set—where was it? A worn children's Bible his daughter couldn't remember ever seeing—hadn't it been on the side of his bed? (*Cathy, did you do something with it? I won't be mad, darling. I just find it comforting.*) On those days, Margaret Bell had ushered him quickly upstairs for a cup of tea with whiskey and an early bedtime, and the next morning, Talmadge might say, *Ah. Silly me. I was feeling a bit under the weather. I'm better now*, or, *What was I thinking? I haven't seen that tea set since Mother passed.*

It wasn't until she was a teenager that the spells became more pronounced. On her way downstairs to leave for school one morning, Catherine discovered Talmadge in his study, still dressed in his clothes from the day before, hair greasy, eyes red-rimmed. He had stayed up all night studying his books and taking notes, like a school boy before a big exam. Catherine stood uneasily in the doorway of the little study and looked around. Every surface—the shelves, the desk, the floor— was littered in sheaves of notebook paper with barely legible scribblings. Mounds of books were scattered about the room, too, open to sketches of trees and flowers. Some of their pages were torn, as though from turning them too quickly.

Margaret Bell had already left for work, and a sickening pit formed in Catherine's stomach. Recalling her mother's remedy from those instances of her father's strange forgetfulness, or occasional fever, Catherine led her father—chattering on about his various readings—upstairs to bed. She brought him a cup of tea with whiskey and helped him sit up enough to drink it. When he fell asleep, she stepped downstairs, tidied his study, and at last walked to school.

Later that same year, he was up until dawn making a vegetable stew—although he had never once cooked anything in their household. In the blue light of a winter's morning, she'd found him there in the kitchen, padding around in his slippers, the too-full pot of stew simmering on the woodstove, bits of brown slop dribbling over its edge and hissing on the stove's iron surface.

"It's my mother's recipe," he said, glancing briefly in Catherine's direction. "But it's far too salty. Far too salty."

Catherine saved the stew for supper and served it that evening to both her parents. Upon confirming its overwhelming saltiness, Talmadge buried his face in his palms and began to cry. She again led her father upstairs, then helped Margaret Bell (her eyes turned downward and away from her daughter) gather their bowls and pour the stew into a pail. She carted the pail next door to the Malverns'—keeping a watchful eye for Pontius Pilate—and dumped the stew in the trough for their pig to lap up.

ONCE, WHEN TALMADGE'S SPELL had either caused or coincided with a fever, Margaret Bell sent Catherine, sixteen years old, to fetch Dr. Oliver.

Dr. Oliver had thick, salt-and-pepper eyebrows and small rectangular spectacles. Catherine had listened from the kitchen as Dr. Oliver stood by the front door and told her mother in soothing tones that it might be helpful for Margaret Bell to think of these spells as a kind of virus. He said many of the men he had known to return from the war were experiencing something similar, that it would pass with enough time, that she should do her best to be kind to him.

"It might help speed them along," said Dr. Oliver, "to go about your business as though everything is normal."

So, that was what Margaret Bell continued to do—had indeed already been doing for some time—and did with the same precision and fortitude (if not the same warmth) that she brought to her teaching. She read the morning paper. She dutifully graded assignments with a red pen in the soft parlor lamplight at night. As she aged, a soft roll of skin began to spill over the starched edge of her old-fashioned, stiffly-starched collar. She kept a small embroidered handkerchief in the same pocket of the same pocketbook for thirty-two years and used it to polish her round, wire-rimmed glasses. She wore the same cropped, curly haircut as her hair faded from red to gray. And as Talmadge's spells increased in both length and frequency, the love Catherine's mother once held for her husband seemed to evaporate like milk in a pan.

THROUGHOUT CATHERINE'S CHILDHOOD, SHE and her parents were often greeted around Portland—at church services, at the general store, at the library—by the parents of the children in Margaret Bell's class. They thanked Catherine's mother for her hard work, for her dedication. They told Catherine how lucky she was to have a mother like her. Each time, Catherine marveled at her mother in these encounters. How she turned talkative. How her cheeks pinkened.

Mrs. Bell—for she'd kept her maiden name in the classroom—was a favorite at Green Acres Grammar School. She was known to be stern but never cruel; she did not believe in striking children and so used a system of both time-outs and rewards, and she maintained order with ease. She kept goldfish in a bowl in her classroom and had the students name them after characters in books. Whenever a goldfish died (which was not infrequently), the whole class planned a funeral—complete with eulogies and flowers and a fish-sized cardboard coffin. Then Mrs. Bell brought in a new goldfish, and the children traded off weeks in which they played the role of Goldfish Keeper. The Goldfish Keeper had to remember to feed the fish and clean its bowl, and had to, if the fish died, lift it from its watery grave in a little net.

It was a great honor, in Mrs. Bell's classroom, to be a Goldfish Keeper.

In the bedrooms of the white house with the green gingerbread trim were various quilts Margaret Bell's students had made for her over the years. In the center of each quilt was a flower, or a heart, or a sun or a moon, each made of various scraps of cloth, in the center of which was always her name and title:

MRS. MARGARET BELL
FIFTH-GRADE TEACHER

Surrounding her name, spread across the rest of the quilt, were other flowers and hearts and suns, and in the center of each of these was the name of one of her students from that year. A student's mother had started this tradition long ago, and each year, another student's mother had continued it, until the Booker household contained small towers of folded quilts in armoires and on bedroom trunks, the names of children stitched across them in neat, black-thread cursive.

ON A COLD WINTER morning, Catherine rose early to make her father breakfast in bed to try and cheer him. The afternoon prior, she'd led him home once more from the post office and tucked him into bed before returning to the law firm. In the kitchen, while Margaret Bell read her morning newspaper over tea, Catherine arranged on a tray several biscuits with butter and honey; a cup of coffee; a small pitcher of cream. But when she pulled open the bedroom curtains and set the tray on the bedside table, Talmadge looked dimly up at her, his eyes sleep-crusted and glazed, then turned his head away and sighed.

"Come on, Daddy," she said. She could feel a gust of chill air come through the closed window. The radiator clanged. "I made you breakfast. We don't want Mr. Washburn to have to do all the work today, do we?"

She sat down on the bed beside her father, the mattress barely sinking under her slight frame. Talmadge squeezed his eyes more tightly closed, unable to let in the daylight or his daughter.

When she tried again—"Daddy?"—he rolled over so his back was to her. The thin cotton pajama top he wore twisted when he turned so she could see a wedge of pale lower back, padded with wiry gray hair. As she reached to pull the quilt over his body, he let out a long, loud fart.

Under any other circumstance, she would have laughed. Now the foul stench, the sight of the hairs on his white flesh, made her stomach churn.

He stayed in bed for the duration of the day and then through the weekend, rising only to shuffle to the bathroom. Even with the window cracked, his room began to smell stale, and faintly of urine.

Catherine pulled him to a sitting position to feed him broth. She tried coaxing him to rise, to join them downstairs for supper, or breakfast, or tea. She told him Pontius Pilate missed his daily treat. She pulled up a little wooden chair and sat bedside to tell him stories like she'd done when she was young. There were fairies in the garden, she said. She had seen them just that morning, darting among the weeds. She reminded him of the wolf who lived in the woods at the edge of the yard; if Talmadge listened, he'd hear him howling.

But the father who had once listened to her so attentively couldn't seem to hear her now at all. He was lost inside his own mind, or inside the past, or inside the belly of a beast no one could see or understand.

Finally, trembling with frustration, her eyes burning, Catherine fell silent. She rose from her seat in the wooden chair and placed it back at the rolltop desk. Outside, in the dying light of the afternoon, a wet, heavy snow had begun to fall. She took an extra quilt from the armoire and put it over her father, tucking it around him as though he were a child, and let him sleep.

THE QUILTS WITH THE names of Margaret Bell's schoolchildren would eventually make their way to Fingertip, stacked in Catherine's closet, spread over the beds of her children in the yellow house and eventually in the pink house across Only Road, over Aunt Lou's bed and over JL's bed and over the spare twin bed that Sunshine thought of as her own. Stacked in the small hallway closet of the yellow house, among musty smelling sheets and faded towels. Over Billy's bed in a room with its shades always drawn tight; over Sunshine's bed in her green wallpapered room, white daisies swimming.

Sunshine—with the lightly freckled nose of her grandmother and the blonde hair of her mother (she assumed), both of whom she'd never meet—would run her fingers across the names on the quilts. She would trace along the cursive loops of her great-grandmother's name, *Mrs. Margaret Bell*, and along the names of the children written among the patched-together flowers and vines, the suns and the moons, and then late on a June night, after spiders had found their way up the skin of her belly and gone searching for her stones, she would pull a quilt all the way to her chin to try and stop her teeth from chattering.

6.
Underwater

A week after the spiders arrived, JL left for summer camp.
Sunshine and Aunt Lou helped load JL's duffel bag and back-pack, both stuffed so completely that the zippers would hardly close, into the shaggin' wagon and then drove her to the Murphy house, which was big and brick and perched among identical big brick houses. The trees in the neighborhood were not even as tall as the houses and were staked to the ground with chains tied around their skinny trunks.

On the drive, JL had shotgun because she was the one who was leaving. Sunshine leaned her forehead against the back window. Billy had made up the name for Aunt Lou's car, the shaggin' wagon; he said it needed a name to give it a boost and make it feel better about itself. Its bumper was dented and stuffing grew out of the seat cracks like fungus. The AC was blasting but the back seat was always hot, and Sunshine's thighs turned slick against the caramel vinyl.

When they pulled up to the Murphy house, Aunt Lou told Sunshine to get out of the car and hug her cousin goodbye, and then she went to talk with Mrs. Murphy, who was teetering down the driveway on clogs, waving and smiling at Aunt Lou.

Mrs. Murphy was as skinny as the little tree in her yard, with feathered blonde hair cut just like Princess Diana's. She wore tight jeans over narrow hips (no biscuits to make a grown man weep) and a strapless terry cloth top.

Joanna Louise wrapped her arms around Sunshine in a hug. The skin of her bare shoulders felt pleasantly warm. "You can still use my room," she said, pulling back. "Maman wouldn't care if you did."

On the ride to the Murphy house, JL had opened her little seashell-shaped purse and taken out makeup and put it on right in front of Aunt Lou, who for some reason did not scold her or take it away. Sunshine watched with disbelief from the back seat: Joanna Louise carefully applying her eyeshadow, Aunt Lou saying nothing. The whole school year, Sunshine knew (for a fact, Jack) that JL put on makeup once she got to school and washed it off before she got home. Once, Aunt Lou had somehow found out, and when JL lied about it, she'd slapped her across the cheek, hard. But this morning, it had been like Aunt Lou didn't care one way or the other.

Now, standing on the sidewalk at the edge of the Murphy lawn with no tall trees to shade them, Sunshine could see that sweat was starting to trickle down JL's forehead and each time she blinked, black smears of mascara smudged the skin around her eyes. Even with the mascara smudges, JL looked pretty. Her cheeks were pink in the heat and her mouth was like a glossy strawberry. Aunt Lou had given her two French braids and tied the ends with mint green ribbons.

"Okay," Sunshine said, crossing her arms over her chest. "Well, bye."

"I'll write to you," JL said. Then she leaned close to Sunshine, so Sunshine could see her freckles and the mascara smudges, and smell the maple syrup from breakfast still lingering on her breath. "But you can't tell *her*"—JL rolled her eyes in the direction of Aunt Lou—"what they say."

"What's *they*?" Sunshine said. She was using the voice she used with JL when she wanted JL to think she didn't care about the topic of conversation.

"What the letters say, dummy."

Over JL's shoulder, Mrs. Murphy and Aunt Lou were still talking in the driveway, and Caroline Murphy had not yet come outside. Beneath her crisscrossed arms, Sunshine could feel the stones.

Once, JL had walked in the bathroom when Nash was just stepping out of the shower. JL said the thing hanging down between his legs looked like the trunk of the baby elephant in *The Saggy Baggy Elephant*. His *thing*, JL said, was all sag and bag. JL knew about that and about bleeding from your clam and about the silky hairs, a downy fur like on top of a baby's head, that had already started to grow on hers. (All year, Sunshine had watched for them on her own body with excitement, but nothing had happened.) JL could explain the stones and then somehow the other thing, the thing that had happened with Billy on the porch, and she wouldn't tell.

But Sunshine didn't know how to ask any of it—what words to use. Deep in her chest, behind the stones, something felt open and raw. JL had started to turn away and Sunshine said, suddenly and all in a rush, "CanyouwaitasecondIhaveaquestion."

JL turned back, wiping the sweat off her upper lip with the back of her wrist. "Okay," she said, glancing back toward the house. "But you know I only have, like, not even one second."

Sunshine lowered her voice so the grown-ups wouldn't hear. "Don't make fun of me, okay?" She tried to unscramble the words in her mind into a question—what *was* her question, really? JL waited, green eyes squinting. Then the door of the Murphy house swung open and Caroline Murphy's blonde head popped out.

"Joanna!" she called.

No one called JL just "Joanna," but JL's face lit up with pleasure and she turned away from Sunshine, toward Caroline. They ran up to one another and embraced in the middle of the lawn, hugging for a long time, rocking back and forth dramatically.

"Aw, they're so adorable together," Mrs. Murphy said to Aunt Lou, and Aunt Lou said, "Oh, yes, the best of friends."

Sunshine watched from the sidewalk. Caroline kissed JL on the cheek with a large, wet smacking sound, and Mrs. Murphy and Aunt Lou turned back toward each other. JL said something to Caroline that Sunshine couldn't hear, then dropped her duffel bag on the freshly trimmed grass and jogged back over to Sunshine.

Sunshine crossed her arms back over her chest again, but JL wrapped her arms around Sunshine for a second time, squeezing so hard that Sunshine's feet lifted off the ground. When had JL gotten so much bigger than her? Sunshine could feel JL's boobs smashed against her own tender chest. Then JL let go, and she leaned in close to Sunshine's face and whispered maple syrup words: "Write me back, okay?"

When she walked toward the house with Caroline, their excited squeals seemed to reach all the way up to the bright morning sky and out across the green yards. Then the door shut behind them, and the neighborhood fell abruptly quiet.

On the drive home, Aunt Lou stared straight ahead in silence, and Sunshine found she couldn't speak, either. Lucinda Williams played quietly and when the tape ended, neither of them switched it to the other side. Sunshine hugged her knees up to her chest and watched the flat green fields and old farmhouses with their rusting tin roofs slip past.

WHEN SUNSHINE WAS VERY little, maybe first or second grade, she and Billy had driven to the Piggly Wiggly after several days of storms inside the yellow house. Billy's truck bumped and lurched over the potholes on the road beyond the tracks. He hadn't yet turned onto 79 when he suddenly said, "You know how I get caught up sometimes, Fred. I just want you to know that it's not your fault. A-okay?" His voice had sounded so shaky that, as he turned onto the two-lane highway and picked up speed, she'd unbuckled her seatbelt and scooted over to the middle of the bench and rested her head against his arm.

His shirt was freshly washed—she had done laundry for them both, and hung it on the line, and folded it neatly—and the cotton against her cheek smelled like sunlight.

Later, though, she thought that maybe Billy had just said that—about the storms not being her fault—to be nice. To make her feel better. She had learned a long time ago to do what she could to prevent the storms from arriving. To watch for signs. To be polite, always remembering to say *yes, sir* and *no, sir*. She brought Billy beers when he asked and she counted to see how fast she could do it. She kept things tidy in the yellow house, putting the groceries away in the right order (peanut butter in this cabinet, cereal on that shelf, bourbon on top of the old fridge). When Billy forgot to buy milk or toilet paper or cereal, she walked up to the Lust and she told Big Jake to add it to Billy's tab, and he did so without asking her about it, and sometimes even gave her a free root beer along with the Dum Dums.

If the storms came anyway, despite her efforts—and if she couldn't stand Billy's sadness, his silence, any longer then she sometimes went to Aunt Lou's house.

JL left her window unlocked and cracked open for her, no matter how hot or cold it was outside, and so on some nights she'd shove it open enough that she could hoist herself inside.

She told herself it was probably okay to leave Billy like this because from the spare bed in JL's room she could keep an eye on the yellow house. If Billy needed her, if water began to pour from the windows and over the porch, she was right there. She could go back. Then, comforted by the sound of JL's breathing in the darkness, she'd fall asleep.

Aunt Lou didn't ask Sunshine why she stayed in JL's room. Sometimes, Sunshine came in after dark and then, in the morning, made up the bed, doing her best to brush from the quilt and sheets the red dirt she'd tracked inside. She'd climb back out the window and walk back across the road to the yellow house before anyone else woke up.

Other times, though, she'd pad into the kitchen barefoot and get herself a glass of water, and Aunt Lou, reaching into a cabinet for plates or mixing pancake batter in the blue mixing bowl, simply glanced over and said, "Hi, sugar," or, "Morning, sleepyhead."

On these mornings, Aunt Lou made it seem like Sunshine was as much a part of her household as the tangerine light in the evenings or the waxed wood floors. As much as JL herself.

And Sunshine knew that neither she nor Aunt Lou had to say anything to understand that they shared a secret.

They seemed to be protecting something, a silent knowledge, and it was something she and Aunt Lou had together that JL and Aunt Lou did not have, which made Sunshine's whole body fill with what felt like warm light—even though JL got to be Aunt Lou's daughter and no matter Aunt Lou's demeanor on those mornings, Sunshine was still just a niece, and being a niece and not a daughter was like winning *Best Effort* at the elementary school science fair.

ONLY ONE TIME A couple years back was their shared silence broken, and it was Aunt Lou's fault.

JL had stumbled, eyes puffy from sleep, into the bathroom to shower before school. She had started showering every day that year, sometimes twice in one day, and Aunt Lou had bought her a bottle of Baby Soft. She'd dress for school, spritz a cloud of the powdery-smelling perfume into the room, and then step forward into it with her eyes closed and her chin high.

That morning, the bathroom door was locked and Sunshine could hear the shower running. She knocked. "I have to pee," she shouted.

"Go to *your* house, then," JL shouted back.

It was the third night in a row that she'd slept over. She banged on the door again in frustration and then shuffled sleepily into the kitchen, still in JL's pale blue flannel pajamas (hand-me-downs, like all of Sunshine's wardrobe, and too big).

Aunt Lou was standing in the kitchen, voluminous red hair piled on top of her head with tortoiseshell combs, pouring coffee into a pink mug. The kitchen was cool and drafty on winter mornings but smelled like hot coffee and toast. Aunt Lou glanced at Sunshine and instead of saying her usual *good morning* or asking what she wanted for breakfast, a kind of shadow settled over her features—almost as if Billy's own storm had slipped out the door of the yellow house and arrived there in Aunt Lou's kitchen.

Aunt Lou set the percolator on the counter, and for a moment Sunshine thought she was in trouble, maybe for staying over or for yelling at JL, that Aunt Lou was coming to grab her arm and drag her toward the front door and say, *Enough is enough, Miss. You go back to your own home, now.*

Instead, she marched past Sunshine and across the living room and out the front door to the porch. Sunshine followed (bladder full, threatening to burst), wondering if she should do something—apologize, maybe—but she didn't know what to say, and so she watched as Aunt Lou slipped on a pair of Nash's boots (too angry, it seemed, to bother noticing that her own rubber boots were right next to his) and stomped toward the yellow house.

Only Road was cold and hard under Sunshine's bare feet and her breath made drifting white clouds in the air. She hitched up her pajama bottoms and called to Aunt Lou, "I think he's sleeping in today," but she could tell that Aunt Lou wasn't listening. Her peach-colored bathrobe was pulled tight around her, and her freckled legs were bare from the knee down. Nash's boots looked large and ridiculous. It was an outfit she would never have been caught dead in had she not been too mad to notice.

She stomped up the dirt drive and over the bridge to Terabithia, Sunshine hurrying behind, and then they hurried single-file up the old stairs and through the screened porch. Aunt Lou's footsteps were so heavy that Sunshine thought the house might at long last punch through the marshy earth and fall down into the underworld.

She wanted to grab her aunt's arm and say, *Just leave him alone, let him sleep*, but this version of Aunt Lou scared her and there was a knot lodged in her throat.

At the edge of the hallway, Sunshine stopped. She stayed by the record player, by the stacks of records that Billy did not play during storms, that gathered dust as they waited for his attention to return once more.

She hadn't closed the front door behind her, and the cold morning was barging its way into the yellow house and making itself at home. She peered around the corner, down the hall. She shifted from leg to leg to keep herself from peeing.

"Billy," Aunt Lou shouted, banging her hand on the bedroom door. "I know you hear me. Get your ass to work! Don't you know you have a goddamn daughter to feed?"

Sunshine looked toward the hallway ceiling over Aunt Lou. Rainwater leaked down along the cracks in the ceiling, dripping down onto the wood floors with a soft *plink*. The plaster bulged with the weight of it.

Aunt Lou banged again. "Don't you give a goddamn *shit* about any-thing?" she yelled.

Sunshine wanted to go pee but that would mean walking down the hall toward Aunt Lou and she felt scared to do that. She prayed Billy was asleep and couldn't hear this, that he was dreaming of something good, like storytelling on the porch, like when he used to play baseball and, at fifteen, had the best arm this side of the Mississippi like Big Jake had said.

When Aunt Lou was met by silence, she said something else that Sunshine would think about for a long time afterwards, wondering what exactly she meant. "You're turning into *him*," she shouted. Her voice was hoarse and sounded shaky, but she was still yelling. "Do you know that? You're going to look in the mirror one day and see his face, Billy Turner, and it'll be too goddamn late. You just think about that."

Aunt Lou banged on the door again with the flat of one palm and Sunshine's bladder gave way. She buckled her knees, pressing her legs tight together, but it would not stop; her underwear turned warm and wet. Trickles of pee ran down her legs and onto the floor. Then Aunt Lou was there, grabbing Sunshine's hand, pulling her out the door and down the porch steps. She didn't seem to notice what had happened, the darkened crotch of her pale blue pajama bottoms. Aunt Lou wiped her face roughly with her free hand and said, "Let's get you some breakfast, sugar. I'll drive you into school today."

THAT NIGHT, SUNSHINE HAD watched the daisies first float past.

The water in her room was different than the rainwater of the storms; it was ocean water born of the wallpaper her Grandma Catherine had pasted on the bedroom walls a long time ago: a deep green background, and the daisies looked like the anemones Sunshine had seen on a field trip to the aquarium in third grade. All the children had been allowed to reach their hands in a cool, shallow pool of water and touch the sea creatures there.

Maybe Grandma Catherine had chosen this wallpaper for the same reason. Maybe the daisies had also reminded her of sea creatures. Maybe she put up the wallpaper to create such magic, an in-between world of both earth and water. Free of *him*.

Whoever *he* was. Sunshine imagined a troll. With gray, dead-looking skin and wispy hair. With red-rimmed eyes.

Perhaps Grandma Catherine, too, had imagined that in this in-between world (no ugly old trolls, no spidery hands), children could breathe underwater.

THE MORNING AFTER MONOPOLY, after the bourbon on the porch and still a week before JL left, Sunshine woke early.

She was too hot and tangled in bedsheets. She had thrown them off and rolled to her back so she faced the ceiling with its cracks like tree branches.

The light outside the window was still the rosy gold of early morning, and over the wall opposite the open window, the shadows of the oak spilled and swayed. Her bedroom smelled like trees. She remembered Aunt Lou the night before, drinking and smoking cigarettes, and how she threw her head back and laughed at all of Billy's jokes. Sunshine smiled up at the ceiling and stretched her arms out in front of her, up toward the cracks, and wriggled her fingers. She shut one eye and blotted out a water stain with her thumb.

For a moment, the June mood from the night before still lingered, and the day was like the sea, spread out wide and open before her.

She'd see if she could go out on the bateau with Moss this morning; she bet if she got dressed quickly enough she could catch him. But when she sat up in bed—excited, now—her shirt brushed her chest and something felt tender.

All at once, she remembered the stones, and with the stones came a sickening feeling in her belly, something stretched taut, like when she felt embarrassed about something only worse than that—and she remembered, too, the spiders inside of her shirt. How they felt for the stones, Billy's breath hot in her ear.

She'd run to find Moss, and she'd spend the day at the lake with him. He'd tell her stories about when her grandparents were alive. How Grandma Catherine always wore the color pink. How she loved the woods like Sunshine. He'd tell her how everyone in Fingertip used to drive into St. Cadence to watch the high school baseball games, and how Billy could throw such a good curve ball they thought he was going to the Big Leagues, and then Moss would let her cool off in the cold clear water while he tied up the bateau.

The sun overhead would dry out and bleach clean this spongy, stinking memory of what happened on the porch.

She rose quickly from the bed and changed out of her clothes from the night before, into a tank top and overalls that Aunt Lou hated but were good if you needed to balance a worm on your knee as you baited a hook, or wipe fish blood from your hands. As she changed, she kept her eyes upward so she wouldn't accidentally look at the stones. She felt guilty that they were a part of her—as though by having them at all, they'd invited what had happened with Billy. She wished she could remove them, somehow—unfasten her buttons and pull them out. She wouldn't pocket them for safe-keeping but reach over the edge of Moss's bateau and drop them one by one into the deep part of the lake. She could hear their satisfying *plip plip*. Like bubbles from a fish's mouth.

She stepped cautiously into the hallway, intending to tiptoe past Billy's bedroom door, but she heard noises from the kitchen.

He was awake.

BILLY SAT AT THE table, reading the newspaper and sipping from a mug of coffee. He'd already showered. His hair, wavy like Aunt Lou's, was pushed wetly back from his forehead. He looked up at Sunshine and grinned.

"Well, good mornin' to you, Fred."

"Mornin'," she said, but her voice was too quiet.

"Hey," he said, setting down the paper. "You hungry? You want an egg-in-a-basket?"

Sunshine nodded, and Billy hopped up. Like he hadn't had too much bourbon last night. Like nothing had happened at all.

"Hey, you want to watch cartoons, Fred?"

He set the little portable TV on the Formica table and turned it to *The Scooby-Doo Show*, adjusting the set until the static mostly cleared. Sunshine couldn't seem to pay attention and instead kept watching Billy from the corner of her eye. He wore pale, grease-streaked jeans and a white shirt so thin she could see the color of his skin from beneath it. At his feet lay the butterfly-shaped stain, a stamp on the black-and-white linoleum from a time long before Sunshine was even born.

Billy took out the eggs, then the butter, and slathered it over both sides of the bread. When he spoke, she started.

"Hey," he said, without turning around. Had he felt her watching him?

"Hey," she said, and her stomach felt funny again.

Then he looked over his shoulder, grinned at her, and turned back to the stove. The butter in the pan sizzled.

"Heya, Fred," he began again. The kitchen door was open to the little side porch and she could hear, above the sizzling in the pan and the spooky music from *Scooby-Doo*, the layered coos of mourning doves. "I know I shouldn't have told you about the job, Fred," Billy said. "I don't want you to worry. Okay?"

He again turned to look at her over his shoulder, and she nodded and tried to smile, but for some reason there was a lump in her throat. She wanted to go put her arms around Billy and hug him and breathe in the smell of his shirt, but she felt awkward around him this morning. She was gripping the edges of her chair with both hands and her bare feet were tense, digging into the chair's cold metal crossbar.

"Okay," she said, and swallowed hard so her lips would stop trembling.

"We okay?" he said, still looking back at her, and she nodded again. She couldn't speak, now, or she'd start crying. She was afraid Billy was going to start apologizing for the way his hands had moved and she hoped he wouldn't speak of it at all. She hoped that somehow, such a silence would mean it wouldn't happen again.

That it had never happened.

"Look, Fred, I've got lots of options here, okay? I've got some connections down on the coast and I'm going down tomorrow to look and see about them. I'll go down every day if I need to, okay? You know old Billy will always take care of you and you don't have to worry about a thing."

As he rummaged around the kitchen, opening and closing cabinets and the silverware drawer, Sunshine quickly wiped away the tears that had started sliding down her cheeks. Then he set down a tall glass of milk and a plate with the egg-in-a-basket sandwich on the table in front of her. He'd cut the crust off her toast to keep for himself, and in exchange he had given her his own buttery circle of toast.

That flat little circle of toast, cut out to make room for the egg, was the best part of any egg-in-a-basket sandwich.

He leaned down so he was looking right in her face and cupped her cheek very gently with one hand. She took a shaky breath, inhaling his Right Guard and fruity shampoo, and looked back at him. There were tiny flecks of gold in his green eyes. He scraped his thumb back and forth across her cheek like a little windshield wiper, cleaning away the tears, and made a funny squeaking sound in the back of his throat.

She smiled.

"Like I said, Fred. Ain't nothing to worry about. Are we A-okay?"

She nodded and let out a sigh. "A-okay," she said.

BILLY SAT AT THE table with her to eat their breakfast and watch the end of *Scooby-Doo*. "Darn you meddling kids!" he kept saying, even before the mystery had been solved, just to make Sunshine laugh. He made them extra toast to soak up the remainder of bright yellow yolk that pooled on their plates. This was even better than going out with Moss—just her and Billy, the mood in the yellow house turning bright again.

Billy said he was going to go run some errands for the day, and after he left Sunshine turned off the television and cleaned up their dishes. The clock on the wall—its round face tired-looking and water-stained—read only nine o'clock, but the day no longer had the open-sea feeling it'd had when she had first woken up.

The heat from the dishes steamed up the window over the sink and the soapsuds made filmy mounds as she scrubbed the pan, and for some reason she remembered the time Aunt Lou had yelled at Billy. She remembered how Aunt Lou had accused Billy, had shouted, "You're going to look in the mirror and see his face, Billy Turner." How she said he had a goddamn daughter to feed.

Sunshine imagined drying her hands and racing across Only Road. She wanted to tell Aunt Lou that she was full from the breakfast Billy had made her, that he'd given her the extra circle of toast. She wanted to shout at Aunt Lou, *See? He's nothing like him.*

Already, the day's warmth had begun to drift in from the open kitchen door.

It was like Billy had said: She didn't need to worry. And if any of that late night (the june bugs clanging against the screen, silent record spinning) still lingered in the yellow kitchen that morning, dirtying Sunshine's own two hands, then she was washing away the last of it now.

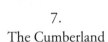

7.
The Cumberland

One early spring morning in 1941, when Catherine's father was just pulling out of a days-long spell but was not yet himself—face still pale, eyes glazed and unfocused, as though learning to see again—Catherine, acting on a whim, started up the Plymouth. She bundled them both in coats and hats and helped her father to the passenger side, rolling the windows down so the cold wind rushed through, stinging their cheeks and fingers, waking them both.

She drove nearly forty-five minutes to the Cumberland River and pulled off on the gravel shoulder just past the iron bridge. Together, they stepped over rocks and grass wet with frost and made their way down to the pebbled shore.

She could have simply walked with Talmadge, arm in arm, to the creek at the edge of town—but that morning, the creek seemed too close, its vines and its branches too tangled with their own everyday lives, and the magnitude of her father's illness required a larger landscape. A wider river.

IT WAS THE FIRST of many visits that spring season. In March, the smell of snow in the air, they stood watching the reflection of clouds skate across the surface of the black water. Over the eddies, a thin glaze of ice.

At the urging of both Dr. Oliver and finally Mr. Washburn himself, Talmadge had retired from his position at the post office that previous year; he was lost in his own dark spells more often than not. He was no longer full of the manic energy that kept him scribbling notes or making stew until dawn. Rather, he simply seemed sad.

He grew quiet. He slept long hours.

During their weekend trips to the river, Catherine no longer bothered with the childish stories that had entertained him when she was a little girl, nor did she try to make small talk, or ask what was on his mind, or how he felt. She simply stood nearby as they watched the water, as they smelled its river smells.

And, incredibly, the Cumberland seemed to have a rejuvenating effect.

By the time the weather warmed in late April, the sycamore leaves were a buoyant green and the air fragrant with mud. Teenage boys with their pants rolled high fished for trout in the shallow eddies. Catherine took her father's hand. Barefoot and laughing, they waded into the river, too, the pebbles smooth and reassuring against the soles of their feet.

That spring, they revived their old game: Catherine pointed to a knee-high sapling, or a patch of blooming grasses, or budding wildflowers, and her father named what he saw.

Oh, he'd say. His voice was hoarse, in those days, with so little use. *That one's a sycamore, of course.*

That's ironweed.

Inkberry. Always loved that name. Inkberry.

That one's milkweed, there.

Coreopsis.

That one? Bergamot!

He offered these names proudly, as though they were secrets only he possessed. And ever so gradually, Catherine began to feel hopeful that whatever had seemed so irrevocably broken inside of her father was slowly, at long last, beginning to heal.

ON A SATURDAY IN late May, Catherine let Talmadge continue sleeping while she and her mother drove the Plymouth into Nashville to visit Aunt Ruth.

Margaret Bell's older sister was more prim and Christian than even Margaret Bell could stomach, and she spent the majority of the visit explaining to Catherine the steps she should take should she wish, at age twenty-one, to at long last escape spinsterhood and find herself a suitable husband. One such suggestion, if Aunt Ruth might be so bold, would be for Catherine to wear colors that complemented her red hair, not clashed with it—greens and blues and so forth. Aunt Ruth's own hair—once also red, now thinning and gray—was tied in a bun so tight that Catherine could see the strain of her aunt's skin along her hairline.

Margaret Bell remained measured and polite throughout their visit, but as she pulled onto the two-lane highway that led back to Portland, she began laughing. Catherine, red-faced with humiliation and close to tears, said, "What on earth is so funny?"

Margaret Bell laughed so hard that she had to pull the Plymouth to the side of the road, verdant hills rolling like the sea to either side of the road. A truck roared past. She leaned back again in her seat and opened her mouth wide and let her laughter rattle the car until Catherine couldn't contain herself anymore, and began laughing too.

Catherine pulled her own hair so tightly that her eyebrows lifted and she turned to her mother and said, "I have some beauty tips for you," and Margaret Bell took off her glasses and wiped at her eyes with her kerchief, and it was still several minutes more before she was able to pull the car back onto the highway.

IT WAS SOMETIME THAT afternoon—perhaps as Aunt Ruth delivered her cutting criticisms to Catherine (each remark dolled up like a child on christening day to vaguely resemble a helpful instruction), perhaps as Margaret Bell and Catherine shared a laugh so visceral that they felt both giddy and exhausted afterwards, or perhaps as the truck roared past and Margaret Bell removed her glasses to wipe her eyes, and as Catherine's humiliation drained away and made way for something else, something she hadn't felt with her mother before—that Talmadge Booker went to the second floor bathroom of the white house with the gingerbread trim.

For years afterwards, Catherine imagined it: The house was so quiet that Talmadge could hear the ticking of the oak grandfather clock from downstairs, in the dining room they never used. The bathroom was muted with afternoon light. Talmadge stood very still, bare feet on the cold bathroom tile, and one by one he gathered the bottles in the medicine cabinet. He gathered his wife's headache medicine, and the medicine his doctor had given him for his ongoing stomach ulcers, and the glass bottle of cough syrup that had sat in the bathroom cupboard for at least a decade. He padded barefoot across his bedroom, and he lined the bottles up on his nightstand in one neat line, like soldiers at attention. He poured the contents of each bottle into his mouth and washed it all down with the rest of the bottle of whiskey.

WHEN HIS DAUGHTER (EYES still pinkened with laughter) found him, it looked like Talmadge had simply lain back on his bed, dressed in pants and tucked-in shirt—his narrow, hairy feet the only part of him unclothed—and fallen asleep.

His hair was combed neatly across his scalp, his hands folded, as though in prayer, across the soft mound of his belly.

LATER, CATHERINE THOUGHT SHE should have known his death was coming.

In her most pained moments, she thought perhaps she *had* known, in fact—but hadn't wanted to believe it.

Although he had not had a spell in a month or more—or at least not the kind she would have recognized—they had visited, that previous weekend, the river by the iron bridge. She'd brought a picnic of ham sandwiches (with pickles on his) and Coca-Colas. The day had been warm and the water had glittered. On the river bank, she had pointed out every vine, leaf, and tree, the bright green snake she had seen in the grass, the trout in the shallow eddy, the honeysuckle swathing the speckled bark of a sycamore—and her father had not named a single one.

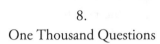

8.

One Thousand Questions

June 1982

Aunt Lou came home from the day shift one hot afternoon and waved to Sunshine, who had peeled back the plywood bridge to Terabithia to look for the toad whose shrill call could be heard at night. Through the open window of the shaggin' wagon, Aunt Lou called out, "I have a surprise for you!"

In the pink house, Aunt Lou opened a beer for herself and poured Sunshine a lemonade. Together, they sat on the back screened porch as Aunt Lou read JL's letter aloud.

It began *Dear Maman (and also Nash and Sunshine because I bet they're listening)*—Aunt Lou rolled her eyes when she read that part, but she was smiling—and gave a formal-sounding and detailed update on life at camp. JL said that she had fallen off her horse when a bee spooked it but don't worry, she hadn't hurt herself; she said she made a craft for her maman but would wait to surprise her with it; she said she learned how to pitch a tent and start a fire.

Her letter for Sunshine was folded in a complex system of various blank sheets of notebook paper. When Sunshine finally reached the letter itself, it had been shaped into a fat, tiny square and read PRIVATE! FOR SUNSHINE ONLY on on both sides.

Sunshine looked at Aunt Lou.

"It's okay, sugar," Aunt Lou laughed. "You girls can have your secrets."

She took her beer and went inside to shower, and Sunshine unfolded the letter. It read:

Hey Sunshine,

Hey how's it going-oing-oing-gone?

If you're reading this and Maman is around, please go SOMEWHERE ELSE. I want to tell you a secret.

OKAY?

ARE YOU SOMEWHERE ELSE?

OKAY THEN.

I met a boy at camp, his name is Henry AND we French kissed.

DO NOT TELL ANYONE.

Silencieuse!

It was like sticking my tongue through a Life Saver. But don't worry, I'm not going to do it until I'm 16, when I do I'll tell you first.

Have you gone to the new house yet? Are Maman and the 'Stache still gross? Is Billy rich now? If you want to stay in my room you can, I don't mind.

L + U + V,

Joanna

Sunshine took the letter and tore it into tiny pieces and flushed it down the toilet in the green-tiled bathroom, still steamy from Aunt Lou's shower.

Aunt Lou called out from her bedroom, where she was putting on make-up. She had a date with Nash that night. "You should write back," she said to Sunshine. "It's always nice to hear from people you love."

AFTER AUNT LOU KISSED her goodbye, Sunshine took one of the spare quilts from the hallway closet and several spare sheets, pilled and soft with age, and carried the heavy pile across Only Road. Billy's truck had been gone that morning when she woke up and still hadn't come back.

The yellow house was dark with the coming storm and filled with the sweet smell of almost-rain.

In her bedroom, she tucked the corner of a borrowed quilt into the top drawer of the smaller of her two bedroom dressers (where old baby clothes and empty picture frames and tarnished silver candle holders were kept in disorganized drawers). The other end she tied to her bed post so the quilt draped down and formed a wall. From the hallway closet, she took a sheet with faded blackberry vines to make a roof—the quilts, she realized, were too heavy—but it wasn't long enough to tie to the far bedpost and when she tried to prop one corner on the nightstand, it only slipped uselessly to the floor.

Over the washing machine on the narrow covered porch off the kitchen was a storage shelf where they kept old boxes of detergent, speckled with mildew, and a rusting toolbox. Sunshine took out a hammer and nails—all of them also rusting—then returned to her bedroom.

When she was finished, the fort was secured with clothespins and various nails, and its walls were made of quilts and the green papered walls of her bedroom. A rush of breeze blew through her window and the roof of the tent rippled, but held. The sky outside her window was a deep bruise.

She shivered with excitement.

As the storm crashed and banged, she outfitted the inside of the fort with piles of blankets and pillows. She took the old porcelain hurricane lamp with the painted flowers from her dresser and brought it inside, and she brought in a spoon and a half-empty jar of peanut butter, too (a snack inside of a fort felt especially exciting), and a dish towel so she could keep the spoon clean.

When the rain let up, and the sunset through the receding clouds lit Fingertip in an eerie glow, Sunshine went back across Only Road, the mud squishing between her bare toes, and took armfuls of children's books and novels from JL's bedroom closet. They had belonged to Aunt Lou when she was little, and their pages smelled old and somehow sweet, and back inside the fort she built a library, stacking the books neatly against the wall. Finally, she settled inside. The globes of the hurricane lamp glowed soft and warm. She ate spoonfuls of peanut butter and wrote JL a letter back:

Dear JL,

Hi summer is great! Billy has lots of C A $ H. The kissing sounds disgusting and when you are 16 and do it I don't want to know about it just so you know.

Sunshine

She didn't actually know what JL meant by "it," and she very much wanted to know, but she was mad at JL for leaving her alone for the whole summer and so she didn't ask.

In fact, she wanted to write to JL a list of questions. She bet could think of at least one thousand of them, and she'd write them all in Pig Latin in case any grown-up was nearby, and very tiny—but still they'd fill one of those old-fashioned paper scrolls that JL would have to dramatically unroll at camp. Sunshine would write the most important ones first:

What're the ones-stay in my est-chay?
Did this appen-hay before you ot-gay oobs-bay?
Did enry-Hay use is-hay ands-hay and did they eel-fay like iders-spay?
Are you orried-way about getting egnant-pray?
Because remember? What you said about the ubworm-gray?

"Oh, it can happen in all sorts of ways," JL told her.

The lake spread out before them like a mirror. They sat with their legs stretched out before them in the shallow water, dribbling soft handfuls of sand onto their shins and thighs. Sunshine's legs in the sun were the color of raw honey. JL's were paler and lightly freckled. They were whispering so that Aunt Lou, sitting on a beach chair in the shade of the oak, eyes closed, wouldn't hear.

"It can happen just from kissing. If you put your mouth on his mouth and he puts his tongue inside, like this"—JL made a donut shape with the thumb and fingers of one sand-covered hand and jabbed her tongue through—"then a teeny tiny beetle type thing—it's too small to see— slips from his tongue to your throat and down into your belly."

"Then what?" Sunshine whispered.

Disgusted. Riveted.

JL's eyes were bright with sunlight and secret knowledge. They matched the green of the water. She leaned closer to Sunshine. "The beetle swells and swells," she said, "and then it cracks open like an egg, and a gross little grubworm comes out—and you wanna know what happens next?"

"What?" Sunshine said, breathless. She was dying to know.

"Well," said JL, "the grubworm grows into a *baby*."

SUNSHINE WROTE AT THE end of her short letter: *PS I don't want to stay in your room thanks.* Then she sealed it in an envelope, wrote, PRIVATE FOR JL on the outside, and, the next morning, left it on Aunt Lou's kitchen table for her to mail.

If Aunt Lou opened it, at least the only secrets inside—whatever *it* was—would get JL in trouble, not Sunshine. Not Billy.

9.

Fruit in Your Hand

B illy and Aunt Lou didn't much like to talk about their parents, but Sunshine had long sensed them in the yellow house, even before she learned anything about them.

She had long sensed the story of the crocodile bride too.

Sometimes stories were like that. It was like you were born knowing them deep in your bones, and when you finally heard them told, they were more like memories.

SHE WAS SEVEN YEARS old when Billy first told her about the Black Bayou. It was an overcast summer afternoon, the sky low and gray, and they were in the iron rockers on the porch. It smelled like rain though the ground was still dry and Billy had started to tell her about the shark in the lake. He said he was once out fishing and a great white had attacked his boat, but Billy bopped it on the nose. Defeated, the shark swam back down the bayou channels and to the ocean and he hadn't seen one there since.

"I like that one okay," Sunshine said. "But you told it before."

"I told that one before?" Billy said, feigning disbelief. "Well shit, Fred. I guess you've about heard them all."

She moved her weight so the rocker went back and forth. "Aunt Lou said you have more stories than anyone," she said.

"Ah, is that right?"

"She says they're not true."

Billy's mouth dropped open. "*Not true?*" he screeched, and Sunshine laughed.

It had begun to rain. The moss in the branches blew like hair and from somewhere down the road, Sunshine heard wind chimes.

"All right," said Billy. He took a long sip of his beer. "I'll admit it. The shark story might be an exaggeration."

Sunshine knew what exaggeration meant. She had learned it at school. It meant to stretch out the truth like caramel. She felt disappointed.

"I knew that," she said, although she hadn't known that at all. Billy looked at her sideways and she thought he didn't believe her.

"I do have a true story, though," he said. "I just hadn't told it to you before because I thought it might scare you. It's one that your Grandma Catherine told to me and Lou when we were little kids—'fact, I guess I was about your age when I first heard it."

The promise of a new story eclipsed her disappointment—and Aunt Lou didn't know everything, besides. "I wanna hear!"

"You sure? There's a crocodile, Fred, and he ain't friendly."

"I wasn't scared about the shark."

"Well, this crocodile is the biggest you ever saw. He could swallow that shark whole, no problem....But wait a minute now. I'm getting ahead of myself. Are you absolutely, positively *sure* you want to hear this story?"

She was sure. Absolutely, positively. Rain drummed on the porch roof. Goosebumps sprouted along her arms and legs.

"All right then. It starts a very long time ago, deep in the forest, at a place called the Black Bayou."

And right then, Sunshine could feel that story like a memory. As soft and true as fruit in her hand.

• • •

THE TENNESSEE ROADS WERE matted with wet, colorful leaves when Catherine drove by herself to see Aunt Ruth again in Nashville. Margaret Bell said she had papers to grade, though Catherine suspected she just didn't have the energy or will to cope with her sister. Catherine brought Aunt Ruth a birthday gift from her mother (a new, soft leather Bible with a watercolor frontispiece showing the angel descending to greet a white-bearded Elijah) and a card from herself.

Aunt Ruth (hair pulled tight) seemed disappointed by the card and delighted by the Bible. Catherine stayed for an hour and then hastily rose, kissed her aunt's dry cheek, and said she must be getting back.

Exhausted even from such a brief visit, she stopped first in a corner café. She sat on a wooden swivel stool at the countertop near the register, her back straight, legs primly crossed. That morning, she'd put on a pink sweater to spite her aunt—but, after glancing one last time in her dresser mirror, had decided to at least add a little make-up to avoid the predicted criticism about her looks, her spinsterhood.

It hadn't worked. Aunt Ruth commented that Catherine's rouge only emphasized her too-long face and pointed out, too, that her mascara was smudged.

In the café, the dusky rose of her sweater complimented her pale skin, her pinkened cheeks—contrary to what Aunt Ruth had insisted—but Catherine couldn't have known that then. She was thinking (perched on that café stool in her pretty pink sweater) not of her own appearance or of Aunt Ruth's criticism of it, but of her father.

In those months after Talmadge's death, grief overtook her at unexpected moments. The sight of a child walking down a Portland sidewalk with bobby socks rolled to her ankles made Catherine catch her breath with the pain of her loss. Another time, it was the waxy skin of apples from the tree in their backyard (though Talmadge had not even cared for apples). Once, it was the sight of Pontius Pilate—at age nineteen, he had lived long past the age of most roosters—whom her father alone had loved.

Now, at the café counter, she could feel it. As though a heavy lid had been knocked off a deep well, as though that grief were rising up from inside of it like water.

She tried to breathe it away, but her throat was tight and her lips trembled.

As though beckoned by her sadness, a man appeared at the café counter beside her. He was tall and slender and handsome. Clean-cut. Dark hair slicked back with pomade.

He looked over at her and smiled as though pleasantly surprised by what he saw before him: a small, red-haired young woman in a pink sweater, eyes full of tears.

"I'd be reminiscent," he drawled, leaning close, "if I did not ask if I might join you."

Catherine, assuming his misuse of the word was intentional, smiled in spite of herself. A small, trembling smile—but still. The well water receded. She took a deep breath.

Settling on the counter stool beside her, the man ordered a fresh cup of coffee for himself and a refill for her. When the waitress turned her back, he took a small flask from his pants pocket and splashed a helping in each mug.

JOHN JAY TURNER WAS an assistant manager of a bank in town—an educated man, Catherine noted immediately, despite the vocabulary words he sometimes got wrong—who had gone to Vanderbilt. She did not mind his bragging about his degree, which he did within the first few minutes of conversation; it seemed somehow charming, a sign of his confidence. (Only later would she learn, from something one of his friends mentioned casually at a bar, that he'd actually come several credits shy of his degree.)

She liked the way his green eyes contrasted with his dark hair, and she liked how in the corner café, those eyes were on only her. Not on the large-breasted waitress behind the café counter, or the attractive college girls in a nearby booth. Only later would he show his interest in other women. On that first day, his interest was in just her, with her small breasts and slight frame, with her red hair and the pink sweater that she loved.

In the months that followed, John Jay frequently drove to Portland to visit her. He took her to dinner at the nicer of the two Portland restaurants (though neither was particularly nice to begin with), then parked his car at the edge of a nearby farm field. She had never had more than a single sip or two of her father's whiskey tea and she was delighted, on these nights, by the way the whiskey in John Jay's flask both warmed and numbed her. In the moonlit front seat she let him lift her skirt, pull down her underwear and put his body inside of hers. It hurt so much the first time that she cried out in pain, and he kissed her neck gently and said, "Shh, shh," which she took as a sign of his kindness.

AT CHRISTMAS, THEY ATTENDED a party at a small brick bungalow in Nashville. Catherine wore a new rose-pink dress, and one side of her hair pulled back in a rhinestone comb. She'd carefully curled the ends and then combed them smooth. Standing next to John Jay in the crowded living room, laughing with the other couples, sipping whiskey that some of John Jay's friends—the Party Boys, he called them—had made in their basement, she barely reached his shoulder. She was petite (narrow-shoul-dered, small-waisted) and John Jay was over six feet tall.

As John Jay laughed and chatted with the Party Boys, she leaned her head playfully against his arm. She liked the scratch of his wool sweater against her cheek and the warm strength of the arm underneath the fabric.

"She can't resist me," he said to one of the men.

There erupted a chorus of chuckles as the blood rushed to her cheeks. She lifted her head and took a sip of her drink. John Jay wrapped his arm around her shoulders, and pulled her close.

It was two or so months into their courtship and he wasn't often affec-tionate in public. When he did touch her, when he pulled her close like this and she could smell the sharp piney scent of aftershave, it felt as though her patience had paid off. Now he was paying her the attention she craved (but that—it was silently and implicitly agreed upon—she did not always deserve).

At the end of the night, John Jay drove her back toward Portland. The car smelled strongly of whiskey and drifted, on occasion, into the other lane.

"Darling," Catherine said, after the third time it happened. "Would you mind pulling over? I'd be happy to drive the rest of the way. I only had one." She spoke gently, as she might to a child—and later, she would regret her tone. Or perhaps her word choice. She actually wasn't sure which, exactly, was the source of her regret, only that she had somehow come across in the wrong way.

Otherwise, what happened next would not have happened.

On the dark highway shoulder, without saying anything in return, John Jay opened his car door to climb out and trade seats. They passed one another in the bright wash of headlights from his car. No other cars were in sight; to either side of the road stretched black, empty hills. The air was bitterly cold.

In the headlight glare, she offered him a smile to let him know everything was fine; she still loved him; they were having a good time—*she* was still a good time. She met his eyes. In the brilliance of those headlights, they were a sharp, cutting green.

"What are you smirking at?" he sneered, and then the back of his hand was raised, and she flinched but did not have time to move or to duck. She heard a loud cracking sound and it took her a moment to realize it was the sound of his hand striking her. The rhinestone comb landed with a cheap clatter on the pavement.

She froze in the blinding glare and held her hand to her ear. She heard ringing and her eyes were hot with tears. John Jay was already at the passenger side door, climbing in, slamming it shut; she bent to look for the comb and saw that he must have stepped on it as he passed. It had broken into several pieces.

Catherine drove the remaining half-hour with her fingers clenching the steering wheel to keep them from shaking. Beside her, John Jay stared out the window, arms crossed over his chest like a chastised child. She fought to control her uneven breathing.

It seemed important not to show she was upset. To act as though everything was fine. To show him that she could take such moments in stride.

When she pulled his car in front of the white house with the gingerbread trim, its windows darkened, she asked in what she meant to be a relaxed, all-is-well tone if he wanted to come in for coffee before he drove home.

He scoffed.

She had not yet reached the front door when he drove off.

IN THE EARLY WEEKS of the new year, Catherine put on white heels, a pale pink suit, and a pair of pearl earrings she borrowed from Margaret Bell. One side of her hair was pulled up in a pearl comb—a Christmas present from John Jay. He had noticed the rhinestone comb, she knew, and although he did not apologize for anything that had happened that night, she believed—she knew—the pearl comb was meant as an apology. She had teared up when she opened the little velvet box.

With the comb and the matching earrings and the pink suit and white heels, she felt stylish and pretty. She hurried behind John Jay. (He almost always walked at least several strides ahead of her in public, and she told herself it was simply because of his long limbs. He was so handsome and so tall. He couldn't help his stride.) The heels of her white shoes made a pleasant clicking sound on the stone steps of the Nashville County Courthouse, where, twenty minutes later, they were pronounced married.

She looked down at her slender hand with its new gold wedding band, then turned her head up toward John Jay and smiled. He smiled, too, a boyish grin, and he leaned down to kiss her. His aftershave enveloped her, pierced her nostrils. She told herself that this—a tall dark-haired man who had chosen *her* to love, to hold, to press his lips against—*this* must be true happiness.

YEARS LATER, IN THE yellow house, Catherine would not talk much to her children about their parents' time in Tennessee.

Certainly nothing about that first moment in the headlights of his car.

Certainly nothing about too much whiskey, the broken comb, the nights afterwards, when similar moments occurred and were immediately forgiven.

In fact, she didn't often mention John Jay to her children in general. As though in omitting the topic of their father from daily conversation, his various abuses and the pain they caused might be forgotten. Or even erased.

When she did speak about their past together, she focused brightly on positive incidents and events and details, most from very early in their courtship. Most embellished. All designed to paint their father in a rosier light than he had ever succeeded in painting himself.

"Oh, listen," she once told them, on a drive into St. Cadence. The bruise behind her sunglasses was tinged a yellow-green. "I couldn't believe the time your daddy bought me that pearl comb. I don't even much wear it now, it's so pretty. Made from genuine oyster pearls. He didn't have much money back then, so for him to spring for something like that comb. Well, mercy."

She told them how affectionate he could be with her at parties, in those early days, and she described that first moment in the café, looking over to see such a handsome green-eyed man, how she admired his carefully pomaded hair. "Such a handsome man," she said. "None of those Portland bumpkins took such care of their appearance as your daddy." She described how she'd been sad that afternoon, but how their father's conversation and good looks cheered her right up.

She showed them the photograph on the courthouse steps in Nashville. She said, "Doesn't your daddy look so handsome? Don't we look so happy?"

She shared with them only her sweetest memories, and she let the other truths of John Jay fall away from conversation like bark from a tupelo grown soft with rot.

CATHERINE DIDN'T KNOW WHAT her two children did or did not notice, did or did not absorb, did or did not believe.

When she sat at the Formica table the morning after a bad night and Billy put his little arms around her shoulders, leaned his ahead against her, or when her two-year-old daughter gently kissed her bruises, or on those nights when they retreated to their bedroom, the door closed against what was happening outside of their bedroom—did her children register the truth of these moments?

Did they register the horror?

Or did they believe it was all a part of some better story? Did they believe that elves had bruised her in her sleep? Did they believe that when he struck her, she had done something to deserve it? Did they believe that his cruelties, his bottomless need for control, for a sense of being *better than*, was truly tempered by those warmer memories she shared with them—by an expensive pearl comb, by a warm gesture at a Christmas party long ago?

She hoped so—that they believed a better story. *The bigger picture.* She hoped that they believed anything but reality.

She hoped for this so furiously that she could sometimes believe her own hopes were true—that her children saw things the way she wanted them to see things, that they knew in their small bodies not the reality of their father and his treatment of their mother, of themselves, but only in the unreality she did her best to create for them.

In the wished-for. In the imaginary.

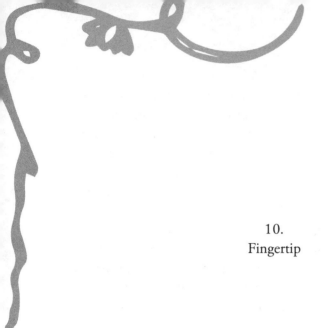

10.
Fingertip

June 1982

J une slid toward July like a slow, heavy train.

(The old wood-slatted freight cars wobbled under the weight of stacked pine logs and bins of salted fish, wide-eyed among layers of ice, and crates of bright oranges—NATURE'S ORIGINAL!)

The mornings were often blue-skied, but by early afternoon, clouds had ballooned overhead, threatening to topple and crush the Atchafalaya under their weight. As the afternoon wore on, they spread like mud across the sky over Fingertip and let forth thunderous sheets of rain.

On a hot, clear morning in early July, before Billy left to go look for work (or odd jobs, or whatever it was he went and did all day that he didn't share with Sunshine), he left a five-dollar bill pinned to the Formica table with a pepper shaker. The milk had gone bad, and so Sunshine took the money and walked up to the Lust. The earth was soft from the previous day's rain, and she had to wipe her feet thoroughly on a patch of grass before going inside.

The Lust was cool and quiet. By the entry, two large glass windows filled the aisles with light. Farther back, the counter where Big Jake stood gave way to the bar with spinning stools, and in the cool shadows beyond that were a handful of small tables and a pool table.

Big Jake had a sweaty, moon-shaped face and a huge belly that bulged out over the waistband of his pants. His eyes were small and shiny, like tiny black candies. He was the same age as Aunt Lou and had grown up in Fingertip. His daddy, Little Jake, owned the Lust before him, and Big Jake took it over when Little Jake died of a heart attack before Sunshine was born.

Aunt Lou said Big Jake had been a handsome man once, but he got drafted to Vietnam and when he got back, he let himself go.

Sunshine was only seven or eight, then, and JL and Sunshine had gone with Aunt Lou to get groceries. It was winter, and Only Road was hard under their shoes. Sunshine's were too large—hand-me-downs from JL that she didn't quite fit into just yet—and she kept tripping over the rubber toes.

"What's *let himself go?*" Sunshine had asked.

JL, walking in front of Aunt Lou and Sunshine, turned around so she was walking backwards. "It means he got fat," she said, laughing.

"We don't call people *fat,*" Aunt Lou said.

JL shrugged and turned back around. Her red pony tail swung back and forth as she walked. Her denim bell-bottoms flapped at her ankles. The pockets on the butt were shaped like hearts, their edges stitched with rainbow thread.

"Did Billy get drafted too?" Sunshine asked.

"No. He was one of the lucky ones."

"Why was he lucky?

"Because Vietnam would've broke him," she said, and then she'd looked down at Sunshine, walking along beside her, and smiled. "Sorry, sugar. I shouldn't say things like that. I'm just glad he didn't have to go into all that mess."

THE CONCRETE FLOOR OF the Lust was smooth against Sunshine's bare feet. Big Jake said, "Good morning, little miss."

"Morning, Big Jake," she said, and went to the cooler for the gallon of milk. Then she remembered the other things they needed—dish soap, a bar of Irish Spring for the bathroom, more Honey Nut Cheerios. She piled these things in her arms and took them carefully to the register.

"Six fifty-four," Big Jake told her.

Sunshine handed him the five. "Could we put the rest on Billy's tab?"

Big Jake consulted the notepad where he kept track of tabs, then raised his eyebrows so the skin of his forehead scrunched into soft folds. "I don't suppose your daddy can come on up here and pay his tab today?"

This had happened before. Billy was always slow to pay his tab. *There's never any money, Fred*, he sometimes sighed. When he couldn't pay his tab, he stopped at the Qwik-E-Mart off 79 for beer instead of the Lust so that Big Jake couldn't ask him about the money he owed, and if they needed something from the Lust, Sunshine went instead of Billy, because Billy said Big Jake wouldn't ever give a kid a hard time.

But on those occasions he'd still been employed, and Sunshine could reassure Big Jake that they'd bring the money soon. Now, her face grew hot. She looked down at her bare, mud-streaked feet. She pretended to be distracted, using one toe to rub off a fleck of mud. She tried to think of what to say. "Um," she said, "I think he's busy today." She was relieved when bell over the door rang out.

"Hell's bells," Big Jake said. "If it isn't the prettiest lady in Louisiana."

Sunshine looked up to see Aunt Lou. She was dressed for work, her long red hair pulled back in two combs. She wore a knee-length denim skirt and a striped, short-sleeve blouse.

She *was* pretty, Sunshine thought proudly, and for a moment she forgot her embarrassment.

Aunt Lou rolled her eyes at Big Jake. "You old flirt," she said, then she pulled Sunshine against her body and kissed the top of her head. "Feels like I've hardly seen you lately, sugar." She kept her arm around Sunshine, holding her close.

It was true, about not seeing her. Aunt Lou was working more often this summer—saving money to help pay for the move to the new house, she'd said—and besides that, Sunshine hadn't wanted to see her, not since the night on the porch.

IN THE PAST, WHEN Billy stayed on the coast for work or went out on the rig overnight, Sunshine would spend the night in JL's room. They'd try to stay up as late as they could, until their eyes closed involuntarily and their words came out jumbled. "Your feet are salamanders," JL had once said to her, half dreaming, and for months afterwards they'd said it to each other, "Your feet are salamanders," and erupt into laughter.

But after what happened with the spiders and with JL at camp, Sunshine knew she couldn't go to JL's room anymore. It wasn't that Aunt Lou would be bothered so much as she might notice. Might ask questions. Might see that something was *off*. And even if she didn't, Sunshine feared that the very act of staying at Aunt Lou's house might somehow reveal the secrets she was keeping. As though Aunt Lou might suddenly realize she was in possession of X-ray vision, and could easily peer straight into Sunshine's chest. She'd see Sunshine's heart, all black and sooty with secrets. Aunt Lou would tell her to scrub it clean before she went out in public—and then she'd squint, and her X-ray vision would come into sharper focus, and she'd see *him*. That ugly old troll—the one Aunt Lou had said that Billy would see in the mirror one day. With gray, liver-spotted skin and red-rimmed eyes, right in the center of that soot-tarnished heart, staring boldly back at Aunt Lou. Licking his lips with the knowledge of Sunshine's secrets.

He wouldn't waste time; he'd whisper them all in his hoarse troll voice.

He'd tell Aunt Lou what Sunshine let Billy do on the porch that night. How she was too big and sat on his lap anyway. How she couldn't speak, how she just sat there. He'd tell Aunt Lou that Sunshine had been keeping Billy's secret about the job, not just for a day or two but all summer.

The anger Aunt Lou had let loose in the hallway of the yellow house, Aunt Lou would let loose on her.

And then on Billy too.

Who knew what would happen then? What punishments might ensue? What words, what silences would slice and sever? What storms would flood the yellow house? And who would stop loving who?

Sunshine's heart, poisoned by *him*, might spill its secrets and then wither (swiftly, irreversibly) to a fine black dust.

"WHAT'RE YOU UP TO today, sugar?" Aunt Lou said. She still had her arm around Sunshine and she smelled like almond soap.

Big Jake was writing something in his notepad. "Nothing," she said.

"I guess there's not much to do around here, huh?"

Sunshine shrugged.

"Well. With your imagination, I'm sure you'll think of something." Aunt Lou turned to Big Jake. "What did we do around here when we were kids?"

Big Jake took his handkerchief from his back pocket and wiped the sweat from his forehead. "Probably not much good," he said, and smiled at Aunt Lou.

JL said Big Jake was in love with her maman but that she hadn't ever loved Big Jake back. Sunshine watched him, now, and how his eyes turned soft when he looked at Aunt Lou. Sweat trickled from his hairline down along his temple. Then he turned to Sunshine.

"Now, look," he said, and she braced herself. She didn't want Aunt Lou to hear whatever Big Jake was going to say. "You let your daddy know I'm happy to help a man out from time to time. Believe me, honey, he knows that. But I can't be running a charity. That's all."

Aunt Lou looked down at Sunshine, frowning. "You got enough cash today, sugar?"

"All good here," Big Jake said, and he winked at Sunshine. "Now what can I help you with today, Lou Lou?"

Aunt Lou laughed. "You're the only one who calls me that anymore," she said.

Big Jake pushed the paper bag with Sunshine's groceries across the counter. "Must mean I'm special," he said.

Sunshine, eager to escape anymore questions or talk of money, took the bag and turned for the door. "Bye," she called over her shoulder.

"Well, don't linger on my account," Aunt Lou said, and Sunshine heard the two grown-ups laugh as she pushed out the door and into the heavy heat of the morning.

JUNE BUGS CALLED FROM the mound of vines and honeysuckle that grew wild all across the old train platform. The commuter train had stopped running this length of track after the sugar mill closed, when Billy was still just a baby, but he said a ghost train still ran past sometimes. He said that when he was little, he and Aunt Lou would walk up to the platform to suck the honey from the honeysuckle blossom, and that now and then they'd hear the whistle of the ghost train and feel the rush of wind blow back their hair as it rumbled past.

Aunt Lou called the ghost train story hogwash. "No such thing as ghost trains," she once said. "Don't listen to him, Sunshine Turner."

This was years ago. They were in Aunt Lou's living room, just the three of them, Aunt Lou and Billy drinking beers after dinner in the tangerine lamplight. Sunshine drank a root beer and listened to them talk.

"Wait just a minute," Billy said, leaning forward in the easy chair. His voice was loud. "Just 'cause you've never *seen* a ghost doesn't mean it don't exist."

"*Doesn't* exist," Aunt Lou corrected. "And I didn't say ghosts don't exist, I said ghost trains don't exist. There's a difference."

Billy turned to Sunshine, who was sitting cross-legged on the sofa. His eyes were sparkly and she could see that he was not really mad. "Don't listen to my sister," he said.

Sunshine turned to Aunt Lou. "Are there ghosts?"

"You're asking *her*?" Billy scoffed. "She doesn't know anything!"

Aunt Lou stuck her tongue out at him. "Well, sugar, maybe so. I've just never seen one."

"Look," Billy said. "Ghosts are all around, Fred. All the damn time. You see one, don't be scared. That's an amateur mistake."

"Why are you looking at me?!" Aunt Lou cried, and reached over to slap at Billy's arm.

"Fred, you see this abuse your daddy suffers?"

But Sunshine could see he wasn't serious, and she was thinking about the ghost train besides. About ghosts being all around. "What do you do if you see one?" she asked.

"Oh, that's easy," said Billy. "Now, in my experience—"

"In your *experience?*" Aunt Lou started laughing.

"*Yes*, in my *experience*," Billy continued, and waved at Aunt Lou like he was brushing away a mosquito. "In my experience, Fred, ghosts come around when they got something for you. But most ghosts have been gone for a while, so their memory ain't so great. You gotta ask questions if you want to know what they've gotta say. If they've brought you any news, any gifts...."

"Billy Turner," Aunt Lou scolded, and shook her head.

"Just telling her what I know! The kid asked."

"Sunshine, you know what I'd do if I saw a ghost?" Aunt Lou said.

"What?"

"*Run*," Aunt Lou said, and all three of them burst into laughter.

SUNSHINE SQUINTED TOWARD THE train platform, which had long ago collapsed under the weight of all that the honeysuckle. Across the tracks, the old soybean fields spread on like water.

For a moment, she stood in the middle of Only Road and listened for the whistle of the ghost train. For the rumble of a train from down the tracks.

In the unshaded road, the sun beat down.

The ghost train didn't come. There was only the chorus of locusts in the drainage ditch, the cries of mourning doves from the pines across the tracks.

• • •

THE TRAIN LINE WAS still running when the Turners arrived in Fingertip. The war was not yet over, but John Jay was just past drafting age, and he took a job as supervisor of a sugar mill run by a distant cousin of Catherine's.

Catherine hardly knew the cousin, but she had written anyway and explained their case: John Jay had been laid off at his job as bank manager in Nashville, and urban opportunities were scarce. She had heard, she wrote, that Louisiana was like Tennessee, but hotter and with its mountains ironed out flat, *ha ha.*

The cousin replied that he not only had a position at the sugar mill, but that he'd heard rumor of vacancies in a New Deal community just one parish over from the sugar mill. Ninety-nine-cent mortgages, and a commuter train to carry employees to work. He included the brochure he'd seen along with the letter, and in the spring of 1942, Catherine and John Jay moved to Fingertip, Louisiana. (Population: 62.)

The Lust was still the Last Outpost, and the houses along Only Road were painted fresh pastel colors, lined up like children dressed for Sunday school. At the end of the road, the little yellow house (vacant since its last inhabitants had left Fingertip, the husband for overseas and the wife and their newborn son to live with her parents in Birmingham) had not yet been placed up on its stilts. The house was a bright yellow and still young. Not an old lady who leaned to one side, tired from all the secrets she kept.

But the first day John Jay left to walk up to the train platform, he made the mistake of wearing his newly polished wingtips and sank up to his ankles in red mud.

CATHERINE OFTEN THOUGHT THAT she had been wrong to show John Jay the brochure, with its flattering photographs of the little village: A single unpaved road. Neat little bungalows. Charming screened porches. There was even a general store and a nearby chapel.

The brochure offered four little pages of sun-dappled promise.

Of a much longed-for break in economic strain. A small plot of land. A place to raise up happy, healthy children.

Catherine imagined that the quaintness of such a place could only influence her marriage to John Jay for the better; it would be like placing an apple alongside a tomato to speed its ripening.

The new place, the new job, the nearness of neighbors, of trees, of water, the quiet single road, the hopeful yellow house—these things would warm John Jay's increasing coldness and cool his temper. They would coax from him the love Catherine imagined was somewhere inside of him (hadn't she seen it, in those first months of their courtship?), waiting only for the right circumstances to emerge.

She had imagined him grilling dinner in the shade of a tree, their various children clamoring around his legs. She imagined pouring coffee at a kitchen countertop with his arm hooked around her shoulder, his unshaven face nuzzling the crook of her neck. Porch cocktails with each other, perhaps with neighbors. The clink of their glasses. And when it got too late, John Jay carrying a sleeping child to bed.

Gently. Lovingly.

Catherine's imagination had ushered her into the marriage with John Jay, and it ushered her further still—to a place where she knew no one, not even her husband.

NOT LONG BEFORE SHE left for Louisiana, Catherine borrowed her new husband's Buick one winter afternoon and drove from their rented apartment in Nashville to her mother's house in Portland.

She wore her best city clothes, hoping to impress Margaret Bell, and they sat at the kitchen table drinking coffee from Margaret Bell's antique teacups. Delicate pansies were painted on their sides. Catherine told her mother that she was in love, that she wanted to have children, that John Jay had accepted the position at the packaging plant and they would be moving to a bungalow that cost only ninety-nine cents per year. She spoke with excitement, with perhaps more excitement than she actually felt, hoping to stir in Margaret Bell some sign of happiness. Some sign of her approval.

But Catherine's mother remained tight-lipped. She stared down at her coffee, still stirring it with a tiny silver spoon although the sugar had dissolved minutes ago. Finally, she picked up her linen napkin and, to Catherine's surprise, dabbed at her eyes.

"St. Cadence, Louisiana," Margaret Bell said, repeating the name Catherine had told her.

"Near there, anyway. *A little village.*" She said those words for the third time: A little village.

It sounded so charming.

Catherine took a sip of her coffee. "I think you'd like it. I saw photographs in the brochure—I should have brought it with me."

Then Margaret Bell did something even further unexpected. She placed one hand on Catherine's wrist. She looked her daughter in the eye. Through her glasses, her eyes were still moist with tears. Her lips were trembling.

Catherine fought the urge to jerk her wrist away. The loss of control in her mother's facial expression, the rawness of her emotion so plainly evident, was frightening.

"It's very far away," said her mother, her voice choked, "to move with a man you hardly know."

Catherine had only seen her mother allow herself to cry two other times—once when she'd discovered the nest of baby robins in the potted hydrangea on the back porch had been eaten by a rat snake, and once (her nose buried in a linen handkerchief) at Talmadge's funeral.

Often after arriving in Fingertip, she remembered her mother's choked voice, like molasses through a sieve, and she wondered if Margaret Bell could see in Catherine's husband what she herself refused to acknowledge.

She hadn't ever mentioned to Margaret Bell the incident in the headlights of the car. And to herself, she explained away that moment and the others. It was the whiskey. Not John Jay himself. Not his conscious choices.

When he occasionally gave her apology gifts—the pearl comb or the necklace he won at a county fair (it was brass, and the skin of her chest turned raw from where the locket rubbed against it, and so she kept it in a porcelain dish on her dresser)—she accepted them as proof that he was not who he was in his worst moments.

When he insulted her hair and her freckles. Her slight frame.

When he slapped her with an open palm, or the back of his hand.

When he shoved her so hard that she fell back against the edge of a table so that, for the rest of her life, a small, calcified knot could be felt along the ridge above her neck where the cut had healed over.

It had always been true that Catherine and Margaret Bell did not say much to one another as a general rule. When they did speak, it was often only small talk about the house. Even after Talmadge's death—or perhaps, especially after his death—they'd kept their conversation constrained to logistics. Who would write the obituary? Who would notify the paper in his hometown, who would write to his brother, what sort of sandwiches should they serve at the luncheon after the funeral—ham or cheese? Would it be too costly to offer both?

The fact that Margaret Bell had nearly cried in front of her daughter the day she shared the news of her move to Louisiana was downright shocking.

Why hadn't she—Catherine later wondered—told Margaret Bell right then the truth of her relationship with John Jay? Why hadn't she asked for her help in extracting herself from it?

By the time she arrived in Fingertip, it was too late.

WHILE JOHN JAY WORKED weekdays at the sugar mill, Catherine often walked along the trails that led from the end of Only Road to the lake, down along its shores, then deeper into the forest where some of the farmers from up the road came to hunt wild pigs. As she walked, she sometimes imagined that Talmadge was beside her, quizzing her on the grasses, the brush, the trees, and she'd show him what she had learned in the books from St. Cadence Library: *That one's moonseed, Daddy. That one's a longleaf pine. You can tell by the bark.* Most often, she only went so far along the pig paths before growing nervous she'd get lost, and she'd turn around to find her way back to the lake.

CATHERINE LOVED THE LAKE, which looked nothing like the black river in Tennessee but which offered that same soothing sense, like a mother's cool hand on a feverish forehead. The alligators terrified her, but she got used to the possibility of their presence, to glancing around for them first—and it was rare that she saw one, not in the cold spring— before stripping to her bathing suit and wading into the jade water.

She did not go past the edge of the spring water; Moss Landry had warned her of that.

Moss reminded her of a younger version of Talmadge. His lean frame, his hair gone gray so early. She liked the way he spoke. "You cross that line, you in gator territory," he'd told her. "Stay where that water is clear an' that, an' you stay just fine."

John Jay did not like to swim. When they first moved to Fingertip, she asked him some weekends to come with her. She suggested a picnic. "We could skinny dip," she said, stroking the back of his neck. They were lying in bed on a Saturday morning. The curtains were open, and the sky outside was a candy blue. They had both kicked off the covers. John Jay smelled like body odor and bourbon, but how easy it could be, even among the lingering smells, to forget who he had become the night before. He was so handsome, with his unshaven face and dark hair loosened from its usual pomaded slickness. The lids of his closed eyes were shiny.

"Those woods are for hicks," he muttered, then turned his face to the other side of the pillow.

SHE KNEW THAT MOVING them to Fingertip was her fault. She couldn't blame her husband's unmistakable and ever-increasing resentment—although before they'd left Tennessee he had bragged to friends, to the Party Boys who had not gone off to war, about their good fortune. "Ninety-nine-cent mortgages," he'd said. "We'll save a goddamn pretty penny."

But despite the fact that the ninety-nine-cent mortgage enabled them to live with a financial ease that would never have been possible in Nashville, John Jay complained about Fingertip relentlessly. He resented Catherine and, like all resentments in his life, he fed and watered it like a poisonous plant, growing it up inside of himself until his every word frothed bitter and loathing, until he no longer seemed to remember that they shared any history together at all. That he had, in fact, once courted her—albeit briefly—and then proposed to her, that he'd smiled at her on the courthouse steps.

That he'd called her by name: *Catherine.*

MOST EVENINGS AND WEEKENDS, John Jay drank with the other men at the Last Outpost—but Catherine was especially shy in this new and unfamiliar place and exchanged only polite hellos with the other wives who lived along Only Road. She found it difficult to sustain small talk for more than the time it took to briefly wave, to comment on the heat. And if she wore too much makeup or oversized pink-framed sunglasses indoors or unseasonably long sleeves on occasion, she did not stay long enough in conversation with those women for them to ask her about it.

She simply waved (revealing the sweat stains in the pits of her long-sleeved dress) and kept walking on—toward the lake, or toward the Outpost for coffee or flour, and the women raised their eyebrows but went back to their gardening, sweat trickling down their foreheads, or to reminding their children to take their shoes off at the door.

On occasional weekend afternoons, while John Jay drank at the Outpost, Catherine went alone to see matinees at the movie theater in St. Cadence. She watched *The Wizard of Oz* alone in the balcony and cried at the ending, when Dorothy returned to the farm. She thought of Talmadge and his plants, and of her mother and the quilts with the names of schoolchildren; she remembered the smell of the whiskey-and-lemon tea and the snow and chimney smoke in winter and the ear-splitting crow of Pontius Pilate at dawn.

Eventually, she rose from the shabby velvet seat and made her way downstairs and out the doors of the theater into the sweltering afternoon, the humidity draped over the Atchafalaya like wet laundry on a line.

In the yellow house, while John Jay was at work, she made herself ham sandwiches with pickles for lunch—not because she liked her sandwiches with pickles, but because the smell of them reminded her of Talmadge—and she wrote letters to her mother, whom she longed for in ways she had not expected. For the stern line of her mouth, her orderly daily routines.

She longed for someone who knew her family, knew anything of her life back home, knew that schoolchildren loved her mother or knew the way the pebbles in the Cumberland felt against bare feet or of her father's love of the natural world or of his illness.

She and her mother had never spoken of it. Now, so far apart, they certainly did not write about it. But they'd both experienced the loss of Talmadge Booker, and no one in Fingertip, or in any part of Louisiana, or in the states stacked between Louisiana and Tennessee, shared the knowledge of Talmadge as he had once been, or of the loss of him.

11. The Heart

July 1982

S unshine sat at the Formica table with the portable television drawn close. Although the clock read ten o'clock, she'd been up for hours. She'd already walked down the path to the lake, the sky overhead still pink with dawn, to look for alligators (unsuccessfully, though she did see a water snake gliding along the surface). She'd picked beetles out from under Moss Landry's fig tree, and she'd read *Annie Pat and Eddie* inside her fort. Billy's bedroom door was shut and, tiptoeing past, she'd heard his soft snores.

Eventually she'd settled at the table, her toast slathered in extra peanut butter. She turned the volume on the little television down low so it wouldn't wake Billy.

When he finally shuffled into the kitchen, puffy-eyed with sleep, happiness filled up her chest like honey. All week he'd gone out looking for work and taking on odd jobs. Some nights he'd come home with cash. He'd looked dirty and tired and didn't much want to talk. Instead, he'd put on a record, taken his beer to the porch, and sat quietly rocking. On one of those nights he'd fallen asleep out there. Sunshine had finished watching TV in the kitchen and, hearing his snores through the open window, had gone to check on him before she herself went to sleep.

"Billy?" she'd said, pressing her nose against the screen. "You wanna go to bed?"

He'd started awake. "I'm awake," he muttered. Then he had opened the screen door, ruffled her hair, and gone past her to his bedroom.

Sunshine had remained, for a moment, in the doorway. She felt both relief and disappointment (like a brother and sister, hand in hand). Relief that nothing strange had happened. That she'd seen no spiders, that her stones were safe inside of her. And disappointment that Billy seemed to hardly notice she was there at all.

NOW IT WAS SATURDAY, which meant he'd probably stay home, and she thought he might make egg-in-a-basket sandwiches and watch *Scooby-Doo* with her like weeks ago.

"Mornin'," she said, through a mouthful of peanut butter toast.

Billy wore jeans and no shirt. He waved to her, hand rising halfway up, and yawned.

All at once, she felt the coming storm. A wind was blowing through the yellow kitchen. The ceiling was sinking heavy and low.

She'd been stupid to say anything at all. She watched, a sense of dread blooming in her like a weed, as Billy took a can of beer from the refrigerator and went to the kitchen sink. The refrigerator door hadn't shut all the way and instead swung slowly open, so that Sunshine could see its bright, almost-empty interior.

She kept her head turned toward the television but watched Billy from the corner of her eye: his handsome profile, the lines that splayed from his eyes and brushed his temples.

On the tiny screen in front of her, Road Runner was saying, *Meep meep, meep meep.*

Billy, staring through the window toward the tree line, brought the beer to his lips and gulped until it was empty. It made a tinny sound as he set it on the kitchen counter, and then he belched loudly. He went to the refrigerator again but still did not close the door; instead he reached inside and took two more beers, and then he passed by Sunshine again.

He didn't speak; he didn't ruffle her hair or even offer another half-wave. The screen door slammed shut behind him, and through the open window over the sofa, she heard the iron rocker begin to go back and forth.

Over the kitchen table, fat drops of rain began to fall. Sunshine stood and moved forward through the downpour—each step making small splashes, like little leaping fish—and closed the refrigerator door.

Past the rivulets of rainwater that mapped the window over the rose-pink sofa, Billy was sitting in the porch rocker. When she turned back toward *Looney Tunes*, she saw that a ghost had joined her: Grandma Catherine was sitting at the table.

Slender-armed. Freckle-nosed.

She wore a pale pink house dress soaked through with the rainwater falling from the ceiling in the kitchen, and her red hair was pulled partway up with two combs, like in the black-and-white picture on the courthouse steps. Like how Aunt Lou wore her hair sometimes too. *Was there something you wanted to ask me?* Grandma Catherine said, wringing rainwater from her hair.

But Sunshine covered her eyes with her hands. She didn't want anyone, not even a ghost, to see the hot tears gathering.

• • •

THE STORIES CATHERINE TOLD to her children arrived in her imagination like familiar old friends she didn't remember ever making in the first place. There was a deep black bayou with an unfathomably hungry crocodile. There was a pair of knowing hands.

As she spoke, she could smell the mineral earth and the bittersweet cypress; she stood on the bayou shore and could feel the old forest breathing all around her.

While her children were young enough to still want their mother to hold them before they slept, she told them the stories almost nightly. Lou often fell asleep within the first few minutes, but Billy usually lasted longer, swallowing his yawns. He loved the stories the most. If Catherine retold a part and left out details, he filled them in. *The crocodile ate the clouds,* too, he'd say. *Mama, you f-forgot!* Or: *You said she had flowers in her hair. Where did they go? Did they f-fall out?*

The warmth of their bodies against her own, Lou's mouth against the side of her breast, drool darkening the fabric of her top—these were moments that made it feel as though there were only two places that mattered in the world: the Black Bayou itself, and the room in which she told of it.

THERE HAD ALWAYS BEEN healers in these parts. Traiteurs burned snippets of a mother's hair and wafted the smoke toward the nostrils of her colicky, red-faced infant. They tied snakeskin to a broken ankle to speed its healing. They offered prayers and various salves.

The crocodile bride was different. She didn't need to speak or be spoken to. She didn't need an explanation of pain, a teary confession or plea. She simply lay her hands on the injured or sickly or heartbroken, and inside of her, an understanding pooled like cool green water.

Placing a hand on a child's forehead, she knew if he needed medicine, or enough food at home, or more of a parent's love. No sooner did the knowledge arrive within her than she knew how, within that same touch, to make him feel better.

To make him loved, seen, satisfied.

When men, coughing and red-faced, came with a problem too humiliating to discuss, she knew what they were suffering and knew the insecurities that had caused their condition to begin with; she knew the absent mother of their childhood or the father who had teased them too harshly, she knew of the time they lost their innocence to a girl who made fun of the size of their johnson.

(*What's their johnson?*—this time, it was Lou who spoke. Billy's eyes were already closed. She had thought both children had already fallen asleep and she'd been continuing the story for her own amusement, filling in details that would have made another adult in the room giggle knowingly—but there was only Catherine and her not-yet-asleep children, squeezed into Billy's twin bed. The nightstand lamp illuminated the bedroom with its gentle light.

Yeah, said Billy sleepily, eyes still closed. *What's a johnson?*

They were each tucked into the crook of her arms, each of which had gone numb.

You little Curious Georges, she said. *Well. Johnson was the name of a special type of horse, and people thought that bigger horses meant you were rich.*

Oh, said Billy.

Oh, Lou mimicked, and they pressed closer against Catherine's body. She leaned to kiss the crown of Billy's dark head and then Lou's red one. A baby-fine curl of red hair caught in her mouth but she couldn't remove it with her trapped and numb arms. So she continued.)

In response to the crocodile bride's hands, a man struggling with the size of his johnson horse discovered a newfound confidence, and swaggered home to his pleasantly surprised wife. The baby's faltering heart steadied. The pregnant woman's color returned to her cheeks and her nausea went away. Broken wrists and ribs and hearts were mended.

Soon, the villagers were so eager for the crocodile bride's touch that they could no longer wait for her visits to the village. They began traveling to the Black Bayou—a place they had always known to never go near.

To appease the crocodile, the villagers brought with each visit a gift for him. They trembled with fear and gratitude on the shore and then tossed into the water one of their few possessions of any value: A brass watch that had belonged to their grandfather. A blue willow plate. A silver locket. A string of pearls.

This arrangement worked well for both the villagers, who could see the crocodile bride and leave the Black Bayou alive, and also for the crocodile, whose belly again began to fill up with the treasures he had once so regularly enjoyed.

But each time a visitor left, the crocodile bride found herself increasingly agitated. She had come to the Black Bayou for safety (though from what, she'd always keep to herself) and she had found it, hadn't she? Hadn't the danger long passed? Her youth had stretched long beyond what seemed possible; her hair was still black, with only a thread of gray here or there. Her skin remained mostly smooth. Might she now venture into the village, even the city? Might she find a handsome man to love, and who loved her back? Might it not be too late to perhaps raise a child of her own—rather than bid hello and farewell, again and again, to those children whose parents begged her to heal their broken bones, their phlegm-rattled chests?

The crocodile wasn't unkind to her. He caught fresh fish and lay them on the shore for her to find each morning. She bathed in the bayou water and he protected her, always, from any wildlife that might cause her harm. When one of her many visitors, having no belongings of her own to offer the crocodile, tossed into the water a crown of lilies, the crocodile left it on the shore for her as he often left the catfish and the trout, and the crocodile bride accepted the gift and wore it in her hair each day.

I'm the king and you're my queen, teased the crocodile.

Ha, said the crocodile bride, and rolled her eyes.

One evening, after the last of the day's visitors had left and the old forest was ablaze with the pink of a setting winter sun, the crocodile bride dug a hole in the soft soil on which the little red house was perched. She dug deeper and deeper until her shovel hit something hard—but when she reached to pick up the crocodile's heart, she found that, over the years, it had grown much heavier.

Again and again she lifted with all her might, and still the heart wouldn't budge. It was dense and hard as iron. She tried lifting again and then again, until she was streaked with dirt and sweat, her muscles trembling with the effort. The sun sank below the horizon. Uncovered by soil, the heart's beating was so loud her ears ached.

Finally, she heard the crocodile calling to her from the water. *Yoo-hoo! My queen? My bride? Please come speak with me!*

Teary with frustration, she stomped down to the shore.

What on earth have you been doing all evening? said the crocodile. *Why has the drumming of my heart grown so loud? I don't think I like it.*

I dug it up, confessed the crocodile bride, tears sliding down her cheeks. *I wanted to give it back to you.*

But I don't want it, said the crocodile. *It's happy enough under the earth— so close to you. Aren't you happy in the house I built for you?*

The crocodile bride sat wearily on the shore. She turned her face to the twilit sky and shook her head. *I was happy*, she said. *But suddenly time has passed, crocodile. My hair has streaks of gray. I'm without a husband or children. I'm without anyone to truly love.*

For a long time, they did not speak. The woman had drawn her knees up to her chest and was weeping, now, into her folded arms; the crown of water lilies slid off and fell, the petals limp and rimmed with brown, on the ground beside her.

Finally, the crocodile spoke in a voice so sad that the whole bayou fell quiet and the soft breeze in the treetops ceased blowing. *Then why don't you go?*

The woman looked up, surprised. A full moon had risen over the far shoreline, and her dark eyes gleamed. *Because I can't leave you here without your heart.*

Perhaps I can simply eat up the shore until I reach it, then I can swallow it down.

But the shore is beautiful, said the crocodile bride. *And besides, I can't leave the little red house. It will be lonely without me.*

Perhaps I can eat that, too, said the crocodile.

But the house is a good house, said the crocodile bride. *And besides, once you swallow your heart and swallow the red house, what more will you hunger for?*

Everything, said the crocodile.

And when you hunger for everything, said the crocodile bride, *who will quell that hunger?*

For this, the crocodile had no answer.

The woman took the crown of lilies and placed it back upon her head. She stood, brushed the mud and leaves from her dress, and waded into the water. She placed her hands on the crocodile, and his hunger quelled. He watched, confused and sad, as she turned and climbed the little ridge that led to her house.

The moon peered through the trees. The beating of the exposed heart in the hole in the earth was deafening, and it seemed to her that it was no longer the beat of a heart at all, but words:

Da dum, da dum!

Wake up, wake up!

It was only then that her sadness transformed itself into something new. Something monstrous. It rose up inside of her like starvation itself. The earth around the heart gaped open like a wound. The shovel glinted in the moonlight. She began flinging mound after mound of dirt back over the heart, burying it once more. When she was too exhausted to go on anymore, she dropped the shovel and fell to her knees. She dug her hands deep into the soil and flung it hard over what remained of the hole in the earth, then pounded that dirt into place, pounding and pounding, the sound of her own fists and of her grunting, angry cries mingling with the heartbeat in an untamed din.

12.
Wednesday Underwear

S ometime in early spring, the air still chilly, the bright green leaves recently returned to the figs and the oaks along Only Road, Joanna Louise had called up to Sunshine's window one morning.

She stood under the oak in front of the yellow house, barefoot and messy-haired, in an old sweatshirt and jeans torn at both knees. "Hey," she said, then lowered her voice to a loud whisper. "Come over. I have a secret."

Sunshine had dressed quickly, then tiptoed past Billy's closed door and down the front porch steps. The two of them climbed back through JL's window, and she drew the curtains shut and locked the bedroom door—something Aunt Lou said she wasn't supposed to do.

Sunshine sat on the bed, legs crossed. The sun had just risen over the tree line and a wedge of light fell across the quilt before her. "Well?" she said, in a way she hoped made it seem as if she didn't care about JL's secret, that JL had wanted to talk to her at all.

JL knelt on the floor before Sunshine and slid something out from under the bed. Sunshine leaned forward to watch. It was the old silverware box where JL kept postcards and trinkets and Bazooka Joe comics, held closed with brass latches. Slowly, JL opened the lid, and from the velvet-lined box removed a carefully folded-up pair of lime green underwear.

WEDNESDAY was scrawled in pink letters all along the white elastic waistband.

She stood and carefully lay them on top of the quilt. Sunshine could see a dark stain on the underwear. Blood.

She gasped.

Her cousin was watching her, eyes narrowed. Sunshine looked again at the stained crotch, the inky, rust-red blot. She imagined JL dying in the back seat of the shaggin' wagon before they even had a chance to reach the hospital, her face white and lifeless, the blood pooling out from between her legs.

But she refused to ask about the blood. Instead, she looked up at JL's smug, flushed face. She raised her eyebrows as though to say, *So?*

JL took a long important breath. "It happened. Do you know what this means?" She stared fiercely at Sunshine. Eyes sharp. Mouth pursed with expectation.

"I guess," Sunshine said. It was not entirely a lie. She could guess that JL had caught a disease that made you bleed onto your Wednesday underwear. She could guess that it meant drama. Illness. Perhaps—fingers crossed—death.

"It means that I'm a *literal* woman," said JL.

Sunshine's curiosity won out. "Oh. So you're not dying."

JL rolled her eyes. "Of course not. It's a period, dummy. Don't you know what that is?"

A period. She had heard the girls at school talk about this.

Sunshine didn't have friends at school, which was something her teachers noted on report cards and that Aunt Lou asked her about sometimes. Mostly it was because she thought the girls at school were stupid idiots who, like JL now, cared only about boys and makeup. And also because no other children lived in Fingertip, which was not even marked on the maps rolled up above the blackboard in each classroom. Aunt Lou said living in Fingertip might have something to do with it—*it* being the way Sunshine did not have friends. *Behaviorally*, one teacher had said,

Sunshine is very sweet and always does her best to follow directions. Socially, she can get lost in her own world. She often eats lunch alone and seems to hang back on the playground at recess.

Aunt Lou said it would help if Billy reminded her to comb her hair now and then or to take a bath. But Sunshine didn't care about combing her hair or taking baths unless Aunt Lou made her, and she wore overalls or jeans and JL's hand-me-down shoes that were usually a little too big and always stinky by the time JL had outgrown them. At recess, the other girls huddled on the playground in one clump, all except Sunshine and Winnie Trudeau, who was fat and picked her nose in class, and Jeremiah Wilbur, who was the only Black fifth grader and also wore unfortunately thick glasses.

But she had heard them talk. She'd heard about it—periods. She had just never asked what the word meant, *my period, when I get my period, my sister got her period*, because to do so would be to be ridiculed, and because, also, she suspected it might be one of the words, like *nipple* and *anus* and *nostril*, that Aunt Lou did not like to say aloud.

In JL's bedroom, the question lingered in the air between them: *Don't you know?* Sunshine felt the heat rising up along her neck and cheeks, all the way to the top of each ear, and she conceded. "No," she said, finally. "I don't know what that means."`

But as soon as she admitted it, she realized that JL could see that already, had known, and that was probably the point of bringing Sunshine over to show her the underwear. To let her know, again, that she knew more than Sunshine.

Sunshine felt a rush of anger. She wanted to take the pair of disgusting underwear and run out of JL's room and wake Aunt Lou and Nash and say, *Look at what JL did, JL's been bleeding from her disgusting hairy ugly white clam, she locked her door to show it to me.* She wanted to take scissors and slice the Wednesday underwear into tiny bits and throw them up in the air like confetti and leave JL to clean up the mess.

JL's mouth dropped open in dramatic disbelief. Then she shut it again. "Aww," she finally said, as though admiring a pet rabbit.

Then she took the underwear into her lap and folded it up carefully again.

Sunshine felt, for some reason, like Joanna Louise was removing a treasure that had just been within grasp—a unique lime-colored gem with a rust-red blot.

"Well," JL sighed. "I guess maybe you're just still too young."

"*Fine*," Sunshine said. She went to the window and tugged it open. There was a lump in her throat. "I don't want to know, anyway. I think it's disgusting."

She climbed out into the chill morning air and stalked toward the yellow house. Blue morning shadows stretched long across Only Road. Behind her, she heard Joanna Louise loudly whisper, "Hey Sunshine, wait! I didn't mean it. I know you're not a dummy."

But she had pretended not to hear her.

THEN, ONE NIGHT IN early July, Sunshine awoke in the darkness of her bedroom with her covers kicked down to the foot of the bed and a thin film of sweat dampening her body. Her stomach hurt and she felt queasy. On the toilet in the hallway bathroom, mid-pee, she looked down and saw what was wrong.

If JL were not at camp, Sunshine could go climb in her window and wake her up. What did you do when you got a period? JL hadn't told her that part, and she'd been too mad at her to think to ask any questions. Her stomach ached and a wave of nausea passed over her.

She took a roll of toilet paper into her bedroom, got out a clean pair of underwear, and wrapped the toilet paper around the crotch of the underwear. Then she crawled into her fort and turned on the hurricane lamp. Its glow felt comforting. She lay back on the pile of pillows and turned over on her side, hugging her stomach with both arms.

She should tell Aunt Lou in the morning, probably; Aunt Lou would tell Sunshine what to do. But they didn't talk about those things like JL and Sunshine talked about them, and the idea of saying any of it aloud to Aunt Lou made her feel more sick.

It was hot inside the fort. Sunshine rolled to her back and stared at the faded blackberry vines that ran along the roof. Billy had said Grandma Catherine went to the Black Bayou once. Aunt Lou said those stories were made up, but Sunshine had felt it, the truth of it. Felt it like a memory, like soft fruit. If Sunshine went then the crocodile bride would lay her hands on her without a word. She'd know how to fix her—the bleeding.

Maybe more.

Maybe Billy would turn all June moods and find work, and his hands would never turn to spiders again, and Sunshine wouldn't have to say a word of it aloud. Hot tears rolled down her cheeks. She didn't remember falling asleep, but when she awoke, the walls of the tent glowed with morning light and she could feel that the toilet paper had soaked through.

AFTER THAT FIRST TIME in early spring, JL started acting like nothing was more annoying and painful than having a period. Sunshine knew she was just showing off. On morning walks to the bus station, she'd clutch her stomach and moan loudly. Once, after school, she took a small square wrapped in pink plastic from her backpack and said knowingly, "I have to *go take care of something.*"

This morning, Sunshine stayed in her room until she saw through her window that Aunt Lou had left for work. Then she went across Only Road and dug around in JL's dresser drawers until she found those pink plastic squares in a cardboard box that read *Always*.

THE NEXT DAY, THERE was only a little bit of blood and her stomach didn't hurt. Outside the open windows of the yellow house, she could hear mourning doves.

After breakfast, she walked across Only Road with a bucket of soapy water and ducked under the sloped arms of Moss's fig tree. She crouched down and picked at the Japanese beetles along the roots like Moss had shown her, then drowned them one by one in the bucket. Last summer, Moss had squatted under the thick canopy of the fig branches and rolled back a chunk of soil near the base of the tree as if it were a rug. (Sunshine had seen dark spots scattered along the shining skin of his balding head, under the white wisps.) He pointed to the rolled-back earth and said that right there—the dirt knit together so tightly like that—was the sign of a grubworm infection. Then he reached into the uncovered soil, pinched a grubworm between his two fingers, and pulled it out to show her: a fat white thing, sickly and translucent.

Aunt Lou said Moss was *a bit of an odd duck*, which JL had told Sunshine meant he was gay, which meant he wanted to kiss men, not women. But Sunshine liked the way Moss talked. Most in Fingertip were from all over, Aunt Lou once explained to her, because houses were cheap and there used to be good jobs at the sugar mill. Aunt Lou said that Ms. Mouton was an exception but for some reason she'd had to stop speaking French when she was a little girl. But Moss Landry was a *true* Cajun. He hadn't ever stopped speaking French and he said things like, *How's your daddy an' them?* when he was just asking about Billy and Billy alone.

It was Moss who taught Sunshine about alligators and what to look out for along the shore so you didn't accidentally stumble into one of their dens. They'd gone out in his bateau a ways down from the swimming hole, and he showed her where the grass along the shore was matted down. "You stumble into a den an' they might swallow you whole, a bitty thing like you."

Sunshine had squinted toward the shore. She could see a gator there, head protruding from the shallow water. She'd asked him, "Could you escape a gator belly if you were swallowed whole?"

"Oh, sure enough, suppose so," Moss said, "if you got a knife on you. The skin of their bellies is the only soft part of 'em. You could slice your way out of there if you got a knife. You got a pocket knife, Miss Sunshine?"

She shook her head no.

"Well. You plan on gettin' swallowed by one of them cocodril anytime soon, I'd get yourself one, sha."

From inside the fig tree she could see the yellow house and all the way down Only Road to the Lust, and Aunt Lou's house and Moss's pale green house behind her. She'd spied through the leafy veil as Moss left his house and walked to the woods, bucket and fishing rod in hand, where he'd spend the whole day out in his bateau. He hadn't noticed her (or if he had, he'd left her to the privacy of her fig tree fortress)—but Aunt Lou always seemed to find Sunshine no matter where she was hiding. At first she didn't notice that the shaggin' wagon had backed down the road and stopped in front of the fig tree.

"Is that you in there, Sunshine Turner?"

Sunshine emerged from inside the branches and jogged over to wagon. Aunt Lou's car smelled of cracked, worn vinyl and Nivea hand lotion. Pinched in between Sunshine's soapy index finger and thumb was one of the green Japanese beetles. She held it up for Aunt Lou to see.

Aunt Lou made a face. "Girl, what in the *Lord's* name is that thing?"

"I'm drowning 'em so they don't turn to grubworms. See?" The beetle wriggled its legs uselessly.

"If you drop that thing in my car, I'll drown *you* and I won't even feel bad about it."

Sunshine squatted down, placed the beetle on a muddy stone—a small altar—and squashed it beneath her bare big toe. She could feel the satisfying little crunch of it.

"Hey, I haven't seen your daddy around much," Aunt Lou said. "He seems so busy, huh? They sending him out on the rigs?"

Sunshine noticed Aunt Lou was wearing a new lipstick, the color of raspberries, and a green polka-dot sundress she hadn't seen before. The dress matched her eyes, which were squinted up in the way they got when she was worried about something.

Sunshine looked back at the beetle—squashed, its glimmering shell crushed flat. She shrugged her shoulders. "Good."

"Good?" Aunt Lou said.

Sunshine met her eyes and nodded. "Yeah. I mean yes, ma'am. He's doing good." But she looked away again, back toward the ground.

"You'd tell me if that weren't true," Aunt Lou said. "Right, sugar?"

The same feeling Sunshine had started getting since the spiders first crawled up inside her shirt was back now, inside her stomach—that tugging feeling, as though strings ran across the inside walls of her torso and occasionally, without warning, grew taut. She imagined a circus tent with tightrope walkers inside, stepping their way carefully across these strings.

"I caught over fifty beetles so far today," she said. She smiled.

Aunt Lou looked back at her a long moment. The tightrope walkers turned and went in the other direction. The strange silence between her and Aunt Lou unraveled down the red ribbon of road. Sunshine's throat felt suddenly tight, like she might start crying.

Aunt Lou sighed, tapping one finger on the steering wheel. Then her face brightened unexpectedly, and she said, "Hey—I'm running some errands in town before work. You wanna come keep me company? You'd have to come to my shift, but I bet we could use you on the register."

Sunshine liked working at the diner. She sat up high on a wooden stool and punched numbers in the register, and the customers dropped coins in a cardboard milk carton lopped off at the top. At the end of the night, she got to split the tips with the waitresses and the cooks.

Next time she went to the Lust, she could pay for the milk and peanut butter herself.

"And," Aunt Lou added, cheerful now, "is it my imagination, or does somebody have a birthday coming up? Maybe we could pick out a present."

Sunshine had forgotten about her birthday. She would turn twelve years old in a few weeks. The feeling in her belly softened. Birthdays were like bends in a winding road—some new possibility on the other side. More money. No more storms. All June moods. JL dying a tragic death at camp (drowned in a canoe, thrown off a horse, kissed to death) and Sunshine the Only Kid Left in Fingertip, given free food and Dum Dums at the Lust for the rest of her life.

In addition to unlimited access to the Magnavox.

"Okay," she said, and she smiled at Aunt Lou. A real smile, this time.

"Okay, then," Aunt Lou said. "But hurry up and get some shoes and clean clothes. And bring a brush so you can do something with that rat's nest on the way."

In her bedroom, hurriedly pulling on a dress and making sure she was not bleeding so much she needed to open a new *hygienic napkin* (she did not know how to pronounce the word *hygienic* on the Always box but she liked the formality of the words, as though the pink plastic squares inside were planning on attending a fancy dinner party), she felt a little bit grown-up. She looked at the mirror over her dresser and shimmied her shoulders in a little dance like JL had showed her how to do. Suddenly exhilarated that, in the darkness between her legs, on underwear sprin-kled with yellow roses, she had a new kind of secret. *A period, dummy.* Undiscovered by spiders.

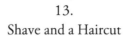

13.

Shave and a Haircut

July 1982

More and more throughout the summer, on her way to and from her shifts at the 79, or to Nash's apartment in St. Cadence, Lou's thoughts ran off like streams that seemed to end, no matter the course they ran, in a pool of worry.

She'd realize that she had driven the last several or more miles and didn't remember them, or that she'd altogether passed the turnoff to Fingertip. On her way to work, she'd suddenly become aware she was pulling into the parking lot of the 79 and time had passed in a blink. Each time, her eyebrows had grown furrowed and her forehead pulsed with a dull tension, so that by the time she reached her destination, she'd search for an aspirin to soothe the worsening headache and take the edge off the knot that had nestled like an egg in the crook of one shoulder blade.

She worried about Joanna Louise, who she thought had seemed unhappy before she left for camp (or perhaps she was just being moody, a typical teenager—it was so hard to tell). She worried about Sunshine, too, who seemed somehow *off* this summer—quieter, lonelier. She thought that JL's absence must be hard on her, and Lou was working so often, stashing away her tips in preparation for their move this fall, that she hadn't had Sunshine over for dinner as often.

She would be better about that, she promised herself. On the nights she wasn't working, she'd make sure she made Sunshine dinner, make sure she was doing okay without Joanna Louise around.

She'd invite her brother too. Billy had more or less disappeared since his promotion at work the month prior. That wasn't necessarily all that unusual; he always went through his phases. They saw each other in passing and waved across the street. She found herself replaying their conversation from back in the spring, and wondered again if he resented her for this upcoming move. But why should she stay? Why should he—a grown man—be her responsibility? He'd be fine.

As for Sunshine, it was barely July and Lou already felt dread at the idea of leaving her behind.

And there was something else she couldn't quite name, something tangled up with the dread of leaving Sunshine in Fingertip. It was like the watermelon vines in Moss Landry's garden; each summer, the vines ran wild, spilling through the chicken wire and into other garden plots. Their tendrils found their way to his tomato vines and snaked up and around their stalks, their weight bowing the tomato plant toward the ground. Moss had to carefully pry loose the watermelon vines, untwirling the bright tendrils from the tight hold they'd found in the span of only one good rain and a sunny afternoon.

The feeling in Lou coiled relentlessly upward, twirling and tugging— but as to what was causing that unease, or as to whether it was just her tendency to be (as Billy would say) too negative, she couldn't say.

Nash couldn't understand her mounting concerns. He saw nothing but excitement—the thrill of a new house, of marrying Lou. "I just wanna marry my girl," he'd said, more than once. "Everything else will fall into place. You'll see, babe."

When she had lamented that no one would ever buy the house in Fingertip, Nash had pointed out that they could certainly afford to continue a ninety-nine-cent mortgage, worst case scenario, and that, besides, would it be so bad to own two properties? "What if JL wants to stay there after she graduates?" he'd said, and she had snapped that Joanna Louise would be going to college, thank you very much, and she'd burn that house down before allowing her to live in it again.

Nash had laughed. "Won't argue with an arsonist," he said.

WHEN LOU FIRST LEFT Fingertip at eighteen years old, she had cried as soon as she crossed the tracks. Her friend Clarissa was driving her in the pea-green Pinto; they were spending this last morning together before she'd take Lou to the courthouse to meet Robert. Despite Robert's Christian devoutness, he wanted a quick and pragmatic marriage. No ceremony. "We don't need all that fluff," he'd told her.

Clarissa drove in silence, her long hair blowing in the rush of wind from the open windows. Neil Young was on the radio. Lou could smell the sweet, sun-warmed pines. She held a balled-up tissue in her hand, damp with tears.

How many times had she and Billy walked to their bus stop along that road as children and then as teenagers, smoking cigarettes, listening to the wind's papery rattle through the stalks in the fields? In many ways, things had felt simpler between them back then. Growing up with John Jay had bonded them in ways no one else could or would understand; only as Billy began to drink more did something dark begin to color their relationship, and it had darkened further, still, after he had knocked that night—*shave-and-a-haircut*—and she had made the mistake of knocking back.

WHEN SHE EVENTUALLY RETURNED, she left no address for Robert Dalton and told no one that she was going.

She packed some of her clothes and most of her daughter's. She packed the blanket her daughter loved—a soft square of brown with a plush bear's head at one corner, crusted with milky drool—and she'd packed a toy that the visiting pastor's wife had gifted them when Joanna Louise was baptized: a small, hand-carved wooden replica of Noah's ark, with animals walking up its ramp, two by two. She took a grocery bag's worth of food from the pantry and the stack of bills she'd been saving—leftover cash from the grocery money Robert allotted her, gas money she'd asked for when in fact she still had half a tank. She only realized, much later, that she must have been planning to leave all along and had not admitted it even to herself.

Then she buckled two-year-old Joanna Louise into the back seat of the wagon—a used clunker Robert had purchased for her—and left one Monday morning while he was at work.

THEY DROVE ALL DAY, crossing out of South Carolina, stopping to eat cheeseburgers and fries in a booth at McDonald's. She bought JL a milk-shake for dessert and let her slurp it down in the backseat of the car. The radio played the country music Robert hadn't liked for her to listen to; he preferred the Christian cassette tapes he kept neatly organized on a shelf in their living room and in the console of his Toyota. Lou turned the radio dial up so loud that in the review mirror, Joanna Louise pressed a chubby hand over each ear and scowled.

Only when she crossed into Louisiana did it sink in what she had just done.

She felt a sudden wave of nausea, and her hands began to shake so hard that the wheel rattled.

She found a pay phone at a rest stop, left the car running and the windows down and Joanna Louise sleeping inside, and dialed the old familiar number. She could see the pale blue phone their mother had kept on the kitchen wall as though she were standing before it herself. It rang six times and no one answered. She hung up, collected her coins from the metal dish, and tried again. This time, Billy picked up on the third ring.

"Hello?" he said.

"Hello," she said. She could hear him breathing, but he said nothing—whether because he didn't recognize her voice or didn't know how to respond, she wasn't sure. She tried again. "Shave and a haircut."

She was relieved to hear him laugh. A short, surprised bark of a laugh—but a laugh nonetheless. "Well, well, well," he drawled, nice and slow. Teasing her. "Two bits, I guess."

In the background, she could hear the sounds of a baby mewling.

. . .

SUNSHINE SAT IN THE passenger side, grateful that JL was not there—that she got to ride shotgun and spend a whole day with just Aunt Lou.

The sky yawned blue overhead with small puffs of clouds. When they turned into the even pavement of 79, Aunt Lou popped in her Sam Cooke cassette, and they sang along to "You Send Me." Here and there along 79 were fireworks stands, painted white and layered with American flags. Sunshine had forgotten about the Fourth of July. She wondered if Billy would bring home Pharaoh's snakes and sparklers to set off like they'd done in the past, but then she thought about how there wasn't any money and decided she wouldn't ask.

But she was in a good mood anyway. Even if there wasn't any money. Even if she had to keep Billy's secrets.

A trip into St. Cadence with just Aunt Lou was rare. When JL was with them, Aunt Lou and JL would bicker, and Sunshine would feel annoyed with her cousin for being a know-it-all, or she'd get her feelings hurt because JL would just stare at her own face in the passenger side mirror and ignore Sunshine entirely.

With just Aunt Lou and Sunshine, the mood felt lighter. Aunt Lou laughed when Sunshine's sweat-slick thighs made a farting sound on the leather seat. She asked Sunshine if there were any boys she liked.

Sunshine was repulsed. "Ew! No."

"Okay, well, you never know. *I* was in fifth grade when I first had a crush."

Sunshine shook her head. "That's *disgusting*," she said, and Aunt Lou laughed again.

When they pulled up in front of the hair salon, she turned off the ignition. "Well," she said. "I think it's about time for a change, sugar."

Inside, the salon smelled like rotten eggs and hairspray. It was empty except for Deborah, Aunt Lou's hairdresser, who studied the cut-out magazine clippings that Aunt Lou pulled from her purse and nodded and said, "Oh, yes, I can just *see* this on you. Yes. Very cool."

Deborah was the daughter of the lady who owned the salon. She had dyed blonde hair cut short like a boy's. (Later, in the car, Aunt Lou would say, "Doesn't she remind you of Mia Farrow with that adorable pixie cut?" and Sunshine would have to ask who was Mia Farrow and also what was a pixie cut.) Deborah wore jeans that came up past her belly button and a yellow macramé tank top that showed off honey-colored shoulder blades and three inches of smooth, flat belly. She had Sunshine sit in the empty chair next to Aunt Lou and deposited a handful of Hershey kisses in Sunshine's open palms.

"You don't think it'll be too, you know, puffy?" Aunt Lou asked.

Deborah was combing her fingers through Aunt Lou's long wavy hair, the two of them looking at her reflection in the mirror.

"No," Deborah said, eyes squinting in concentration. "I'll give you a product. Do you have any good products?"

"No," Aunt Lou laughed, but her cheeks turned pink. "I sometimes use a spritz or two of Aqua Net. But it's so sticky."

Deborah stroked the waves again. Aunt Lou's hair was getting bigger and bigger the more Deborah touched it. "Aqua Net just dries it out. What you need is a good leave-in and then this conditioning mousse. I'll show you—you'll love it." She turned to Sunshine. "Doesn't your mama have the most magnificent hair? Such a color!"

Sometimes people mistook Aunt Lou for Sunshine's mother and she didn't know how to correct them. But Aunt Lou fixed it. "She's my niece, technically, but it doesn't make a difference to me. People say we have the same nose."

Sunshine had not ever heard that, and she looked at Aunt Lou's nose. It was a nice nose, she thought, straight and even and not too big or small. Sunshine had just a sprinkling of small freckles, whereas Aunt Lou was covered in freckles—but maybe their noses did have the same slope.

Deborah washed Aunt Lou's hair and then poured Sunshine a teacup of lemonade and poured herself and Aunt Lou little teacups of white wine. The teacups were different pastel shades. Sunshine's was lavender. "Mama's been serving refreshments to our customers for years in those stupid little Dixie cups," Deborah said, running a wide-tooth comb through Aunt Lou's long, wet hair. Droplets of water occasionally flew out and sprinkled across Sunshine like the start of a sunshower. "But I told her she needs to bring in a little Southern charm, you know? The teacups were my idea. Bought a whole box full of them for one dollar at a thrift store in New Orleans—would you believe it? Aren't they cute?"

Deborah talked without ever seeming to pause for breath. Her voice was low and breathy in a way that Sunshine would later try to imitate in the privacy of her bedroom. (*What sort of hair products do you use?* she'd say to her mirrored reflection. *Your blonde hair is just so lovely, just like something out of a fairy tale.*) Deborah told them she was saving money to open her own shop in New Orleans. Her boyfriend played music every weekend in a bar there, and sometimes she sang a song or two with him. "He's Black," she said, "which Mama certainly doesn't like very much, but she can't really do anything about it now, can she?"

Sunshine was listening so intently that she hardly noticed what Deborah was doing to Aunt Lou's hair, the long clippings that fell to the tiles below. Sunshine only ever saw Black people at the Piggly Wiggly, and there was also Jeremiah Wilbur, who kept quiet and was good at math and bad at reading aloud.

Somehow the idea of a boy didn't seem so disgusting now that Deborah had mentioned it. Sunshine wondered what it would be like to be Jeremiah's girlfriend. She used one foot to kick off the tiled floor and spin her chair around and tried to imagine holding Jeremiah's hand as they walked down the hallway at school, tennis shoes squeaking on the tiles. She knew the same girls who had sung at her to clean her hair and clean her belly would make fun of her for holding hands with Jeremiah, but she could squeeze Jeremiah's hand tighter and reassure him with Deborah's words: *They can't really do anything about it now, can they?*

"When I open my own shop," Deborah said, "I'm going to have a pitcher of gin and tonics handy. You know I saw in *Vogue* or *Life* or somewhere an article about a stylist in L.A. who makes seventy-five dollars per haircut? That isn't counting color or anything extra. She cuts celebrities' hair. Diane Keaton and people like that. I love her style, Diane Keaton's." Deborah put the scissors down on the vanity, and Sunshine noticed Aunt Lou's hair.

It was wet, still, but cut high above her shoulders. Aunt Lou looked through the mirror at Sunshine staring at her. "Where have you been all this time?" Aunt Lou teased.

Deborah pumped the mousse into her hands and showed Aunt Lou how to massage it into her hair. "You'll like the way this makes your hair feel," Deborah said. "Very sensual. It'll drive your boyfriend crazy. What's his name again?"

"Nash," Aunt Lou said, drawing his name out. Her cheeks had grown pink at the mention of hair products earlier and then stayed that way, pleasantly flushed. Around Deborah she seemed younger, Sunshine thought. It occurred to her for the first time that thirty-five years old was not so old as she'd thought.

"Nash!" Deborah sighed. "Like Graham Nash. Don't you wish him and Joni Mitchell were still together? Don't you just love her? I do."

She led Aunt Lou to the row of chairs and lowered one of the enormous bowls down over Aunt Lou's head, then came up behind Sunshine's chair and swiveled it to face the mirror. "Okay, Miss Sunshine," she said. "How about you?"

In the mirror, Deborah's long, slender fingers ran through Sunshine's hair, gently undoing the tangles. Last week, Aunt Lou had given Sunshine one of JL's old training bras: two triangles of pale pink cotton with skinny straps that constantly slipped off of her shoulders. But she'd forgotten the training bra today, and now, seeing the small swollen lumps on her chest under her thin, candy-striped dress, she felt embarrassed.

"I'm supposed to comb it more," she said, and glanced toward Aunt Lou, expecting her to chime in—but she was looking through the pages of a magazine, the corners of her mouth turned down in concentration.

"I think it's pretty," Deborah said. "I like it kind of wild like this."

Deborah's fingers running through her hair made Sunshine feel that she could fall asleep right there, the lingering taste of milk chocolate on her tongue, the fan whirring overhead. She forgot to feel embarrassed. She'd like to see Deborah singing songs with her Black boyfriend, she thought. She'd be old enough to drive by then. Maybe she'd have a little maroon Volkswagen like Deborah and she and Jeremiah (they would be friends by then, she thought, not just classroom friends—bound, as they were now, by the unfortunate fact of being different than everyone else) would take gummy worms and a cooler full of root beer and drive themselves to New Orleans, and Joanna Louise would ask to go but Sunshine would tell her no, it was just her and her friend Jeremiah, but that she'd bring her back a souvenir *if* she thought of it, though she might be too busy having fun. So.

"What about this?" Deborah asked, and Sunshine opened her eyes. "You know what I'm thinking? I'm thinking you'd look darling in bangs. Like Heather Locklear's—you know, sort of long and maybe a little feathered." She folded up a section of Sunshine's hair over her forehead and said, "See? Squint your eyes a little. If you make things kind of blurry, you'll get the gist."

Sunshine squinted and watched the blur of her face in the mirror: Long blonde hair, all combed out and fluffed, green eyes, and Aunt Lou's straight, even nose. A pink mouth. Squinting like this, she thought she almost looked pretty.

Aunt Lou's voice rose up from the row of hair dryers. "If you convince her to do something with her appearance, I will owe you more than the cost of a cut."

Deborah laughed. "Sunshine, honey, what do you think? Try a little something new?" She held Sunshine's pretend-bangs with her left hand and rested the fingertips of her right hand on Sunshine's shoulder and squeezed, just a soft squeeze (like testing a fig for ripeness) and Sunshine saw in the mirror that Deborah's hand was spidery, with fur on its legs and a fat fleshy torso the size of a squashed plum.

Sunshine flinched, and she made a sound, but it got caught in her throat so it came out oddly, a choked, "Ugg."

As soon as the sound left her mouth she saw that of course Deborah's hand was just a hand. But Deborah, also startled, had leaned back. "Did I hurt you?" she said, and laughed a little. Heat crept along Sunshine's neck and into her cheeks.

"Sunshine?" Aunt Lou said.

Sunshine looked at her aunt, her hair concealed under the bowl of the dryer. Aunt Lou was smiling but her eyes looked concerned again, just like in the car that morning, but then they relaxed. "Jumpy as a bullfrog," she teased.

Deborah stepped closer behind Sunshine and looked at her in the mirror. Very slowly, she put both of her hands on the back of the vinyl chair, then leaned down so her face was almost alongside Sunshine's in the mirror. She smiled with her lips closed and said, very quietly, "Maybe bangs some other time."

For some reason, Sunshine felt as though Deborah knew what had happened better than Sunshine knew it herself.

The haircut did not make Aunt Lou look like a Cheeto.

Sunshine had spent the last of their time in the salon looking at magazines, her cheeks burning with shame for the way she had reacted to Deborah's hands, but then Deborah had at last proudly swiveled Aunt Lou's chair around to face Sunshine, and Sunshine's mouth fell open and no sound came out. Aunt Lou's hair was cut chin-length, and with full waves that didn't look frizzy at all.

"I think it shows off her jawline and these *dimples*," Deborah said, and Aunt Lou's cheeks turned pink.

Sunshine finally said, "You look so *pretty*," and for some reason, they all laughed. For a moment, Sunshine forgot to be embarrassed about thinking Deborah's hands were spiders.

But by the time Sunshine and Aunt Lou had paid and hugged Deborah goodbye and climbed back into the shaggin' wagon, a fat lump had formed in Sunshine's throat. She felt embarrassed about how she'd acted and wished she could run back to the salon and tell Deborah she was sorry for being so jumpy—but that would be what JL would call étrange, and so she slid inside the shaggin' wagon. Aunt Lou looked over at her, beaming. Her green eyes seemed bigger with the new haircut and matched her dress. Her freckled skin glowed and her cheeks were rosy. "You okay, sugar?" she asked.

Sunshine nodded, but found she couldn't speak.

"You seem kind of grouchy or something. Maybe you're just hungry, huh?" Aunt Lou started up the shaggin' wagon and turned on the radio.

Whether Aunt Lou was in a particularly good mood after her haircut or whether she sensed Sunshine's own mood had changed, Sunshine didn't know, but Aunt Lou took her through the drive-through at Jack-in-the-Box and they got milkshakes, vanilla for Aunt Lou and strawberry for Sunshine. Aunt Lou said that before they went to work, she wanted to go to Leggett's for a couple things. She purchased a new bottle of perfume for herself—Chantilly, which she said she'd read that Christie Brinkley wore—and then they went to the children's clothes department to look for a birthday gift.

Sunshine didn't care about clothes, though, and besides that she felt sad for some reason. Each time Aunt Lou held up a skirt or a denim jumper or even a pair of overalls and said, "What about this? You like this one?" she just shrugged.

"I had no idea you were so picky," Aunt Lou said, seeming annoyed.

They were on their way back out to the car, passing by rows of shoes lined up on giant, white plastic cubes, when Sunshine saw them: bright, banana-yellow Converse All Stars.

She had seen some of the girls in her fifth-grade class with these shoes last year. They came in all different candy colors. Maddie Giroux (who had led the chorus of *Cinderelly, Cinderelly...*) had them in purple; Tonya Lubbock had them in red and also in sky blue.

"Yellow shoes? They'll get muddy as soon as you put them on," Aunt Lou said.

Sunshine swallowed. "I won't wear them on the road," she promised. "Only at school."

Aunt Lou said she'd think about it but that they seemed a silly birthday present all things considered. "And you're growing like a weed," she said. "Look at how skinny and tall you've gotten this summer. You'd grow right out of them." She nudged Sunshine with her elbow and grinned down at her. "By the time school starts, your toes'll poke right through like a hobo's."

"Okay," said Sunshine, but she couldn't resist adding: "They'd be the *best* birthday present. The *best.*"

Aunt Lou rolled her eyes. "Don't push the issue," she said.

Sunshine did not *push the issue*, but as they walked back to the car, she pictured what it would be like to start middle school with yellow Converse All Stars. She thought that finally she would have a seat at the main lunch table. Where the girls who passed notes in class sat. She might not be stuck with Jeremiah and Winnie. She might make a friend, and sixth grade would unfurl before her with possibilities she hadn't even known to consider back in elementary school.

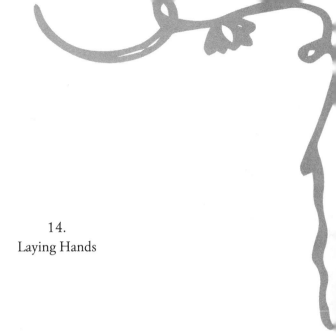

14.
Laying Hands

In the passenger seat beside her, Sunshine was staring out the window at the stretches of flat green fields. Her arms were sun-browned and she looked especially skinny; Lou thought she was probably going through a growth spurt. She seemed moody these days, too—her face was turned toward the window and her mouth looked tense. The sight of Sunshine's tiny little breasts—hardly breasts, really, but especially obvious under the thin cotton of her dress (some other time, when the mood seemed right, Lou would remind her about the training bra)—made Lou's heart lurch. Her daughter and niece weren't little children anymore. In fact, after Sunshine grew up, Fingertip would have no more children at all.

As she turned onto 79, she brought one hand to the back of her neck. With her haircut, the skin there was fully exposed, and somehow the bone structure felt more delicate.

She wondered what Nash would think. He'd loved to play with her long hair and she hadn't mentioned the decision to cut most of it off.

When Janey, a young waitress who had worked briefly at the 79 Dine, got married to a high school sweetheart, she told Lou she was putting a paste of egg whites and vinegar on her scalp each night so her hair would be long for the wedding. But Lou had already been married, and she didn't hold stock in the upcoming occasion in the way Janey had for hers. The shaggin' wagon heaved itself into a higher gear, and it occurred to Lou that perhaps this was part of why she had cut her hair off—to declare herself unconstrained by marriage. By a man's expectations of her.

JUST A FEW NIGHTS back, Nash had been hurt when she'd told him she didn't care about a ceremony. He'd told her he wanted at least a small one; he said you only got to marry someone once. "No offense to the divorced among us," he'd added, and squeezed her shoulder.

They were sitting on the couch in her living room, sipping a drink before dinner. She reached out and put her hand on his leg. Beneath the worn denim, his thigh was muscular. She said, "All right, baby. Let's have a little ceremony."

Now, she touched her hand to her exposed neck again. It occurred to her that ceremony was at least intentional. You had to plan for it. Something about that was a comfort; she wasn't just repeating old mistakes, playing her own history on a loop.

Years ago, just out of high school, she hadn't planned to marry Robert Dalton. It always felt to her as though it just *happened.*

It had been like slipping on a patch of red mud.

SHE MET ROBERT WHEN she was a senior in high school and accepted her school friend Clarissa's invitation to attend youth group in St. Augustine Parish. The youth group was held in the basement of a Baptist church.

The New Covenant of God called itself Baptist Charismatic. Lou, always shy, had followed Clarissa that first evening into the fluorescent, whitewashed basement. They'd served themselves Dixie cups of fruit punch, and Lou had begged Clarissa to sit in the back, where the metal folding chairs were cold through their jeans.

Clarissa had silky brown hair parted in the middle. She was dating one of the leaders, Mickey, who was twenty years old, wore a bandana around his forehead, and didn't seem at all how Lou had imagined any church leader. Robert, the other leader, was more conservative. He wore pastel-colored polos and a close-cropped, neatly-combed hairstyle. But both Mickey and Robert were compelling speakers. They raised their voices and preached with their whole bodies. They read and interpreted Biblical passages and applied them to the mounting tensions in Vietnam and to war protests. At the end of each meeting, anyone in attendance could make prayer requests, and everyone circled around, reaching their hands out to rest on that person's head and shoulders and back and wrists, and a kind of energy seemed to pulse all throughout the church basement as Robert and Mickey spoke with firm confidence to the Lord.

As if the Lord were someone they could command into submission even as they asked Him for miracles.

Her first night there, when they prayed for a girl whose mother was sick with cancer, the girl turned pale and began to shake, and the other members of the youth group backed up, although they seemed neither alarmed nor concerned. Clarissa leaned over to Lou and whispered, "Don't worry, sometimes this happens"—and as Mickey went on praying, commanding healing, Robert knelt and held the girl's head with two hands as she convulsed on the beige tile floor, eyes rolling to the back of her head.

Lou soon learned that such moments did, in fact, often happen. Prayers were said, hands were laid, and often the person for whom the group was praying fainted or convulsed. Some spoke in tongues, an indecipherable language that flew rapidly from their mouths, their eyes closed, touched by all those hands, or by Robert or Mickey kneeling tenderly, holding the person as their body gave way to the Holy Spirit.

She attended the group each Wednesday night throughout the rest of the school year. Clarissa—the only friend she had ever allowed to see where she lived, that tiny dead-end town—drove her home afterwards. The headlights of the pea-green Pinto illuminated the red dirt of Only Road. The dripping, dust-green moss.

On those nights, walking into the yellow house (the sputtering of Clarissa's car engine receding into the distance), Lou was relieved of the anxious knot in her stomach that she usually felt upon entering her home, wondering what sort of mood her father would be in. If he was going to pick a fight with her mother, if the fight would end in violence.

It was as if the Holy Spirit had lifted that burden of fear, however temporarily, into His own two arms.

FOR AS LONG AS she could remember, her father had gone to great and often creative measures to establish his position of power in the household. He cheated on her mother and made no effort to hide it from her or his children. More than once, he came home with lipstick on his mouth and the collar of his shirt, his buttons halfway undone, his normally carefully-pomaded hair sticking up at various angles.

If on any occasion her mother argued with him (which meant simply voicing her own feelings or ideas—meant quietly claiming, *Well, I don't know...*, or *Don't you think?...*), John Jay insulted her until she backed down. Or, he slapped. A backhand or an open palm shut down any argument as firmly and abruptly as a period silenced a sentence. And if her mother remained quiet, he told her she was spineless as a jellyfish. Quiet as a mouse. Homely as one, too, he'd remind her.

Still other tactics were more original, almost comical.

Almost.

On weekend mornings, John Jay had the odd habit of taking a newspaper into the bathroom, sitting down on the toilet, and leaving the door open so that whoever passed by in the hall had no choice but to both see and smell his business.

If one of the family was feeling particularly bold, he or she might lean into the bathroom, take the brass doorknob, and close the door quietly— as though he were a napping child they didn't want to disturb. But it was much easier to walk past as though they didn't see him at all, to breathe through their mouths rather than their noses and act as though both the noise and the stench of his shit did not waft down the hall and into the living room.

He did not call their mother by her name. When he addressed her at all, it was *Hey you*, or *Dummy*, or *Hey Stupid*.

He did not address his children by anything at all. If he wanted one of them, he simply barged into their bedroom, whether they were dressed or not, whether they were asleep or awake, and barked for them to follow him.

Depending on his mood, on what he'd had to drink, on how work had gone that day, on whether or not his bad molar was aching, he might then sit one of them down on the pink couch and lecture them for fifteen minutes, thirty minutes, an hour or more, the volume of his voice rising and falling over mountains and valleys. Billy had left a wet towel on the floor, or Lou had not straightened her shoes on the porch, or Billy was stuttering again.

Still, his most effective tactic of rule was not violence or belittlement; it was ignoring his wife and his children altogether.

He brushed past them in the hallway, smelling of bourbon and after-shave, not seeming to notice if he knocked against them, not seeming to notice if they stepped to the side, pressing themselves flat against the wall to let him pass, not seeming to hear when one of them had again grown brave enough to say, *Hi, Dad.*

One evening, Lou returned home from church to a darkened house but for the porch light through the window. She was giddy with the energy in that basement room, of Robert Dalton's eyes on her as he spoke of the apostle Paul. In the living room, her father sat in the La-Z-Boy, feet propped up, a drink in hand. She was startled to see him there, illuminated only by the sickly glow of the porch light. Billy and her mother were elsewhere—hiding in their bedrooms, probably, as they all often did when John Jay was home. She flicked on the light switch.

"And where have *you* been?" John Jay said, squinting into the sudden light.

"At church," she replied, but she felt guilty, for some reason—his tone implied she had done something wrong.

It was difficult, when John Jay saw the worst in his children, not to believe him.

"Huh," John Jay said, and he crossed his feet, moving slowly, pausing to flex one foot mid-air before letting it rest delicately across his other ankle. She stood frozen in the doorway but hoped if she left now he might let go of whatever argument he was trying to pick with her, but as soon as she moved toward the hallway, he spoke again. "Did you wear that to church?"

She was wearing bell-bottoms and a gauzy white blouse she had borrowed from Clarissa. She'd worn a little lip gloss too. She and Clarissa had checked their make-up in the car mirrors and giggled with each other before going into the church.

"Yes," she said. "It's just a youth group. It's more casual than a church service."

John Jay raised his eyebrows. "And did you ever consider that when you wear a transparent shirt like that, you look like a slut?"

Her father's eyes were on her breasts—she knew her bra showed, faintly, through the shirt, and she wished she had thought to step back toward the hallway, out of reach of the light she regretted turning on—as though to remind her who in this room had the power. (The gazer, his eyes taught Lou. The gazer is the one with power, and never the gazed upon.)

She hunched her shoulders as though they might fold over her body, expanding like wings—inside of which, she could disappear.

Throughout her adult life, she would work on undoing that hunch, on reminding herself to roll her shoulders back. She would place her arms on either side of a doorway and lean forward to stretch her shoulders and reverse their tendency to slump forward. She would constantly remind her daughter and niece not to slouch.

She didn't want them, too, to feel as though it was preferable to disappear than to be seen.

AT CHURCH WITH CLARISSA and the others their age, with Mickey and Robert commanding assistance, relief, miracles, Lou began to learn what her father had long communicated otherwise: that she, like all children, was deserving of love, and that there was a Heavenly Father—if not an earthly one—who was always there to offer it.

The lessons unraveled, offering infinite possibilities and hope.

From Robert Dalton, from his meaty hands and neatly combed hair and booming prayers, she also learned that even her father was a child of God. That he was capable of redemption. (She learned that it was her responsibility to forgive him for his actions. Time and time again.)

During a prayer circle one evening, Clarissa raised her hand. "Lou gets embarrassed by attention," Clarissa said, and hooked an arm around her waist. "But I think we should pray for her family."

Lou glanced at Clarissa. Annoyed. She could feel that her cheeks were bright red.

"Oh, it's okay," she protested. "We can pray for someone else."

But Robert Dalton, standing next to her, rested one hand gently on her shoulder and beckoned the others to move in close. "Friends," he said, "let us lay our hands on Lou Turner. Let us pray her family finds the healing it needs."

Hands had come from all directions, pressed warmly on the crown of her head, her shoulders, her back. She had felt it, then: The Holy Spirit moved His way through her, like electric currents running from those hands and into her body. Her knees buckled and somehow more hands emerged and helped lower her to her knees and Robert Dalton's face was before her and so many hands were holding her and she rocked back and forth, crying, as Robert Dalton's voice boomed out like the voice of God Himself.

WHEN HE BEGAN OFFERING her rides home, a sense of shame about her home and about Fingertip—its very existence, and that she should reside within it—boiled up inside of her. She told Robert something about her house being on Clarissa's way home, anyway, but she thought to add that she had some spiritual questions she'd like to talk over with him, and Robert suggested she arrive early some time and they could walk the grounds of the church and discuss.

The next week, Clarissa—giddy with excitement for Lou—dropped her off early.

Together, she and Robert walked at sunset around the churchyard, visiting the old gravestones in the little gated cemetery, strolling under a large oak whose branches arched overhead and concealed them from the outside world, and it was there that Robert Dalton leaned forward and kissed her, gently, on the lips.

In the coming months, Lou let his hands wander up her shirt and over her breasts in the kitchen of the whitewashed church basement (the kitchen smelled of always graham crackers and apple juice, the snacks of St. Cadence Sunday school attendees), and she let his tongue push its way into her mouth and she thought about him at night, on her side of the bedroom, and when she knew that Billy was asleep, when she could hear his snoring and occasional oblivious fart, she let her hand wander down inside the waistband of her underwear and recall Robert Dalton's hands on her body.

But she had seen the way her mother had trapped herself at the end of a muddy red road, in a too-small house with a man whose love could not be earned no matter how hard she tried.

Robert Dalton was only ever *for now*. Not for the future.

She had a full scholarship to Louisiana State University for the coming fall. Clarissa would be there, too; they'd talked about rooming together. She thought that eventually, she'd like to teach English. Maybe after she graduated college she'd get married, but she didn't care about that then. She wanted to leave. To learn. To read and talk about books. To make her own money. She wanted to buy a house someplace else and have her mother come live there with her.

She wouldn't have even considered marrying Robert Dalton if what happened to Catherine and John Jay had not happened.

AFTER THE SUGAR MILL closed down, John Jay had found work at a packaging plant, where he worked throughout all of Lou's childhood and high school years. On New Year's Eve of her senior year of high school, her parents were attending a party at the owner's house, all the way in Lafayette.

John Jay, always eager to impress with appearances, spent nearly an hour getting ready in the hallway bathroom. When he emerged, a great cloud of cologne followed him, burning Lou's nostrils as he passed her at the kitchen table. She had no interest in parties; she was doing homework. Her father went to the refrigerator, took down the bottle of bourbon from its place on top of it, and poured himself a drink.

"Ready yet?" he barked over his shoulder. He meant it for Lou's mother, who was getting ready in their bedroom, and it was not so much a question as an order to hurry up. His drink was to take with him on the road.

Lou heard the bedroom door open and the clicking of her mother's heels down the hallway. On the porch, she would take off the heels and slip on her rubber clogs, which she'd wear to the car so she wouldn't get red dust on her party shoes—but Lou could see her mother wanted to make an entrance.

She stepped into the kitchen. She was smiling.

AT FORTY-EIGHT, CATHERINE COVERED her fully gray hair with Technicolor-red dye. Wrinkles lined her forehead, the edges of her mouth, the fine skin under her eyes. Her small shoulders seemed hunched in a position of perpetual defeat.

But on this night, she had put on the richly colored paisley dress Lou had helped her pick out. She had wanted pink—she always wanted pink—but Lou had insisted she try something new. "Paisley is hip," Lou had told her in the dressing room of the little Lafayette clothing shop. Now, the greens and burgundies of the dress complimented her hair, which fell to her shoulders and was held up on one side by an emerald barrette. The blousy sleeves of her dress tapered at a wide cuff, emphasizing the slimness of her wrists, and the cuffs were lined with a neat row of silver buttons. She wore dark eyeliner. Her lips were a soft mauve.

She looked stylish, luminous.

"Mom," Lou gasped.

Catherine curtsied, and Lou had giggled. Then, a further surprise, still—John Jay had turned toward his wife and daughter, his drink in hand. "What about me?" he said, and held out his arms, gesturing for their approval.

It was a rare moment of levity. Both Lou and Catherine had laughed.

"You look very handsome, Dad," Lou said, secretly thrilled by the moment. His nonchalance. His humor.

John Jay bowed as if on stage. "We don't look bad," he said. "Not bad at all."

For many years, Lou would remember how her mother had beamed in that moment, as though she and her husband were still in their twenties, and John Jay were courting her for the first time. And Lou would point to this moment—her father's good humor, his inclusive *we*—as evidence that he loved her mother. That he could be kind. That he wasn't the person that Billy thought him to be. That he wasn't the person his daughter had known him to be for her entire life.

When she completed her homework that evening, she took out the Bible that Robert had given her, and she read the chapter he'd told her about—in Luke, where the father forgives the prodigal son his exorbitant spending. But the house was too quiet and she felt scared, for some reason, and so as she read, she brought the portable television over to the table and switched the channel to *Bewitched* and let it play in the background. She did not so much enjoy reading the Bible as she enjoyed the idea of telling Robert she had done it. What she *wanted* to read, what she planned to spend all of her time in college reading, were the books she loved in her English classes—books like *Jane Eyre* that made her believe she was not in Fingertip, Louisiana, but on a moor in nineteenth-century England, books that she would soon require herself to forget about entirely.

LATER, WHEN LOU REMEMBERED this night, she allowed herself to imagine that the owner of the packaging plant who was hosting the New Year's Eve party was wealthy.

She imagined he lived in one of the huge old plantation homes with enormous wraparound porches, and she imagined her mother's delight as they walked up to such a house, the spaciousness of that land so unlike the close, crowded woods at the end of Only Road, the tangled backyards. She imagined that inside, they served small triangular sandwiches and cocktails in elegant, gold-rimmed glasses, that the room where the party had gathered was softly lit, that the furniture was velvet, and she imagined that her mother felt just as wealthy as the other women there.

She loaned her mother, in this imagined version, a fur wrap like something out of an old movie and she filled the room with warm light so the lines of her mother's skin softened, too, and the silver buttons on the cuff of her sleeves glittered. She imagined that on that night, the brief moment of good humor John Jay had displayed in the kitchen—his pride in his appearance, the bow—had continued. That the glass of bourbon he'd taken with him as they walked out the door had only brightened his mood.

Sometimes she even went so far, in her imagined version, to believe that perhaps that night it had dawned on her father, at last, that he loved her mother. All night, moving from room to room in the enormous old house, her father kept his hand on her mother's lower back. A cocktail in her mother's hand, the mauve-colored lipstick marking the rim of her glass.

Jesus, as Robert Dalton always reminded the youth group, was a worker of miracles. Under His guidance, anything was possible.

The truth was that it drizzled all that night. A cold, wet rain. The temperature dropped to a record low in Atchafalaya, and a black, razor-thin layer of ice formed on the roads.

Lou imagined that on the drive home from that party, her mother had been nestled against John Jay, sleepy and content, letting her eyes close, so that when the tires lost their purchase on the ice, and John Jay, head spinning with bourbon, could not regain control of the Buick, her mother did not see the blinding headlights of the oncoming truck.

• • •

THE AFTERNOON SUN REFLECTED off the aluminum siding of the 79 Dine.

Sunshine worked the register and Damien, the cook, brought her free snacks from the kitchen. He liked to make miniature food when she was there—a grilled cheese sandwich a quarter of its usual size, a small stack of pancakes no bigger than silver dollars, a miniature cheeseburger patty. When Sunshine giggled, he said he was making food that was Sunshine-sized, nothing to laugh about, and winked at her. Embarrassingly, she felt her cheeks grow warm. The night was punctuated by the dinging of the bell on the door of the diner when customers came and went, by the miniature pancakes and cheeseburger patties, by the clink of coins customers dropped in the milk carton tip jar. By the end of the shift, Sunshine's belly was full and her mood had lifted. Tammy, Aunt Lou's favorite waitress, said that the customers always tipped the most when Sunshine worked the register.

Aunt Lou had seemed sad on the drive from Leggett's to the 79, and Sunshine had wondered if she was regretting her haircut or if she was upset with Sunshine's bad mood earlier or for asking about the All Stars, and Sunshine spent much of the drive trying to think of the right thing to say. But when they stepped inside the little diner, the regulars told Aunt Lou how pretty she looked and how flattering that cut was on her, and Tammy gasped, and Sunshine could see that Aunt Lou was beaming, now, in her green polka-dot dress.

When Nash arrived after work and saw Aunt Lou he shouted, "Holy hot tamale!" and didn't seem to care that everyone turned their heads to look at him.

Aunt Lou blushed. "Keep your damn voice down," she said, but as she passed by she rested one hand on his cheek and smiled up at him.

WHEN THE SHIFT WAS over, Nash asked if Sunshine wanted to go by the new house. "It's coming along," Nash said. "You won't even believe it, Sunshine girl."

"I need to get her home to bed," Aunt Lou said, untying her apron strings. "We've been gone all day. We're exhausted."

"I'm wide awake!" Sunshine protested, and Aunt Lou said she was too tired to argue and okay, fine, and Sunshine could see that Aunt Lou was still in a good mood. They ordered to-go cups of coffee and let Sunshine fill hers with cream and sugar, then Aunt Lou and Sunshine followed Nash's truck over into Lafayette Parish.

They drove down a single-lane road lined with large old houses with big yards and wraparound porches, then turned onto another single-lane road and drove through a tunnel of pine trees, the bark silver in the headlights. Then Nash's truck pulled into a darkened lot and he turned off the ignition.

They picked their way through the yard, past a dumpster and various stacks of plywood and two-by-fours. The moon was bright, and the house rose up before them—two stories high plus an attic, an old farmhouse surrounded by pines and crawling oaks. It looked nicer than when Sunshine had last seen it; even in the darkness she could see that the paint was new, and the large windows were no longer boarded up but fitted with new glass. Nash said they didn't yet have the electricity turned on, but he had several battery-operated lanterns and a flashlight, and he led them on a tour.

THE HOUSE SMELLED OF sawdust. When they climbed to the second story, Nash held a lantern up into a bedroom at the top of the stairs. "This room'll be yours, Sunny Delight," he said, the lantern light casting long shadows around the empty room. "When you visit, I mean."

Sunshine stepped inside the room. The floorboards were wide and smooth, and two windows faced the side yard and another two the backyard. The bedroom was bigger than her room in the yellow house and there were no sea anemones on the walls, but she liked the smell of the sawdust and how she could feel it underneath the soles of her tennis shoes, like dirt from a forest floor.

Behind her, Nash had set down the lantern in the doorway and taken Aunt Lou into the hallway. He was describing something about the bathroom and Aunt Lou was saying, "Oh, sure, babe, I can picture it. Yes, yes, I can imagine."

NASH DROVE AHEAD OF them back to Fingertip, and Sunshine finished the last of her sweet coffee. Aunt Lou left the radio off and they drove in silence but for the wind rushing in through the open windows.

Sunshine wanted, all of a sudden, to tell Aunt Lou about Billy's job. She thought that with the mood just so, Aunt Lou might not get mad. Maybe she might be able to tell Sunshine what to do, or maybe she and Nash knew about a job and could help out Billy. She looked over at her aunt; her profile in the darkness, her newly cut hair blowing around in the wind, and she said, "Aunt Lou?"

But if she told about the job, would she also tell about the bourbon? About the rain that had been falling inside of the yellow house all summer? Would she tell about the spiders?

Maybe, instead of telling her Billy's secret, she could just ask Aunt Lou about the stones in her chest, or what *doing it* meant—she could leave JL out of it so she didn't get her in trouble. She could say she'd overheard someone at the 79 talk about tonight.

Aunt Lou glanced over at her. "What's up, sugar?"

But the tightrope walkers in Sunshine's stomach were marching furiously, waving their batons as though in warning. She caught her breath. "I forgot," she said. "Nevermind."

"Today was really nice," Aunt Lou said, her voice slow and dreamy. "Spending time with you like that, for starters. Isn't it good to just get *out* sometimes?"

Sunshine nodded, and smiled, and said, "Yeah. Today was real nice."

"*Really* nice."

"Really nice."

All at once, her own good mood flitted away—like a scrap of paper accidentally dislodged from the glove compartment—and for the first time in a long time, Sunshine wished that she had a mother.

SHE HAD ASKED AUNT Lou about the Florida orange crate, once. Billy said the God's honest truth of it was that a great blue heron had brought Sunshine, bundled up in a blanket and tucked inside the crate, to the porch of the yellow house and left her there. She was so small and so pink that Billy had mistaken her for a strawberry at first. When he realized his mistake, he had no choice but to do what any good honest man would do and take her in.

She was old enough now to know that probably wasn't true, no matter how many times Billy had sworn it, but when she asked Aunt Lou about it years ago, Aunt Lou had said she didn't know, she genuinely didn't know, and that she supposed if Billy wanted to tell the story of Sunshine's mother he would have to do it in his own time.

Aunt Lou had guesses, though. She said she suspected that Sunshine's mother may not have been ready for the responsibility of a baby, or was maybe too young, and when Sunshine asked more about what she meant by these guesses, Aunt Lou had looked suddenly tired and sighed loudly and said, "Oh, sugar, I like the story about the heron the best. Don't you?"

Now it felt to Sunshine that a mother would know what to do about all of the secrets, about who to tell what, and how much to say and how to say it.

She tilted her head against the window and watched the tall grass in the roadside ditches rush past. She didn't remember closing her eyes, but when they pulled into the driveway behind Nash's truck and Aunt Lou said, "Sugar, you wanna sleep in JL's room tonight?" she realized she had been dreaming. In the dream, JL was with them in the car and she was whispering something to Sunshine, though Sunshine couldn't remember what. She followed Aunt Lou and Nash inside and lay down on her side of JL's room, not bothering to climb underneath the quilt.

• • •

LOU OPENED TWO BEERS and brought them into the living room for her and Nash. An old rerun of *The Dick Van Dyke Show* was on the Magnavox, and Nash was laughing, face glowing blue in the television light. She handed him his beer but stood, for a moment, watching the show with him.

She'd read somewhere that Mary Tyler Moore preferred pants, that she thought it was unrealistic for housewives to always wear dresses and that she wrote it into her contract, a clause requiring her—or allowing her, or something like that—to wear pants each episode. Throughout Lou's childhood, her mother had worn dresses. They were not particularly stylish, as John Jay did not give her much of an allowance and St. Cadence did not exactly offer the best shopping opportunities, anyway, and her mother was not enough of a seamstress to make her own. But she sometimes ordered them from a catalogue or made the trip into a Lafayette department store. She kept her dresses clean and pressed and on hangers in her bedroom closet. She preferred, always, shades of pink.

"I'm just going to check on Sunshine," she told Nash, setting her beer on the coffee table.

Lou pushed open the bedroom door cautiously. Light from the hallway slid slowly across the room. She opened the door further, still, until the light reached just the edge of Sunshine's bed.

Sunshine moaned, but didn't wake.

Quietly, Lou stepped closer. Sunshine's tangled blonde hair fanned across the quilt, and strands of it were matted across her face. Her lips were parted. Her body itself was tangled, one leg bent, pulled up almost to her chest. One arm draped back toward the door so her chest was turned upward, toward the ceiling. She hadn't bothered to change into pajamas and her dress was twisted around her torso.

One little button peered out.

These last weeks, she'd told herself that Sunshine's absence was a good sign: Billy must be doing well. But the tugging inside of her, the sense that something was *off*, had not gone away, and she was glad to have Sunshine here. Her tan and tangled body. Her breathing deep.

15.
The Rat Snake

In the summer, Sundays in Fingertip were slothful days.

In the weedy lot that stretched out behind the Lust, the sun beat relentlessly on the old chapel, its only congregation the wasps that nested in the eaves. Perhaps an occasional rat snake. So far as Lou could tell, most everyone stayed in on Sunday mornings, and if there was any kind of Sunday ritual it was beers on porches from the afternoon on past dinner. Even Ms. Mouton, a devout Catholic for as long as Lou had known her, had stopped attending Mass in St. Cadence after her husband died some years back.

On Sundays, Lou felt both a relief at the lack of expectation, and a lingering sense of obligation—for whom, or of what, she wasn't sure. The few times she'd taken the girls into St. Cadence for an Easter or Christmas service, they'd wriggled in their seats or giggled uncontrollably at nothing at all and had to be sent—by Lou, who gave them her sharpest, most thin-lipped look of warning—to the bathrooms to collect themselves.

Of the family she'd known in her lifetime, only Robert was religious.

AFTER SUNDAY SERVICES IN Charleston, there were potlucks in the park across from the chapel: a triangular wedge of grass, shaded by sweet-smelling pine trees and bushy-topped palms. There were tables covered in checkered oilcloth and big cardboard boxes of fried chicken and biscuits, and jars of honey to drizzle over the biscuits, and lemonade in Dixie cups.

Robert shook hands with the men and women in his congregation and smiled. His teeth were white and straight. He held Lou's hand tenderly in his own, and whatever sins he had committed during the week began to fade.

When the pregnancy began to make itself known through her floral Sunday dresses, congregation members came up to her, rested their hands on her stomach, and offered blessings and prayers. To someone else this may have felt intrusive, but to Lou (barely twenty years old) these gentle hands felt healing. She imagined all of those hands were protecting her unborn baby girl, curled up like a moon in her belly. Keeping her safe.

On one of those Sundays, a story Catherine used to tell her and Billy resurfaced in her memory and then returned to her again throughout the coming months, then years. She could never remember the details, but she remembered enough: something about bruises disappearing. Broken hearts instantly cured. A cut turning to scar tissue and then all together invisible, all within a few hours.

Billy would know the details she'd forgotten. He loved those stories. But after Lou left Fingertip, she hadn't reached out to him for reasons she couldn't explain.

What she did remember of the story was what she wanted to believe throughout those years in Charleston—that wounds could be healed simply, by a laying of hands. Hadn't she felt it in the whitewashed basement of the church where they'd had youth group meetings? Under a South Carolina sky, in a green, neatly trimmed park, her own bruises could cease to ache. Robert's behavior could fade, could be forgotten. He was forgiven by the Lord; he could be—he should be—forgiven by her. Those weekly sins rinsed white and clean as the walls of that church basement.

On one of these afternoons, Lou found herself making small talk with a visiting pastor's wife in a corner of the park. The sun was bright and Lou kept raising her hand to her forehead to shade her eyes. In the grass nearby, their daughters were propped on a picnic blanket, sucking on orange wedges. Each little girl wore a dress and ruffled underwear. Juice dribbled down their faces and onto their dresses. Joanna Louise looked up at Lou and grinned, flecks of orange stuck to her chin.

Then, without any words, the pastor's wife was taking Lou's hand down from her forehead, into her own. The woman was trim and blonde, dressed in pale blue linen and a matching pillbox hat. She ran her fingers gently along the four blue smudges that lined Lou's wrist.

"Oh," Lou said, but she didn't attempt to pull away. She met the woman's eyes.

"Honey," the pastor's wife said, nodding. "Can I offer you some advice?"

Lou's heartbeat quickened and her breath felt suddenly shaky. It was easy to believe that others didn't notice her bruises. Or, perhaps that others knew what she herself believed: Somewhere along the way, she had done something to deserve the life she now led.

But standing across from the pastor's wife, her perfume thick in Lou's nostrils, Lou found herself hoping for relief. She hoped this woman would offer her permission, or instructions, to get out. *Can I offer you some advice? Leave him.*

The sudden force of this hope—that's why she was shaking, she realized. That's why her teeth had begun to chatter.

The pastor's wife looked down at Lou's wrist again. She placed her own four fingers lightly over the smudges and let them rest there. Covering up the marks with her well-manicured fingers.

"In my experience," said the pastor's wife, "the best you can do is submit. It's our duty to trust that the Lord will offer His just rewards."

In the moment, Lou didn't pause to question this advice. She didn't allow herself to even acknowledge the hope that had sent shivers throughout her body. She only nodded. "Yes, yes, you're probably right," she said.

Eager to appear knowing. Dutiful.

The pastor's wife smiled as though to reassure—then she let go of Lou's wrist and turned away.

It was a week later that Robert beat their small daughter (her pale, pudgy toddler legs) with a belt, whipping furiously, with rage, and something inside of Lou abruptly and fully awoke. It was that snake again at first—bucking and arching—and then it was more. It was hot and alive and tremendous, like a giant roaring to life.

It had been five years.

IN FINGERTIP, IT SOMETIMES felt as though Lou's current lack of duty to a God in which she only half-heartedly believed anymore was surely disappointing someone, somewhere. Robert. Or a pretty pastor's wife in a blue pillbox hat. Perhaps God, if there was one. So when the Fourth of July fell on a Sunday, she was grateful. There could be no real expectation on a holiday.

It was not often that her house was entirely empty. Nash had gone out with buddies in Lafayette the night before, and Lord knew where Sunshine was off to these days. Lou slept in, then sat drinking her coffee on the screened-in porch out back, rereading her daughter's letter from camp. In the pines outside the porch, wrens chirped. The morning light through the trees cast quiet shadows.

When she and Billy were children, and there had still been other children in the pastel bungalows, too, some of the parents would go to the old train tracks and set off fireworks on the Fourth of July. Families gathered on picnic blankets in the middle of the road and watched the colorful explosions overhead. Then three of the sons in Fingertip were drafted to Vietnam and only Big Jake had returned, and their deaths somehow made for the final straw in Fingertip's declining population. Both the Martins and the Lanes moved shortly after the death of their sons; those who had stayed had grown children, and no new families—besides Lou and Joanna Louise—had moved into the unoccupied houses.

Fingertip, even with its ninety-nine-cent mortgages, was a forgotten secret, and those still here had little use for fireworks.

Only when Joanna Louise and Sunshine were younger did they celebrate—Billy would buy sparklers and the girls would make shapes and words in the air. But she thought Sunshine was probably too old to care about that this year. She remembered that in a couple of hours, Channel 10 was showing the *Columbia* landing; maybe Sunshine would want to come watch it with her. Not exactly a raucous celebration, but still.

She loved time with just her niece. She missed her.

Sunshine was young enough that she was still sweet. "Your house feels good," she sometimes told Lou, and Lou loved knowing she could provide that for her—something good-feeling. Pancakes when she slept over. Swims at the lake. Sunshine didn't resent her yet like Joanna Louise seemed to—though for what reason, Lou didn't understand. Just two years ago, they'd still been close. Joanna Louise used to wrap her arms around Lou's waist for no reason; even at age eleven, she'd still wanted Lou to draw her a bath at night. Sometimes, at night, she'd even let Lou read to her.

"She's just being a teenager," Nash had said recently, before Joanna Louise left. "You didn't act that way with your mama when you were a teenager?"

And perhaps she had. Once, on a drive back from the diner this summer, a memory had resurfaced: her mother turning to her in that old Buick and asking Lou about Billy's drinking.

She was fourteen, then—the same age as Joanna Louise—and something in her stomach had flipped over. It felt like the black snake that once got caught in a rat trap in the Laurents' kitchen. The whole neighborhood, it seemed, had gone about trying to figure out how to kill the poor thing—it was doomed anyway—without shooting it, as the rat trap was wedged between a wall and a gas-fueled stove. Eventually, Moss Landry had lifted up a shovel, but before he could bring it down the snake had lunged—a desperate, defensive lunge. It was useless; the lower half of its body was caught between the steel brackets, and the force of its attempted attack flipped it over, belly-up, so that it twisted upward in a grotesque arc.

"Have you noticed?" her mother had said. Catherine's hair was still been long, then, and as she drove, wisps of it had blown across her face; her mouth had scrunched tight in the way it did when she was upset about something. Over the years, small vertical lines had cut into her upper lip.

Inside of Lou, the snake had arched and bucked.

She'd feel it again throughout her life. When John Jay hurt her mother. Those sickening sounds.

She'd feel it after Robert first hit her, before she learned how to numb herself, and the snake would suddenly lunge again, would arch its muscular body, when she saw that, despite all of her promises to herself when she was growing up, despite her plans for college, her love of reading, she was where she was—with this husband, in this life.

In a green park with pastor's wives in blue pillbox hats, whispering of just rewards.

"No," she remembered snapping at her mother—as though her mother was an idiot for even wondering about her son's drinking. As though she'd asked something entirely unreasonable. For some reason Lou had felt protective of Billy, and her impulse wasn't to connect with her mother—to admit that yes, she'd noticed, she'd seen—but to put her down. "You worry about *everything*," she'd added, rolling her eyes, and her mother had not brought it up again.

COFFEE IN HAND, BAREFOOT, Lou walked across the hard mud road and knocked their old familiar rhythm on the door.

Billy came padding barefoot from the kitchen. He wore torn jeans and no shirt. "Two bits," he said, and grinned.

She hadn't realized she'd felt worried about seeing him—but at his appearance in the door, she felt herself relax. Through the screen door, she could smell the familiar smells of the yellow house—something nameless and sharp-edged, almost like turpentine, mixed with both coffee and the faint but unmistakable scent of their mother's gardenia perfume. As though that perfume had seeped, long ago, into the walls themselves.

"Happy Fourth," Lou said.

"Oh yeah," he said. "Hey, Happy Fourth." He reached his arms up and braced them on the door frame, stretching back.

She smiled. "Is Sunshine home? I thought she might want to come watch the space shuttle landing."

"She's out playing." Billy jerked his head in the direction of the woods.

"Oh. Well, when she comes back, tell her I came by?"

He nodded. "Ah. So that's it then. I see how it is."

He was teasing, but it annoyed her—his way of making *her* decisions about *him*, somehow.

With Billy, though, it was important to soothe. Not to stir up.

"Well, how are you?" she asked. "How's the job?"

Through the screen, his eyes met hers. "All good," he said, nodding. "All good. Mostly the same as before, really, but with more time on the rigs." He drummed his hands on the door frame. "So when's the big move? Coming up soon, huh?"

Lou bristled. "As soon as the house is finished," she said, and took a slow sip of her coffee. "Late August, probably. We're hoping it will be before school starts."

"We gonna see you anymore?" he asked.

Lou laughed. "We're not going to the moon," she said. "So I'd hope so."

He shrugged. "Well, you know. Last time you left, I didn't see you for five years."

"Okay," she said, though she said it only to buy herself time. She never knew how to respond to Billy when he got like this—when he acted like every choice she made, she made specifically to hurt him. But tempering her anger at his childishness was guilt. Nibbling away at her insides. Taking tiny but relentless bites.

"Sunshine loves you, you know," he said. He wasn't looking at her, but over her shoulder—toward her house, maybe. Her future absence from it. "Thinks of you like her own mama."

She nodded. She wrapped one arm around her ribs, protectively, still holding her coffee in her other hand. "I know that," she said. "That's why—well, I actually thought she could even come stay with us for a while."

She said this cheerfully, as though it wasn't a big thing, as though it was hardly a thing at all.

Billy slid his gaze back to her. "As in for a weekend?" he said.

Now her free hand had found its way to the hollow at the base of her throat. She stroked the soft skin there. Her heart was beating fast. "As in for longer, I guess. She'd be welcome to stay for longer, I mean. For the school year, anyway. I mean obviously only if you wanted that too."

"Ah," Billy said, his voice flat. "You think I'm not so good at being her daddy, huh?"

Lou could tell by the way his eyes had hardened, by the tone of his voice, that this conversation would go nowhere good. How had it begun in the first place? She'd simply come over to offer something fun for her niece to do, and in hardly anytime at all, she and Billy were on the verge of a fight.

She hadn't known if she wanted to even bring up this idea, ever—and she'd assumed that if or when she *did*, she'd do so in a way that seemed appealing to Billy. Even comforting. A relief from being a single father, perhaps. But why *would* it feel that way? If he'd suggested taking Joanna Louise along on a move, she'd have laughed in his face.

"No," she said, and she tried to keep her voice even. (To soothe, not to stir.) "That's not it, Billy. It's just closer to her school, for starters. And I guess I thought it might be nice for her to be with Joanna Louise. Closer to other kids her age....I think this place can be kind of lonely for kids. Don't you?"

Her brother stuffed his hands in the front pockets of his jeans. His belly was bare and hard. Even with all of his drinking, his body had stayed lean and strong over the years. It was hard to understand how he didn't have a girlfriend or a wife by now—though she'd long wondered where he stayed when he didn't come home from the coast. Maybe Jimmy and Marie's. Maybe elsewhere.

There were some things they just didn't discuss.

"I don't know," he said, and shrugged. "We were kids here and it never felt lonely for me. I had you. Clearly you felt otherwise."

John Jay's arguments, too, had been childish and obtuse, looping over on themselves so the person he was talking to—or more often, yelling at—stood no chance of escape.

That feeling in her belly—it arched and coiled.

She pursed her lips. She waited for the feeling to retreat. When it was gone, when she could trust herself again, she said, "Billy. It isn't about you, okay? Just think on it."

Then, shaking in spite of herself, she turned for the steps. She could sense him there in the doorway behind her, and because guilt was nibbling away, and because she did want to make things right, she turned before stepping out the screen door.

"I love you—"

But Billy had already left the doorway and disappeared inside.

16.
Elves and Giants

A gain and again, Catherine decided that the best she could do, living with John Jay at this southern edge of the world, was bear it.

Her husband's mood swings. His temper. How, when he was upset, he might strike her, or ignore her entirely, and she didn't know which was coming, or when, or which was worse.

How he shoved himself inside of her, whether she wanted him to or not.

For three years after their marriage, she longed for a child but didn't conceive. Her doctor in St. Cadence informed her that she likely never would. And so she lived with John Jay only and feared that her life would be always just the two of them—until eventually, on a mild winter day, that same doctor confirmed that Catherine was pregnant.

She started crying right there in the doctor's office and threw her arms around him.

Lying in bed that night, John Jay asleep beside her, she ran her hands along her still-flat belly and privately, silently changed the story about the night of the baby's conception.

She imagined that she and John Jay had left their home for a night-time picnic. He carried a bottle of white wine, a secret bar of chocolate in his back pocket. It had been November when Billy was conceived and the weather for her imagined picnic was cooler, crisper, than it had been in reality; instead, she imagined the night was wrapped in Tennessee weather, teetering on cold. In her mind, she wore her favorite green sweater, the one John Jay had once said—when he still had kindnesses left to offer—matched her sea-colored eyes.

Along the imagined path to the lake, Spanish moss hung where there was none in reality and made a tunnel for the two lovers to pass through, and somehow the coppery smell of the Cumberland River filled the woods and the pines weren't pines but sycamores, their bark glowing silver in the moonlight.

They strolled through the dark trees. They were arm in arm. They made love on a blanket in the sand and afterwards, John Jay curled up behind her, wrapped his arm around her, murmured words she could not understand into her neck. His hot breath warmed her, and she drifted in and out of sleep with her husband pressed against her back; it felt as if she were curled inside a seashell, snug and protected.

Loved and in love.

Catherine allowed herself to imagine and reimagine this scene so many times that night, stroking the skin of her belly, that she felt for days afterwards a kind of tenderness toward John Jay, as one does after dreaming something delicious, something intimate, with a person one doesn't really know in life.

WHEN CATHERINE WROTE TO Margaret Bell, she left out the parts of her life she knew would upset her. Instead, she described the things she thought would please her Christian sensibilities and reserved nature. She praised, for example, John Jay's work ethic. He never called in sick. He brought home money for his family. He made sure Catherine had a weekly allowance for groceries and such. (She did not mention how small the allowance; she did not mention the money he spent on liquor, pouring it into his coffee each morning.)

She praised his parenting skills. He was strict, she wrote, but did not hit the children.

She left out the part about how, when he struck her with the back of his hand one night, his wedding ring knocked against her tooth, and within the weeks that followed, her tooth turned ash-gray and she took to smiling with her lips pursed.

She wrote about the Last Outpost (it wasn't until several years later that someone would paint over the A and it would become the Lust) and how a man they called Little Jake ran it, and how his son was called Big Jake, and wasn't that a funny pairing of father and son nicknames?

In her letters, she left out the part about how Billy, the more sensitive of her two children, had a stutter that came out when he was nervous, and so he avoided speaking in front of his father. She described how Billy, in some ways, was like Talmadge. How he loved the purple wildflowers that grew in their backyard in the springtime and in the ditch that ran along Only Road, and how he would pick them and hold out clumps of them for her in his chubby fist. She described how he called his sister "Lou Lou."

Little Lou, her sweet, redheaded youngest. Her soft Lou Lou Littles.

She left out the time that John Jay came home drunk, woke his five-year-old son up from the bedroom he shared with his sleeping sister, commanded him to sit on the pink sofa in the living room, and made him repeat S words after him.

S words were the words Billy found most difficult to pronounce.

Snake. Sally. Sofa. Soft. Silly. Stupid. Son.

"Repeat it after me, boy. 'How did I get *s*tuck with a *s*tupid *s*on?'"

No, CATHERINE DIDN'T DESCRIBE this scene to Margaret Bell. She could hardly stand to remember it herself, much less admit to anyone that she had let it happen to her son.

Her Billy. Sweet. Sensitive.

She'd watched from the hallway as Billy sat in only pajama pants and no shirt, stifling yawns at first and then tears. His feet did not touch the floor.

He repeated after his father as he had been told. "S-s-stuck," he said, voice choked.

She didn't write to her mother that she had been watching (cowering, a coward, a stupid coward who deserved to be hit, she thought) from the dark of the hallway, and when she heard Billy begin to repeat these words she emerged, at last (too late, she knew—years, a lifetime too late) and she braced herself to be struck as she passed John Jay, who towered in the middle of the dark living room. He reeked of liquor.

She hurried to her boy, scooping him up. She said to John Jay, more firmly, more fearlessly than she even intended, "That's enough. It's past his bedtime," and although Billy's body was still trembling, he was already falling asleep by the time she reached his bedroom at the end of the hall.

His hot, teary cheek pressed wetly against her neck.

SHE THOUGHT THAT PERHAPS they would get lucky—that in the morning, Billy would think this had been some sort of a bad dream, or, because he was small, he wouldn't remember this at all. She tucked him into his bed. Lou Lou slept in her nearby crib, still undisturbed.

After that night, Catherine did not write to her mother that she stayed awake as John Jay climbed on top of her and how she did not resist him or plead for him to wait.

How, as John Jay nearly smothered her with his panting, heaving weight, she planned an escape.

She would gather the children in her arms, Billy and two-year-old Lou with her bright red hair curling in every direction, and get Little Jake to drive them to the bus station east off 79, and together, they'd ride all night and all day until they reached Portland, and she would never come back to this place.

• • •

ON THE LONG DRIVE from Charleston back to Fingertip, Joanna Louise in the review mirror (sleeping, or chattering to herself, or slurping her milkshake), it occurred to Lou for the first time in her life that it had been a choice.

That her mother had chosen to stay with him.

Wasn't Lou making her own choice, right now? Wasn't she leaving her husband? Her financial security? The idea that her mother hadn't done the same for her was irritating. She drove another several miles, her body growing increasingly tense.

It wasn't just *irritating*. It was enraging.

She took a ramp off I-10 and pulled the wagon into a Burger King parking lot, in the corner where no other cars were parked. In her booster seat, Joanna Louise was slumped far to one side. Eyes closed, cheeks flushed, red hair matted against her temples.

Lou balled up one fist and put it to her mouth. Shaking, she bit down, hard. She bit down so hard that her teeth broke the skin and she cried out in pain.

In the back seat, Joanna Louise stirred, groaned, and then resumed her nap.

In the front seat, Lou pressed the heels of both trembling hands to her eyes, the knuckles of her right hand beaded with blood. She rocked back and forth, and from deep in her chest rose heaving sobs.

• • •

AFTER JOHN JAY HAD what Catherine sometimes referred to as *a rough night*, Catherine went about her morning routines as usual. She made the children eggs-in-a-basket; she set the percolator on the stove; she asked Billy and Lou about their good or bad or funny dreams and she shared about her own. Letting them know, in other words, that everything was all right.

By morning, the urgency of any plans she'd made to leave John Jay had somehow lessened. Somehow, the routines, the food, the conversation all seemed of more importance. With John Jay gone at work, the kitchen was filled with good smells, its warmth bright and golden, and the two children were happy to be with just their mother. It was easy to feel, on these mornings, that such happiness couldn't help but last; it was easy for the night prior to take on a different shape. No longer a black, monstrous thing that terrified them all. Ugly, yes, but manageable. The shadow of a monster only—not the actual beast.

In the bright kitchen, tending to dishes, tending to her children, to the soothing mundane details of her life, Catherine told herself it was better to keep things stable; it was best for her children to have a father in their life than none at all; things were not as bad as she'd imagined them to be; that she'd been dramatic to think that the only solution was to leave.

One warm spring morning, Billy asked about the bruises that ringed both of her arms. Catherine was sitting at the table with the children, buttering a piece of toast. She paused to look down at each bare arm in surprise. "Mercy. I hadn't even noticed!" she said (and this was true—she hadn't, or she would have worn her robe), "But you know what?" She lowered her voice and spoke solemnly. "I'd thought I'd dreamed it. I guess not."

"Dreamed what?" Billy said, eyes wide.

"About the elves," Catherine said, and set the toast in front of Lou. She'd dreamed, or *thought* she'd dreamed, that angry elves had visited her in the middle of the night. She said that in her dream, they'd marched up Only Road from the woods and then right up to their yellow house, slipping in easily through the gap under the front door. They made their way into her bedroom, where they attacked her with their tiny, toothpick-sized weapons. "It was all so strange that I thought surely I was asleep."

"But why were they angry with you?" asked Billy, and his lower lip began to tremble.

"Yeah," Lou said, too little to understand the story but alarmed by her brother's concern. "How come, Mama?"

"Oh, mercy—there's no need to cry! It didn't hurt very much. Fair-skinned people like me—like your sister here—we have sensitive skin. We bruise easy. Tender-skinned is what my mother calls it."

"I don't like the elves," Billy said.

"I don't like the elves," Lou parroted.

It was early, and both children were still in their pajamas, hair uncombed. In an hour, Catherine would walk with both of them up Only Road, across the tracks, and the remaining half mile or so to the bus stop. She loved watching them climb on board, carrying their oversized knapsacks and their lunch boxes. They were young enough that they weren't embarrassed to kiss her goodbye on those mornings, were not even aware of the pale faces of the other schoolchildren watching from the bus windows.

"Aren't my children so sweet to be concerned," she said, handing Billy his second piece of toast. "But it wasn't the elves' fault, really. One time, a giant destroyed the trees where they had lived. Elves are so tiny that they think all humans are giants, so whenever they feel sad about what happened to their trees, they gather together to seek revenge. They try to find the giant, and when they don't find him—giants are surprisingly good at hiding—they find a regular old human. Last night," she shrugged, "I guess they found me."

She got up from the table to refill Lou's milk and Billy's orange juice, and once she put their cups back on the table she raised both arms over her head and stomped her bare feet on the linoleum and said, in a deep, giant-like singsong: "Little elves, little elves, look and see, look and see! I'm a big fat giant who will crush your tree!"

Billy giggled and Lou squealed. Neither of them asked about the bruises after that; they asked instead about the elves. They asked, too, about the crocodile and the crocodile bride. They asked if the elves ever tried to attack the crocodile bride and their mother said no, no, the elves were far too scared of the crocodile to go near the Black Bayou, and rightfully so.

The woods were one thing, but the bayou—oh, no. That was far too dangerous a place for such little things.

. . .

DRIVING HOME FROM HER evening shift one night in late June, it occurred to Lou how much easier it would be, between two people in love, if a person's history could be unfolded like map. She would spread that map before Nash and show him life inside the yellow house as it had been when she and Billy were younger.

She'd point out the smell of coffee percolating in the yellow kitchen, of gardenia perfume. She'd show him the pink dresses her mother insisted on wearing despite regularly claiming pink clashed with red hair. She'd point out on this map the noises she and Billy heard from beyond their green wallpapered bedroom, the sound of blows landing, of skin on skin. How her mother only ever said, "Oh!" as though surprised, as though someone had simply pointed out something mildly disconcerting—a stain on her white blouse, a spider on the living room wall. *Oh!*

When they were little, Billy tried to distract Lou with stories. He told her the stories Catherine told them, adding details he thought would make her laugh. Sometimes they curled up in bed together and pulled the peach-colored coverlet up over their head, the lamplight filtering through. When Billy made their fort they hid there, surrounded by the daisy-strewn walls and a sheet covered in lush blackberry vines.

On the paper map of her history, Nash would be able to see all of this with a simple gesture, a wordless pointing-out. As if she were a schoolteacher showing a student the direction in which a river ran.

SOON AFTER LOU RETURNED to Fingertip from Charleston, she and Billy argued on the porch late at night for the first of many times in that particular season. It was a drunken argument, sloppy, and the following morning, they muttered shameful apologies as they passed each other in the kitchen, poured their coffees, swallowed aspirins.

But for a long while—and even now, so many years later—she couldn't shake the accusation he'd hurled at her that night.

She'd been criticizing him for something or other. She didn't remember what. Maybe that he didn't have a girlfriend—maybe that she suspected he did have girlfriends, several of them even, and kept them secret. Maybe it was his spending, all the concerns about paying bills but a case of beer in the fridge at all times. Whatever it was, he lost his cool. He shouted, "I'm doing the best I goddamn can after the one person in my life who gave a *shit* went and got the hell out of my life as fast as she could."

When his door slammed, she heard a single, open-mouthed screech; Sunshine had woken up. She went to the door of the bedroom she'd once shared with Billy and listened, but her niece had already settled again. Joanna Louise, who could sleep through anything, hadn't made a peep.

Standing in the darkened hallway, she leaned her head against the door of their old bedroom and thought that her brother was right. She *was* the one person who gave a shit, and she'd abandoned him anyway.

AFTER THE CAR CRASH, the remainder of Lou's senior year passed in a dark blur.

She didn't remember signing the form to have her parents' bodies cremated. She only vaguely remembered going with Billy and some of their neighbors to the lake and scattering the ashes; she remembered that everyone sang "Amazing Grace." (As an adult, she couldn't stand to hear that song; it made her feel as though something had cracked open inside of her, a crevice exposed, impossibly deep.) She didn't remember until well into her adulthood that Moss Landry—who was her father's age, and who John Jay had always referred to as a faggot—had come over to check on the two of them one evening in the week after the accident, and how when he stepped inside the living room, Lou had let her head rest against his shoulder and sobbed. She didn't remember that Billy had gotten so drunk the night after the funeral that he vomited on the living room floor and passed out beside the vomit, his hair sticky with bile, and that she'd woken him up the next morning, led him to his bed, and cleaned up the vomit while he slept off his hangover for a full day. (It was during her time back in Fingertip just after leaving Robert Dalton that they pieced together, over beers on the porch late at night, what they recalled of that time, filling in each other's gaps in memory.)

Her grade point average slipped in those last months of school, and it only occurred to her during those first months back in Fingertip that the likely reason she'd passed her final exams at all was because her teachers had taken pity on her.

She hardly even remembered, on the day she graduated high school, Robert's proposal. She was still in her cap and gown, but she didn't remember that, either—not really. The circumstances of the proposal came alive in her memory only as a result of Robert Dalton's telling and retelling of the story. When members of his congregation asked, in that first year in Charleston, how they had met, he'd describe the atmosphere of celebration. Graduation caps flying, proud family members snapping photos. He'd decorate the circumstances like one would decorate a party, stringing up garlands, tying bundles of balloons, setting out vases of white carnations.

Perhaps because he was oblivious to it or perhaps because the truth might paint him as a predator, homing in on a vulnerable young woman in the aftermath of a traumatic event, Robert Dalton always left out the part about her parents' recent death.

Of course, Robert Dalton wouldn't have known the details of it, the way it felt.

No one knew except Billy.

How the lights of a police car woke them up that night. It must have been two in the morning. Together, she and Billy met the officers at the door.

Somehow their mother, in her new paisley dress, had been thrown from the Buick. John Jay had died right away. Upon impact, they said. But their mother had landed on the edge of a nearby field, in the brittle winter grass, and according to a witness, she had still been breathing. Unfortunately—that's what the officer said (*Unfortunately...*), by the time the ambulance arrived, her breathing had stopped.

Lou still hadn't ever allowed Robert inside her home in Fingertip— only after his proposal did she allow him to drive her as far as the Lust Outpost (which she called, so she wouldn't offend him, just the Outpost)—and so he certainly could not have known the abrupt and shocking emptiness of the yellow house.

For months after her death, they left their mother's shoes on the porch by the front door, side by side. She'd had small feet. Size six-and-a-half. The shoes had once been white, but the canvas was stained with red dust and streaks of mud. That spring, inside one of them, a moth made a webbed cocoon.

A WEEK AFTER HIS proposal that May, Lou and her new husband drove a car stuffed floor-to-ceiling with belongings (most of them his) to Charleston, South Carolina, where Robert had taken a position as pastor.

For reasons Lou would never understand, Robert's behavior toward her changed the moment they were married. He went from the kind youth group leader who lay his hands gently on her shoulders, summoning the spirit of God, to rage-filled and domineering. She was too weary with grief for the loss of her parents, too disoriented by her new life as a pastor's wife in South Carolina at age eighteen, to resist what was happening, to let herself see clearly the ways in which she was following a path she'd sworn to never step foot on.

On a Monday morning, after Robert had left for his office at the church, Lou made her daughter's breakfast (Joanna Louise's white legs slick with Neosporin and covered in a patchwork of Band-Aids) and a flood of indisputable facts came rushing back.

She remembered that because the government had more or less forgotten about the village it had created, or had misunderstood the Roosevelt administration's paperwork, or had simply lost its records, the mortgages in Fingertip had always remained ninety-nine cents per year.

She remembered the uninhabited houses—specifically, one just across from the yellow house. The Laurents had left the year before she graduated—the house was likely not dilapidated like so many of the others, empty for a decade or more, and chances were slimmer, still, that it had since been reinhabited.

She had always liked its pink siding—the color her mother had most loved (despite her hair).

She remembered that she had never once allowed Robert to see her home.

She remembered how, once more due to a lack of either clear or organized records, Fingertip residents were not listed in the phone book.

How Fingertip itself was not even marked on a map.

The place she had wanted nothing more than to escape would be, she could see clearly, the safest place for her to begin anew.

While that seething giant awoke inside of her (crashing into tables, smashing plates, knocking over furniture, stirring up in its rampage old memories and longings and emotions she had forgotten she ever possessed),

Lou moved about their Charleston house on that last morning in total silence.

She moved calmly and with a complete clarity of purpose.

She gathered her belongings and her daughter, and just as quietly as she slipped into her marriage to Robert Dalton, she slipped back out.

ONE YEAR LATER, SHE received notice of Robert's divorce filing in her P.O. box in St. Cadence. The letter came from a law office in Charleston. She read the letter in the post office, and she borrowed a pen from the postal worker and signed the papers right there. Joanna Louise tugged at her pants, whining that she was hungry. Lou heaved her daughter up to rest on one hip, then licked the envelope, folded it shut, and mailed the paperwork back to the lawyer.

She drove the two of them, just her and her daughter, to the 79 Dine. They slid into a booth and she ordered Joanna Louise pancakes and herself a club sandwich—a celebration, though she didn't tell that to Joanna Louise. She whispered it to Tammy when she came by to refill their drinks.

Tammy was several years older than Lou and had been through her own share of bad relationships. She rested one hand on Lou's arm and smiled, her eyes soft with compassion. "Good for you," she said. "You're free, honey."

EVENTUALLY, AS LOU'S FINGERS traced the map of her history, she would show Nash the shame she still carried with her for even marrying Robert Dalton at all.

The shame, too, that she'd abandoned her brother; the sense that maybe he'd have turned out differently—drunk less, been happier, found himself a wife—if she hadn't left.

How easy it would be, with a map.

She could show and tell each painful part of her life, each meaningful smell and color and sight and sound, without ever having to crack open any part of herself in the process, without having to feel a single bit of the pain she was asking Nash to witness, without having to risk being swallowed by it.

No one could be angry, disappointed, disgusted, or heartbroken because of a simple map; it was made of paper and ink. She could point out what she wished and then fold it back up.

Tuck it neatly away again.

And that would be that.

17.
The Black Bayou

Billy's absence wasn't so unusual. It was the lack of knowledge as to his whereabouts that caused the tightrope walkers in Sunshine's belly to prance. Toes pointed, leotards glittering.

It was the secrets she carried. Small but heavy.

Already, it was mid-July. Locusts sang in the tall grass along Only Road. June bugs whirred. The pale blue sky was mottled with fat, silvery clouds. By noon, any mud along Only Road had hardened to a thick crust in the day's heat. Sunshine noticed her armpits were always damp and had taken on a smell like soured milk.

In the yellow house the groceries were dwindling. The cabinets held only a few cans of tomato paste, dust gathering on their tops, and an old box of Honey Nut Cheerios. When she opened up the cereal box, tiny moths fluttered out. After Aunt Lou left for work each day, Sunshine went to her house to borrow food. She borrowed bologna and slices of American cheese. She borrowed an almost-empty box of vanilla wafers. On Aunt Lou's dresser was a jar of change, and Sunshine dug out enough quarters to go buy peanut butter or a loaf of Wonder Bread at the Lust.

Sunshine had always been allowed to help herself at Aunt Lou's, but now she felt sneaky. Aunt Lou wouldn't care about the food or the quarters, either, but she'd wonder why Sunshine needed these things, and why Billy hadn't left her with money.

One afternoon she returned to the yellow house, food and quarters in hand, and saw that it had grown dirty. Dust bunnies gathered in the little living room and crumbs littered the tiled countertop in the kitchen. The coffee in the coffeepot was topped with greenish mold.

It was like Aunt Lou sometimes said. How *somebody* had to do the taking care.

She blew the dust off the Robert Johnson record and turned the volume up loud. She swept and tied rags to her feet and skated on them over the hardwood floors. She swept the porch and wiped down the Florida orange crate, sticky with beer, and emptied the ash tray, which was still full from the night Billy and Aunt Lou had celebrated the promotion. Sweat trickled down from her hairline and into her eyes, and because Aunt Lou was working and Billy wasn't home and so she didn't need to be modest (she didn't think, anyway), she took off all but her underwear and padded around in her bare feet. Her tangled hair fell around her face like a curtain as she bent over to reach the drain in the bathtub or the crevice of a baseboard, furred with dust.

Cautiously, she opened the door to Billy's room. The blinds were lowered and it was dark and smelled stale and she shut it again quickly.

Finally, she tidied up inside her fort. Straightening the blankets. Replacing the used peanut butter spoon with a clean one. Neatly restacking books in the library.

SHE'D STAYED IN HER fort each night since Billy left because she didn't like staying at the yellow house by herself. She heard funny noises. The oak branches scratched at her window like the fingers of a restless giant. The rooftop creaked and groaned, and she imagined a haint was up there, a black shadow with a knife in hand, waiting for the right moment to slink down through an open window and cut her to bits.

But she'd decided that nothing dangerous could get inside the fort. No haints holding knives. No spiders searching for her stones.

That night, the hardwood floors dust bunny–free, the house smelling like lemon oil, Sunshine crawled inside the fort and turned on both globes of the hurricane lamp. The daisies on the wallpaper turned orange in that light. She dipped her spoon in the peanut butter jar and washed it down with the last of the milk and stayed up reading *Thimble Summer*, a novel she'd decided was her favorite in part because the girl on the cover, Garnet, looked a little like Sunshine. She wore overalls and had blonde hair that looked uncombed. Sunshine wondered if Garnet's armpits also smelled like soured milk.

She didn't remember falling asleep and woke when headlights slid across the walls of the fort. She heard the grinding of the brakes, the truck engine shudder into silence.

Relief joined her in the little fort.

The tension she'd felt each night since Billy hadn't come home left her body faded. She let out a sigh. She sat upright, yawning.

The threat of a rooftop haint seemed suddenly ridiculous. Through her open window, she listened as Billy's boots clomped across the bridge to Terabithia and up the porch steps. She heard the pause as he pulled off the boots and the soft thuds as they landed, first one and then the other, on the row of shoes Sunshine had lined up neatly along the yellow siding. The screen door slammed shut behind him.

But as soon as he entered the house, Sunshine felt the tightrope walkers in her belly again.

She wished they'd quit.

There wasn't anything to be scared of, she told herself.

Billy's car keys landed with a clang on the kitchen table. There was the opening and closing of the refrigerator door and the crack and hiss of a beer. Then, bare feet padding down the hallway.

She heard him pause in her doorway. She could feel his presence there but for some reason she stayed quiet. She waited.

"Heya, Fred," he said. "You awake in there?"

She thought she might not answer; she'd pretend she wasn't home, that she'd gone to Aunt Lou's. But her bedroom door was open—he'd seen the light in the fort. There was probably the silhouette of her shadow inside, sitting upright.

"Heya, Billy," she called, and she tried to make her voice sound normal. It was Billy, she told herself. Just Billy.

"House smells nice and clean," he said. "Aren't you the little Betty homemaker."

His voice was light and teasing. Relief returned. It cozied up next to her like a housecat and purred reassurances.

"I cleaned," she said proudly.

"And look at that fort. Whew-ee, Fred. Some advanced architecture."

"It's got a library," she said. "And peanut butter."

"Peanut butter! Hell's bells, Fred. That's not a fort, it's a goddamn palace."

Sunshine laughed and pulled the quilt aside just enough that one eye could peer up at Billy. The hallway light was behind him and she couldn't see his face very well, but she thought he was grinning.

"There's my girl," he said.

She smiled. He'd returned in a good mood. "I missed you," she said. "Any luck?"

He rubbed at his eyes with one hand. "Bah," he said. Disappointed. "Not a lot, Fred. Some, but not a lot. Your Aunt Lou keep an eye on you okay?"

"Yeah," she said—although in truth, she'd been avoiding Aunt Lou. She pulled the quilt a little further back. "But she didn't have to," she said through a yawn. "I stayed here by myself. I washed and folded your laundry and I got more peanut butter."

"Look, Fred," Billy said, and then he came and squatted near the fort entrance, eyebrows knit with concern. "You're gonna turn into a jar of peanut butter if you're not careful."

She giggled again.

"I'm serious. I've been meaning to talk to you about it. I'm surprised it hasn't happened already."

She was really laughing, now. "I am not," she said.

"Hey," Billy said, peering past her shoulder. "Good lord, Fred! Queen of England over here!"

Sunshine moved aside so he could better see inside. The tightrope walkers in her belly had come back without her noticing but she tried to ignore them. Billy was home again, and it was just the two of them. Both in a good mood. Maybe even a June mood.

It was hard to tell.

Billy was muttering exaggerated comments about Sunshine's fort ("Fred, where'd you get the money for this nice carpet? It looks just like a blanket we used to own..." and "The gold ceiling fan is a little much. Now you're just showing off") as he crawled clumsily forward. She had to move aside, squealing with laughter, as his grown-up, too-big body made its way inside her space. She scooched backwards to make more room, all the way until her back was up against the dresser, where the corner of one quilt edge was secured in a top drawer.

Billy swung his legs around so he sat cross-legged, like her, and suddenly, in the now-cramped fort, it didn't seem that funny that he was there. She wished he would leave. Then she felt a rush of shame for wishing that. A rush of shame, too, at the tightrope walkers in her belly, performing dramatic flips and handstands all because Billy was spending time with his Sunshine, his only Sunshine.

He took a sip of his beer. "That ain't the most graceful entrance I ever made," he said. Sunshine tried to laugh.

Billy squinted toward the stack of books, nodding his approval. She could see his face, now, illuminated by the lamp. His eyes looked puffy and tired, and his forehead and nose were oily. The whole tent smelled like beer and she realized that Billy had probably been drinking before this too. His eyes slid back to her, then glanced down toward her chest. Or did she imagine it? She was wearing a tank top that tied with two strings at each shoulder. It was blue-striped and the ties were red, and she didn't have a training bra underneath.

"Heya, Fred," he said again.

She didn't reply. Her voice was trapped inside her throat. At the start of the summer, had Billy joined her inside a fort like this, she'd have laughed with him. She'd have let her folded knees touch his, and asked for a story, and she wouldn't have minded too much if he smelled like beer because beer was better than bourbon. (*Beer is A-okay, Fred.*)

Billy said, "Whaddaya need all these books for when you've got old Billy here?"

Somehow, her voice rose up from where it had been trapped in her throat. "It's my library," she said.

"Hey," he said, still looking at the books. "I was thinking. You ever get lonely, Fred? Down here in Fingertip, no other kids around?"

The question surprised her. Billy didn't usually ask about her thoughts or her feelings. He teased her and made jokes and told stories. Did she feel lonely? She wasn't sure. She thought maybe she might. But Billy glanced up from her library.

"No," she said, and shook her head for emphasis. "I don't."

He grinned at her. "My sister and I made forts like this when we were kids. I ever tell you that before? Just not so fancy."

"Oh." She pulled at the edge of her tank top so it came up higher on her chest. "You didn't tell me that before."

"Probably used these same blankets. Kinda funny, huh? We came in here when we were scared." He sipped his beer again. The sheet with the blackberry vines hung low, grazing the top of his head. "It's hotter 'n hell in here, Fred."

And it was hot; she hadn't noticed until he said it. Her armpits were damp and sticky. On Billy's forehead, beads of sweat glistened in the lamplight.

"What were you scared of?" Sunshine asked.

"Lots, I guess." He turned toward the books again and ran one of his fingers down their spines, nice and slow. "Scared of swimming. Scared of crocodiles."

"But there aren't crocs around here."

"Well, sure. Except the one."

In the oak just outside her window an owl called, but it sounded far away from inside the cramped tent. They were like two children. One big and dark-haired with gold-flecked green eyes, one skinny and blonde. With light freckles on her nose and damp, soured-milk armpits.

Billy continued, "You remember the crocodile, don't you, Fred?"

"You were scared of the crocodile from the story?"

"Sure, Fred. You ain't?"

"I guess," she said.

"Hey," he said. "You want to hear a story I ain't told you before?"

"Okay," she said. And she did. She wanted Billy to talk so much she forgot to be afraid. She wanted the tightrope walkers to grow sleepy and stop their performance. She wanted to feel like how she felt when Billy used to tell his stories, before the spiders. Before that nasty troll had wormed his way, with his secrets and his misery, into the middle of her heart.

"I went, once," he said. He was still looking at the books, one finger resting on top of the stack.

"Where?"

His eyes cut back to her, somber with the story he was about to tell. "To the Black Bayou, Fred. I went to see about the crocodile bride."

Sunshine waited to see if he was joking. But he didn't wink or laugh. He only took a long sip of his beer.

And the story was working already; her belly began to settle. She wiped at a rivulet of sweat that was trickling down one temple.

"I went one night because things inside this old house just felt too sad, you understand."

(She did understand. How the yellow house could feel like that.)

"Our mama had gone too. I ever tell you that? You know she brought a letter opener for that old crocodile, Fred. It'd been a gift from her own mama, this nice sharp brass blade and a handle made from mother-of-pearl. She loved that old thing, but she let the old crocodile swallow it up so she could see the crocodile bride."

In the fort, the air was beery and somehow even the glowing orange light seemed to make everything pulse with summer heat, the daisies and the blackberry vines and Sunshine and Billy. Sunshine forgot to be scared and lay down on her side. She folded her arms up under her head and curled up her knees and one of them touched Billy's knee.

Her bedroom and the world outside the fort was quiet—as if the cicadas and locusts, the toads and the barred owls outside had all paused to listen to Billy's story. As if even the ghosts and the haints had stopped their tricks and were leaning close, just beyond the blackberry vines.

"Anyhow, I guess I was too old to just go on listening to the stories—I guess I had to see for myself. I snuck out at night and I walked for hours—down that pig path by the lake, then farther and farther. The trees started to thicken up, not those spindly pines we got up here but big, fat cypress, with ferns taller than I am now. Taller than a grown man, Fred. Can you imagine ferns that big?"

She could. She could imagine it; she smelled the wet dirt of that lush forest floor, and felt the ferns brushing her shoulders as she stepped in between them. Without meaning to, she closed her eyes.

Billy's voice went on, soft and low. "The moon was out that night," he said, "so that everything kind of glowed silver. I wandered for a good long while, not even knowing where I was going, really, just that it looked like how Mama had described in her stories and so I thought I must be close. Then, finally, I saw a light—only it wasn't a light. It was the moon, and it was reflecting off the water, and I knew I was there."

Sunshine's eyes were closed and she could see it too. The moonlight on the water.

She rolled sleepily over on her stomach and stretched her legs so they reached off the blanket beneath her and under her bed. The hardwood felt cool against her skin. She kept her eyes closed, face turned toward Billy, head in her hands, and then she felt Billy's fingers rest on her back.

Slowly, they began to track. One finger running slowly up. And slowly down.

"So I went toward the water, Fred, and I saw it spread out before me: the Black Bayou. And nearby, like it was just waiting for a kid to come along, sat the little boat, just like my mama had said. I dragged it into the water and I climbed inside. It was child-sized, and I was thirteen, almost fourteen. I was taller than my mama by then." (Up and down his finger traced, and she thought how it didn't feel like how the spiders had felt that night. It felt like when she was little and in bed sick, or when she'd woken up crying from a bad dream and Billy had come. To clean up her vomit from the floor. To comfort her. It felt nice and soothing, and she didn't know if it was okay to enjoy it or if she should guard herself against the spiders—if they'd find the exposed gap between her shorts and her blue-striped top, if they'd crawl inside her shirt, searching for the stones that were now pressed, a little painfully, between her body and the floor of the fort.) "She'd have fit in that boat easily," Billy said, "but I remember thinking that for once I was glad I was so skinny, else I might've sunk the thing. And you know your daddy can't swim."

When she was little, his finger would first trace along her back in squiggles and loops. He'd tell her he was writing her name: Sunshine Turner. He said he didn't want any nasty, child-thieving haints to think that, as sickly or sad as she was, Sunshine Turner wasn't looked after. Wasn't loved.

Anyone with a name, Billy told her, is loved by someone in this world.

"Over my shoulder, out there in the middle of the bayou, I could see this small, flickering light. I knew if I could just reach that light, I'd get the help I need."

Sunshine wanted to ask what Billy needed help for, but she thought she knew, anyway. *Him.* The liver-spotted, wispy-haired troll. Hunched and sallow skinned, with secrets to spill.

"I must've been halfway there when I realized it, Fred. I couldn't believe it. Desperate as I was to see the crocodile bride, I'd gone goddamn blind. I'd forgotten the most important thing."

Sunshine was in the boat herself, now, the oars rough against the palm of each hand, as Billy traced his finger up and down—and it felt so nice, so comforting, that she'd drifted halfway asleep.

The thin ribbon of beach where Billy had found the boat was a silver-blue.

On her back, the hand reached the exposed skin at her waist. Her body tensed. She kept her eyes closed, unwilling to open them and see what (if his hands had turned to spiders) the rest of her daddy had turned into. Instead, she peered at the beach in the moonlit distance. At the fat globe of yellow moon. A breeze blew across the water and little waves lapped at the boat.

"You can probably guess, can't you, Fred?"

Tonight, the spider on her skin wasn't searching for the stones, it seemed—it was running up and down the skin of her back, it was tracing its squiggles and loops—*Sunshine Turner.* She thought she'd perhaps been wrong. Perhaps it was just a hand: Billy's hand, warm and dry.

"I'd forgotten the damn gift, Fred. Can you imagine? And no sooner had I realized it than something hit that little boat, hard. I felt it, just under my feet. *Thud.*"

(She felt the thud under the boat. As if that crocodile was swimming just under the floorboards of her bedroom.)

"Oh boy, Fred. I was so scared. I knew what it was. I knew what it was, and I began to row as hard as I could but that thump came again—"

(Again, Sunshine felt it below the floorboards. *Thud.*)

"—and then suddenly the boat was tipping to one side, and I'd dropped the oars and was using both hands to grip at the side, there, but my feet slipped off, and I, I—"

Sunshine's eyes flew open. "What happened?" she whispered.

Billy's hand on her back had stopped moving. Not tracing and not searching. Just still.

She could see that he was just Billy. Not whatever she feared was attached to a spidery hand. Just Billy, sitting still and cross-legged, one hand resting on her back. He was looking up toward the roof of the tent, at the faded blackberries, and he pulled his hand out from under her shirt. He wiped both hands on his jeans, and she wondered if her back was sweaty and he was wiping himself clean.

His eyes found hers. The skin under his eyes formed shadowy half-moons. "That's it, Fred," he said, and she wasn't sure but she thought he seemed sad. "That's the whole story."

He took his beer and crawled over her legs and out of the fort.

"Goodnight, Fred," she heard him say, and the bedroom door clicked shut behind him, and the fort, with its faded fruit and glowing-orange daisies, fell quiet again.

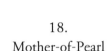

18.
Mother-of-Pearl

S ome months after Billy was born, Catherine received a letter from her mother, asking if Catherine would like her to visit Louisiana. She didn't want to impose, she wrote, but she remembered how hard it had been to raise a child, the nights of waking up countless times over or getting no sleep at all. Margaret Bell recalled in this letter that Talmadge, for the first whole year of Catherine's life, had not fallen into a single spell. Even with his spells, he had been a dedicated father, she wrote, and perhaps she never gave him credit enough for that.

This particular letter—its offer to visit, its recollection of Talmadge—was filled with an openness, a tenderness, that Catherine couldn't remember ever experiencing from her mother.

She politely declined the visit with a brief list of excuses: the smallness of their house, the difficulty of such a drive. All of which were true, none of which made up the full truth.

SHE'D SAT DOWN TO draft a letter, once.

Despite the May heat, she wore long sleeves. The children were napping and the afternoon sunlight filtered through the kitchen window. Beyond it, the trees that surrounded Fingertip were a hopeful green.

Her pen hovered over the paper—for ten minutes, then fifteen, then twenty. She rose, made a cup of coffee, and returned to the table. Still she could not bring herself to write a word, and eventually, she threw down the pen and burst into tears.

Should she write to her mother honestly, should she shape the truth with language, who knew what other truths Catherine might be forced to see? Such as the kind of person she was to have let herself come to this place at all, and with a man—as her mother had said—she hardly knew. Such as the kind of person she was for staying. Such as her shame that she was too scared, too cowardly, to try and change it now.

WHEN, IMPOSSIBLY, YEARS HAD suddenly passed—Billy almost four, and Lou walking, speaking full sentences—Catherine decided that if she didn't want Margaret Bell to see the yellow house (and all that happened inside of it) she and her children could at least visit Tennessee.

The bus ride was eighteen hours. They ate soggy cheese-and-tomato sandwiches, and Catherine told Billy and Lou true stories from when she was a little girl, in the place where they were going.

She told them about her daddy once going out the door pants-less and they laughed. Billy asked why and she explained that her daddy got sick sometimes, like everyone did, but that the sickness was in his head and it made him do funny things like forget pants, no matter the cold.

When the children caught sight of the sign that said they were crossing into a new state (WELCOME TO MISSISSIPPI! WELCOME TO TENNESSEE!), they cheered and clapped along with the other passengers.

At last they arrived, bleary-eyed and bloated. When Margaret Bell greeted Catherine at the station in Nashville, both women had tears in their eyes.

SINCE CATHERINE HAD LEFT seven years prior, Margaret Bell had grown plumper. The effect was such that her wrinkles were not so pronounced, and she looked younger. As though she were aging in reverse. She no longer wore the old fashioned, high neck blouses she had worn throughout Catherine's childhood; her skirts were shorter, reaching mid-calf rather than ankle-length. She seemed happy and vibrant. "Your Meemaw is going to show you so many things!" she said to the children, driving them home from the bus station.

In the white house with the gingerbread trim (little about its appearance had changed, since Catherine had been gone) Margaret Bell showed Billy and Lou how to make ambrosia salad, which was not a salad at all but a sweet and gooey pile of marshmallows and canned oranges and shredded coconuts and pecans all tossed together. She made them eggs-in-a-basket and always made them seconds. She showed them how to make Million Dollar Rolls, a recipe she said was so delicious it won the *Better Homes* Baking Contest and the woman who invented the recipe won not one million dollars, as suggested by the name of the treat, but one thousand—which was fine enough, she told them, but seemed unfair.

They stayed for ten days.

In the evening, Margaret Bell read the children bedtime stories until they fell asleep in the bed that had belonged to Talmadge. Margaret Bell had made it up with a new set of sheets covered in zoo animals dressed up in human clothing. She had stacked children's books on the nightstand and fixed a night light into an outlet so they wouldn't get scared.

One night, Catherine kissed each of them goodnight and then, while her mother read to them, slipped quietly down the stairs and into her father's old study.

It was the first of many nights she would visit the study. She liked its familiar smells of leather and paper. She sat at Talmadge's kidney-shaped desk and ran her finger along the brown leather inlay with the gold-painted leaves along the edges. She opened the drawers and smelled their musty insides. Her throat caught unexpectedly.

Another night, she pulled a volume of Talmadge's encyclopedias about plants of the eastern United States, sat in his old familiar easy chair, the leather velvety with age, and slowly paged through it. She covered the names with her thumb, looked at the sketches, and quizzed herself.

Most, she was pleased to realize, she remembered.

When she heard the creak of her mother's footsteps on the staircase, she sat upright, closed the book, and went to the doorway.

"Did the children go to sleep all right?" she whispered.

Each night of Catherine's visit home, the two women retired to the kitchen table with the big bay window facing the sidewalk outside. Her mother, who had never been a drinker during Catherine's childhood, who had regularly called alcohol "the Devil's tonic," would open a bottle of red wine for them to share.

Each night, they drank it down to its last drop (until their teeth were slightly darkened, their lips the color of gooseberries) and talked about more than they had ever talked about in Catherine's lifetime, more than they had talked about even in their letters. Some nights they opened a second bottle, and the evening unspooled deliciously, long past midnight. Their feet grew cold. They hugged their sweaters or robes more tightly to them.

Her mother told Catherine that she liked retirement more than she thought she would—a fact, she said, that she'd never admitted to anyone else.

She told her daughter, too, about a gentleman caller. That's what she called him—a *gentleman caller*. She pursed her lips as she talked about him, repressing the pleasure Catherine could plainly see.

He was a widower, also a retired schoolteacher—he had moved to Portland after Catherine had left—and, Margaret Bell said, he sometimes took her dancing.

Catherine nearly spit out her wine. "You *dance?*"

"Of course I dance," Margaret Bell said sharply. "Who doesn't dance?" Then she leaned across the table to refill Catherine's glass.

THROUGHOUT THESE CONVERSATIONS, CATHERINE found herself slipping small bits of the truth of her life in Fingertip.

"Tell me about the village," Margaret Bell said one evening. "What is there to do there?"

"Well, there's the bar," Catherine said, "at the northern side. It's part bar, part shop. John Jay spends most of his nights there." She paused. "Or sometimes in St. Cadence."

"Without you?" Margaret Bell had asked.

"Yes," Catherine said, looking down at her glass of wine. "Without me."

Sharing these small truths that she'd so carefully omitted in her letters was like dropping a stitch while knitting a scarf—easy to do, and easier still to continue on afterwards without realizing anything had gone amiss. She shared with Margaret Bell that she suspected John Jay of an affair. Of multiple affairs, maybe. She assured her mother that men would be men, of course. She knew that.

And still—the knowledge, she admitted, did hurt.

For the most part, Margaret Bell seemed to sense that asking questions might demand too much, and so she let her daughter drop her stitches, and she listened, and she didn't ask for more than Catherine was willing to give.

One night, snow began to fall beyond the bay window. Together, like giddy children, they grabbed their coats from the mud room and went outside into the front yard and stuck out their wine-stained tongues and let the snowflakes melt on them.

DURING THE DAY, CATHERINE bundled the children up in coats and scarves and walked with them around Portland. She led them to the creek. She told them about her daddy, how much he loved the plants there, how when it wasn't winter time those brown vines and branches filled up with bright green leaves of all different shapes, and she told them how her father had taught her the names of all of those beautiful plants.

They asked what happened to him, where their grandpa had gone, and she said, "He died before you were born, but you would have liked him. And boy, oh boy, he would have liked you."

As their time in Portland continued, and as she and her mother grew closer with each day, Catherine began to consider the obvious: That she did not, in fact, need to return. That she could, in fact, stay right where she was, raise the children attending the same church on the other side of town—only a half-mile walk away. Raise them in her childhood home. Teach them the names of the plants Talmadge had taught her. Show them the river by the iron bridge, where they could swim when the water levels dropped and the temperature rose.

Leave Fingertip and its stories and its omissions, leave its forgottenness and maplessness and its single red road that couldn't decide between dust and mud. Leave the fig trees and the lake and the alligators.

She considered that she could simply stay.

SHORTLY BEFORE CATHERINE LEFT for the trip to Portland, when John Jay was passed out one night, she had reached into his wallet and taken several bills, which she used to buy Christmas presents for the children in Portland. For Billy: a baseball, a red baseball cap with a blue rim, a box of malted milk balls (his favorite), and a lucky rabbit's foot. For Lou there was a large doll with red yarn hair in two braids and a blue polka-dot dress and a separate set of two outfits. There was a new set of hair ribbons and a small, pink, patent leather purse, inside of which Margaret Bell had dropped a whole silver dollar.

Margaret Bell and Catherine exchanged presents too. Catherine gave Margaret Bell a bottle of nice wine for them to share that evening and a brass brooch in the shape of a swan.

Margaret Bell gave Catherine a silver watch that had belonged to Talmadge and a blue sweater she thought would look pretty with Catherine's hair. Catherine wore it the remaining three days of her time in Nashville, along with the silver watch. Its largeness felt comforting against her wrist.

After they had finished opening presents, they let the children run to a neighbor's house with gifts of candy canes. Outside, it had begun to snow: white flakes drifted from a cloudy, yellow-gray sky. The flakes clung to the blades of grass in the yard but melted on the sidewalk and road. Margaret Bell was making more coffee for both herself and Catherine when she said, "Oh, mercy. I almost forgot."

She went to a cupboard and took out a small, lean package wrapped in brown paper. "It's just something small I found at a secondhand shop. I thought it might come in handy."

Inside the brown paper was a sharp, shining brass blade like a small sword, and a mother-of-pearl handle: a letter opener.

The gift seemed a tender nod to the communication that had finally opened between them since she had left for Fingertip; and it seemed, too, a reminder that she'd be leaving again.

"Thank you," she said.

Margaret Bell set a cup of coffee in front of her daughter and joined her at the table. They sat together for a long while without speaking, content to watch the snow falling outside the window, to sip their coffee in the winter quiet of the morning.

BUT SHE WENT BACK.

Perhaps it was a matter of pride—the same pride she had seen in her mother, with her high collar, her downturned eyes—for all of those years as her husband grew increasingly ill.

Perhaps it was easier to follow what was expected of her than to change course.

Perhaps changing course—perhaps change, at all—felt somehow more frightening than anything or anyone else.

THE MORNING THAT MARGARET Bell drove them to the bus station in Nashville and said goodbye, a lump formed in Catherine's throat so full that she could not speak.

Margaret Bell put her hand on her daughter's cheek. Her face was so close to Catherine's that Catherine could smell the powder her mother had dusted across her nose and forehead, the coffee still on her breath. "Come back and see me again," said Margaret Bell, and Catherine could only nod.

When Billy and Lou at last fell asleep on the bus, Catherine pulled the blue sweater up over her face and cried until she felt she couldn't breathe.

IT WAS JUST A few weeks later that she received a phone call from her Aunt Ruth.

"A heart attack," Aunt Ruth said, voice softened with grief. "Mercifully, it was sudden."

A neighbor had found her in the yard, Aunt Ruth explained, where she appeared to have fallen on her way back from the post office. Envelopes had scattered on the cold ground. (Aunt Ruth did not describe that part—but Catherine could see them there, like brittle leaves).

They didn't have the funds to send her back for the funeral, John Jay said. "Not *again*. Money, in case you haven't noticed, doesn't grow on goddamn trees."

Stunned by her mother's death, Catherine did not reply.

Instead, she sat upright in bed, resting back against the headboard, staring ahead at nothing as he lectured her. He explained the ins and outs of their finances (although their finances never stopped him from spending money to tailor a suit; to buy the expensive cologne he insisted on wearing; to buy bottle after bottle of bourbon; to pay his bar tab at the Lust). As he applied layer after layer of shame like a painter applying spackle over cracked drywall—for her daring, for boldness, for the fact that she had dared *assume* she might leave for such an event.

"No," he said again.

She hadn't even asked. She had simply told him, her voice quiet and flat like a small pond: "The funeral is in a week."

"No, no, no." He unbuttoned his work shirt. Dark, coiled chest hair sprang and spilled over the edge of his white undershirt. There was a hard line where he shaved so the hair would not grow up his neck and tumble out over the crisp line of the collared shirt.

Seeing that line between her husband's shorn neck and the unruly hair below always felt to Catherine like seeing something that should be private: A white thigh too long untouched by sunlight. The underbelly of a fish. The blue-white of her own shaven armpit.

Perhaps John Jay sensed her pity and disgust; his eyes grew suddenly dark and angry. They seemed to dare her to argue back. To see what happened to wives who argued. "You can't go running back home whenever you please like you're still a child," he said. "Your children need you *here*, for godsake."

John Jay was right that the children needed her, but incorrect that they needed her there, in Fingertip, all of them under the roof of the yellow house. The reality was they needed her with them, and they needed her to take them all, the three of them together, away from him.

They needed for her to take a job, to find a new husband. To call Aunt Ruth and tell her they were coming back to live in her mother's house. To do anything to leave.

She'd grieved the death of a parent before, but this was somehow different. She was grieving not only Margaret Bell but their newfound closeness.

She was grieving the change she'd been on the verge of making.

Just a single breath of courage away from making.

And although in the years to come, the facts of what she knew her children needed would occasionally arise in her mind once more—suddenly and in stark clarity, like a too-dark room illuminated by a camera's brief flash—Catherine couldn't, in the end, bring herself to step into those choices, those changes.

The flash subsided; the room fell dark again; and she stayed.

WITHOUT CEREMONY, THE WHITE house with the gingerbread trim was sold to pay off the last of the family's debts and funeral expenses. Aunt Ruth sent Catherine a letter with this update and three cardboard boxes packed with the schoolchildren quilts.

One night, when John Jay did not come home on time, and Catherine assumed he was out again with the secretary at the packaing warehouse or another girl he had met in town, she put the children to bed, went to her bedroom closet where the stacks of quilts lined the top shelf, and took them down.

One by one, she spread them out on top of the double bed.

She read the names:

Joey Follin, Allison Dougherty, Jeannie Peters.

Libby Sanders and Bobby Franklyn appeared twice, she noticed; she vaguely remembered her mother mentioning, with genuine sadness, that these children had been held back to repeat their school year. Those were Catherine's favorite names to see on the quilts: poor Libby and Bobby.

She read her mother's name in the center flower of the quilt.

She ran a finger across her favorite scraps of cloth. She liked the patterned pieces the best: a flower petal of blue calico; a yellow polka-dot sunshine; a heart made of two separate halves, one with lavender stripes and the other covered in tiny red flowers.

When she had finished looking and touching and reading and tracing, she stacked all eighteen quilts one on top of the other and lay down on the mattress of them, covering with her body the names of the children and her mother's name in the middle of them all, and wept. She bit the fabric of the quilts and let it absorb her angry, bereaved moans. She cried until her teeth chattered and her whole body shook with a violence she hadn't known was possible in herself, an earthly violence like the Cumberland River after a hard rain, the water mesmerizing in its rushing, white-foamed rage.

In the drawer of her bedside table, she kept several of the letters her mother had written her, a birthday card Talmadge had once given her when she was a child, and the letter opener with the mother-of-pearl handle.

How easy it would be, she thought, to reach into that drawer, take the letter opener, and drag its sharpened tip down each of her forearms.

She imagined John Jay finding her there, blood soaking through the quilts, but it would be too late. She'd be elsewhere, far away from him. If she didn't make it to Heaven because of her chosen mode of death, perhaps she stood a chance of at least seeing her mother briefly, one last time, as she crossed over. Perhaps her mother would hold her hand as the blood drained from her wrists and she faded blissfully from consciousness.

But she thought of her children in the next room. Who would wake them in the morning with little jokes, with kisses? Who would make their toast, their eggs-in-a-basket?

Slowly, Catherine rose from the stacked quilts and, one by one, folded them up. She was exhausted from crying; the next morning, her eyes would still be swollen, the eyelids pale and shiny like a hard-boiled egg.

She returned the stacks of quilts to their high shelf, and then closed the closet door quietly, gently, so as not to wake the children sleeping on the other side of the wall.

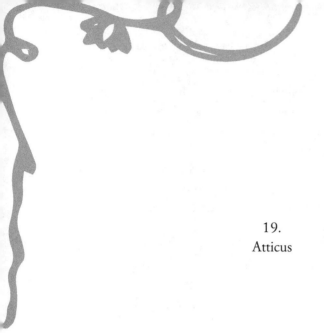

19.
Atticus

July 1982

E arly one evening, Nash took Lou to see *The Thing* at the Magic
Multiplex, a new movie theatre in Lafayette.

The Magic Multiplex was about ten times the size of the St. Cadence
Theatre, with six different movie screens laid out in a maze of dimly lit,
red-carpeted halls. Its seats did not smell like a disturbing mixture of
popcorn and vomit. The armrests were not uneven with flattened pieces
of old chewing gum, but nicely cushioned and pocked with individual
cup-holders. The air-conditioning in the Magic Multiplex was always on
full-blast so that Lou had to bring a sweater, whereas the St. Cadence
Theatre did not have central air at all.

Still, Lou felt sentimental about that old theatre. Catherine had taken
her and Billy to the double features on summer afternoons. They saw *The
Sound of Music* and *Bambi* and *Gone with the Wind*. When she was thirteen
or so, she and her mother watched a matinee of *To Kill a Mockingbird*,
fingers sticky with popcorn butter and peanut M&Ms. At the end of the
movie, Lou slid her eyes toward Catherine and seen tears streaming down
her cheeks when Boo Radley came to visit Jem.

On the drive home, Lou slouched far down in her seat to put her knees up on the dashboard. Out the windows of the Buick, a storm was on the horizon. The green of the bean fields always looked especially bright, an electric green, against the dark gray of a stormy sky. As the first raindrops splattered the windows, Lou imagined they were driving home not to John Jay, but to Atticus Finch. A rabid dog would follow their car down Only Road, and everyone would cower in their houses, watching from windows, and Atticus Finch would step out from the screened porch and come down fearlessly to the car and usher the two of them inside.

No—he would take hold of her mother's wrist (the dog would be ambling down Only Road, mouth foaming, just like in the movie) and say sternly, "Take Lou inside!" and he would kiss her on her cheek the way Mr. Laurent did to Mrs. Laurent when they encountered each other in their driveway. Then Lou and her mother would watch, horrified and proud, as Atticus Finch raised the rifle to his shoulder and shot the dog dead.

Lou replayed this in her mind, Atticus Finch waiting for them, as they drove home through the rain that afternoon. She replayed it again and again, changing details of the story to further delight herself. In one version, Atticus Finch took her mother out on a date, just the two of them, and in another he kissed Lou on the forehead and then took Billy out in the yard to play catch, and the neighbors were jealous of Billy and Lou Finch, whose father was so kind and steady, a killer of rabid things.

EACH TIME THE ALIEN emerged on the movie screen—from a dog, from a man—Nash nearly leaped out of his movie seat, shouting expletives, and Lou clapped her hands over her eyes, peering out from between her fingers. The third time Nash yelled out, someone behind them whispered, "Shhh!" Nash craned his neck toward the row behind them and said in a whisper so loud it could hardly be considered a whisper at all, "Sorry, sorry—but it's so *scary*."

Lou shook her head at him; he put a hand on her thigh and squeezed.

They rode home in his Ford pickup, the sky at the tail end of twilight. Nash lit a cigarette and tapped the ash out the cracked window. The AC made Lou's arms prickle with goose bumps. Over the soybean fields, fire-flies blinked.

As they drove, her thoughts skipped like stones on water from that storm through the Buick window to Atticus Finch to her father, stand-ing in the bathroom, shaving. Then again to her brother announcing his promotion at Devereux & Co. in the middle of a recession that even her daughter knew something about. She remembered how, when Billy had told her about the promotion, inside of her were two reactions—elation and doubt—and how the elated part of her had shushed the other part, had said it was no use to have that kind of attitude.

Just let the man be. Just let him feel, for once, that he'd had some degree of success in this world.

Then inexplicably, the image of Sunshine in the pink vinyl chair at the beauty salon unfolded: her niece flinching when Deborah touched her shoulder—or her head, or her neck (did it matter?). She hadn't thought of it at all, not a second glance, until just a moment ago, when the two-lane highway led the Ford through a thicket of pines, their bark the color of ash in the headlights, and the starkness of the trees in the headlights and the blackness beyond made her feel uneasy—and then there it was, the memory of Sunshine in the salon, the sulphury smell of hair products filling the room. Deborah playing with Sunshine's hair and chattering on as Lou flipped through the pages of the newest *People*.

"Hey," she said to Nash. "Can I ask you a weird question?"

"'Course, babe. Shoot."

Deborah had, what, touched Sunshine's head? Or shoulder? She had touched her in some capacity and Sunshine had flinched—but, no. No, not flinched. She had started so violently that Deborah had stepped back.

"Babe?" Nash said.

She'd gotten lost again. In the rivulets and streams.

"You might think I'm crazy," she said.

Nash laughed. He had a drawling, lazy sort of laugh. "I already know you're crazy," he said.

"Uh huh. I knew you'd say that before you even said it."

The road emerged from the woods again and into the open space of more farm fields.

"I was just thinking," she said, unsure of exactly what the question was, exactly. "I wonder if everything is okay with my brother right now. You know, with the new job."

Nash tossed his cigarette butt out the window. "Why wouldn't it be?"

Lou shrugged. "I don't know. Just a sense, I guess. And for one thing, he's not exactly the world's most respected truth-teller."

Nash chuckled. "Just part of his charm, I always thought. He's more of the storytelling type."

And that was true. Billy was the storytelling type and that was, indeed, a part of his charm.

"I can't explain it." She felt guilty. Something good had happened for her brother, finally, and her instinct was to doubt him. What did that say about her? About the kind of sister she was to him? "Maybe it's the move," she said, rubbing her forehead. "It's just stirring up all of these negative emotions."

Nash kept his eyes on the road. For a moment, they drove in silence.

"Look," he finally said—and she could sense in his tone that she'd hurt his feelings again. It had happened before. Her anxiety about the move, about leaving Billy and Sunshine, came across as doubt about her relationship with Nash, about their future together. His sensitivity about it always surprised her. "If now isn't the time, babe, you just need to tell me. I just need to *know* that, you know?"

She reached out and tucked her fingers in the hair at the base of his neck. She gently scratched. "Babe, I can't wait to move in with you," she said. It was in these moments she wished for a map. It would be so much easier. "It's hard to explain, with Billy. Things between us are complicated. And, look, I wish I understood why I have a weird feeling—but I don't know what it's about. Maybe it's nothing."

(But as she spoke, she knew that wasn't entirely true. She knew that the feeling was not nothing, that it was in fact a *something*. Solid. Ugly. She'd dropped it in the bathtub that hungover morning earlier in the summer and let it sink like a stone. *Plunk*.)

"Can you understand that?" she said.

Nash reached across the seat and rested his hand on her thigh again. He loved her thighs, even though they were thick and dimpled, even though they had, in recent years, developed patches of little veins along their sides.

"Honey," Nash said. "I'm doing my best to understand. I promise you that."

THE FIRST FEW TIMES that Sunshine had emerged, as a very small child, from Joanna Louise's room, wearing an oversized T-shirt of Billy's, her bare legs downy with blonde hair and speckled with mosquito bites, Lou had assumed Sunshine and Joanna Louise had been playing the night before and that Sunshine had fallen asleep there.

The girls often played together without Billy or Lou knowing where exactly they were. They were the only children in Fingertip, even back then, and the neighbors looked out for them. Ms. Mouton (who was always watching and who was always, ever since Lou was a girl, a gossip) eagerly shared with Lou anything rude or disobedient that she had seen one of the girls do. Big Jake often gave them treats at the shop and babysat them when she or Billy could not. Moss Landry, all kind eyes and slow steps and few words, sometimes took them out in his bateau, or showed them how to make a pie with the figs from the tree at the front edge of his yard.

Then Sunshine had showed up again, and then again, and when Lou asked her when she'd come, Sunshine said, "At night. Anna's window was open." Back then, Sunshine still called Joanna Louise *Anna*. Lou didn't question Sunshine's arrival, in part because she loved Sunshine like the girl was her own and felt glad when she showed up as though the house was hers, too, and in part because she didn't know how to speak to Sunshine about Billy's moods.

She didn't understand them herself.

This summer, Sunshine had stopped coming over, which Lou told herself was probably just evidence of her niece growing up—though it made her want to cry if she thought about it too much. She had noticed similar changes in her daughter around the same age—Joanna Louise not wanting to do anything that might seem too childlike.

If a person could unfold the map of their own history out before them, perhaps there could be a way to see the present day on that map too—to look and see which dots or which lines looked strange, and where they led, so that you could make anything wrong right again.

And then no sooner would the thought cross her mind that something was *off* with her brother, was *off* in the yellow house across the road, than guilt would show up, too, fresh and full-bodied as a passenger in her car, and she'd find herself suddenly filled with embarrassment and shame.

She never gave Billy a chance to improve, she knew. Hadn't he said it, so many times? And he was probably right. Couldn't she see the good in people? Couldn't she see the way they could change? Couldn't she see that in her own brother—after all they had been through?

But it wasn't just the job, was it? It was something about Sunshine.

And then the thoughts veered once more, cut along a new stream, and she would remind herself that no, no, Sunshine loved Billy and Billy loved her.

When Billy walked in the room, Sunshine's eyes followed him. Watchful. Hopeful.

She waited quietly, patiently for his attention, and when he gave it—when he hugged her to his side, or picked her up and turned her upside-down and said, "Lou, honey, I'm sorry, I just noticed your floor is too dirty and I've got to mop it up—will you excuse me?" and swung Sunshine back and forth so her long and perpetually tangled blonde hair dragged back and forth along the floor—Lou had always thought that no matter her brother's shortcomings, no matter his mood swings and his depression and his drinking, his love for Sunshine was so powerful that what could be wrong, really wrong? What could be really wrong when that much—Billy's love for the daughter he had raised—was so right?

AFTER NASH HAD TURNED onto the road that led into Fingertip, the truck cruising slowly in third gear, he put his hand on Lou's neck with his free hand. "You're a worrier," he said. "I can feel all that worry right here. Right here in your neck, a knotted-up feeling."

She let her chin tilt forward as Nash massaged her, and she took a deep breath.

It was just that, she told herself. It was just a feeling.

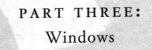

PART THREE:
Windows

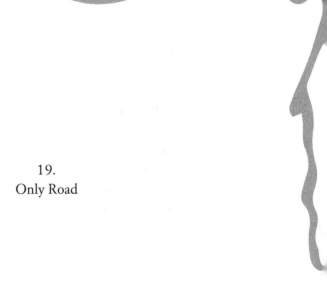

19.
Only Road

Most of the families that settled in Fingertip were not from those parts. It was not a village of Cajuns or Creoles, of folks grown up on the bayou.

The people who occupied the houses along Only Road were from the Southeast and the Midwest, from Florida, from Alabama, from Washington, D.C.—they were young couples or families who had been hit by the Depression for one reason or another and applied to live in the New Deal communities Eleanor Roosevelt had created. In the place whose original name no one could remember, a ninety-nine-cent mortgage and all bills paid. Pastel bungalows in two neat rows down a single unpaved lane. Nearby jobs at a sugar plant and a commuter train to take you there. Weather so hot and humid that on dead-of-summer afternoons, residents—new to Louisiana, and many unfamiliar with the South's suffocating heat—felt like they were drowning.

The houses in the place they called Fingertip were built under the shade of oaks, with screened windows and screened-in porches. Before the early sixties, when air conditioning units were finally installed (several years after the rest of the country had begun using them) in the living rooms and some of the bedrooms, the windows and doors along Only

Road remained open throughout the green, humid days and on through the night. To keep cool there were endless pitchers of iced tea, and cold baths, and swims in the lake until the palms of your hands shriveled into something dead-looking. Some swore by soaking a bed sheet before dinner time, furiously wringing it out, and then hanging it on the line in the yard until bedtime, until it was just damp enough. In bed, they pulled the sheets over their naked bodies like shrouds. Fans, those simple and wondrous appliances, were placed strategically around the house, offering a soft and constant shushing.

Still, over that gentle shushing, outside noises found their way with relative ease in through the open windows and doors.

The great barred owls that frequented the crawling oaks, for example—the people in the houses along Only Road could hear their hoots. They could hear the chirping of cicadas, and the moths that fluttered at window screens, moving hopelessly toward a bedside light. Waking chilled and sometimes even shivering under those still-damp sheets, the neighbors could hear, over the shushing of the fans, the strange, tinny sound of the tiny wings.

Their bodies cooled, they kicked aside the damp sheet and pulled up the dry one waiting at the foot of the bed. They let the shushing of the fan grow louder and louder in the shells of their ears so the nighttime noises receded and they could sink back into sleep.

Come morning, what other noises had they already let recede?

Let dip beneath the oil-black surface of their humid dreamy nights, along with the moths and the moon?

20.
Swiss Cheese Shirts

July 1982

Aunt Lou invited Sunshine over for coffee one morning in late July. Sunshine remembered to wear the pink training bra and also to comb her hair, and Aunt Lou made her coffee how she liked it best, with extra sugar and so much cream the coffee turned a pale beige. She served them both sliced orange wedges and peanut butter toast, and after they ate they poured more coffee and sat side by side on the couch, watching *Good Morning America* and then the weather report on Channel 10. The weatherman said a severe storm was predicted for later that week.

"Ooo," Aunt Lou said. "Could be a lightning storm."

When Sunshine was little and there were night time summer storms, everyone went up to the Lust to watch from the big front windows as bolt after bolt of lightning lit up the sky over the soybean fields across the tracks. Once, Sunshine and JL watched from behind the glass as lightning struck a pine tree, and the grown-ups who had missed it (the grown-ups always lost interest in the storm after the first couple of minutes and sat along the bar or played pool instead) had made Sunshine and JL describe in detail what it had looked like, the struck limb exploding off the tree in a flash of orange heat.

But no one really went to the lightning parties anymore. JL said it was because everyone was too old. She said it was like her maman sometimes said: Fingertip was dying on the vine.

BEFORE FINGERTIP WAS DYING on the vine and before JL had turned into what Aunt Lou called *a pill*, she and Sunshine had spent their summers and all of their weekends together and there were no secrets between them.

JL had not yet become best friends with Caroline Murphy.

There was no summer camp.

There was no Wednesday underwear with its rust-brown stain; there were no stones.

Once, they went into the woods and climbed the pine tree with the low branches and sat with their legs dangling over the rough bark of the loblolly, the space between Sunshine's legs tingling pleasantly from the way the tree pressed against her, and JL told her that she had overheard her mother say something to Nash about Sunshine's birth—about a girl-friend of Billy's who left Sunshine on the porch, not a heron at all.

"I know that, dummy," Sunshine said, though she hadn't known that then, not yet. She was getting old enough to realize that it was unlikely that herons or birds of any sort would carry children in Florida orange crates, and she was certainly old enough to notice that there were body parts that grown-ups did not like to talk about, and that the two secrets were somehow connected, but she wasn't sure she believed JL. Sometimes JL told her things, true or not, just to make her mad.

"Well, did you know that we have five holes in our butts?"

"*Five?*"

"Want to check?"

"Check the holes in our butts?"

"Yes," JL said. "Let's count them."

It was early winter, and one of those days that began with frost on the ground and then melted under a sky so clear and blue it almost hurt to look at.

Overhead, the pines tilted and creaked in a chill wind. Sunshine could feel its cold fingers waggling their way through the holes in her sweater.

JL climbed down from the tree and stretched her arms up overhead as though in a victory pose. For no reason, she twirled once and then twice. Nearby was a large fallen branch, forked in two, and when she was done twirling Joanna Louise instructed Sunshine to lie down under the branch while JL sat on the forked part, butt cheeks spread.

Leaves and pine needles stuck in Sunshine's hair; she could smell pine sap, and the ground was cold. Then JL was sitting over her, naked from the waist down.

Sunshine giggled. "*Ew*," she said.

"Do *not* tell Maman about this," JL said above her, and then she started laughing, too, and when she caught her breath she twisted around so her upside-down face was almost level with Sunshine's, her red hair now brushing the ground, and she said, "Count them! My butt cheeks are getting cold."

"Don't fart," Sunshine said. "If you fart, I'm leaving."

"Just count." JL flung herself upright again.

Sunshine looked for the five holes. The star-shaped butthole was the most obvious. Dark pink. Small, considering all that came out of it. Years ago, JL had screeched at Sunshine and Aunt Lou from the hallway bathroom to *come here, come quick*, and revealed an enormous, coiled-up turd. Sunshine had looked at it, fascinated. Aunt Lou had started laughing and then cleared her throat and said, "Joanna Louise Turner, what on *earth* possessed you to show us this?" and JL had said, proudly, that it was the longest turd she'd ever pooped out and that it looked like a snake.

Now, under her cousin's pale, spread-wide cheeks, Sunshine held her breath so she would not breathe in any accidental or intentional farts. She did not trust JL.

Around the star-shaped butthole, the skin was stretched taut, fawn-colored. Closer to the middle of the crevice the skin got fleshier and soft and wet-looking. It was hard to tell how many holes were in that fleshy part, exactly. She was tempted to touch them.

"Okay," she breathed. "Your butthole is one. And there's one in the middle."

"My pee hole?"

"How do I know?"

"I could pee. You could see where it comes out."

Sunshine reached up and flicked a section of white butt cheek. "If you pee, I'm telling Aunt Lou."

"Okay, any others?"

"I think so. A tiny one."

"Where?"

"Kind of by the middle one. Like, sort of above it." She was pointing as though JL could see her, as though she were drawing a map of cities: Butt Hole. Middle Hole. Tiny Hole.

"Huh. Only three. Okay. Your turn."

They traded positions. When Sunshine straddled the pine branches, pants all the way off, the cool air rushed in between her legs and again her clam tingled. Twigs dug into the soles of her feet.

JL was silent for a long time.

"So?" Sunshine said.

"It's weird," JL said. "I see seventeen holes."

"What?"

"At least."

"Nuh-uh. Count again."

"I'm trying, but I keep losing track...."

Sunshine squealed, "Shut up! Liar!"

JL poked at Sunshine's butthole, hard, and said, "Oil check!" Sunshine yelped and leaped up and fell awkwardly off the branch.

"You're disgusting," she said, scrambling for her pants. "You're going to smell like poop."

JL, still lying on the ground, poked her head out from underneath the fallen tree and sniffed her finger. "Mmm," she said, and Sunshine, pants not yet all the way up, laughed so hard she fell again, the blue sky and pines wheeling overhead.

As THEY WALKED BACK down the pig path that afternoon, pulling pine needles from their hair, scratching where bits of twigs and leaves had gotten caught inside and outside their pants, JL told Sunshine about her plan to find the library books that would tell her about these things.

Sunshine could look, too, if she wanted, JL had said.

"I know I can," Sunshine replied, annoyed.

But secretly, Sunshine was afraid of Aunt Lou finding out, and so on their trips to the library she stayed in the section of children's books, among *Caddie Woodlawn* and *The Loner* and *Anne of Green Gables*, books Aunt Lou had first introduced her to and that she loved. When she was still little, Aunt Lou used to read to her and JL at bedtime. Together, they had all read *Caddie Woodlawn* twice by the time Sunshine was nine. Both JL and Sunshine hated how Caddie started to become a lady by the end.

"She just *gives up*," Sunshine said, outraged.

Now, that Joanna Louise was going into ninth grade, she didn't change in front of Sunshine or talk to her about buttholes or the words she discovered in the library or elsewhere. She wore makeup (which was the same, according to Sunshine, as Caddie Woodlawn deciding to start sewing) and whatever she'd discovered in the library books, she kept mostly to herself.

Earlier this year, after climbing in through JL's window and plopping down on top of the quilt, Sunshine had asked if JL wanted to have a frontal wedgie contest. This was a game JL had invented and meant you pulled your underwear all the way up in the back and the front so that it was caught between your butt cheeks and your clam and hurt and tickled a little at the same time, and then you saw who could last the longest wearing it like that, and Sunshine always won because she would sleep all night with her underwear like that no matter how uncomfortable.

But that night, reading a book in bed, JL did not glance in Sunshine's direction. Still staring at the page in her book, she said that game was for babies, and then, even worse, she said, "Besides, I always picked mine out early. I just never told you."

• • •

LOU LEFT FOR WORK in a good mood. The morning with Sunshine had helped dull the longing she'd been feeling for Joanna Louise and put her mind a little more at ease about Sunshine. It had been several weeks since they'd spent the day at the salon and then the 79 and the new house; it had been so nice to spend time with her again.

She drove under the crawling oaks along Only Road, then crossed the tracks.

Maybe, she thought, she could revisit the conversation with her brother that had gone so poorly a couple weeks back. Things had probably cooled by now. Maybe he'd had some time to think on it, to see the sense in Sunshine living closer to school, staying close with her cousin. Maybe he'd reconsider.

LOU HAD BEEN BACK in Fingertip for nearly five years and working at the 79 Dine for most of that time when she first noticed Nash. He'd been coming to the diner after work for ages—two years at least, he would later claim—and always ordered the grilled cheese sandwich with tomatoes. It was approximately his five hundredth order of grilled cheese with tomatoes when at long last, Lou looked him in the eye and said,—*with a side of chips and an extra pickle?*, thus completing the order he'd made four hundred and ninety-nine times prior without her ever bothering to show she recognized his face or order.

That was the story as Nash told it.

What Lou noticed that evening, whether it was for the first of five hundred times or not, was that he had kind eyes, with those lines that crept outward so his eyes always looked like he was smiling even when his mouth was not. And he was handsome, with a thick handlebar mustache and careless stubble everywhere else. The dirty blonde hair and tan, muscular arms of a man who worked outdoors. She noticed his T-shirt was covered in holes: a Swiss cheese shirt.

That evening, he didn't leave after he finished his tomato and grilled cheese sandwich, side of chips, and two dill pickles stacked neatly on a single toothpick. He stayed until Lou told him they needed the booth for a four-top, and then he moved to the counter and started a new tab. He drank coffee there at the counter, finished it, and then ordered a refill and a slice of pie. He finished the pie and requested another coffee refill. He read the newspaper cover to cover and then a brochure on Gulf Coast fishing tours.

One and then two full hours passed.

Then another.

Outside the 79 Dine, the summer sky turned pink and violet. The setting sun flashed a brilliant, blinding orange on the big semis that occasionally roared past. Then there was only darkness beyond the diner glass, and when Lou reached to refill a water or a cup of coffee, she could see in the window reflection the man at the bar behind her: his broad shoulders under the Swiss cheese shirt, his unkempt, dirty-blond hair.

But he didn't bother her or distract her from her work or comment on her body the way other regulars did. He only glanced up from time to time, smiling with his eyes, until, finally, the night shift staff clocked in.

Lou completed her side work, rolling the silverware and slicing the lemons. She slipped into the cramped back hall, hung up her apron, and checked her hair in the mirror. She wore it in a ponytail, and fine strands had long ago come undone and curled in wild wisps around her face. Her forehead and nose bore the sheen of carrying heavy trays all afternoon and evening.

She rummaged around in the other girls' aprons hanging on pegs until she found someone's lipstick, then applied just a little, so it wouldn't look like she tried too hard. She took out her ponytail, combed her hair with her fingers, and pulled it up again. She slipped into the bathroom and dabbed her nose and forehead with a fold of toilet paper. Then she went to the bar and sat down on the green leather stool next to the man with the Swiss cheese shirt (and the side of chips, extra pickles).

NASH WAS NOT FAZED by the facts of Lou's *situation*, as she called it. By her seven-year-old daughter or her five-year-old niece who she explained might as well be a daughter to her. He wasn't fazed by the fact that she lived across the street from her troubled older brother—that's how she described Billy: *Well, he's troubled.* She stirred her root beer float. They had not left the diner. (Later, the staff would tease her about this, ask when the wedding was, make kissy sounds when she walked in for her next shift. "Caught yourself a big one," Tammy would say, winking.)

He was not fazed, apparently, by spending no fewer than four of his after-work hours waiting for a woman to finish her own work. When she first sat beside him, he'd said, "Oh, wow. Done so soon?"

SHE AGREED ON A drink at a nearby bar. "Just one," she said.

When rose to leave, Lou could see the lower halves of their bodies in the reflection of the diner glass. She couldn't see her face but she saw her torso and her hips, her blue-striped blouse tucked in at the waist of her faded jeans. For the first time, she could see—as though through an entirely new pair of eyes—the appeal of her own body.

IN THOSE DAYS, ON nights she worked, Joanna Louise and Sunshine often stayed with Big Jake at the Lust. He let them sit at the bar and drink Shirley Temples, and he brought out his small television from the apartment where he lived in back of the building and set it on the bar and turned the station to the *The Patty Duke Show*. (They liked that it was about two cousins, and sometimes they combed their hair back in headbands and wore collared shirts buttoned all the way to their necks to look like Cathy and Patty Lane.) Sometimes, when Billy took a fishing gig offshore and Lou picked up the girls after she got off her shift, she arrived at the Lust to find the girls asleep on the far pool table.

If she was too tired to bring Sunshine up to her house, and if Sunshine was too tired to murmur tearfully that she wanted to be in *her* bedroom with *her* blankets—as she sometimes did—then she simply tucked them both into bed in JL's room, made herself a gin and tonic, and read *Elle* in the living room.

When she'd left Fingertip and married Robert Dalton, she'd left behind the books she'd loved as a teenager. *Jane Eyre* and *Wuthering Heights* and *Pride & Prejudice*. Later, after she'd left Charleston behind, she told herself she no longer liked to read those books. They were too romantic; they'd tricked her into a false idea of love. What she wouldn't or couldn't admit to herself is that she had given up on the possibility of her own romance along with her own education. She'd resigned herself to motherhood. To work. And that was that.

That first night at the bar, tipsy from no dinner and most of a beer, Lou told Nash about Robert. Not much, but a little. "He got physical," she admitted, then she left it at that.

Nash nodded at her. His eyes weren't smiling then; he looked a little sad.

"So," she said, changing the subject. "How come I've never seen you at the 79 before?"

"Very funny," he said.

ON HER EVENING SHIFTS, Nash would come in and eat his usual meal, then wait, as he'd done that first night, for her to get off work. Tammy would lean in as she and Lou passed one another in the narrow aisle, both balancing trays. "I see your man is here again," she'd say under her breath. "Been trying to get him to notice me for the better part of a year and all you had to do was ignore him."

Nash shared with her that he'd been the quarterback of his high school football team. He owned a construction company that built and renovated houses. He explained, when she asked how it was he didn't have a girlfriend, at least, that he had been too busy running his own business, hustling to make it work. Besides, he added, he had a thing for redheads—and there just weren't too many of them around.

Lou felt the color rise to her cheeks, and she covered her mouth with one hand as she laughed—a gesture her mother had often done to cover up her bruised front tooth. Lou's own teeth were not bruised (despite Robert Dalton), but her own joy sometimes embarrassed her anyway—as though it was something best kept hidden.

The first time they kissed, Lou pulled away and laughed nervously, her hand automatically flying up to cover her mouth. Nash took her hand gently in his own.

"There's that smile," he said, and kissed her again.

THERE WAS SOMETHING ABOUT Nash—his all-American love of foot-ball, his house-building—that made her feel he was solid. Rooted. Like the cypress trees that grew along the lake. And although Tammy teased her—"Oh, we all know why you like him. Believe you me, honey, we get it"—it was not just his build. It was the way his eyes stayed twinkly, how his mood stayed steady, how he could make her laugh. Whereas Robert Dalton had carefully gelled and combed his hair in the mirror each morning, clipped his nose hairs with a tiny pair of scissors, and plucked his eyebrows in the middle so they wouldn't be one furry brown bar across his forehead, Nash didn't seem to be aware of his own looks—unless he was trying to make her laugh. Sometimes she'd emerge from the restroom to find him naked in bed with her bed sheet wrapped around his body like a toga, his body frozen in some Grecian pose, his biceps obviously flexed. When she laughed—and she always did—he'd feign ignorance. "What?" he'd say. "I'm just more comfortable this way."

He mentioned marriage more than once over the years. He brought it up casually, testing her out, knowing that after her first husband, she found marriage suspect. Even downright stupid.

"What do we need to get married for?" she'd say. "I'm happy with how things are."

Then last year, he took her to the old farmhouse in Lafayette one afternoon before her shift. He talked about his plans to renovate; he showed her all the bedrooms, the large old windows. "See? It's got good bones," he kept saying. Then, as they walked across the lawn to his truck, he grabbed her hand. His eyes were not smiling; he looked, in fact, like he might start to cry.

"Marry me, Lou."

She squeezed his hand. She nodded. "Yes," she said, and he scooped her up and spun her in dizzying circles. When he set her down again, they were both teary-eyed and laughing.

JOANNA LOUISE ROLLED HER eyes at Nash's jokes and, Lou was well aware, called him "Nash the 'Stache" behind his back, but Lou thought her daughter liked him well enough—could maybe even love him. For Sunshine's part, it had been love at first sight. The first night they met, Nash had pretended to be a horse, giving Sunshine—only just turned seven—a ride around Lou's living room, glimpses of sun-browned skin showing through the gaps in his Swiss cheese shirt.

He owned, it turned out, a whole collection of Swiss cheese shirts.

In their first year together, *Born Free* played on television and they all watched it in her living room—Nash and Lou on the sofa, Joanna Louise and Sunshine sprawled on the floor among pillows and blankets and a bowl of popcorn.

Billy wasn't there that night; since Nash had come along, he'd made himself scarce. It was a given that Sunshine would stay the night. By then, the attentiveness Billy had once given her appeared intermittently and unpredictably. Lou was not sure where or when he abandoned the parenting he'd thrown himself into as a younger man.

One year, on Halloween, Billy had taken the girls trick-or-treating in St. Cadence. The three of them, Joanna Louise reported back, had gone on a mission to get more candy than any trick-or-treater had ever gotten before. He drove them all the way to Lafayette and took them to the wealthier suburbs. Sunshine and Joanna Louise traipsed from house to house, dressed as an owl (Sunshine) and a witch (Joanna Louise, in a hat she'd made from cardboard and black Magic Markers), with pillowcases so heavy they could hardly carry them.

Like Nash, Billy made the girls laugh. He teased. He told Sunshine the stories their mother had told them, stories Lou no longer remembered and dismissed—though she had loved them when she was younger—as hogwash.

But when Sunshine got a little older, Billy often seemed tired and overwhelmed. He often fell into one of his moods and did not seem to pay much attention to anyone for days on end. It was a huge stroke of fortune that it was Jimmy Devereux, his old high school baseball buddy, who had employed him at the coastal job years prior—otherwise, he would have been fired a long time ago.

Lou did not, would not, let herself get caught up in her brother's life, in his choices. She had decided this soon after returning to Fingertip. His business was his business. She would help care for his little girl, she would be a mother to her as best as she could, but that was her limit. She wouldn't care for the girls and also a grown man.

And so when Billy did not want to join them on movie nights, she didn't press him. When Sunshine slept in her daughter's room because Billy was in one of his moods, she cared for her niece as best she could and left it at that. After a lifetime with her father, after several more years with Robert Dalton, after parenting a daughter and a niece and waiting on customers day in and day out, she did not have the energy to care for someone who couldn't muster up the energy to care for himself.

THE GIRLS FELL ASLEEP during *Born Free* with the half-empty popcorn bowl between them. Nash put his hand under Lou's shirt on her bare stomach. On screen, Elsa the lion was running across a field, and Joy was crying. Lou cried, too, and didn't know if it was because of Elsa the lion or because of Nash and his gentle and unrelenting love for her, for her body. How sweet it was to just watch a movie with him and the girls, eating popcorn.

In bed that night, the lights off, they lay awake talking in low voices.

"I could build us a house someday," Nash said.

Lou laughed. She was lying on her side, one hand resting on his bare stomach.

"You laugh, but you'll see. Don't you know how talented I am?"

"Oh, I don't doubt it."

"I *could* do it, though. For you and me and the girls. Shit, Billy too, if he wants to join."

"Not for Billy," she said, too forceful.

"Well, okay," he said. "But for the rest of us."

If in that moment in the darkness Nash had asked more of her—about her history, about her feelings about Billy (*Why the tone, babe? What's he ever done to you?*)—she might have told him everything. She might have let it all tumble out, right then. About anger at Billy for the way he drank, at the way he sometimes seemed to disappear so that his own daughter didn't like to be in her house. She might have told him about that night when she was sixteen. About knocking back. She might have cried—she would have said that Billy had been so sweet once, and what happened? More and more he was reminding her of their father.

And she might have admitted how she hated herself for still *missing* her father—something she found enraging, missing this person who had done nothing, absolutely nothing worth missing.

But Nash had not asked, had let it go, had focused brightly on the future, and although the words were right there—she could feel them, waiting to be spoken aloud—the moment had passed.

When over the years there were other such moments, intimate moments when it felt like anyone could say anything, could dream about the future or share about the past, she turned away from it—and the more time that passed, the more it seemed impossible to put words to such memories, such feelings.

WHEN NASH EVENTUALLY BEGAN the renovation, he showed her the blueprints: a bedroom for the two of them with their own bathroom. "We'll have those his-and-hers sinks," he said. He pointed at the room for Joanna Louise, then the room for Sunshine, for when she came to visit. "Or she could stay longer. Either way. We'll have the space, babe."

Lou had never brought herself to mention it, the idea of a room for Sunshine. She'd felt nervous, for some reason—but why? It was Nash himself who had first brought up the idea years ago. Did she think his capacity to love had shrunk in that time?

But here before her was a thoughtful blueprint, and here was the man who made it. Who loved her, and loved the people she loved.

21.
The Yellow Rope

July 1982

S unshine tried to put her one thousand questions out of mind, but still the questions piled up anyway. Like clouds on the horizon.

She thought of new ones when she was watching TV at Aunt Lou's, and walking through the paths in the woods, and riding with Aunt Lou to the Piggly Wiggly, and lying awake in the quiet sea cave of her bedroom at night, wondering if the spiders would appear.

(They hadn't. Not yet.)

She wondered about the stones inside her chest and how big they would grow, or if the stones stayed small and the boobs formed on top of them like jellyfish? What about the white crust on her underwear and the weird salty smell of it? What about the thing that shifted and hardened inside of Billy's jeans? Recently, he'd taken her hand in his—it was not a spider, just Billy's own rough hand and her own was small inside of it—and guided it to the outside of his jeans and pressed it, just very gently pressed it, against his *thing* and she could feel it moving on the other side of the rough denim. (It was only for a moment in the kitchen late at night when he smelled like beer, and her stones were safe.) And what about the hair growing on Joanna Louise's body—the soft, downy hair Sunshine had seen when JL was getting dressed that spring morning and had not known that Sunshine wasn't asleep but watching through two barely open eyes? What about Miss Collins's baby—had it come out by now? How did it breathe in there? Did the baby start off tiny, like the green beetles on the fig leaves? Was it like JL had said, its body swelling so that it burst through the iridescent green shell—a puffy, squirming blue-white grubworm? Did the grubworm sprout legs and arms and a mouth? Did it eat your belly from the inside out like the crocodile gobbled up the clouds and the trees and the shoreline, so the space inside of you got bigger and bigger and the grubworm got bigger and bigger inside of it, until it wasn't a grubworm at all anymore, but a baby?

THE DAY WAS HUMID. Even in Aunt Lou's living room, with the AC unit on, Sunshine felt too hot. She watched another episode of *I Love Lucy* and then walked back across Only Road to change into her bathing suit.

She wanted to swim but Aunt Lou had reminded her countless times that summer that she could not swim alone. So far, she had obeyed. She had waded, only, or she'd asked Moss Landry if he wanted to swim and the two of them had strolled to the lake together. But Moss was old, and slow. Before they swam, he stood on the shore and rubbed suntan lotion all over his chest and his back and his face and his legs. It seemed to take hours. His skin stretched in all directions as he rubbed, like putty. Sunshine, who didn't ever wear sunscreen, waited for him in the ankle-deep water, but even when he finally waded in to meet her, he didn't like to swim in the way that Aunt Lou did, in circles and circles. Moss was ready to leave soon after they got in, and then they walked slowly through the woods back to Fingertip, sweating again even before they reached Only Road.

Billy had left for the day and the yellow house was quiet. In her bedroom, Sunshine put on her swimsuit bottoms and JL's old top. (It had two red triangles attached to strings that tied in back. The triangles sagged like deflated balloons.) She decided that she would make a sandwich and go to the lake and lie down in the shallow water. Just enough to cover her body and cool her off.

That wasn't swimming, technically.

Even Billy could do that, and he couldn't swim.

Moss would probably be out in his bateau, anyway—fishing was what he loved to do more than anything, more than swimming—and if he was in eyesight she wouldn't, technically, be swimming alone.

In the kitchen, there were only the heels of the bread loaf left, and both were moldy. A jar of peanut butter was in the cupboard, but when she opened it there was not even enough for a spoonful. The two remaining bananas had rotted, and fruit flies hovered over them. On the floor by the oven was the butterfly-shaped stain.

Sunshine stooped down and pressed her fingers against the checked linoleum.

When she looked up, Grandma Catherine was standing at the sink again. Young and bare-armed. Her back was to Sunshine and she wore the white canvas Keds that Aunt Lou said she always wore, and her red hair was pulled partway up in combs.

He was *a sunnavabitch*, Grandma Catherine said over her shoulder.

Sunshine could not see her face very well against the afternoon light streaming through the window. It spilled all around her. It spilled over to where Sunshine was squatting, touching the mangled linoleum, the brown butterfly stain.

But, Grandma Catherine added, *he could be so charming. That's what got me at first. Mercy, he could be charming.*

Sunshine looked back at the butterfly stain and then back up toward the sink again, and the light still streamed in but nobody was in the kitchen except her.

OUTSIDE, ONLY ROAD WAS so quiet that it felt to Sunshine as though she were the only person in all of Fingertip. She looked toward Old Mouton's porch but even she was inside, watching *The Price is Right*, probably, with blue tissues jutting from her nostrils.

Sunshine walked down the exact middle of the road.

What if everyone in Fingertip was dead? What would she do first?

She'd raid the Lust Outpost. Obviously. She'd eat all the candy bars she wanted and all the potato chips and take all the peanut butter. Then she'd swim in the lake and go out past the rope, even if there were alligators.

THE LAKE STRETCHED WIDE and flat under the hot sky.

No one was at the shore or out on the water. Sunshine sat in the shade, tracing her name in the sand with one finger. She dug a hole and buried her feet. The sand was cool just under the surface, but sweat ran down her temples and the back of her neck. Even in the shade it was hot. She left her clothes on the sand and walked in her bathing suit down to the water's edge and stepped in up to her ankles, then her shins.

She looked around.

There were the trees, their green muted with midsummer. Grayish Spanish moss. The rhythmic whine of locusts. On a nearby tree sat a tremendous blue heron, but even he was watching something else. No one was there to see if she were to swim alone. Just the once. Just quickly, to cool off, and then she'd dry off and go home and Aunt Lou would never know.

She waded in, thrilled with the knowledge of her aloneness.

She'd only meant to dunk herself under and then walk back out again, but once she was in deep it felt so good that she allowed herself just a little more. She did backstroke like Aunt Lou, looking up at the wide blue sky, kicking her feet. She flipped forward on her belly and swam the breaststroke back the other way. On the shore was the crumpled pile of her clothing and besides that there was nothing else. She pulled her red goggles down over her eyes and swam underwater for as long as she could hold her breath, watching the minnows dart back and forth. She didn't like swimming with the bathing suit top on; the strings itched, and she wasn't as sleek and quick in the water.

She surfaced and gathered her breath again and then dove under and swam to the edge of the yellow rope. She held it with two hands and kicked her legs out in front of her, like she was a trapeze swinger and the yellow rope was her trapeze. If Aunt Lou were here to see that, she would kill her. Or if she didn't kill her she would at least drag Sunshine out of the lake by one arm, slapping with her free hand. She would ban Sunshine from the lake for a whole month.

But Aunt Lou was not here.

Sunshine took another breath and slipped feet forward, a trapeze artist performing her trick, under the yellow rope, and let go.

ON THE OTHER SIDE, the water was the color of boiled peas. She stayed close to the cold spring side at first, looking around every other moment to make sure she hadn't missed Moss out on his boat somewhere. But today the lake was all hers, and she swam forward with smooth strokes. She ignored the too-loose fabric of her top and the itchy strings. She was a mermaid. No—she was an alligator, gliding with ease, without fear, and she forgot about everything back on the shore. Her crumpled clothes and being modest and the spiders and the secrets.

She changed her swimming to a backwards crab-crawl. If it was storming in the yellow house this very moment, so be it; she was a swimming fish, a gliding gator, a flash of light on the water.

The yellow rope and the shore just past it were getting farther and farther, her clothes a dot in the sand. She kicked her feet under her and treaded water for a moment, taking in her surroundings, and saw that the swampy edge of the lake, the forest of cypress and tupelo, was now just behind her. She had swum almost clear across. Out here was where the gators hunted. They built dens in the frogbit and sawgrass, and she could see the thick green patches through the trees.

The colors of the swamp in summer were also different than on the cold spring side. Over here, the water was murkier, but the green of the trees and the grasses seemed brighter. Sunshine had only seen the swamp from the times Moss had taken her fishing with him, but from down in the water it looked different, ancient. The cypress reached up like those Roman columns she'd learned about that year. The canopy of moss was like a vaulted ceiling, dappled in light and leaves. She treaded water for a moment, losing herself, taking in this lush green world from the surface of the water, and then one foot kicked something.

It was hard underfoot but moved when she kicked it. In her stomach, a quick flash of recognition. Of fear like an electric current.

Sunshine crab-crawled backwards, trying hard not to splash. To swim fast but smooth. She glanced over her shoulder—how long would it take her to get back? Five minutes? Ten? More? Then she turned back toward the swamp and saw it, not five feet in front of her: the snout of a gator, pointed at her like an arrowhead.

Its eyes were black and shining and rimmed with yellow, its nostrils black. The mound of its back rose above the water.

Moss had showed her how you could guess the length of a gator—how the inches between the tip of its nose and its eyes equaled the number of feet from nose to tail. Sunshine could see there were six or more inches between those nostrils and its yellow-rimmed eyes.

She was not yet five feet tall.

Her breath was ragged. People drowned when they panicked, Aunt Lou had told her. *If you get scared on the water, you float, or you crab-crawl. You take deep breaths. You do. Not. Panic. You hear me young lady?*

She crab-crawled back toward the opposite shore as noiselessly as possible, watching the gator watching her, trying to reach the yellow rope. The arrow kept its aim but stayed still, as though guarding the swamp, that ancient church, from a little girl who was supposed to remain on the other side of the yellow rope.

Sunshine glanced over her shoulder from time to time, quickly, terrified that when she turned back again she would see the jaws right there, wide open, as big as the crocodile in Billy's stories. When she at last reached the rope, she ducked quickly under and swam the remaining distance as fast as she could, sputtering and coughing, until it was too shallow to swim anymore. At the little pile of her clothing she plopped down, shaking, heart pounding, nauseated with fear and with the effort of her swim.

She looked out at the still, empty surface of the water. Then with a start, she felt around her neck—where were her goggles? She stood up and looked under her clothes. But she remembered she'd taken them off when she was close to the swamp so she could see better. She usually put them on her head, but this time, she'd held them. She must have been holding them still when her foot kicked up against the alligator. She must have dropped them without even noticing.

Somehow, losing her goggles seemed like the saddest thing that had happened all summer, and she pulled her knees to her chest and put her forehead on them and began to cry.

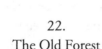

22.
The Old Forest

After Margaret Bell died, it felt like something inside of Catherine had been pulled apart like fibrous wet paper. The edges softly frayed.

When her children were near, when she could focus on tending to them and loving them, she was able to forget her grief, her loneliness. How few friends she had in Fingertip. How isolated she felt—and indeed how isolated she was, down at the tail end of Only Road. With her children nearby, she could forget about her husband, about her longing for him (for his attention, for his affection). She needed only to care for Billy and Lou.

After school each day, she made them snacks, slices of bread spread with peanut butter and dotted with raisins to make the shape of a smiley face. On Saturday mornings, she made them egg-in-a-basket sandwiches. She told them stories about everything, about growing up in Portland, about Talmadge, about the haints in and around the woods that surrounded Fingertip, about the crocodile bride. She told them these stories until they were old enough that they did not want story time before bed anymore, and it was then that she separated their books according to each of their favorites and strung up a series of sheets to divide their room in two.

She allowed herself to believe that if she arranged the household just right and kept the right food on hand and let her stories fill their imaginations and if she loved, loved Billy and Lou with a fervor and attentiveness that her own mother hadn't known how to offer during her own childhood, then John Jay's presence in the household, and in their lives, would be outweighed by her own.

That light would replace dark.

Perhaps, as her children grew, he'd become just a shadow at the edges of their memory. Perhaps, with true fortune, her children might eventually confuse memories of their mother's love with memories of their father's, and the two would intermingle in their minds so that the truth of how he ruled their lives in the yellow house would be eclipsed entirely.

And Catherine was able to go on believing this until the children were older—Billy fifteen, Lou only thirteen and still in middle school—and she began to notice that on some days, Billy came home from baseball practice later than he should have, and that, on those days, when she stood on her tiptoes to kiss his cheek hello, he smelled unmistakably of bourbon.

(Unmistakably. And yet. How easily she convinced herself she was mistaken in the face of even the most glittering of truths.)

Eventually, driving to St. Cadence one weekend, Catherine asked Lou if she had noticed anything about her brother's drinking. Her daughter (long red braids, a smattering of pimples across each cheek) had snapped at her that no, she hadn't, that Catherine worried too much, and Catherine had felt swift, ready relief.

Billy was only testing his limits. Pushing his boundaries. As teens would do.

She reached out her hand and playfully tugged one of Lou's braids, and her daughter's pout lifted itself into a small grin.

THE LAST TIME BILLY asked her to tell him a story, he was eleven years old. Lou was spending the night in St. Cadence for a friend's birthday party, and perhaps because it was just the two of them, and Billy didn't have to act the part of the big brother, he'd felt free to ask, and happily she climbed in bed alongside him. He'd rested his head against her shoulder. It was winter, and he wore pale blue flannel pajamas.

"What happened to the crocodile bride?" Billy said, yawning. "Did she die?"

Catherine pulled the quilt up over him. "I'll tell you," she said.

As time passed, the land surrounding the Black Bayou began to change.

On the plantations, the weevil ate the cotton and sugar grew up in its place. Men traveled from all over to the nearby swamps. They balanced on shallow boats shaped like bananas and hacked at the ancient cypress with axes and saws. They dragged the great trees out in long, straight rows. The enormous trunks dug deep trenches in the earth—miles-long scars that even one hundred years later did not fade.

(*Is this part true?* Billy asked. He'd outgrown his stutter, by then.
The whole story is true, Catherine replied.
How do you know? Who told you?
Mercy. Please watch your tone.
Yes, ma'am, Billy said. *But who did tell you?*
She told me, silly. The crocodile bride.)

Without the trees to take up all that water, the floods became monstrous things. The turquoise sea to the south grew hungrier and gobbled up the shore.

When it rained, now, the tree-stripped land sank, flooded, turned to miles and miles of swamp. More trees were felled, more land was farmed. Sugar stretched on for hundreds of thousands of acres, and then soybeans came and went, and then there was not much of anything at all—just dry stalks in a field that flooded too often for a farmer of any reason to bother with sowing more seeds. In the wind, the stalks whispered like ghosts.

City parlors boasted imposing sideboards, little round tea tables standing primly next to wing-backed chairs, and large armoires and ornately trimmed dressers furnished bedrooms, the wood finely polished.

This wood was cut from a tree so old it was born before the country met any white faces at its shores. In hours, it fell at the hands of only two men. They stood on either end of banana-shaped boats. But the wood was fine, the grain ornate, the resin making its destruction nearly impossible; its warm hues glimmered like gold in the new electric lights.

The men who took the trees had heard of the Black Bayou, and none wanted to risk his life to do this job in the kingdom of a crocodile. They agreed amongst themselves that they might conveniently misunderstand the red Xs that marked, on their company maps, their various destinations across the Atchafalaya. Besides, they had already felled whole forests. What were just a few more cypress by then? Might as well leave them alone, leave that misplaced old crocodile to himself.

And so it was that much of the old forest surrounding the Black Bayou remained more or less untouched, and then concealed by the new growth that soon sprang up around it.

But the Black Bayou was not, could not possibly be entirely unmarred. Its water ran to other channels of water, which ran to the sea, and all of that water began to rise. It first covered the shore where the crocodile bride had once stood (a dark-haired young woman with strawberry-colored bruises on her arms, a cut along one cheek) and then flooded the ridge upon which the little red house was perched, and the water spread like spilled oil through the forest.

The deep water suited the crocodile, who was by now beyond enormous. He swam in slow, lazy circles, guarding the red house that now sat on an island (once the ridge that rose just inside of the forest, some distance from the water) in the very center of the bayou. On a quiet night, the crocodile bride could still hear the beating of the crocodile heart buried deep below.

LONG AGO, RUMORS HAD spread that the crocodile bride aged more slowly than everyone else—that perhaps her bond with the crocodile, marriage or no, extended her own life. Perhaps living with a crocodile heart beneath your home did strange things to a person in ways they could not understand—as none of them had ever, in fact, buried a crocodile heart anywhere at all. The crocodile bride's youth had lasted long throughout the years.

But as the forest changed, so did she.

Her skin grew thin and lined; her gray-streaked hair grew white. Her bones turned thin and frail. The rising water transformed the hill on which her house was perched and it became an island. A person could no longer walk up on shore, stand a safe distance from the water, and throw a gift to the crocodile. Some brave and hopeful soul left a small boat on the shore of the bayou so that a visitor might row out to her, but most did not dare head out on that open water—a broad, flat lake—even if they'd brought a gift, even if their gift was the most precious thing they owned.

So it was that over time, the crocodile bride became a story to tell rather than a healer to seek.

The villagers told the children of her—of the healing touch they had felt on their bodies. They boasted of the precious objects they'd given away in order to experience her touch. They were proud of what they'd been willing to pay.

When their wives were not there to overhear, the men spoke in awed whispers of the beauty she'd once possessed. Of the water lilies she wore in her hair, of the long braid she wore down her back, shining and black. Of the haughty lift of her chin and the caramel brown of her skin.

Some said that when the crocodile bride was still young, when her house was still perched on its ridge, before the forests were stripped and the land flooded, they had stayed after they were supposed to have gone. They had come to her, they had been healed, and then they had lingered outside the house, hidden.

The sun set. The moon rose.

They crouched behind a fern, or among the large, knobby roots of a cypress—a safe enough distance into the forest that the crocodile could not reach them, and they watched as the crocodile bride walked down the ridge and through the trees, to the narrow crescent beach, and undressed.

They watched as she slipped into that water and glided out into the bayou, watched as the crocodile and the woman he loved swam circles around each other.

(*Was she afraid?* Billy asked.
Oh, no, she was never afraid. Would you be?
I don't know, said her son. He paused. *Yes.*
Yes. Me too.)

Eventually, most forgot about her all together. They forgot to tell the stories. They had long ago forgotten to seek her out.

But if one thing loves us—a child, a crocodile—then we stay alive, and so the crocodile bride went on living in her little red house.

As you know, she lives there still.

If someone wants to find her, they can to this day.

So long as the little boat is still there on the shore, so long as it's not so overgrown with muscadine that it's entirely hidden, then a person can simply climb into that boat (so small it seems almost made for a child) and paddle toward the cypress swamp that grew up in the center of the bayou.

So long as this person drops something precious in the water for the crocodile, then they'll reach the little red house.

They may not *see* the crocodile bride anymore, but they'll feel her warm hands on their body, and she will, as she always has, understand their pain, and mend the wound they desire mended.

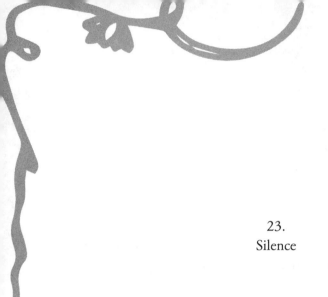

23.
Silence

July 1982

T he day before the lightning storm, Sunshine turned twelve.

Aunt Lou had her over for pancakes in the morning. Nash ate with them and said, "Happy birthday, Sunny! How old are you? Wait, wait." Nash paused and scratched his unshaven chin. "Okay. Best guess. Fifty-two?"

"Twelve," she said through a mouthful of pancakes so it came out, *Chweff.*

"Ah yes. *Chweff,*" Nash said, nodding.

Sunshine laughed harder, clapping her hand across her mouth.

"Don't make her choke," Aunt Lou cautioned Nash. "Not on the poor girl's birthday, at least." Aunt Lou was getting more Sunny Delight from the refrigerator, something that was too sugary, she said, but that she'd bought just for today. A birthday treat. Sunshine didn't even like the taste so much as she liked the name. Sunny Delight for Sunshine.

"All right, but seriously," Nash said. "*Twelve?* Good god. The years've been hard on you, huh?"

Aunt Lou rolled her eyes. Sunshine did start to choke, then, and Nash reached over and pounded her on the back. Aunt Lou said, "Drink this," and pushed the refilled glass of Sunny Delight into her hands.

Billy had already left for the day and had not yet had a chance to say happy birthday or give her a present or anything. Last year he had given her the red goggles and a birthday card she kept on her dresser. He'd woken her up before he left for work and made them egg-in-a-basket sandwiches and coffee with milk and sugar and he sat down to eat with her as the sun rose and cast pink-gold light through the porch screen and into the living room.

She thought he probably forgot this year, and she'd walked across Only Road with a lump in her throat, but when she saw that Aunt Lou had made pancakes and that Nash had made a tinfoil birthday hat (which he took off his own head and attached to hers), her about-to-cry feeling went away. After they finished breakfast, Aunt Lou handed her a box wrapped in newspaper and tied with a yellow ribbon.

Sunshine shook the wrapped present, shoebox-sized.

She thought she knew what was inside, but the package was rattling and she didn't want to be disappointed. She told herself it was probably just a book. Aunt Lou was beaming at her and Nash was watching, too, his eyes smiley in the way that Billy's could sometimes get.

Inside the shoebox were the banana-yellow Converse All Stars. She gasped. "Aunt Lou!" she said.

"Well. It was no big deal."

Stuffed inside the All Stars was the source of the rattling: boxes of Runts and Nerds—all treats Sunshine was never allowed to eat unless, like the Sunny Delight, it was a birthday or unless Billy brought them home for her and made her promise not to tell Aunt Lou. She put on the shoes—a bright, clean banana-yellow, free of red dust or red mud or scuffs from pavement or the smell of Joanna Louise's feet, which had always been the first to occupy any shoes Sunshine wore—right there at the table, then Nash gave her a Mason jar filled with seashells he had found on the property where he was renovating the house; he said they were there from a time forever ago when ocean had covered the land here. He said if Sunshine was still alive when the ocean eventually made it all the way back up here, then she could dump the seashells back in the water. "For now," he said, "they're yours to keep, and I heard shells bring good luck." He shoved another bite of pancakes in his mouth and winked at her.

"Did you see your daddy this morning?" Aunt Lou asked. "He wish you a happy birthday before he set off?"

Nash gave Aunt Lou a funny look, and Sunshine wondered again if Aunt Lou suspected or perhaps even knew about the secrets this summer. Suddenly the tightrope walkers were back in her belly again, kicking their legs high, showing off.

She looked at her yellow shoes and clicked her heels together like Dorothy.

"Yes, ma'am," she lied. "He gave me two new books, and also a necklace."

"Well, that's nice," Nash said. "Isn't that nice, babe?"

"Yes. Sounds like a nice gift, sugar." Aunt Lou's voice sounded far away, though. "Hey, look—I know those shoes are a little too big but it's so you can grow into them. I bet even by the time school starts, they'll be just right. I think you're going through a growth spurt."

"Thanks," she said, and for some reason she didn't understand, she was choked up, her eyes filling with tears.

Aunt Lou said, "Oh, sugar! Birthdays always get me emotional too." She came over to Sunshine and pulled her up against her chest, against the peach-colored terrycloth, soft against Sunshine's cheek.

• • •

UNDER THE DIN OF running water and clinking dishes as Nash cleared their birthday breakfast, Lou told her niece to go on and take a shower or a bath. "I don't mean to nag, sugar, but your hair could stand upright on its own." Sunshine, still wiping at her eyes after her sudden bout of tears, had—to Lou's relief—laughed.

Maybe, Lou thought, Sunshine was hormonal—maybe she was already going to get a period. It was early, but possible. Would Sunshine even know what it was, when it finally happened? She would have to discuss this with her at some point, what it was and what it meant. But for reasons she had never understood herself, discussing sex, discussing body parts in general, had long stirred up so much embarrassment—so much shame, really—in Lou that she'd always avoided these types of conversations. Joanna Louise was her curious one; Lou had caught her reading books at the library. She knew her daughter knew plenty. Knew enough, anyway.

Sunshine was different—she was so sweetly innocent. She followed rules. If there were questions to be asked or knowledge to seek, she wouldn't seek it out on her own.

Lou resolved to discuss it with her soon, now that she was twelve years old.

She stood on her tiptoes to kiss Nash on the cheek, then left him to finish the dishes and went to get herself dressed.

Afraid to ruin her own good mood, she brushed aside any less pleasant thoughts that had been fluttering at the edges of her mind. Like moths at a window screen.

• • •

THAT NIGHT, SUNSHINE HEARD Billy's truck out front, and she didn't run to her bedroom and close the door as she had done earlier this summer. The banana-yellow Converse All Stars and the jar of seashells and the fact that it was her birthday had lifted her mood. The yellow house was still mostly clean. Robert Johnson was singing about giving his soul to the devil, and she had put wet laundry on the line outside, which is what she and Billy never remembered to do, and she felt accomplished and grown up. Nash had slipped her five dollars when Aunt Lou wasn't looking and said to buy herself a treat, and she'd bought milk and a box of Lucky Charms and peanut butter at the Lust, and Big Jake accepted her $5 and didn't mention Billy's tab. Sunshine told him it was her birthday, too, and he gave her a Dum Dum and let her take a free bottle of root beer, and she drank it on the walk back down Only Road, the paper bag full of milk and cereal hooked in one arm and pressed against her chest, the sweating bottle of root beer in her other hand. She'd walked barefoot so as not to dirty her new shoes, and only when she stepped inside the yellow house and set down the milk and cereal and peanut butter, did she put them on again.

When she heard Billy arrive home, she thought maybe her own mood might carry over into him in the way that, if a grown-up was in any given mood it carried over into her, too, and she could feel what they felt right in the center of her chest.

Billy kicked off his boots on the porch then came through the door. He walked into the kitchen and she turned to smile at him, a big birthday grin. But he didn't smile back at her, and she could see he was tired, or maybe even sick. His forehead was knit in a scowl, and his face looked splotchy and red and a little puffy.

He set a bottle of bourbon on the counter, took a glass from the cabinet, and walked with both the bourbon and the glass past Sunshine and back to his bedroom.

She had been stupid not to notice, she thought, that it had been storming in the yellow house that day before Billy even set foot in the door tonight.

She let her cheek fall to one side and rest against the cool Formica table. She could see the dingy butterfly stain on the linoleum. It fluttered its ugly brown wings once, then twice, then gave up and settled back in its place.

From the record player, Robert Johnson sang out:

Tell me, milkcow, what on earth is wrong with you?
Now, you've left you a calf, hoo hoo
And your milk is turnin' blue

. . .

JOHN JAY BOUGHT THE record player not long after he lectured Catherine about their finances (which were never, in fact, as bad as he liked to claim). He treated it like a prized pet, brushing it with a feather duster on weekends, checking the settings before placing a record gingerly on the turntable.

He treated it with far more love and care than he treated his wife or his children, who were allowed to touch neither the records nor the record player itself.

He preferred Big Band music—Kay Kyser and Glenn Miller and Benny Goodman. When he listened to his music, it was always with a drink in hand, and usually in the same place he always sat when he was home—a La-Z-Boy he had bought several years ago (without consulting Catherine, he'd taken the chair that had been there—a green, raw silk club chair Catherine had found at a furniture store in Nashville—and driven it to the dump).

The La-Z-Boy was upholstered in a brown nubby fabric. It not only didn't match the rose-pink sofa—and was, Catherine privately thought, unfathomably hideous—but was also too large for the little room.

One Christmas morning—Billy twelve and Lou ten, both young enough to still be excited about the promise of unwrapping gifts and eating sweet treats and the pleasure of being near their Christmas tree— John Jay sat in the chair like a throne, his screwdriver cocktail in hand, the record playing Christmas music.

The music, Catherine noted that morning, made the little house feel bright and cheerful. That whole season had been unusually cold, with flat gray skies in the afternoon and a brisk wind that blew down Only Road and slammed the screen door, with its long-broken latch, open and closed at random. But inside the house that Christmas morning, it was cozy, pleasantly noisy, the children in high spirits.

Catherine had stayed up late the night before stuffing stockings for Billy and Lou. A new baseball, a set of colorful hair ribbons. Candy canes and oranges and milk chocolate. She'd set out a stocking for John Jay too. She always did. She filled it with packs of Werther's Original and the aftershave he liked and a soap-on-a-rope. She included in his stocking small bottles of liquor (two bourbons, one vodka) as though to say to him: *I fear nothing.* At the very top of the stocking, she put a card she'd bought and had the children sign.

Billy wore pajamas and sat cross-legged on the floor. His hair was dark and wild and needed trimming. Lou was curled up on the sofa next to Catherine, wearing one of Billy's old Little League sweatshirts (ST. CADENCE WILDCATS: 1956 CHAMPIONS) over her nightgown.

John Jay opened his gifts with small grunts of what, Catherine assumed, was meant to be pleasure. That morning, he had poured himself the first of his drinks, put *Kay Kyser: A Big Band Christmas* on the turntable, then settled himself in his bathrobe in the La-Z-Boy.

His feet, to Catherine's dismay, were bare.

John Jay's toenails had developed fungus in recent months that turned them a strange color and texture, like raw wood, and the sight of them made Catherine's stomach churn. He wore only briefs under the bathrobe, and the robe had slipped open to reveal a wedge of hairy white thigh. Catherine could tell that by the second screwdriver he was beginning to feel tipsy, no longer bothering to close the gap in the robe. He nodded his head back and forth as his Big Band Christmas records played. He rose only to flip the record; when he needed a refill after the second drink, he held the glass toward Catherine expectantly.

The children and John Jay finished unwrapping their presents, and the children gave Catherine the handmade ornaments and cards they'd made in school, and she'd immediately hung them on the tree and taped the art work to the refrigerator, claiming she had never received better gifts. When she came back to the living room, she reached under the small Christmas tree in the corner and pulled out a package. On it was written, TO MY WIFE. LOVE, JJ.

"For me?" she said to John Jay. Her children looked to her and then their father.

John Jay only stared at his wife with red-rimmed eyes. When he'd been drinking his eyelids had a way of dropping lazily, almost halfway closing, and the effect of his staring was not one of sleepiness but coldness.

She knew, though, he wouldn't disagree with her—not about this—in front of the children, and she unwrapped the gift and revealed a small velvet box, then pulled from inside of it a silver necklace with a small silver seashell on the end. She looked at her husband and smiled at him. "You shouldn't have."

John Jay paused, just for a moment. He stared at her. "Of course," he said, and cleared his throat. "Merry Christmas."

She rose from her seat on the floor and stood at the arm of the La-Z-Boy. John Jay looked up at her. For a moment he looked almost scared.

"That's sweet, Daddy," Lou offered.

"It is sweet," Catherine said. She was pushing it, she knew, but she didn't care. She bent down and kissed her husband's cheek, his whiskers rough under her lips. He smelled of vodka and yesterday's cologne. Then she went to sit beside her daughter, who clipped the necklace on for her.

John Jay watched from over the rim of his cocktail glass. The knowledge that he had not bought the present for her at all, but that she had bought and wrapped it and written out its loving note, swelled between them.

She let it swell.

In truth, she had put the present under the tree mostly for her children—so they would think their father had done something kind—and she had done it for herself, too, so she would have a gift to open on Christmas morning. But she could have, she knew, told John Jay about it in advance. She could have whispered, *I bought something for myself. Just go along with it.* Instead, she let the moment surprise him, and she sensed his humiliation. That he not only had bought her nothing, but that she had taken him off his guard.

She couldn't help herself. She hadn't anticipated it, but now she sensed the power this moment afforded her, and she reveled in it.

Her children collected the bits of wrapping paper, and Billy took it all out to the trash bin on the side of the house. Lou asked her mother if she'd make cinnamon buns. Billy stretched out on sofa and read the new Archie comic books that Lou had given him.

John Jay didn't hold the glass out to his wife expectantly, this time; he rose to pour another drink and then, still in his bathrobe, took it to the porch. He spent the rest of the morning there, despite the cold, and the holiday inside the yellow house continued on inside at a steady, cheerful hum, the best any day there had felt in a long while.

But john jay did not let his private humiliation go.

He didn't strike her, or yell, or belittle. He did not hold her down and climb on top of her in bed that night, as he had done so many others. In some ways, his behavior after Christmas wasn't unusual. For the remainder of the holiday season and on into the new year, he spent most of his nights out and came home smelling of women's perfume and liquor. Before work in the morning, he spiked his coffee with whiskey. This all had become common enough by then. The difference was the complete and total silence.

Silence like a well-sharpened knife. Silver and gleaming.

He did not hit her, pick a fight, or scoff when she spoke. He didn't say, *Hey dummy* or *Woman*. He didn't yell at her to hurry up in the bathroom. If he sat down with his family at the little Formica table for dinner, he made his usual complaints about the food to his children, not to Catherine directly. (They looked nervously from their father back to her, saying nothing.) In the morning, when she offered a timid greeting, a comment on the weather, a question about how he'd like his toast or his eggs, he didn't reply.

He simply acted, day after day, as though she wasn't in the yellow house at all.

At first, Catherine took a kind of pleasure in knowing she'd at least reached him—that she had punished him in some way. That he could do nothing of significance about it because to do so would be to humiliate himself further in front of his own children, to admit, even if indirectly, that she had outsmarted him. In doing so, he might have to admit that he hadn't once, since they'd been married, bothered to give his wife a gift on Christmas.

But when early in the new year he lay down beside her in bed at night, reeking so powerfully of the liquor and perfume and cigarette smoke that her sinuses stung, and said no word to her at all—not an insult, not a pass at her—and did not reach out to touch her or even to harm her, she found herself overcome by a sadness she hadn't known since the months after her mother had died.

WEEKS LATER, WHEN JOHN Jay slid into bed beside her late one night, she could take it no longer. It was nearly February. How much longer did he intend to go on punishing her?

"John Jay," she whispered. As usual there was nothing, though she knew he was awake. "John Jay. You can't go on forever like this. Pretending I'm not here. Pretending I don't exist."

Still, nothing.

Tears rose abruptly and spilled over. She was suddenly shaking.

She sat up. "Can't you *say* something?" she said, forgetting to whisper, forgetting that her children might hear. "Can't you say anything to me? Don't you know I only want your attention? Your love? Don't you know that? Can't you just bring it in yourself to *q* at me—to show that I'm here? That I exist? That I'm your goddamn wife?"

But his back was to her like a wall. He was so still and breathless that she knew he had not fallen asleep, and yet still he refused to reply.

Eventually, she turned over, buried her face in her pillow, and wept. She did not remember falling asleep, and in the morning, when she finally woke, both the children and John Jay had already left for the day, and the yellow house was quiet.

THAT AFTERNOON, CATHERINE SORTED through a stack of mail she had let accumulate during those last weeks. She opened the letters with the brass blade with the mother-of-pearl handle—aware, as she always was, of the absence of her mother's letters. Although it had been nearly a decade, some part of her still wished for, if not expected, just one more letter. Perhaps describing the coldness of winter in Portland. Telling her news of her *gentleman caller*. Describing a dance she had attended. Suggesting they plan another visit.

She put the bills in one stack, coupons in another.

Her eyes were still puffy and raw from crying the previous evening. She tried to will herself to forget what had happened between her and John Jay: her desperate begging. His insistent silence.

She set the letter opener down on the stack of mail, and she suddenly remembered the way she had let bits of truth slip into the conversations with her mother. She had never told her mother the full truth, about John Jay's beatings, about the way he lorded over their household, but there had been hints.

And her mother's gift to her had been a sharp blade. Had Margaret Bell meant for her to use it to defend herself? It had only ever occurred to her to harm herself.

Not her husband.

She fingered the edge of it, but only the point was sharp, surprisingly so. She pressed her finger against it until the skin broke, and a small bead of blood appeared. She winced.

It was a ridiculous, morbid thought. Catherine knew that if her mother had intended her daughter to do anything about John Jay, it would have been to simply stay in Portland with her—not to harm anyone. The letter opener was simply a letter opener. A gift with a meaning understood by the two of them.

Outside the kitchen window of the yellow house, snow had started to fall—something she hadn't seen since that visit to Tennessee. She went to the sink and leaned her hips against its edge and gazed at the snow drifting over the weedy backyard. Not far beyond rose the piney woods, a hushed blue-green—and the color of those pines also reminded her of Tennessee, of the rolling hills and the mountains that rose in the distance on the long drives to the river with her father.

Catherine turned abruptly from the window, as though she had remembered something she needed to get, right then, and walked out to the screened porch. She walked with purpose down the steps and toward the woods where Only Road abruptly ended. She had not put on a coat or shoes; she wore only the loose dress and fur-lined moccasins she wore around the house and the blue sweater her mother had given her years ago—but she didn't notice the cold. She walked down the path, snowflakes catching in the blue fibers of her sweater. She realized, as she walked, that she was still holding the letter opener, and she slipped it into the pocket of her dress.

Although she walked briskly, with confidence, she didn't actually consider where she was going—only that she wanted to walk through the woods that were the color of Tennessee, and that she wanted to smell the snowflakes and let them fall in her hair and on her tongue as she'd once done, laughing, with her mother. And so when she passed the wider path that veered toward the lake and instead took one of the narrow pig paths some still used for hunting, she did not even notice, really. She walked and walked. Her bare legs grew cold but she didn't much mind; she hugged her sweater more tightly against her and kept on.

The snow grew heavier; it frosted the oak leaves and gathered along the path, softly crunching under the rubber soles of her slippers.

She remembered the previous evening—how she had wept and begged, how John Jay had kept his rigid back turned toward her, how she had seen the glow of his white undershirt in the darkness, how her nose had burned from the smells caught in his clothing and hair. But the memory seemed to bury itself under the falling snow; the shame of it grew fainter.

Then, suddenly, Catherine realized the sky had turned darker.

It was already early evening.

The snow was still falling. With the realization of how long she'd been walking, she realized, too, that she had indeed grown cold; she was shivering. Snow had gathered on the exposed skin of her feet, melted, and run into the fur-lined slippers, the soles of which had cracked in the course of the afternoon. She looked back down the path and saw it did not look like a path at all, but dense woods. She must have strayed from the path at some point, or else it was narrower than she'd first noticed and was hidden by a thin layer of snow, blue in the fading light.

She turned to go back in that direction—she could follow her own footsteps, she thought, but they were hard to see in the coming twilight, and with the snow falling over them. The trees around her seemed thicker and taller than she remembered; she realized, snapping out of her cold daze, that she'd stumbled into a cypress grove. It felt quiet and comforting among the huge old trees, with the red of the tree bark and the blue-white snow. Then through the trees, through the dying light, she glimpsed water.

She felt a wave of relief.

She had come to the lake, and all she'd have to do would be to follow the curve of it back to the beach—then she'd know plainly enough how to return to Fingertip. She just had to keep the water in her sight, was all, and she'd make her way back to familiar woods easily enough.

And so she stepped carefully down the shallow bank, slipping here and there on the snow, pressing her palms against the trees for balance, toward the dark water.

THE CHILDREN WERE still awake, though it was after midnight. They had waited up for her, the bedroom light still on, and she left her wet shoes on the porch and went straight to them.

Her bedroom door was closed and there was no light coming from under the door. John Jay must have gone to sleep.

She was no longer shivering, despite the cold. Her cheeks were flushed with warmth. Quietly, she pushed open the children's bedroom door.

"Hello," she whispered. "Little night owls." She closed the door behind her.

She curled in bed with Lou, the mattress groaning beneath her weight as she adjusted herself, pulling the covers up around them both. Outside the window over Lou's bed, the snow had stopped falling.

"Where did you go?" asked Lou.

Catherine pulled her daughter close. She kissed her on the cheek, once and then twice. She held her close against her, tightly, until Lou squirmed away.

"*Mama*," Lou protested. "Where were you?"

Although he no longer asked for stories, she could sense Billy listening from the other side of the room, on the other side of the sheet with the blackberry vines.

THE WATER WAS WIDER and blacker than I'd imagined.

There in the center, just as I've described before, was an island, and on that island was a little red house. A breeze was blowing, and tiny waves blew across the surface of the water. Snow blew into my eyes. I could see that in a window of the house, a candle glowed.

(Billy's voice rose from the other side of the curtain but she didn't hear what he said.

Billy! Lou grumbled. *Stop interrupting.*

Her Lou, her Lou Lou Littles, her head resting in the crook of Catherine's arm. Catherine's hand was in her hair, stroking the tangled curls.

Shh, she told Lou. *Let him talk. What is it, Billy?*

I said: *Did you have a gift for the crocodile?*)

I DID; I HAD, in the pocket of my sweater, a letter opener with a brass blade and a mother-of-pearl handle, and knowing my life might very well depend on it, I didn't hesitate—I threw it into the water, and then I climbed into the little blue boat, and I rowed toward the little red house.

(*What was she like?* Lou whispered.

It's not true, said Billy, but Catherine could hear he was not so sure.)

BUT I CAN'T TELL you what she was like; you have to imagine for your-self. I can only tell you that I went. I tossed into the water my gift; I heard the heart beating from under the earth; I saw the candle in the window.

Those who go see the crocodile bride know better than to tell of the details afterwards. What she offers is exactly why you go in the first place, isn't it? So the story belongs to you, and you alone.

But you can imagine it—can't you, my littles?

Can't you imagine stepping inside that little house, and the flickering candlelight, and its comfort and warmth?

WHEN SHE EMERGED FROM her children's room and went into her bed-room, she could see through the darkness the shape of John Jay, perhaps asleep; she couldn't tell.

Exhausted, not bothering to undress, she slipped under the covers beside him. His back was to her again, but it didn't matter.

Then, at last—after over a month of silence—he spoke. "I thought you left," said his voice in the darkness. It was strange; it sounded so thin. "I thought you weren't coming back."

It was something of what she'd longed for, in those weeks of silence: for him to admit, even indirectly, that he cared. But she was aware that his admission wasn't complete. It wasn't exactly what she'd wanted—it wasn't that he cared for *her*. He'd feared that he'd been left alone, without a spouse. Without someone to watch the children. He cared for himself, and for himself alone.

She'd come back to the yellow house that night and stood under the oak branches in the yard, all of it dusted with snow. She'd looked up at the house and seen the light of her children's bedroom glowing warmly. Although it was cold, she was no longer shivering. In the bed now she could feel, in the center of her chest, an openness—as though something ugly had been rooted out and left behind a small open space. An empty bowl to be filled.

Not with useless longing for someone who would never know how to love. Not with the rage that had, for years, risen up inside of her when she was alone, so that, driving to the Piggly Wiggly, say, and glimpsing at a stoplight a bruise on her forearm, she'd find herself taken over by an urge to scream. She'd bend forward and scream so loudly, and for so long, that she frightened herself. Her throat would turned raw and hoarse. Her shoulders would cramp; the muscles of her stomach would ache. And each time afterwards, she'd find herself crying.

But that night when she returned to the yellow house, she simply didn't care what her husband did or didn't say. She had no words left for him, anyway. She'd given them to her children. She'd give them to her children again and again. She'd fill that bowl only with love for them.

For Billy and Lou. Her littles.

When she slept that night, she dreamed of flickering candlelight, of a warm hand pressed upon the center of her chest.

24.
Hidden Things

July 1982

O n her way home from her day shift that Friday after Sunshine's birthday, Lou stopped at the Lust for a bottle of wine to take with her to the new house. There was a lightning storm predicted tonight, and already a warm breeze was blowing up Only Road. Lou thought she could feel the prickling of electricity already in the air.

Lightning storms happened almost weekly in mid- and late summer, but a lightning storm coming up from the south at night was a special kind of sight. You could see it from the big front window at the Lust: The treetops at the end of Only Road laced against a sky turned backward in time, from the velvet-black night to the hushed blue of twilight in bright, shuddering bursts.

When the storm spread itself out over Fingertip and then over the old farm fields across the tracks, you could see from the window, too, the great bolts of lightning like reaching claws.

Lou vividly remembered the lightning parties from her childhood. This was back when the houses on Only Road were not yet boarded up—their frames so heavy with humidity they bowed out, the houses growing rounded and plump, like aging bellies—and most everyone in Fingertip gathered at the Lust. The grown-ups drinking, the children kneeling on folding chairs, pressing their foreheads against the glass windows.

These nights had been filled with excitement and fear, with the sense that anything could happen.

Little Jake was still alive back then and in fact had started the tradition. He stayed open as late as it took for the storm to pass so folks could walk safely home, and if he'd had enough bourbon, he'd stay open later still, and the kids fell asleep in their mothers' arms, or on top of the pool table, or else they raced home through the storm before their parents were ready to come with them.

There had been other children, then. They ran barefoot, slipping in the red mud, holding hands with each other to protect against the haints they'd been told might snatch a child awake after bedtime. On dimly lit front porches the children wiped the mud from their feet and their legs with the rags their mothers kept folded by the door, whispering prayers against any evil that may have snuck inside their darkened houses while no one was at home.

Lou remembered being very young and standing with Billy against the window of the Lust and realizing that he was scared. She remembered their mother appearing at their side and the clinking of beer bottles and loud, raucous laughter in the Lust and the drumming of rain on the roof, and Billy burying his dark head in their mother's pink skirt. She remembered the way Catherine had knelt and gathered him close to her and said, "It's all right, Billy. It's just a storm."

The last time Lou had been to a lightning party—she had taken Lou and Sunshine there several summers ago, just before a nighttime storm had broken loose—it had not felt as it once had. It had been, in fact, hardly a party at all, despite how Big Jake had turned the music up loud. A handful of the neighborhood men sat at the bar. The place had felt large and empty, made more so by the too-loud music, and she'd noticed how shabby the building had grown. The smell of mildew in the bathroom. Its buckled, mold-spotted posters of John Wayne and Marilyn Monroe.

Lou had drunk a single beer and chatted with Big Jake, but Joanna Louise and Sunshine had grown bored, slouching and sleepy on the barstools, and when the rain slowed, the three of them had walked home.

Still, even now, carrying the white zinfandel to the register, Lou felt the familiar sense of excitement.

And then all at once, she was yearning not just for the feeling of those lightning parties but for her mother. For her comforting presence, her ready arms and soothing words. For a moment Lou could almost see her, sitting at one of the wood-paneled tables, drinking a sloe gin fizz. Her mother had never been a big drinker, but she came along to the lightning parties and ordered a drink, or sometimes two, to try and be a part of things.

Then Lou's longing deepened further and she missed Joanna Louise, who wouldn't be home for another two-and-a-half weeks.

It was too much, missing the two of them like this. It was like a blade in her breastbone, so painful that a quiet grunt escaped her mouth. Big Jake looked up from behind the counter and said, "You all right, honey?"

THAT MORNING OVER BREAKFAST, Nash had suggested to Lou that they spend the night in the new house. And like a child excited to show off his items for show and tell, he listed the ways he'd already begun to prepare. He'd brought a mattress inside and put fresh sheets on it. He'd already bought gin and ice for the cooler. Later he would make cold chicken sandwiches—"What do you think, babe?"—and potato salad, and he'd have chips and some kind of dessert. "I got everything but the dessert," he said. "But I'll figure that part out."

"Good Lord," Lou had said, rinsing clean their cereal bowls. "Are you feeding an army?"

Nash patted his belly and said, "Well, babe, I'm a growing boy."

Her plans with Nash felt comforting enough that, arriving back home with the wine, the pain in her breastbone began to dull. She showered, scrubbing the smell of fryer grease from her hair and skin, then put on the green polka-dot dress. She used the product Deborah had given her so her curls dried in soft, pretty waves. Sunshine stopped by and lingered in the doorway of the bedroom as Lou leaned toward her reflection in the dresser mirror, putting on makeup. Sunshine seemed to like watching her get ready these days; Lou wondered if Sunshine was starting to get interested in makeup the way JL had around her age (though Lou hadn't allowed JL to wear it).

Sunshine's presence felt comforting, and the sadness Lou had felt so acutely at the Lust further receded.

"Which lipstick?" she asked, and held up two different tubes.

"The pink," Sunshine said. "You look real pretty."

"*Really*. Not real. And thank you."

Lou blotted her lips on a tissue. Outside the bedroom window, the sky was thick with clouds, the air still and gray, as though bracing itself for the coming storm. "There's a lightning party tonight," she said. "Maybe you and your daddy could go on up to the Lust."

"You're not going?" Sunshine asked, and Lou glanced over to see Sunshine had braced all four limbs against the door jamb and was now balanced so her head craned sideways against the top of the frame.

"Girl, please get down."

Sunshine dropped to the floor. She leaned her back against the door jamb, instead. Hands tucked behind her back.

"What'd you get into today?" Lou asked. "Do anything fun?"

Sunshine shrugged. "I started *The Summer of the Falcon*," she said.

"You did?" Lou said, touched. She'd tried to encourage Joanna Louise to read it a couple summers back, but she had said it was boring. "That was one of my favorites when I was your age." Lou paused. "Well, I guess a little older than you. But do you like it?"

Sunshine shrugged. "I like it. I'm not that far along. What're you getting ready for?"

Lou examined herself in the dresser mirror: shoulders tan and freckled. Under the green fabric, her breasts (smaller than she'd like). Her hips (wider than she'd like—though they did look nice with the dress, the way it curved and draped). "I'm going to the new place with Nash tonight. We're having an indoor picnic."

Sunshine's face brightened. "Oh! Can I come?"

Lou did want her to come; she felt a strong urge to bring her along.

"Well, sugar, I would actually really like that, but it's kind of a date. Just the two of us." And then she added: "You'll be all right here."

Never one to talk back, Sunshine nodded. "Okay," she sighed. Disappointed.

Later, Lou would wonder why she didn't phrase it as question—will you be all right here? Why she said the words as though patting down a blanket around Sunshine. Tucking her in. You'll be all right.

"Hey," Lou said—and these next words, too, she would wonder about later. "Is your daddy home?"

"Yeah," Sunshine said. She was gripping both sides of the door frame and bending all the way back so that she looked at Lou from upside down. Sun-bleached hair hanging down.

It had been weeks since Lou had seen Billy, since they'd stood on either side of the screen door and fought. Whether or not he'd told Sunshine about her invitation to watch the space shuttle land, Sunshine never had shown, and Lou had stood in front of the Magnavox and watched the distant white blur as it grew larger and then took form in a swath of clear blue sky.

"How's he doing?" she asked. She felt guilty for how things had gone in that last conversation. She felt guilty that she hadn't reached out at all since then.

But Sunshine, staring at her from upside down, said, "He hasn't been in a very good mood."

"Huh," Lou said, carefully applying mascara. Her general rule—often unsuccessful—was to ask questions about Billy while keeping her tone light enough that Sunshine didn't pick up on her concern. "Not in a good mood today, or for longer?"

Sunshine paused, moving side to side in the doorway, hair swinging. Her eyes were closed, and between being upside down and keeping her eyes closed, it was difficult for Lou, when she glanced over, to get a sense of what Sunshine might be thinking, might be feeling.

"Just today," Sunshine finally said.

Lou nodded. She took in a deep breath.

Billy's moods, they both knew, weren't just moods. They tipped easily into a depression so heavy and black that Lou had sometimes allowed herself to wonder if he shouldn't be hospitalized. Was that something people did anymore? Or perhaps he should at least *talk* to a doctor, something he hadn't done in decades so far as she knew. Not even for a checkup. "I can take care of my goddamn self," he'd say.

Perhaps it was that pain in her chest, that longing for absent family. For her mother. For Joanna Louise. Perhaps it was guilt that Sunshine wanted to come with her and she was leaving her with Billy, whose mood might be turning for the worse at this very moment, and perhaps it was guilt, too, that she wondered if their argument had in fact contributed to whatever mood he was in now. Whatever the reason, Lou decided she'd go make things right with him before she left for St. Cadence. She'd apologize. She'd reassure. "I didn't mean to insult you," she'd explain, and her humility and kindness would override his tendency to see the worst in her, to think she was, somehow, out to get him. She'd help pull him out of his mood.

"Hey," she said to Sunshine. "I've got a whole list of things I've been needing from the Lust and just cannot seem to remember to get. Wanna run on up there for me?"

Sunshine pulled herself upright and said, "Okay!" She loved running errands. She loved to please. She was like Lou in that way.

Lou wrote down things she needed and things she did not need and things she knew Sunshine would have to ask Big Jake to order for her, like vacuum bags, which she would normally just buy at the Piggly Wiggly. She wanted just a few minutes with Billy, enough to offer him an apology without Sunshine overhearing anything.

The last time she'd lost her temper with him—something she'd sworn she would never do again, not like that—Sunshine had been with her. Lou hadn't known it was going to happen. One minute she was checking on him, and the next she was pounding on his bedroom door. When she'd turned (her face wet with tears, her body shaking) to collect her niece, she'd seen that the crotch of Sunshine's blue pajama bottoms was dark. She'd wet herself. The sight had filled Lou with so much shame that she'd felt queasy and lightheaded—but she'd worried that saying anything to her niece, even words of comfort, would only embarrass her—and so she'd pretended not to see.

It wasn't that she anticipated fighting with Billy, now; she wanted to smooth things over. She was good at smoothing. (Usually. Just not in that last conversation, which had gone so awry.) But Sunshine didn't need to know that anything was wrong between them. She could protect her from that much, give her something do for a bit. Let the grown-ups have some privacy.

Lou watched from the living room window as Sunshine went barefoot up the road, list in hand, legs picking their way over the hardened mud. Then Lou stepped out on her porch, barefoot herself, and walked across the road to their old yellow house.

Heavy clouds had begun to crowd the sky over the woods, though over most of Only Road it was still bright. The evening light had turned golden. Far in the distance, she heard the low rumble of thunder. The big lightning storms, the ones that had once been worth gathering to celebrate at the Lust, often crept in slowly. The clouds like thick silver stuffing, the smell of rain in the air for hours before the storm broke.

She passed under the branches of the oak tree, its ashy moss blowing gently in the breeze, and toward the steps leading up to the yellow house.

She was aware, vaguely, of a quiet warning in her. Like a little elf beating on a little door.

WHEN SHE LEFT ROBERT Dalton to come home to Fingertip, Billy was already caring for Sunshine: a bald, three-month-old infant with a quiet disposition (even then, even as a baby). He didn't tell his sister the truth of how Sunshine had arrived, and she didn't ask. Too much time had passed, too much silent grief, for her to feel as though she could question her brother's private life, his heartaches.

Sometimes she wondered, though, if Billy's reluctance to share with her the truth of Sunshine's mother was a means of spiting Lou. Of saying, *You left me here when I needed you most—you went ahead and made your own goddamn life, and I went ahead and made mine.*

But she was surprised—shocked, even—by her brother's ability to care for a baby. By his devotion. By the way it seemed, in the years she had been gone, he had shed his black moods, the hard drinking. She could no longer make out the scars that had been scattered across his forearms when she'd last seen him.

It wasn't until his daughter was older—old enough to care for herself, more or less, old enough to climb through JL's window—that Lou saw that this side of Billy had in fact not disappeared at all. It had simply been lying dormant.

But that darkness was not to resurface for many years, and when she first returned to the yellow house, Billy seemed happy.

DURING THE DAY, LOU went to work at the 79 Dine and Billy went to work on the coast. They traded cars; she drove the truck and he took the shaggin' wagon with the car seats for the girls in the back, then dropped them off each morning with Jimmy Devereux's wife, Marie. (It had been Marie, in fact, who'd first shown Billy which car seat to buy for Sunshine, which baby formula, how to pat and shush Sunshine when she was crying.) On his lunch break he drove to Marie's to check on the girls. He held Sunshine. He used their kitchen phone to call the 79 and tell Lou how they were doing that day—that Joanna Louise ate all of her ham sandwich at lunch, that Sunshine had a good morning nap—and then he drove back to finish his shift.

When Sunshine was old enough, Lou showed Billy how to cut up turkey and green beans and sweet potatoes very small. He changed swollen, stinking diapers and clipped his daughter's tiny fingernails. He bathed her in the sink of the yellow-painted kitchen (holding her so carefully, running the washcloth over her so gently, that Lou teased him: *It's like you're washing fine china,* she said). At night, Billy laid his daughter in the double bed they had made by pushing their old twins together, right next to Joanna Louise, each side of the bed bolstered by gates that Billy had built himself to prevent either little girl from falling off.

He often sang to her: *You are my Sunshine, my only Sunshine.*

This was before Lou got the paperwork from the Laurents, who were relieved to release their old mortgage, however miniscule, to someone who could and would use the property—someone they had watched grow up right across the road. Until then, Billy slept in his room and the girls slept in Billy and Lou's old room. Lou slept on the pink sofa. Sometimes, when just starting to fall asleep, she thought she smelled her mother. The distinct smells of the coffee she made each morning and her gardenia perfume.

After her day shift, if she didn't bring home food from the diner, Lou made them dinner—mostly beans and hot dogs or canned spaghetti with meatballs—as Sunshine emitted soft, dissatisfied cries (but rarely more than that—she was always so quiet). To soothe his daughter during that disgruntled witching hour, Billy would dance around in the living room to the blues records he loved, Lead Belly and Louis Armstrong and Robert Johnson.

John Jay had once done the same to his Big Band records, though if he'd held his own children and danced along with them, neither remembered it. Instead, he'd hold his drink in one hand, close his eyes, and sway back and forth in the middle of the living room, the ice in his glass clinking—as though it was just him in the house and no one else.

Billy and Lou didn't discuss the memories of their own childhood. They didn't discuss anything but their own children, most often: bed times, meals, the frequency and texture of poops. Whose turn it was to run up to the Lust for the baby wipes or diapers or formula they'd asked Big Jake to start keeping in stock again—now that there were two children in a place where no children had lived since they'd been small themselves.

But Lou could sometimes feel it between them: an inexplicable nostalgia.

A yearning for a past that hadn't earned their yearning.

When the mood was right, she'd sometimes leave the beans or the hot dogs on the stove, scoop up JL in her arms, and dance along with Billy. Lead Belly sang, *Down here wonderin', would a matchbox hold my clothes? She says, Daddy, don't be worried like that!* And as she and Billy danced, each holding their daughters close against their bodies, nostalgia rose up like prayers from a congregation and filled the rooms of the yellow house.

It worked its way around the hulking brown La-Z-Boy and into the bright yellow kitchen; it slid underneath the pink sofa, where the dust bunnies gathered; it brightened the dingy front window. It filled the spaces in the yellow house so completely that—for that witching hour, at least—it displaced any tension, any grudges, any grief.

INSIDE THE SCREENED-IN PORCH, Lou peered through the screen door into the yellow house. Golden evening light spilled into the kitchen and part of the living room. She could see Billy at the kitchen table, a glass in front of him. The little portable television was turned to the news. She knocked—*shave and a haircut*. He didn't turn around and she thought maybe he couldn't hear her over the television.

Only upon entering the yellow house did Lou realize she had been afraid of what she might find, what Billy's mood might entail. She'd imagined dishes teetering in the sink. Filthy floors. But the little living room had been recently swept and it smelled of lemon oil—Sunshine's doing, probably. On the Formica table where Billy sat was only the television, a glass, and a bottle of bourbon.

Worry flickered in her chest like a candle flame. But she wasn't here to criticize. If her brother wanted to drink—it was a Friday night, besides—then so be it. She herself was looking forward to wine. What was the difference?

And she had come to apologize. To make right. To soothe, not stir.

Behind her, it was already growing darker. The thunder sounded no closer, but she heard a rush of wind through the oak leaves. Somewhere inside the house, the wind slammed a door shut. She flinched. Perhaps this wasn't one of the slow storms. Perhaps she shouldn't have sent Sunshine.

Billy either hadn't noticed her there or was ignoring her. It was hard to say. She felt awkward and hesitant.

Lou cleared her throat. "Hey," she said.

He turned to look at her, and grinned. She let out a breath. A smile in return. Things would be fine.

"Well hey there," he said. His hair had grown long this summer; it was nearly to his shoulders, dark and curling and peppered with gray. His bearded face was a bit drawn—but still handsome. His drinking had not ruined his looks in the way it did to some. Not yet. He nodded toward the television. "Lightning storm tonight," he said.

"I heard," she said, and crossed the living room. "It's started rolling in already."

The storm clouds still had not entirely passed over the sun to the west, and the kitchen was filled with light. It was a comfort. Lou pulled out a chair and sat with Billy. Channel 10 was showing the forecast for the weekend using little cartoon clouds and lightning bolts and, for tomorrow, a sun wearing a smile and sunglasses.

"Sunshine's running an errand for me at the Lust right now," she said. "Maybe you all should go on back up there for the party."

Billy laughed. "Not much of a party there these days," he said, his eyes on the television.

She smiled. "I guess that's true," she said, then impulsively stood again. She got a glass from a cabinet and went to the freezer for ice, but the trays were empty and something smelled rotten.

Billy turned down the television volume, then leaned back in his chair and watched as Lou took his bourbon and poured herself a glass. She took a small sip and winced. It burned her throat, but she felt a little more brave.

"Look," she said. "I feel bad about last week. About arguing with you. I wanted to apologize."

Billy looked down toward his glass. He ran one finger back and forth across the rim.

"I didn't mean to hurt your feelings. About taking Sunshine. I know she loves you, and if you'd rather keep her here with you, I of course understand."

Billy grunted. Or maybe scoffed. She wasn't sure. She looked at his face, trying to discern if he was angry or if he was hearing her, forgiving her, but it was hard to say with his eyes still downcast, watching his own fingers on the bourbon glass. Outside, the clouds passed over the sun and the kitchen fell into bluish shadows.

Lou felt a familiar pang. That snake, again. Arching belly-up. Where had it come from? She took a deep breath. "Are we good here?" she asked. "I can't tell if you're hearing me or not."

Despite the wind outside and the disappearing sunlight, it was hot in the little kitchen. For some reason, both the window over the sink and side door were shut. She could feel the fabric under her arms growing damp.

The light from the television flickered across Billy's face. "I'm hearing you," he said, nodding. When he finally looked up at her, she was surprised that his eyes didn't look angry—she had been bracing herself for anger, for some biting, blaming comment—but sad. In the flickering light from the television, they were glazed with tears. "I've got something

I feel bad about, too," he said, and he breathed deep. "Something I've been wanting to tell you."

Lou nodded.

"I lied," he said. "When I told you I got promoted. I got laid off, Lou."

She watched him, wondering at first if he was joking. But he was wiping at his eyes. Offering none of the venom he'd offered last time.

Why, then, was something in her swelling? Not sadness—she was in no mood to let herself cry, even at the sight of Billy's tears—something she hadn't seen since they were teenagers. She didn't understand it, the rising-up feeling, where it came from or why it brought a hot flush to her cheeks, why she was suddenly trembling.

"Why?" she finally said. "Why would you lie about that?"

But she knew the answer even as she asked: He must have known he'd disappoint. He'd known he was no better than what their father had told him he was so many times over. Lou could almost hear John Jay, drunk and angry for reasons no one could understand. His words intended to humiliate.

"Look," Billy said. "I'm trying to be honest now, at least. I'm trying to tell you the truth." He took another deep breath, and she could hear his earnestness.

It startled her.

She felt something inside of her, a door she hadn't known was open, slam shut.

"So you have no job?" she said, and she was startled, too, by the edge in her own voice. "No money? How're you paying bills? How're you buying groceries?"

She knew she was justified to ask these questions. He'd lied to her. And she knew, too, that what she found herself saying now would hurt him. The words came out anyway, as if of their own accord.

"How're you feeding your *daughter*, Billy?"

"Don't," he said, in a voice like a warning. "Don't talk about me and her like that."

"And you dared to give *me* a hard time?" she said, voice rising. "As if I'd said the wrong thing to even *ask* about her coming with us. But look at you. Look at all this."

She gestured toward the bourbon, but she meant more than that alone. She meant the lack of a job, the lack of money. The lying. She meant something she couldn't even define. Something that had started, perhaps, that night when she was sixteen and Billy had stepped from behind the blackberry sheet, when he had thrown his hands up and said, "I'm sorry. I'm sorry."

Lou pressed her palms flat on the Formica table, as though to steady herself in the chair. Billy crossed his arms over his chest and looked toward the window of the side door. It still was not raining, but the light had faded to a premature dusk. Billy was ready to back down, she saw— but Lou could feel it inside of her, a craving for a fight she'd come here to prevent.

The desire was overpowering.

"You were right about what you said before," she said, and though some part of herself, some small, quiet part tried to warn her, to say, *Slow down, hold on now,* her words were coming out faster than she could control them. "You were right that you're not so good at being her daddy."

The ghosts in the yellow house there with them. They were real; Lou could feel that now. She could feel them cheering on this bubbling, brewing, much longed-for release in a household of hidden things. Hidden sadness. Hidden rage. A household of secretly plucked blackberries and stories told at bedtime. Of a secret, swollen black eye behind the tinted shade of pink sunglasses. Of a secret tongue in a silent mouth.

"Don't talk about her," Billy said. His voice was low and shaky. "Don't talk like I'm not caring for her right! I love her. She's the only good thing in my life."

But Lou was past the point of feeling sorry for him. She didn't recognize the person leaning forward, eager to put Billy down. To hurt him. To devastate. And still, she couldn't seem to stop that person from saying more. "It isn't about love!" she shouted, and spittle flew from her mouth and landed on the table. "It's about doing the things that need to get done. Buying goddamn food instead of booze. Finding a job. Being a goddamn *adult.* What *happened* to you, Billy? I mean what really *happened* to you?"

She had stood up without even realizing it. She'd stood and was leaning forward, standing over Billy like she had once seen her father stand over her mother at this same table. (He'd leaned forward, he'd sneered, "Are you *stupid*, woman? Didn't I tell you to shut up?") Her forehead was tense; pain pulsed from somewhere just behind its center. Dull but persistent. Like a distant heartbeat.

"Look," she hissed, "We're moving next month, and that's it, that's it. I'm taking Sunshine with us. I'm taking her with us, Billy. And when you get your *shit* together, when you snap out of whatever *lifelong, down-and-out pathetic depression* you've been in, we can talk about a different situation. But until then, I don't keep on *worrying* that you're fucking her up. That you're fucking her up just like he fucked us up." Lou's whole body shook and her voice had grown so loud it felt as violent as if she were hitting, as if each word were a physical blow. "Do you hear, you *stupid* asshole? Do you fucking *hear me?*!"

Then she suddenly was hitting. She was standing over Billy, slapping his shoulders, his arms that had moved to cover his head, as hard as she could. His shoulders and his head and his arms.

She slapped wildly, furiously, punishingly.

He didn't move to get away. He only covered his head, hunching forward, as she hit and hit and hit.

When she was finally done, she could hear her own quickened heart pounding in her ears. She was panting. The kitchen was unbearably hot and still. Slowly, Billy moved his arms from his head. He looked up at her with wide green eyes, and her stomach churned. She remembered his face when John Jay would yell at them. His eyes like they were now. In them, real and irreversible heartbreak.

She had never in her life lost control like this. It was different than the time she knocked on Billy's bedroom door and yelled at him to get up, to pay attention. Different than the time she had smacked the girls when they were so late getting home she had almost called the police. Those outbursts had been brief and to the point. A brief bout of shouting, a *whap, whap, whap*, and she was done.

Her hands ached from the blows. She was suddenly aware of the sweat that trickled down the back of her neck.

Billy opened his mouth as though he was about to speak, and then closed it again. He was not looking at her anymore, but she continued to stare at him, unsure of what to do or say next.

Before she could speak, his lips began trembling.

"Billy—" she started, but it was too late. He pressed his face into both hands. He let out a single, terrible choking sound, and then his shoulders shook with sobs.

Stunned at her own behavior, at how cruel she'd been, Lou turned from Billy and saw that, standing just inside the front door, was Sunshine.

Eyes wide. Clutching grocery bags against her chest.

All was quiet but for the soft sounds of Billy crying.

Lou wanted to do something, anything, to make right what had just gone so wrong, but she had lost all ability to speak. She had nothing left. Only hot, sickly shame. Quietly, gently, she turned back to the table again, away from the sight of her niece, and picked up the chair that had fallen over. Hands shaking, she placed it neatly in its place. Then she walked past Billy and then past her niece, who would not look at her— who was staring, open-mouthed, at her crying father.

What had Sunshine seen? How much had she heard?

But Lou couldn't stand to know the answer. Instead, she kept walking out of the yellow house, down the steps, and across Only Road.

It wasn't yet raining. She wanted it to—she wanted to be soaked and shivering. To be exposed to the lightning overhead. But the thunder still sounded far away, and she saw only distant flashes of lightning over the tree line.

Inside, Lou gathered her shoes and her purse; she took the white zinfandel, opened it, and drank several warm gulps.

Then, still shaking, she carried her things to the car. She avoided looking at the yellow house. She drove up the red dirt road, the clouds hanging low overhead, the Spanish moss draped across the oak branches like tired old memories.

IT WAS NEARLY AN hour later when Lou pulled into the drive of the new house in an early twilight brought on by the storm clouds. Thunder clapped loudly and a strong wind blew back her hair as she climbed out of the car. Nash burst with enthusiasm from the front door, in faded blue jeans and an old football T-shirt with the number forty-two on it. The T-shirt dotted with countless holes.

He jogged down the gravel drive. "Baby girl!" he said. Grinning. Joyful at the sight of her. Then, drawing closer: "Babe? What is it?"

She pressed her face into his shoulder, wrapped her arms around his waist, and only then did the tears she'd been holding back—her throat aching and raw with the effort of restraining them—finally come out in guttural, aching sobs.

Nash said softly, "Whoa, hey now. Hey now," and wrapped his arms around her. He rubbed a palm up and down her back and swayed, slightly, side to side. He held her until she had emptied herself of tears, until she had taken several deep, shaky breaths, until the first drops of rain at last began to fall.

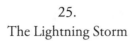

25.

The Lightning Storm

S unshine hadn't meant to come to the yellow house first.
　　　 She hadn't been paying attention. She was holding the groceries bags, careful not to drop them, and crunching on a Dum Dum, and
watching the dark clouds stretch like taffy overhead, dragging behind
them the rest of the storm.

She was thinking about middle school and the rumors JL had told
her. That kids smoked in the back by the dumpster. That someone had
given someone else a blow job. They were in JL's room one afternoon
after school, the windows open, an autumn breeze sending the sheer pink
curtains billowing like a woman's skirt. On the ceiling above Sunshine's
side of the room were stuck glow-in-the-dark stars. That afternoon was
one of the rare days that school year when JL still wanted to talk to her.
By winter, she was mostly ignoring Sunshine alltogether.

"So," said JL. She was lying on her stomach, facing Sunshine, her chin
resting on top of two stacked fists. "Do you even know what that means?"

Blow job. She did not know what that meant. Of course she didn't.
"Yes," she had lied.

What's a low-bay ob-jay? she added now to her imaginary scroll of questions for JL, and then she turned toward the yellow house, forgetting about the groceries she had meant to take to Aunt Lou's, and walked up the steps.

WHAT SHE HEARD WAS different than the time Aunt Lou had yelled in the hallway. Her voice was not only angry but mean. A sharp blade, aimed straight at Billy.

For the first time in her life, Sunshine thought her aunt was ugly.

Her eyes too small and her nose too big. Her face blotched red. When Aunt Lou passed by Sunshine at the door, Sunshine could feel the heat radiating from her body.

Now, Sunshine swallowed back the hard lump in her throat. Her legs felt wobbly and the tightrope walkers were in her belly again. Flipping forward and backwards. Doing cartwheels. A rain-smelling breeze blew through the screened porch and into the yellow house. She set the grocery bags down right there by the front door, trying not to make too much noise, and she went to her room.

Even from her room, she could hear Billy's deep, uneven breaths. It sounded like he'd stopped crying, but she wanted to plug her ears anyway.

A heavy breeze blew again, rustling the leaves in the oak outside her window, and the rain smell filled the green bedroom. Hands trembling, she took her banana-yellow All Stars out of their still-new box and put them on.

The rubber smelled new. The canvas was clean. The color was as bright as the yellow taffy Billy sometimes brought home for her from the coast (that Aunt Lou did not like her to eat, and so he always said, "Don't tell your aunt," and winked). Laffy Taffy shoes that made her feel somehow ready to return to the living room, where the groceries still sat. She could see Billy still at the table, his face still buried in his hands, though his shoulders weren't shaking anymore and his breathing had quieted. She picked up the grocery bags.

In the kitchen, Sunshine turned off the television and turned on the light. Billy wiped his face off inside the collar of his T-shirt.

"Hey, Fred," he said, and he sounded tired. "Were you there for all that?"

"It's okay," she said. "I'm not going with Aunt Lou, anyway. I don't like her. I'm staying right here. Okay?"

He laughed without smiling, and rubbed his forehead with his hands. Then he rose to use the bathroom, and Sunshine poured them drinks. She poured milk for her, from the carton Aunt Lou had just sent her to buy, and more bourbon for Billy. Sometimes she heard Aunt Lou say, "Oh why not, I deserve it," if she made herself a second drink. Sunshine told that to herself now: Why not? Billy deserved it.

She felt like a grown-up. She was doing the taking care.

Sunshine went out to the porch and set their glasses on the Florida orange crate, and then she went back inside and put away Aunt Lou's groceries. She didn't care if she was stealing, technically. She hoped Aunt Lou wouldn't be able to afford more and would feel hungry all week and be sick with remorse for how mean she'd been to Billy.

When Billy emerged from the bathroom, Sunshine took his hand. "Let's have a lightning party," she said, pulling him toward the porch. "We can watch it from the porch. Here, I poured you a drink."

She hadn't known how much to pour so she'd filled it to the top. When she handed it to him, he grinned, but he sat obediently in the rocker and he sipped it a little. She sat down in the rocker next to him and they looked out past the oaks at the charcoal sky. There were flashes of lightning here and there but she couldn't see any bolts yet, and only spits of rain came down. She glanced over at Billy now and then, making sure he was okay. Almost a grown-up in her bright new shoes. A grown-up taking care of things.

He looked at her, eyes bloodshot and puffy from crying. Maybe from bourbon too. She didn't know. But it didn't matter, anyway. All that mattered is that she helped him feel better. He said, "Thanks, Fred. Thank you."

WHEN THE STORM AT last began, great sheets of rain slammed the tin roof of the yellow house. The wind blew so fiercely it opened the screen door and slammed it again, startling them both. They jumped. Billy got up to latch the door closed and they laughed. Together, they watched as lightning turned the rain silver and illuminated the drenched branches of the oak. The bolts were huge and bright and deliciously frightening. Thunder shook the yellow house.

Sunshine noticed the tightrope walkers had ceased their back-and-forth. (Maybe they, too, were watching the storm. Standing in the open flap of the circus tent, in sequined leotards and yellow sequined tight-rope-walking slippers.)

The worst didn't last too long. The thunder rumbled on, but farther away now. The rain turned steady and rhythmic. And perhaps because, if she ignored the smell of bourbon and everything that had happened, the mood during the storm felt almost like a June mood. Or perhaps because Billy had laughed when they were startled by the screen door blowing open, or perhaps because she wanted for things to feel normal and right again, Sunshine stood from her own rocker and went to Billy and climbed onto his lap.

Since the spiders had first appeared, she'd avoided touching him, or asking for a story, or doing or saying anything much at all. But on the porch, wrapped up in the smell and sound of the rain, sensing the space that the sudden bout of laughter and weather had seemed to crack open between them, she was making things A-okay, Fred. She wanted her ges-ture—going to him, settling herself down on his lap—to say to Billy the things grown-ups said in movies: *Let bygones be bygones. Let's just sweep it under the rug.* She wanted her gesture to say, *See? I'm still your Sunshine, your only Sunshine, remember, Billy? Remember?*

She could hear Miss Collins telling her this choice was *inappropriate.* Shaking her head. Eyebrows knit with deep concern. But there was noth-ing to be scared of, nothing inappropriate. It was just Billy, her Billy. She took inventory:

Sad swollen eyes (he had cried so much).

A beginning-to-brighten mood (despite the bourbon).

Two hands (not spiders at all, she remembered—she was always remembering).

If her gestures were just so and she did not say the wrong thing, then the mood of their entire summer, as bruised and worm-chewed as the flesh of a rotting fig, would die off for good.

She thought that tomorrow it would feel the way it had first felt at the lake back in June (she was sure it would feel this way, if she did the right thing), with Aunt Lou reading magazines and Joanna Louise turning into an Oompa Loompa. With clouds on the horizon and a blue sky overhead. And later, an Irish jig in the kitchen, not for a promotion that had not actually happened but for fun, because it made them laugh. Tomorrow, there would be no stones, no spiders. No losing her red goggles on the other side of the yellow rope.

Her longing for this hoped-for tomorrow was so powerful it eclipsed all knowledge and lessons. (*Sunshine does not always pay attention during the lesson. She has an active imagination and she sometimes seems to drift off.*)

She made her mistake. She nestled her head against Billy's warm neck, and he wrapped his arms around her again, just like before, and she swallowed down the bile that rose swiftly, unexpectedly, in the back of her throat.

The thunder had receded far in the distance. Music from the Lust drifted down through the almost-darkness. The storm had passed and it was almost dark, the wet sound of rain dripping from the oak branches and eaves, the smell of it all around them. She told herself that everything was A-okay, that she would not throw up. His hands moved up her shirt. Rough human hands. She was holding her breath.

Then he did something he hadn't done before. He took one hand out from under her shirt and he turned her face gently to face to his, and then his mouth was on hers, pressing. Tongue pushing through.

She thought of what JL had written about kissing the boy at camp. About it feeling like putting your tongue through a Life Saver.

It was not like how JL said it was.

She tasted bourbon, and the slick wet tongue in her mouth felt huge, like a slug swollen with rain. For one brief moment, she had the foolish idea that she would get to brag to JL in the same way JL had bragged to her that she had felt it too. She had kissed someone.

But, no sooner had she considered the future opportunity to gloat than she remembered what JL had said about getting pregnant.

Sunshine could see it as clearly as she'd seen the grubworm Moss had once plucked from the earth under the fig tree. Curled up in her belly like a fat, milky noodle. Through the translucent tail, a dark mass visible.

She pulled away from Billy, suddenly. His face was close to hers, still open-mouthed. He looked at her dimly through his puffy eyes and he said, "Oh, shit, I'm sorry, Fred. I'm sorry."

But with the realization of the grubworm she felt something else too. It was not like tightrope walkers anymore. The circus tent—and the tightrope walkers in it—had blown away in the storm. It was a hot current in her, something electric. It ran through her whole body. Without thinking about making things A-okay or about Billy's feelings, she pushed herself off his lap and backed away from where he sat.

"Shit," he said again, like he was disappointed in something. His words were slurring, and she could tell now that he was very drunk. He started to stand up, but he stumbled, and quickly sat back down.

As his face moved in and out of shadow she could see it—that it wasn't Billy. She could see the liver spots. The wispy hair. The sallow skin on a hunched body.

"Hey, Sunshine, I'm sorry about that. Just forget it, okay?" but the bourbon made his words run together, and then she was pulling open the screen door and running down the steps, slick under the new rubber soles, feet pounding across the bridge to Terabithia. She was running away, running hard as she could—the yellow shoes slapping the mud— toward the woods and down the trail that led to the lake. She kept running, down a path too dark to see.

She heard Billy's voice behind her, calling and calling. He was following her, she realized—but it wasn't Billy. She knew it wasn't. The voice only sounded like Billy. But it belonged, she knew, to an ugly thing.

It belonged to *him*.

PART FOUR:
The Crocodile Bride

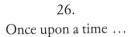

26.
Once upon a time ...

... THERE WAS a young girl who lived with her father in a little yellow house.

The girl's father was a trickster. He could tell stories for days on end and then fall abruptly silent, as though his mouth had been sewn shut. His hands could turn to spiders without warning, and from his tongue he let slip small eggs that hatched into worms. He could turn, without warning, into a hunched and hideous troll, with liver spots and wispy hair.

One night, when one of the eggs had found its way down inside her belly and hatched, the girl ran away. She could hear her trickster father—now a troll—following her, calling her name.

She knew better than to reply, and she kept running until his voice faded behind her and she heard only the sounds of dripping rain.

The woods smelled bittersweet, like wet earth dug up. Like how a kind old man had once told her it felt to be truly happy. But it was dark, and the girl was scared. She was tired from running and slowed, little by little, to a walk. Her bright yellow shoes had turned thick with mud.

It felt as though she walked for days. As though the night stretched on for more hours than was possible for a night to last. Several times, she tripped and fell. Once, she banged her knee so hard she began to cry.

She considered turning back, but she could feel the ugly little grub-worm in her belly and knew it would grow into something monstrous if she did not get help, and so she went on, although she was no longer sure she was following any kind of path at all.

At last, tired and thirsty, her knee aching, her feet raw and blistered where they'd rubbed against the canvas of her yellow shoes, the girl noticed she was no longer stepping along a muddy path, but on moss, and she saw that the trees around her were enormous, rising up around her like ancient temples, and through the canopy far above she could see that the moon had come out from behind the clouds.

Then, just up ahead, the girl saw it—the glint of water. As she drew closer she saw that out on the water was a house, its windows warm with candlelight.

She made her way down the bank toward the water's edge, where there sat a little blue boat. It was like her father had once told her; it was just the right size for a child. She climbed inside and began rowing toward the house. In the distance, she could hear the beating heart. *Da dum. Da dum.* The light from the moon and the distant windows seemed to wake her up. She rowed hard. The oars made little lapping sounds.

But she had forgotten, in her haste that night, the cost of this watery passage.

Despite her daddy's warning: *I'd gone goddamn blind, Fred. I'd forgotten the most important thing.* No sooner did she remember than there was a thud against the little boat.

And then another.

The boat began to tilt, and though she scrambled to hold tight, she felt herself slipping—and all light (the moonlight, the flickering candlelight) winked out.

INSIDE THE CROCODILE, IT was hot and heavy and wet.

She was lying on something. On many things. They dug into her knees and the palms of her hands. She pushed herself up so she was standing, and then she heard something—someone, a little ways away, breathing in the darkness.

She felt a flash of relief. Someone was there with her! They could find their way out together. It would be A-okay.

Hello? she called, and her call echoed back: *Hello hello hello.*

In response, there was the *shkk* of a lit match. As if to say, *See? Here I am.* The match and the hands accompanying it were some distance from her, down a long tunnel of shadowy darkness. At her feet were strange shapes, but it was too dark to see clearly what was making them. She could see only the hands in the glow of the match, at first, and then the hands lit a lantern on a table and the lantern released a brighter glow and cast long shadows toward her. Beside the table with the lantern sat a boy, or maybe a small man? It was hard to say in this light.

Oh, hello! she called out. Her words again echoed in this strange chamber. *Hello hello hello hello hello.*

Hello, said the person at the other end of the belly. (*Hello hello hello hello hello.*)

She could make out dark hair, but the face was washed out in the light of the lantern. Shadows stretched long and black on the walls. *Come on down here,* said the person—she could tell by his voice that he was young. *Don't be afraid. I'm glad to see you!*

She made her way slowly forward. Something crunched and broke under her bare foot. Sweat trickled down her forehead and beaded along her upper lip.

As her eyes adjusted to the light, she saw what it was that cast the strange shadows in this dark tunnel: Piled up all around her were various objects. It was like Billy had told her: ... *his belly filled up with treasures.* She looked down in wonder. In the flickering light the gifts glimmered and shone. There were piles of coins and rubies and emeralds, earrings and strings of pearls; there were black-and-white portraits in ornate, gilded frames. In the humidity, a silver tray had tarnished. A framed oval mirror was peppered black with mold. A brass book-end shaped like a music note had gone green.

Sunshine forgot, for the moment, to be afraid.

She stopped a short distance from the table with the lantern and the boy sitting beside it, arms crossed over his chest. He was about her age, or maybe a little older, with dark hair that fell over his eyebrows and a dusting of freckles over his nose and wide green eyes. He was looking at her with his dark brows furrowed. Then he grinned.

He had a friendly grin.

They were both naked but for their underwear. No socks or shoes. No training bra or T-shirt. No being modest, not really.

Hi, she said, and they were close enough, now, that she did not need to call out and her voice did not echo.

Hi, said the boy. He pulled one leg up to his chest and hugged it with two pale, skinny arms. *You lost your clothes.*

Yeah. Sunshine looked down at her bare feet and wriggled her toes. *But I don't remember how.*

It's too hot in here for clothes, said the boy. *I don't remember how I lost mine either. I think when I was being swallowed, maybe.*

Maybe they got caught in the crocodile teeth, Sunshine said.

But we didn't, did we? the boy said proudly. His thighs, too, were skinny and very pale. Sunshine could see blue veins running just under the skin.

Yes, she said absently, but she was looking up toward the shadowy space above them and then back over her shoulder, down the tunnel of this great belly. Her stomach churned, and she realized there was suddenly a smell of rot in the air—or at least, she hadn't noticed it before. At the same time as she noticed the smell, she remembered the grubworm in her belly. Blueish-white and wriggling.

She looked around her, as though searching for help in the sloping surface of the crocodile's belly, dark and shadowy and colorless in the flickering candlelight.

It came out of nowhere, she said, *and I was so close to the house.* All of a sudden, she felt as though she might cry.

The boy didn't seem to notice the rotting smell, or her sadness. His eyes lit up. *What house?* he asked.

The little red house, with the candle in the window.

You know about that, too? said the boy, and he let his chair fall forward again. He ran both hands through his hair. *Oh, gee*, he said, and his eyes twinkled with excitement. *Did you go there?*

No. I was on my way, but—and Sunshine gestured around them.

I tried to go, said the boy. *A long time ago. But I didn't have a gift for the crocodile.*

Me neither, Sunshine said.

I guess that's why he ate us, said the boy.

He unhooked his arm from his leg and leaned forward so that both elbows rested on his knees. He made a fist with one hand and lightly punched the palm of his other hand. It made a soft slapping sound. *So I guess*, said the boy, *it's gonna be just the two of us down here.* He smiled at her again. That friendly smile. Who did he remind her of? *Gee, I'm glad you're here. It's been real lonely.*

How long have you been here? Sunshine asked.

I dunno. A real long time, I guess. He paused and turned his eyes up toward the black shadows overhead, thinking. *Yeah, pretty much lost track, I guess.*

He shrugged and grinned again, but his eyes looked so sad, she felt sorry for him. Sorry and scared, and suddenly desperate to get out, to get them both out. She felt it like a surge of electricity, right down to her bones.

She had felt this earlier in the night, too—something hot, something alive.

Have you ever tried to leave? she asked.

To leave? said the boy. He looked confused. *I dunno how,* he said.

Sunshine looked at the treasures at her feet. Piled high all around them. Gold necklaces. A charm bracelet. A porcelain pony with both ears chipped off.

She remembered what Moss had said, ages ago: *The skin of their bellies is the only soft part of 'em. You could slice your way out of there if you got a knife.*

She said to the boy, *But have you tried?*

Tried what? said the boy.

To get out. She knelt down and began rummaging through the objects. They clinked and clanged against each other, their sounds magnified in the vast space of the crocodile's belly.

The boy laughed. *I can't swim,* he said. She looked over her shoulder at him. His arms were wrapped around both legs again; he looked very small like that. *So even if I could get out, what would be the point?*

Hey! I know. Let's play a game. Or sing a song. Do you know any? Or let's tell each other s-stories all night. I know some good ones. My mama used to tell them to me.

But Sunshine was now crawling through the tunnel of treasures, picking up her findings, examining, tossing aside. She reached for something that looked sharp, but it was only the tarnished lid of a jewelry box.

The boy rose from his seat and began to follow her, stepping with care. He held the lantern in one hand and it cast a wide shaft of wobbling light over the tunnel of treasures.

Whatcha looking for? he asked.

We need to get out, Sunshine said. In her bones, the hot thing was still running its course. She was trembling, slightly, from its energy. The crocodile heartbeat drummed on. Keeping time. *My aunt will wonder where I've been.*

She'll be okay, said the boy. *She'll probably forget after a while. Besides, it's not so bad in here. You can s-search through the treasures for hours. I've seen some dolls I bet you'd like. Girls like dolls, don't they? Once I found a cat's eye marble....*

The boy sounded cheerful when he talked about all the treasures to be found, but when he moved the lantern aside and she could see his face clearly in its light, his eyes were not smiling. She turned away and dug through the objects again, faster, with more urgency.

Why did you want to go see her? she asked—holding, examining, tossing aside.

See who?

Each time she moved further into the shadowy tunnel, the boy followed, and the lantern light shone on the objects she held. *I mean the crocodile bride. Why'd you try to find her in the first place?*

Oh. I dunno. I don't even remember. He squatted down beside her. *Say, what are you looking for, again?*

She again felt a wave of nausea. The rotting smell was stronger now. It wasn't the boy—he smelled sweet, like cut grass and honeysuckle and wet dirt dug up. He smelled so sweet that she wanted to bury her face in his neck. She could survive, she thought, on these June mood smells.

No, the rotting smell must be from something else in this place, but she couldn't tell where from.

She didn't want to tell the boy what she was looking for. She said only, *We have to leave. Okay?*

When she turned back toward the treasures in front of her, she saw what it was she needed: a strange-looking knife. The brass blade dull and tinged green. The mother-of-pearl handle as smooth as glass.

The handle felt cool to the touch. She gripped it tightly, then rose to her feet.

The boy stood up too. *Hey,* he said. In the lantern light she could see the dark fuzz along his upper lip. Maybe he was older than she had thought—older than Joanna Louise. It was hard to tell. His arms, which had looked skinny from a distance, were more corded up close; he was lean but strong. Stronger than she was.

What are you doing with that thing? he asked, and though he smiled, his teeth looked too large in this light, so close.

She held the brass blade tightly in one hand. She took a step back, away from the boy.

Look, he said. *Why don't you just g-give me that thing, okay? No one needs to get hurt here. I just want you to p-play a game with me. It's been so lonely down here. I just want you to sing a song or tell a s-s-tory.* He looked like he might cry.

She couldn't listen to him, though. She knelt and shoved objects aside until she saw the dark pink tissue of the crocodile's exposed belly, glistening in the lantern light.

I can try to help you swim, she said.

S-swim? said the boy, and he moved again so he was beside her, crouched down among the old treasures. *I told you, I don't know how. B-b-but look, how about you just put down that knife thing, and we'll p-play a g-game, or else I can tell you a s-s-story, huh? I know a lot of good stories. I just have to remember them.*

But Sunshine was crying, now. *No,* she said. *You have to try.*

And then there it was again, what she had felt before: a live current inside of her, so hot and gut-deep it could light fires all on its own.

It could kill.

She could feel the boy, smell the cut grass and honeysuckle and wet earth there beside her, hear his breathing. The crocodile heart beat on and on. Then the boy was saying something else but she was not listening; she was already raising the blade up high.

She brought it down with all her strength, as hard as she could push it, into the soft underside of the crocodile. She dragged the blade, hard. She cut open that belly like a fish.

The lantern went out. There was the roar of water rushing in, and she thought the boy was trying to tell her something but she couldn't hear him over the rushing sound or over her own voice, which was screaming, now, louder than she thought capable, not a scream of fear but of rage, guttural and wild, and the force of it propelled her forward and then the black water was in her eyes and her mouth and all around.

IT WAS BLACK LIKE a night sky.

It would be so easy to let fear overwhelm you, spin you around. To sink you like a stone. Like a string of pearls, like a cat's eye marble.

Like a brass letter opener with a mother-of-pearl handle.

But there were two strong, smooth arms pulling her up. A woman's arms. They pulled her up out of the water and she took great, gasping breaths. The arms carried her along until she could feel the soft ground underfoot. The arms continued to hold her close, to keep her safe, as they waded—the woman and Sunshine—through the shallow water toward the little house.

27.
The Grubworm

We step inside the little house with its flickering candlelight. She's skinny and wet and shivering. Our toes are caked with mud. My dress clings wetly to my thighs.

In the house, the smell of hot candlewax and cold ash and pine. The woodstove is pocked with rust. Dust and twigs and brittle cypress needles have scattered across every surface. The grit that coats the floorboards, gone soft with rot, presses into the soles of our feet.

She's crying and our arms are still wrapped around one another, her head pressed to my chest.

I want to go on holding her like this for the whole night. For all of time. I want to wrap her in blankets, to pull her to me like I once, long ago, held my own children. I want to tell her stories that will soothe, that will make her forget.

I open my mouth. *Once*, I intend to say. *Once*—

But I realize that I can't remember what story I wanted to tell her. I can't remember any stories at all. What were they, again?

My memories, like twigs floating downstream. In dark river water scattered with red maple leaves, the pebbled shore at our feet. A nearby iron bridge.

In the yellow kitchen of a yellow house, a percolator with a broken handle.

And something, *once*, about a crocodile and a woman's hands. Once, the story had begun. *Once—once—*

Then those bits and pieces, the glimpses (the silver, the brass, a dark river) are drifting, are gone.

AND SO I HOLD her. I feel her soft skin and the bony wings of her shoulder blades just beneath. Her damp, tangled hair presses against my cheek. It smells familiar, like water and sunlight and something else.

She's so small.

As she cries, her body shakes and so I keep my arms steady and I rock her slightly, back and forth, the two of us just barely swaying.

I don't know how much time has passed, but she leans back and tilts her head up toward me. I'm not very tall, and her face is so close I could bend to kiss it. I want to kiss her cheek, as flushed and bright as an apple. I want to feel its warmth, its aliveness, against my lips.

But I don't. I take in her face and I try to memorize it.

I let her look at me too. My hair is—I think—red. My still-soaked dress is pink. Rivulets of water run down my legs. Droplets fall from the hem, tapping softly on the floor.

Are you...? she begins, then pauses. A question lingers.

I can smell her sweet child breath, I can smell the water in her hair, and these smells are so tender, like a ripened fig (I remember, briefly: the taste of summer figs, the dusted-velvet feel of their leaves under my fingers), that my eyes burn.

There was a boy, she says, and her lips tremble and tears spill over again. *But I think he drowned.*

I don't remember seeing a boy; I remember waking already in the warm dark water, the fabric of my dress billowing around me, and seeing only her. Her hair like light. I swam for her and wrapped her small body in my arms. I brought her here.

I don't know about the boy, I admit, and I'm relieved to find my voice still works. *But you'll be all right.* Then I say it again. I mean it. *You'll be all right.*

She's looking at me again, lips again on the verge of speaking.

What was it you wanted to ask? I say.

Are you her? she whispers. *Are you the crocodile bride?*

The crocodile bride.

I so want to remember. My chest aches to remember. I can feel it, the story. I can feel it drifting and churning in the dark water, pulled deeper by the current, then rising, roiling toward the surface, closer—the stone steps of a courthouse; a white dress in the water, trailing like a veil—and then the memory is pulled below again. Down in that black water.

I know it's gone.

No, I say sadly. *I'm not her.*

Why did she leave? she asks.

Then somehow, something does surface—not a memory, exactly, and not a story, but rather a bit of truth. I plunge my hand into that dark water; I hold the thing tight in one fist.

Now that he's gone, I say, *she was free to finally leave.*

I cannot remember the *he,* but I know that this is true. (Another strange memory: a sound like a beating heart.)

But she was supposed to help me, she says, and another something surfaces, and I reach for that, too—but I can't hold too much, it seems, and with each single rising truth, the rest rushes away, and so I simply bring her to me again and rub my hand along her back. I brush her tangled hair with my fingers. I smooth it down.

And then: I remember.

I smile. *She left something for you,* I tell her.

I go to the nearby shelf that runs along one wall. On it sits a jar with the lid screwed on. It is not dusty; the glass is clear and smooth under my fingers.

The handle of a silver percolator was also smooth under my fingers. The skin where I was burned, on my calf, was smooth, too—taut and mauve—and I once held my children close in a room with green flowered wallpaper and told them stories I no longer recall.

The girl takes the jar in both hands and holds it closer to the candle-light that brightens the window. We can feel its warmth on our faces. Light falls through the jar like water.

At first, I don't see anything—just the glass, and the candlelight through it—but then she takes one finger and points to something at the bottom, and I see it then, the gift.

A grubworm. Milky blue-white with a translucent tail, curled up like a moon.

When the girl sighs, it's with a breath that has been held too long. A breath that has been held for years, perhaps. Perhaps for decades.

THE SKY HAS TURNED pink outside the windows and the early dawn light spills in. Dust motes float. Something skitters under the floorboards. We're at the table, sitting on the long bench, facing the window. The water glows the same color as the sky. There is a small boat tied to the shore. She had fallen asleep leaning against me, curled against me like two children I once loved, whose names I cannot remember but who I still love, but now she's awake and I know it's time for her to leave. The dawn is pink on the water.

Still, before she goes, I stand in the open doorway and embrace her small body. Just once more. Before my mind gives way to the dark water with the scattered maple leaves, before I entirely forget myself, forget her, I smell her hair again and remember the taste of a fig under a dark afternoon sky, the muted green of the leaves. My two children underfoot: my dark-haired boy, my small redheaded girl. I remember the red mud on our feet, the smell of coming rain.

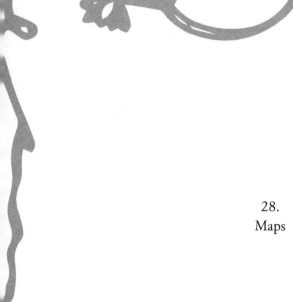

28.
Maps

On a mattress on the floor of the new house, among the smells of sawdust and melting candlewax and Nash's warm body pressed against her own, Nash asked Lou if she wanted to talk.

Earlier, when the storm had first begun, they had gone to the windows and watched the bolts of lightning out over the tree line. Nash had pulled her in close to him again and kissed along her neck, then he'd pulled the neckline of the green dress aside and kissed the exposed skin of her shoulder. A sweet shudder had run down her body, as though a door had just been opened and a burst of welcome cool air had come through. They had made love on the mattress he'd made up on the floor, and now they were sipping wine from paper cups.

To her surprise, she did want to talk.

She wanted to talk about it. About earlier at the yellow house and about much more.

Naked, heady with wine, Lou laid out for Nash the map of her history.

Not the map in its entirety, but enough, for now. Lines here, points there. She showed him what life had been like in the yellow house; she showed him when she and Billy had hid in their bedroom as children and about the noises (skin-on-skin, a surprised *Oh!*) outside the door. She showed him the moment Billy had put his mouth on hers, and she showed him all these years later, the way Billy had looked at Joanna Louise that day, the feeling that something was *off* and how it was not just the job, she knew that, how that was the least of it—only she had been too ashamed to admit her real concerns and she hadn't realized that until now, tonight.

She showed Nash all of this—and because she did not have a paper map to spread before him on the mattress on the floor of the new living room, she used words.

It was, at least, a start.

29.
At the Lake

The morning after the lightning storm was humid. The swimming hole was silt-stirred, pea green, and the water beyond the yellow rope was all dark-brown golds and blue where it reflected the bright sky.

Moss Landry's shirt was already damp with sweat. He bent to start the engine, pulling the cord once and then twice before it clattered to life.

The lake had not much changed over the years, since he'd first arrived in Fingertip—though it was not called Fingertip back then, of course. He'd been such a young man then, his hair still brown and only just barely beginning to thin at the crown of his head. He and Sarah were newly married, and they'd been happy to move into the house at the end of the road, in this new little village. It was rumored that Eleanor Roosevelt herself had inspected each home in her New Deal communities: had walked the floors, tested the water taps, opened and closed each kitchen cabinet.

Each morning, Moss had caught the train to the sugar mill a parish over and each evening, he went into the town after work with his manager, an older man, also married, with close-cropped gray hair. In the alley behind the bar, wedged between a fence and a brick wall, they first kissed. The man's skin smelled, always, of Palmolive soap. His name was Charlie, and he could somehow make Moss, who was shy and quiet by nature, talk for hours.

When Sarah left him later that year, the lake brought him comfort. He liked the solitude out on the water. He liked crossing to the other side and weaving his bateau between the cypress trees. He wanted to take the long way today, skirting the perimeter of the lake, to enjoy the shade of the trees there. In his old age, he preferred to move slowly—though he had always preferred slowness, really, and it was something that had annoyed his wife. She'd always shucked corn with the quick, constant motion of a whirring fan blade. She drove their Ford too fast down 79. Always impatient to finish whatever it was that needed finishing. Even the divorce was over and done in a single blink.

Charlie had liked this about him, though. Charlie told Moss he was not slow but *deliberate*. He said his pace was just right for this part of the world. It was a Cajun pace, Charlie said, and the only time he said he'd seen a Cajun move quickly was on the dance floor.

It hadn't worked out, of course. The wife had found out; Charlie had told Moss he couldn't speak with him anymore. Once, years later, they had seen each other in the Piggly Wiggly, the two of them standing at either end of the frozen foods aisle. They had made eye contact and then Charlie had quickly turned his back, grabbed a bag of frozen peas, and walked away without looking back.

Still, Moss thought of him often. The gray, well-kept hairline along his neck. His friendly brown eyes.

He was thinking of Charlie as he steered the bateau through the morning shade, the caramel water rippling out from the bateau. He was thinking of Charlie's Palmolive smell and the roughness of his shaven cheek at the end of a work day—Moss could almost feel it, even now—when he saw something in the sawgrass and the reeds that grew up along the shore, near a big cypress gone hollow with fungus.

He steered the bateau up alongside the shore and cut the motor, letting it drift closer.

His eyes took in the sight without registering, at first, the what or the who. His eyes saw bare, suntanned arms. A white T-shirt and jeans stained at the hem with red mud, despite being in the water. Floating closest to Moss, the wrinkled white soles of the man's feet. He took in the tangle of dark hair that floated, waving softly in the ripples from the bateau's slow drift. He climbed into the shallow water and turned the body over. He took in the face. Eyelids mercifully closed, blue lips parted, slightly, as though Billy Turner was, even in death, on the verge of saying something.

30.
Gifts

THE SKY WAS PALE, the sun not yet up over the trees, when Sunshine returned to the yellow house, aching with exhaustion. She passed the closed door of Billy's bedroom and she curled up, naked but for her underwear, on top of the quilt on her bed. When she awoke, sun was streaming in and Aunt Lou was sitting on the edge of her bed, saying, "Sunshine, honey. Wake up."

Nash was standing nearby. Sunshine had never seen the expression on their faces before. She sat up. No one seemed to notice or care that she wasn't dressed.

Maybe, she thought hopefully, she was dreaming.

But before Aunt Lou spoke, she knew, somehow, what they were both there to tell her, and she started to cry.

JOANNA LOUISE CAME HOME from camp early.

Mrs. Murphy drove her all the way to the pink house and brought a casserole for Aunt Lou, who took it from her in the driveway and returned Mrs. Murphy's long hug. Sunshine watched from JL's bedroom.

JL looked different than when she had left. She was taller and softer. She was larger-breasted. Her shorts had grown so tight that Sunshine could see where they outlined the curve and crevice between her legs. She wondered if that was allowed or if Aunt Lou was too distracted to notice.

When JL stepped through the bedroom door behind her, Sunshine didn't know what to say or do and so she didn't look over. She continued kneeling on the bed by the window, looking out toward the yellow house. Then JL was kneeling next to her, and she put one arm around Sunshine and rested her head on Sunshine's shoulder, and they stayed like that for a long while, in silence.

• • •

AT FIRST, LOU GRIEVED only the loss of him.

She cried often, and at unexpected moments. At the sight of a truck that reminded her of Billy's. At the memory of that night on the porch earlier that summer (at how easy things had felt between them). At the sight of Sunshine asleep when she checked on her at night, which, in the months that followed Billy's death, Lou found herself often doing.

Other times, she blamed herself. Privately, she confessed her guilt to Nash. She described the argument with Billy and how she'd humiliated him. She said, through tears, "I was a monster, Nash. I didn't recognize myself."

They were lying in bed in the pink house. Nash rubbed her back, watching her, listening.

What if he had done it on purpose—because of her? What if the things she had said to him that evening had caused him so much pain he had to end his own life?

Nash reminded her gently, "Naw, babe. It's not anyone's fault." It was the way Billy's mind worked, he said. It was the pain he carried and hadn't known how to heal.

Nash began keeping a packet of blue tissues in his back pocket. When Lou found herself overcome with tears—for her guilt and her shame, for the tremendous loss of her brother—Nash's hand would often appear, holding out the blue tissue as if offering her a flower.

MUCH LATER—YEARS LATER—when Lou had moved through the worst, the most acute, of her mourning, she would begin to see the truth in what Nash said.

That the loss of her brother wasn't her fault but something much larger than herself or even Billy. Larger than the stories their mother told. That it was history itself—a chain of grief, passed from generation to generation. From a father who had destroyed all he touched, perhaps even from his father or mother before him. From a war fought by a sensitive, rooster-loving grandfather she'd never met. From silences and heartaches in a past impossible to visit. A grief with no words to give it shape, to give it light.

If she and Billy had the words, perhaps they could have held it. Examined its insides and outsides, run their fingers across the patina etched in its surface. Perhaps, even if they couldn't know its source, they could have helped each other carry it.

• • •

THE FUNERAL WAS HELD at a small Methodist chapel in St. Cadence with no air conditioning. Fans whirred lazily overhead. The edges of the hymn books were mice-chewed. The minister asked them to sing songs, but Sunshine could not sing. She stood between Aunt Lou, who was holding a crumpled blue tissue to her face, and JL, who did not look over at Sunshine but whose bare arm brushed Sunshine's own.

Outside in the cemetery, they lowered the black casket. In its waxy, polished reflection shone the image of the sky and of the other mourners gathered around, their bodies miniature and warped. Sunshine could smell JL's apple-scented hair.

That night, after they had turned the lights out, her cousin whispered to her. "Hey—you okay?"

Sunshine couldn't answer; her face was buried in her pillow, muffling the sobs she had held back all that day so that Aunt Lou wouldn't worry. Wouldn't feel sadder than she already felt.

She heard her cousin's footsteps as she crossed the room, then her body (newly softened) stretch itself against her, cupping Sunshine's own body protectively. Lovingly.

"Ça ira," JL whispered. "Ça ira, ça ira."

IN LATE AUGUST, SUNSHINE went to say goodbye to the yellow house.

Aunt Lou hadn't wanted to go with her. She said she'd cried enough for a lifetime and instead she was loading the last of the boxes from the pink house into the shaggin' wagon. They had taken the furniture from Sunshine's bedroom to the new house, along with the Formica table and the record player and records. Aunt Lou said Sunshine could keep the record player in her new room, but the pink sofa that Grandma Catherine had loved, and the La-Z-Boy that she'd hated, and the furniture in Billy's bedroom were all staying.

"We can't take everything," Aunt Lou said that morning, when Sunshine asked about the other furniture. They were standing in Aunt Lou's kitchen, wrapping dinner plates in newspaper. Aunt Lou turned from Sunshine with pursed lips, and Sunshine could see she was annoyed. Silence fell between them.

Sunshine left the kitchen and walked barefoot across Only Road. She went across the bridge to Terabithia and past the iron rocker and the Florida orange crate. She walked through the living room with furniture that looked lonely. She felt sorry for the couch. She decided that when she was a grown-up, she'd drive back to Fingertip and rescue it. Maybe the La-Z-Boy too. She'd put them in her grown-up home so they wouldn't feel sad on their own.

She didn't go in Billy's room. For some reason, she had never liked to go in there anyway, and now she felt too sad. She went instead to her empty bedroom.

All the seawater had drained out and dust bunnies skittered across the floor in the draft from the open window. The daisies on the green wallpaper seemed, she thought now, nothing like sea anemones.

On a particularly cool morning in November, Sunshine sat with Aunt Lou on the steps of the front porch at the Lafayette house.

They were drinking coffee. It was cold, and their breath came out in little white puffs. Overhead, the sky was a brilliant blue, like clear water.

Sunshine liked to sit on these porch steps and look out across the yard, which was not muddy like at the yellow house. She missed the bridge to Terabithia, but this yard was carpeted in a green grass that Nash mowed with a riding mower, and sometimes he let Sunshine hop on and steer. There were tall pine trees and three crawling oaks on the property, their branches low enough to climb.

When Sunshine sat on the front porch, she forgot about all that the house did not have. Green wallpaper with daisies. A slanty floor to send jawbreakers rolling, rolling with a mouse-sized roar. A butterfly-shaped stain on linoleum. No redheaded grandmother standing at the sink. No *Heya Fred.* The house had no spiders, either, and she hated how this knowledge brought her relief.

But on these mornings on the porch, any hatred or sadness or longing she felt drifted away, at least for a while.

Visiting, is what Aunt Lou called these mornings. Every Sunday, the two of them just visiting, just sitting next to one another, not even talking much of the time. On this morning, Sunshine was wrapped in an old green sweater of Aunt Lou's, and Aunt Lou was still in her bathrobe, feet tucked into slippers.

Then Aunt Lou said, "I've been meaning to ask about you, sugar—" She paused and cleared her throat. "About how you're doing, I mean. About how you're feeling with everything, with school and the house and Billy. Just with—well, you know. Just with everything, with everything that's happened." She sighed. She laughed, a little, at her struggle to speak. "Do you know what I mean?"

Sunshine looked at her. They were close, their knees almost touching. Aunt Lou had not put on makeup yet, and her freckled face was bare and smooth. She always complained about the lines that jutted from the corners of her eyes, but Sunshine liked them. They reminded her of Billy and were friendly looking besides. She wanted to reach out and trace them with her finger but didn't want to offend Aunt Lou.

Sometimes, the ways Aunt Lou reminded her of Billy made her chest hurt so badly she thought it was going to cave in on itself. Other times, like right now, the small resemblances felt comforting, like he wasn't all the way gone.

Aunt Lou took another deep, shaky-sounding breath, and then suddenly her eyes filled with tears and her lips wobbled, and that made Sunshine's own eyes tear up, too, though she did not know why either of them would start crying right at this moment, right out of the blue.

"Oh, sugar," Aunt Lou said, her voice choked. "All I'm trying to say is that if you ever need to talk to me, I'm here. I'll listen to you. I'm listening to you."

Aunt Lou had tried to talk to Sunshine since Billy had drowned, to ask how she was doing, and although Sunshine always said she was fine, she was okay, she liked the new house—there was something about the coolness of the day that seemed to run like a river through Sunshine's body, making her feel bright and alive, like how it had felt at the start of each summer when they'd walk to the lake and the water was clear and glittering and inviting, and just as suddenly as Aunt Lou had begun to stammer through what it was she'd been trying to say, Sunshine answered her honestly for the first time.

"It feels really hard," she said. It was hard to talk. It was hard to cry, too—or not to cry, but to feel so much. She wiped at her eyes.

When Aunt Lou didn't offer words of comfort but simply nodded, wiping at her own eyes, too, Sunshine found herself continuing on. "I have to tell you a secret," she said.

Aunt Lou nodded again. She didn't hesitate or look mad or suspicious. She said again, "I'm listening. Go ahead, Sunshine."

With that feeling somehow bright inside of her (and it was still there, even as she cried), with the blue sky like water and the smell of their coffee, Sunshine continued to talk. She told Aunt Lou about that summer. About the stones and about the things the spider hands—Billy's hands—had done to her that she still didn't understand (even as the words tumbled from her mouth). She told her about touching his *thing* under the rough denim and about his tongue, about her fear of a grubworm.

She told Aunt Lou she had run away into the woods that night and how she thought she'd heard Billy call after her and how she had been too scared to reply.

(She left out the parts about the Black Bayou, about the crocodile bride. That was a story she wanted, needed, to keep to herself. *To keep right there in your pocket, Fred.*)

As she talked, she paused to ask Aunt Lou questions, to ask what something was called, what it meant. She wanted to find the right words so she could better say the things she was trying to say. When she asked, Aunt Lou answered and explained; and when Sunshine shared her secrets, Aunt Lou did not deny, or interrupt, or brush aside.

She didn't tell her niece (as she had so many times told herself, remembering, with shame, the night that Billy had climbed on top of her on her side of the blackberry vine sheet): *He was probably just being weird.*

She did not say, *Men will be men.* She did not lecture on forgiveness.

She did not cringe when Sunshine asked her what words meant what, or when she told her about the stones behind her nipples, and how they still sometimes hurt.

She simply listened. She caught her niece's words in two upturned palms. She caught them with care, as though the words were precious gifts—a quilt with the names of schoolchildren, a brass letter opener—and she did not let them go.

Acknowledgments

The eight years of writing this novel, and the two more spent fine-tuning, were not in total solitude. More people than I can possibly name supported me and my vision for this story.

First, for his encouragement and humor, and for fearlessly ushering this novel out of its nest, I am beyond grateful for my heroic agent, Jon Curzon at Artellus. I am incredibly lucky. Editors Meg Reid and Kate McMullen were further additions to what I have described countless times as my "dream publishing team"—patiently supporting and executing my vision for this book, and putting the utmost care into every aspect of publication. Thank you also to Kendall Owens, Larissa Melo Pienkowski, and the entire glorious Hub City team. Emily Mahon, I am so grateful for this cover.

The subconscious sparks of this novel and many of the conscious sparks belong in large part to the Jackson family, especially the siblings: Lois Hines, John Jackson, Laura Pedersen, Eileen Manuel, and Peggy Scolaro. Thank you also to my late grandma Elizabeth Jackson, who inspired more than she knew, and to David Walton.

A late night of porch storytelling with Melissa Andrews planted the seeds from which this novel wildly grew: thank you.

Jaime deBlanc-Knowles hands down played the most critical role in the actual completion of this book, from its very first draft until publication. I owe her more than I can express. Matt Rumley offered countless reads and encouragement; I am deeply grateful for our long, winding friendship. Kyle Seedlock, the third Pedersen sister, believed me an artist long before I ever saw myself that way. Michelle Bright and Vince Colvin are long-time family—a true gift. Thank you to Kelley Janes and Nate Janes, for everything. Thank you to the Blue Bonnet Four: Jules Buck Jones, Audrey Stewart, and Anna Stewart. Infinite thanks to Dorothy and Eddie Gumbert, as well.

For major support and encouragement along the way, thank you (in no particular order) to Brandon and G'nell Price, Lindsay Bishop, Justin Follin, Brannon Via (my muse!), Drew Liverman and Veronica Giavedoni, the Fry fam, Alex Chew, Meg Halpin, Crystal and Mike Franz, John and Monique Mulvany, Danielle and Kevin Sweeney, Virginia Reeves and Luke Muszkiewicz, Caroline Wright, Gretchen Fox Roberts, Carlos Delgado, Walt and Rebecca Seedlock, Geoff Peck, and the Lighthouse Works on Fishers Island, NY. Thank you so much to Bailey Toksöz for her photography skills. A deep thank you to Georgia Carr, Breana Field, and Corey Miller; Megan Scolaro, you were part of a shared childhood that informed much here. Thank you Zelie Duvauchelle, Lindsey Morgan, and especially Ellie Burke. Thanks to Sarah Harris Wallman for her creative partnership, and to Kara Hughes for her thoughtfulness and baked goods. Thanks to "the Grinneys": Rachel Grinney, Matt Grinney, Marta Thompson, Borna Emami, and Jay and Melanie Grinney.

In researching Louisiana land in particular, I owe thanks to: Thais Perkins for her tree knowledge; C.C. Lockwood for a helpful conversation in 2017 and both *The Alligator Book* and *Discovering Louisiana*; *Eyelids of Morning* by A.D. Graham provided the perfect biblical epigraph for my book. The brilliant people at Cajun Country Swamp Tours in Breaux Bridge, LA, taught me about the beauty of the bayou in all seasons and patiently answered my numerous questions in both 2015 and 2017. Loretta Watkins took me on a terrifying but informative kayaking excursion in Breaux Bridge.

I am grateful for all of my teachers and mentors: Mrs. Banye at George C. Round taught me to love sentences; Jeffrey Rosinski taught me to love literature; Diane Cecily provided me with late night grilled cheeses and endless words of encouragement. Thank you Mia Carter, Susann Cokal, Irina Reyn, and Tom Zigal. The late great Chuck Kinder's spirit was with me when I was beginning cancer treatment, reminding me to just keep making shit.

Because I finished the final draft of this novel while undergoing chemotherapy, I also want to thank the incredible nurse Pat Balzac at Texas Oncology, who made a challenging experience lighthearted and gave me the gift of human touch when I most needed it. Dr. Debra Patt and Dr. Julie Sprunt quite literally saved my life.

Very deep gratitude for Miriam Klotz, who continues to teach me how to be with myself.

Thanks to my grandma Kathleen Pedersen; so many of the indelible impressions left on Sunshine come from Rainbow Brite sheets and stories of roller skating in New York City. My sweet grandpa Martin Pedersen no doubt inspired the quiet ways of one character in particular.

I owe endless thanks to my nearest and dearest "wf" Erin Scolaro for her incredibly generous read of my earliest, messiest draft and for informing my imagination, from the moment I was old enough to keep up with her, with grapevine forts and committed games of "Old-Fashioned."

Thanks to Jordan (JD) Pedersen for his sweetness, humor, generosity of spirit, and for keeping me well fed when I took a break to come home—I love you so much.

Thank you to my loving, hilarious parents: Mimz for her creativity and egg-in-a-basket sandwiches; and my sweet dad Bob Pedersen (Oils), who taught me about the elusive "special special" time.

And finally, thank you to my brilliant and hilarious sister Kathryn, best known as KP. I got through the most difficult experience of my life because of her humor and support; I arrived at major decisions in the novel because of our long and water-deprived hike in Big Bend National Park; and I am in general able to keep on a bit more easily because of her. Love "ya," Harry.

The COLD MOUNTAIN *Fund*
S E R I E S

NATIONAL BOOK AWARD WINNER Charles Frazier generously supports publication of a series of Hub City Press books through the Cold Mountain Fund at the Community Foundation of Western North Carolina. The Cold Mountain Series spotlights works of fiction by new and extraordinary writers from the American South. Books published in this series have been reviewed in outlets like *Wall Street Journal, San Francisco Chronicle, Garden & Gun, Entertainment Weekly,* and *O, the Oprah Magazine;* included on Best Books lists from NPR, *Kirkus Reviews,* and the American Library Association; and have won or been nominated for awards like the Southern Book Prize, the Ohioana Book Award, Crooks Corner Book Prize, and the Langum Prize for Historical Fiction.

Child in the Valley • Gordy Sauer

The Parted Earth • Anjali Enjeti

You Want More: The Selected Stories of George Singleton

The Prettiest Star • Carter Sickels

Watershed • Mark Barr

The Magnetic Girl • Jessica Handler

HUB CITY
PRESS

PUBLISHING
New & Extraordinary
VOICES FROM THE
AMERICAN SOUTH

FOUNDED IN SPARTANBURG, South Carolina in 1995, Hub City Press has emerged as the South's premier independent literary press. Hub City is interested in books with a strong sense of place and is committed to finding and spotlighting extraordinary new and unsung writers from the American South. Our curated list champions diverse authors and books that don't fit into the commercial or academic publishing landscape.

Garamond Classico 11/14.4